Joy shifted closer, until her breasts pressed into his chest.

He was hard, taut muscle, above and below. He parted his legs to hold ground, receive her flush against him. Enfold her.

The heat—

Too sudden, and with it the reflex to hesitate, pull back, the sense she was going into perilous territory. But to say no against Wade's mouth was impossible.

She wanted him, every female sinew and nerve in her body shouted it at her with sure sexual conviction. She found her voice again. "What about you? Do you believe in fate?"

Wade caressed her skin, brushed kisses along her cheek, her jaw, her parted lips. "I do now. There's something about us together. Something inevitable." He lifted his head and his dark eyes poured heat into hers. "I like the taste of you, Miss Cole, the feel of you in my arms. And I've been wanting more of both." He smiled.

<u>BOOK YOUR PLACE ON OUR WEBSITE</u> <u>AND MAKE THE</u> <u>READING CONNECTION!</u>

We've created a customized website just for our very special readers, where you can get the inside scoop on everything that's going on with Zebra, Pinnacle and Kensington books.

When you come online, you'll have the exciting opportunity to:

- View covers of upcoming books

- Read sample chapters

- Learn about our future publishing schedule (listed by publication month *and author*)

- Find out when your favorite authors will be visiting a city near you

- Search for and order backlist books from our online catalog

- Check out author bios and background information

- Send e-mail to your favorite authors

- Meet the Kensington staff online

- Join us in weekly chats with authors, readers and other guests

- Get writing guidelines

- AND MUCH MORE!

Visit our website at
http://www.kensingtonbooks.com

ROOM 33

E.C. Sheedy

ZEBRA BOOKS
KENSINGTON PUBLISHING CORP.
http://www.kensingtonbooks.com

ZEBRA BOOKS are published by

Kensington Publishing Corp.
850 Third Avenue
New York, NY 10022

All Kensington titles, imprints and distributed lines are available at special quantity discounts for bulk purchases for sales
promotion, premiums, fund-raising, educational or institutional
use.

Special book excerpts or customized printings can also be
created to fit specific needs. For details, write or phone the
office of the Kensington Special Sales Manager: Kensington
Publishing Corp., 850 Third Avenue, New York, NY 10022.
Attn. Special Sales Department. Phone: 1-800-221-2647.

Zebra and the Z logo Reg. U.S. Pat. & TM Off.

First Printing: May 2004
10 9 8 7 6 5 4 3 2 1

Printed in the United States of America

For Tim, always and forever.

*And Gail Crease, who gave me the you-know-what
to put in the you-know-where.*

*And John Hamilton, for being so smart about so many things
and tolerating my not-so-smart questions.*

Finally, and especially, *to Kate Duffy, my editor from heaven,
who while faced with a thousand deadlines,
mountains of manuscripts, and endless demands
on her time—not to mention my personal contribution
of writer's angst—makes this business fun.*

Does the Hotel Philip Have a "Room of Doom"?

SEATTLE, Wash. Oct. 13, 1946 (AP) Has the Hotel Philip, the luxurious hotel designed and built by Joseph Miller Emerson, had a run of bad luck, or does it have, as Mrs. Margaret Purdeen, a local spiritualist, concludes, a nest of evil spirits?

Since its opening in 1935, the small, exclusive establishment, with its towering ceilings, marble foyer, carved oak pillars, and grand ballroom, has hosted the famous and the ultra-rich, those who happily pay for the best without concern for their pocketbooks. It has been the preferred site in Seattle for important business meetings, evening soirees, high society weddings, and intimate private dinners of foie gras and truffles.

But neither Mr. Emerson nor his staff can explain the strange events that continue to plague Room 33, such as:

1935–One week after the Hotel Philip's grand opening, Mr. James Enwood killed his wife, Claire, then shot himself. A gruesome murder-suicide.

1936–Mary Ann Jenkins, 23, jumped from the room's window onto the street below. The jump did not kill the determined Miss Jenkins, who told the authorities "something in the walls told her to jump," but she did suffer two broken legs and a fractured pelvis.

1937–A mysterious fire broke out in the room. It was put out and little harm was done. Cause never determined.

1939–Another fire, this one serious enough to spread to the adjoining rooms. The blaze was attributed to a careless smoker.

1941–A chambermaid discovers the body of guest Franklin Hanner, 53, who died during the night of an apparent heart attack.

Last night there was another incident in Room 33 when Mr. and Mrs. Janeway, guests of the hotel, were rousted from their beds in the middle of the night by two armed intruders who attempted to rob them. Mr. Janeway, during his effort to thwart the brazen criminals, was shot in the shoulder. Mrs. Janeway, who "very much feared for her life and that of her husband," was unharmed in the skirmish.

Mr. Emerson, the hotel owner, has no explanation for these events and considers them merely "a run of bad luck, unrelated and random." Mrs. Purdeen is not so convinced. "It is not at all uncommon for restless spirits to wreak havoc on the living," she says, adding, "Mr. Emerson should seriously consider conducting a séance in the room with the goal of discovering the source of such tribulation." Mr. Emerson's response to Mrs. Purdeen's suggestion was, "Fiddlesticks."

And so, *Dear Reader*, it appears the unhappy events in Room 33 will be left unexplored, and it will continue to host the Hotel Philip's well-heeled guests. Although this writer humbly suggests they sleep very lightly indeed.

Chapter One

Lana lifted her gaze from the gleam of the polished oak table, rested it on the serene ocean outside her window—and gripped the phone so tightly her knuckles showed bone-white through her pale skin.

She hadn't expected him to be angry. Disappointed, maybe, but coming at her through the phone line was barely leashed rage. It made her stomach ache.

"That can't be right," he said, his words hard, tight with shock. "You misunderstood. Stephen would never do that."

"But he did, David. I've just come from his lawyer. He told me Stephen, except for this house, left everything—and there wasn't much, really—to Joy." She kept her tone level, her attention on the sun-kissed sea.

"Unbelievable." A harsh breath hissed into her ear. "After all my plans—" He stopped. "And why in God's name would he pick Joy? He knew you two didn't get along. You haven't seen her in—how long has it been?"

"Four, maybe five, years. I really can't remember. I assume she's busy with whatever it is she does. Some kind of writing."

David snorted, apparently unmoved by her limp defense of the daughter who stayed as far away from her as the planet allowed.

"And I have a letter for her. Stephen's lawyer suggested I keep it sealed until she opens it. He says I'll be pleased, because it says something about her taking care of me." Lana wasn't sure what that meant, but she already didn't like it. Because whatever the intent, it meant trouble. She walked across her expansive living room to the window and leaned her head against the glass. The unruffled ocean stretched below her, bright and glittery in the late morning. She envied its calm. "It's all ridiculously complicated."

"And the Hotel Philip," David said. "That, too? You're certain?"

"It's hers."

"Christ!"

Lana tamped down her mild impatience. "I know this affects *our* plans," she said, reminding him that more than his interests were involved in their agreement. "But there's nothing I can do until I talk to Joy." Which she was *not* looking forward to. Her daughter was arrogant and difficult. David knew this. He should be more understanding of her concerns, less invested in his own.

"Do you think she'll sell?" he asked.

"I can't imagine why not. When I saw her last, she was traveling a lot and didn't show any signs of wanting to settle anywhere. I doubt she'll be interested in that queer old place. Why would she?"

"I need that property, Lana. We had a deal."

"I know, and I'd have sold it to you as we agreed, if Stephen hadn't dropped whatever marbles he once possessed. You know that. God knows, it's not as if I don't need the money."

Frustrated, she tugged at a loose thread on her cashmere sweater, was dismayed when it freed a string of red wool.

A thousand dollar sweater, unraveling, exactly like her life.

She needed a new sweater. She needed lots of new things, and for the first time in years she worried about how to get them. Stephen was generous, always gave her everything, and promised the rest. Then he'd died on her. Just days ago, but it seemed like forever.

She'd assumed there'd be money, and she'd simply go on as before, but there was very little, and what there was, in a truly mind-boggling move, he'd left to Joy, the daughter who made no secret of the fact she thought her mother was calculating and selfish. And what was the other thing? Oh, yes. High maintenance—whatever *that* meant. If Lana had to depend on Joy for the milk of human kindness, she'd die of thirst. Thank God for David. She pressed a hand to her stomach. Their plan was simple. Lana would inherit the musty old Philip, sell it to David, and plump her sagging fortunes with a considerable deposit—ten million dollars. Now everything had changed.

"Lana, are you still there?" David asked.

"Yes, darling, I'm still here. But I need to rest a while. It's been a stressful morning. Why don't you come over, say, in an hour? We'll have a drink, talk then."

"Good idea. We need to talk." His tone gentled. "You'll be fine, don't worry. I'll see to everything. Do you have a copy of the will at the house?"

"Uh-huh."

"Good. I'll look it over when I get there. We'll see what can be done."

Lana pushed the OFF button on the remote phone, tossed the receiver on the blue damask chair beside the window. She quelled the tears behind her eyes but could do nothing to calm the simmering turmoil in her mind.

She didn't need David to confirm that nothing could be done. According to his lawyer, Stephen made certain the will would stand "any and all scrutiny." But no matter how many times she turned it over in her head, she couldn't understand why Stephen—who loved her insanely—had made her subject to Joy's generosity, when Lana wasn't at all sure Joy had any. At least toward her.

She picked up the phone, sat in the chair, and stared at the silver receiver in her hand.

She'd have to call Joy, of course. But not yet. First, she'd straighten herself up, freshen her makeup.

She didn't intend to be red-eyed and puffy for David. She needed him, now more than ever. She went into her bathroom and soaked a facecloth in cold water. She draped it across her eyes for a moment, then blotted her heated face and neck.

When she again looked in the mirror, she tilted her head, touched the faint spray of lines at the corners of her wide blue eyes. She thought about the cosmetic vacation Stephen had promised her for her forty-ninth birthday. Her expression was wry when she said aloud, "Stephen dearest, if you'd truly loved me, you'd have had the courtesy to die *after* the damned surgery." She stepped away from the mirror and, suddenly chilled, rubbed her upper arms. "And you'd never have forced Joy back into my life."

She remembered what the lawyer said after their meeting. At the time it had confused her, but now she understood him completely.

Death changes everything—and then they read the will.

Wade propped the damp mop against the wall, looked down the hall, and surveyed his work. Not bad. The old gent was looking better. Amazing what a little soap and water would do.

"Mornin', Wade." Sinnie Logan stepped into the hall, waved at him, and turned to lock her door. When she looked back, she sniffed the air. "Smells a lot better around here since you came along." She gestured toward the mop. "You should get help with that."

"You volunteering?" He winked at her.

She made a show of rubbing her lower back. "No way. I've enough trouble getting these seventy-six-year-old bones to swish a broom around old Rupert's place—and he pays me."

Christian Rupert had occupied the Hotel Philip penthouse practically since the hotel was built. Somewhere along the line, he'd started doing the Howard Hughes recluse thing and hadn't stepped outside his door for years. He had to be ninety by now, at least. Sinnie had cleaned his place for years. "How's the old guy doing anyway?" he asked.

"Goofy as ever and sharp as a pin. He's going to outlive the lot of us." She didn't look as if the idea particularly pleased her. She settled her felt hat closer around her head. Winter, summer, fall, Sinnie wore that hat. "What about Gordy?" she asked. "Can't he help you out? Or that new fellow, Mike, who moved in on four?"

"Working. He got a job, part-time anyway."

Sinnie stopped fussing with her hat, peered up at him. "A job? Doing what?"

"Bike courier."

She went back to tugging her hat, looked amused. "Now there's one for the books. Any bike that man sits on will flatten to scrap for sure."

Wade picked up his mop. "It's work, Sinnie. A man needs that." Like he needed to clean this musty old hall. There'd been a time it was carpeted in rich red wool, luxurious and dense, plush enough to soften the footfalls of the hotel's wealthy guests. All that was left now was rutted and scarred oak floor, the ghost of the carpet only a creamy shadow running down its center.

Sinnie looked down the hall, as if she, too, remembered, and nodded. "What you're doing here? It's good, Wade. These old halls haven't been clean like this in too many years to count. Your granddad? He'd a been proud." She cocked her head, fired up her dog-with-a-bone look. Wade knew it well. "Have you thought any more about what I said?"

Sinnie was on him about the hotel. His legacy, she called it. "I think about what you say all the time, Sinnie," he said, not above a lie if it made her happy. "Now, you better get on your way. You'll be late for your gin rummy game." He knew that would get a rise out of her—and change the subject. Family and legacies weren't up for discussion in these scabby walkways.

"You kidding me? Gin rummy!" She snorted. "That's an old lady's game. It's stud poker, and you know it." She marched the few feet down the hall to the Hotel Philip's ancient and unreliable elevator. She pushed the button, looked back at Wade, and raised her voice. "You fixing to stay, Wade Emerson?"

"A while yet."

"That's what you said a couple of weeks ago, when you landed on the doorstep like a bird tossed from its nest. You haven't left yet."

"No, I haven't." He'd come to see Sinnie, sure. God knows, he owed the woman. But he had no idea why he was still here or when he'd leave. A shrink would have a field day with that mental waffle.

"So what's a 'while' in Wade-speak?

"A slice of time somewhere between yesterday and whenever."

"Humph." The elevator came and Sinnie stepped in. She held the door open. "That's no answer, boy. Time you figured out what you're hanging around here for.

Time you made plans. Got yourself involved in something other than mops and buckets." She let the door go and it closed.

Wade listened to the elevator clatter its way down.

Sinnie was right. It was time for him to make plans. Too bad his brain wouldn't oblige, but it, like the rest of him, was jammed in neutral. He reached for the mop and picked up the pail of brackish water. The irony of his situation wasn't lost on him. Wade Philip Emerson, high-flying mergers and acquisitions specialist, on the business end of a mop.

Nobody could tell him life didn't have a sense of humor.

He stowed the mop and pail in the fifth-floor storage room and headed for the stairwell and the third floor. On his way to his room, he glanced at the door to Room 33. In his grandfather's day the numbers were raised, gleaming forth from a shiny brass plaque anchored to the door with matching brass screws; now they were scratched into the wood and filled in with black felt pen, the words "KEEP OUT" scrawled under them.

Wade hadn't yet gone in there. Would. One of these days. Not today.

The door to Room 36, his door, was open. He didn't bother to lock it, because he had nothing in there anyone would want. Pointless during the day anyway, because most of the remaining tenants didn't bother to lock their doors either—or knock on someone else's. They just streamed between rooms as the mood hit.

"Gordy. That you in there?"

"Yeah, it's me." The voice lifted over the chatter of cartoon dialogue and the sound of warring spaceships—at least the whirrs, beeps, and roars that TV sound technicians had decided sounded like spaceships. Nearly boiled his ear drums.

When Wade stepped into his room, a dog barked,

then stopped when it recognized him and wagged its tail furiously. "Aren't you supposed to be walking him?" Wade switched off the TV, ruffled the soft fur on the mutt's back. Part terrier, part poodle, part hound, Melly was a stew of a dog with the disposition of an angel.

"Uh-huh. Want to come? Melly and I've been waiting for you." Gordy looked at him expectantly, a bright smile on his face. "Mr. Rupert wants me to take him 'a good long way.' "

"Not today, sport. I'm bushed. You and Rupert's mutt are on your own."

"Please, come. Please," Gordy begged.

"Nope." Wade flopped down on the sofa he'd bought from a local garage sale. Not bad. He stuffed a cushion under his head. "My plan is to grab a twenty-minute nap, a sandwich, then start on the sixth floor."

"I can help." Again the bright expression, the expectant stare.

Wade eyed him. Gordy was a big guy, over six feet, with more than enough muscle to man a mop. And the help would be appreciated, but he hesitated. Maybe it was the eight-year-old brain in the twenty-four-year-old body that made Wade uncomfortable—some weird thing about using child labor.

Or maybe he wanted to be alone in the dark, dusty halls, think of better days, better times.

He had to go a long way back for those.

"Please," Gordy begged. "I work good. Honest."

"Okay," he said. "Why not? You can give me a hand on six. Fair enough?"

"How much?" Gordy turned all business.

"So now you turn union on me?"

"Huh?"

Wade laughed. "Standard rate, Gordy. It's the best I can do."

"Okay." Gordy looked pleased, even though Wade

guessed he had no idea what standard rate was. Wade also knew he'd take a handful of quarters if that was the offer. "Now beat it. Go walk Mr. Rupert's dog, and when you're done come back here, and we'll go to work."

When Gordy was gone, Wade got up and walked into his tiny kitchen—added to the suite sometime in the seventies. He'd spent hours repairing the cupboards and painting. Hell, since he'd come to stay at the Philip, he'd become a regular home engineer. But he'd barely scratched the surface of what the Phil needed.

It was a good thing old Joe hadn't lived to see the decline and fall of his precious hotel—or his grandson. Wade didn't know which would bother him more. Damn, but he still missed the old man, more than ever since coming back to the Philip.

He worked on building himself a sandwich, glanced out the window to the street below in time to see Gordy and Melly turning the corner. They'd be going to Blackberry Park. Wade frowned. That place was a half-square-block nightmare, and anybody in there after dark was looking for fresh scar tissue. Why the hell Seattle's finest didn't clean it up, he couldn't figure. He also couldn't figure how Gordy managed it every day and met with no trouble at all. Maybe the locals knew better than to tangle with his mom, the woman who taught Gordy to ask *How much?* every time someone hired him— even if he couldn't assess the answer. It was her way of being sure he got something. No way was Cherry Ripley letting Gordy be taken advantage of. She was passionate about two things—her AA meetings and her son.

Wade went back to making his sandwich, the idea of passion, any kind of passion, a distant memory.

He stopped abruptly, braced both hands on the counter, and dropped his head between his shoulders, rigid with suppressed tension.

Shit. He felt like shit. What kind of man didn't go to

his father's funeral? What kind of man carried a load of shame—and hate—around heavy enough to sink him? And what kind of man had a north wind blowing through the hole where his heart should be?

A guy who fucked up, that's who. A guy who'd driven the fast lane, foot hard on the pedal, with a four-inch stiletto heel holding it in place.

Deanna.

He let the name loose in his brain, tested its impact. Not hate. Not love. Not even regret. Just a sea of humiliation, born of his own pride and stupidity.

His head ached, so he went to the bathroom and downed a couple of pain relievers. He needed a drink. But like a lot of other goddamn things in his life, the slow burn of amber down his throat was off limits. Hard liquor and drinking alone didn't do anything for his head two years ago; it sure as hell wouldn't now.

If he didn't have that mop waiting for him, he'd have to start weaving baskets.

Joy Cole breezed into her rented condo, walked to her desk, and stowed her laptop and briefcase. It was July, and hot as hell in Victoria. Unusually hot over the whole Pacific Northwest. Anxious to pare down, get rid of her jacket, she headed for the bedroom and tossed on cotton shorts and a spaghetti-strap tee.

In the living room, she turned on the stereo, tried to find soothing, mellow music. But for all her twirling and button pushing, she found only loud guitars and heavy doses of rap.

She gave up and gave in to her agitation.

She should be happy. It wasn't every day she got a contract for twelve feature articles and a travel budget dreams were made of. Her move to *All-World Travel*

Magazine had really paid off. After this stint in British Columbia, she'd fly to Bali, then from there to Singapore and on to Australia and New Zealand. A great trip that paid great money.

And she was apathetic as hell.

One hotel room too many? Maybe. Or one too many nights alone. She could barely remember her last relationship, but she was pretty sure it ended in an airport bar, sandwiched between Timbuktu and Zanzibar . . . or somewhere. As she recalled, it wasn't much of a relationship, and the sex was barely a five on the one-to-ten meter. Right now she'd settle for a three and a decent conversation.

Okay, she wasn't going there. The minute she started admitting to something as sappy as loneliness, she was doomed. Joy Cole didn't do sappy.

Maybe if she poured iced tea on her inertia, she'd roust it, get a grip. She was always okay as long as she kept moving—and avoided thinking too much. She made a line for the kitchen and along the way hit the message button on her phone.

The voice on it stopped her cold.

"Joy, it's La—your mother." There was a pause as if the mother concept had disrupted her thought process. "Something has come up, so would you call me, please. I'd like you to come to Seattle. It's about Stephen? . . . He died, you know. It's important, Joy, so please call me right away." The voice mail ended on a click.

He died, you know. The words echoed.

Joy didn't know. She plopped on the edge of the sofa. Not sure how she felt, she sorted through a few feelings. Regret? Some. As stepfathers went, Stephen Emerson hadn't been bad, just not particularly good. During the time she'd lived with him, aged twelve to seventeen, she'd rarely seen him—or her mother. The last time had been strictly by chance, in a San Francisco hotel lobby. She frowned, tried to remember. Maybe eight months ago?

They'd had a drink together. He'd looked a bit downcast, she'd thought then, and he'd been a lot mellower than she remembered him.

He'd asked a lot of questions and seemed genuinely pleased to hear her life was, as he put it, "on a good and sensible course."

Naturally she'd left out the bad bits. The bits that were anything but sensible.

Their hour together was pleasant enough, and they'd parted with his hugging her—a first, as far as she could remember. Then he'd made an odd comment about parent-child relationships, what he called the "sad mess of them." When he'd said he wished things could be different, she didn't know if he meant her and her mother's twisted bond, or his and his son Wade's, who'd bolted within days of when she and Lana had moved into the Emerson family home. Looking back, she should have followed his lead. But barely twelve, she'd been painfully confused about where she stood in the bright new world created by Lana and Stephen's marriage. She'd even made a half-hearted attempt to fit in.

Joy got up, shook her head.

What a pair they'd been! Hopping from one place to another, Switzerland for skiing, Hawaii for sun and surf, The Hague to see the tulips, Paris because it was spring, and they just *had* to get some "truly good food," then to Italy for the grape harvest.

She could still hear her mother's smooth voice, "Be a good girl for Nanny, Joy." There'd be a quick peck on the forehead while Stephen called impatiently from the limo waiting to take them away. That damn kiss, intolerable at twelve, and by sixteen, a serious maternal misstep. Then off they'd go.

Away, away, away . . .

The little girl that was Joy wanted to go, too; see all those exotic, tempting places; be grown up enough, free enough, to get lost in a mysterious world that offered unending promises. It was never about the Herculean task of trying to bond with Lana, be with Lana. Through time she'd learned that wasn't possible. No. It was about getting away from her.

She veered off Memory Lane. Nothing but wasted emotional gas. In a remote corner of her heart a remnant of love for Lana remained, a tiny silk knot that couldn't be untied, but it rested tenuously beside a vein that had bled too often in the cause of mother love. Maybe, someday, she'd have the courage to open it again. But not now. For now, she'd keep her shields up, her questions—particularly about her father—in the same locked box they'd been in for over twenty years. Repression had its rewards.

She got up. No point in slogging back through her childhood, that barren landscape she'd traversed without a guide. Worse than some, better than others, it was her cut of fate's cards, and she'd dealt with it years ago. Or thought she had.

She retraced her steps to the kitchen and replayed her mother's message. She was sorry to hear of Stephen's death, but she reminded herself it had nothing to do with her. Unless Lana needed something . . .

With Stephen gone and unable to provide, there was a chance Lana was looking for a stand-in.

Her mouth went dry and every self-protective instinct she'd honed so carefully through the years sparked to life. Rising to the top of her mother's toady list was not a good thing.

If Joy were smart, she wouldn't return the call. Miserable excuse for a daughter that she was, she didn't relish a reentry into her mother's life, couldn't suppress the flutter of panic at the thought of talking to her.

As mother and daughter they were an uneasy fit, always had been; Joy doubted the length of time they'd spent apart had changed that.

"Give your head a shake, woman. You're a big girl now. Able to leap tall buildings in high heels and spandex. You can manage a normal conversation with your mother"—she slapped her forehead—"and you're talking to yourself."

Disgusted, she made her iced tea, took a long, satisfying drink, and walked out to her balcony—if you could call two square feet a balcony. She'd phone her mother in the morning, but she didn't intend to go to Seattle. She had a trip to organize and less than a month to do it—a prospect that held as much appeal as talking to Lana. But Joy knew one truth. Her mother was the black hole of attention-getting, and she didn't plan on falling into the pitch again. She'd worked too hard for her own life.

Her life. Drum roll, please . . .

A sterile, windswept land of hotels, airport lounges, lost luggage, ever-creased clothes, cell phone calls, and laptops with dead batteries. Oh, and not to forget the mountains of fast food slowly turning her thighs into fat-cell incubators.

She laughed at herself. What a self-pitying, ungrateful idiot she was. She had it good, damn good.

She just didn't have it right.

She sighed, pressed the cool glass to her forehead, told herself she'd feel differently tomorrow. And as far as Lana was concerned, she'd learned how to hold her ground years ago. If she were lucky, she hadn't forgotten the drill.

* * *

"Shut up!" the boy hissed at the girl. "Keep it down, will ya!"

The fire escape, with its noisy metal stairs, was bad enough, but if Nelly didn't stop with the chatter, someone would hear them for sure. Luke should have known that last beer would put her over the top, but—he smiled—it would make the sex easy.

The girl slapped a hand over her mouth, but it didn't stop either the giggle or the hiccup. "Okay, but are we almost there?" She spoke through the hand covering her mouth, but at least she was quieter.

"Yeah," he whispered back. "Just one more floor."

The good thing was the stairs were on the alley side of the hotel, and most of the rooms on this side, except one, were empty. Hell, most of the hotel was empty. He'd been scoping it out for a month. Of the thirty-six rooms, less than half were occupied. Getting in, and getting out, without being seen would be a piece of cake.

Nelly giggled again, and again he shushed her. Christ, if it wasn't for those boobs of hers, he'd have brought Christa instead. "Here it is." Luke put his face to the window and looked in. Black as tar in there. Good. He worked the crowbar under the old, wood-sashed window, added a bit of muscle, and it lifted. He stepped over the sill and gave Nelly a hand in.

He opened his backpack and pulled out a blanket, a six-pack of beer, and a candle—no harm in a little romance. The finger of flame offered by the lit candle barely formed shadows in the blackness of the room. Luke spread the blanket over the bed's sagging mattress.

Nelly took her hand from her mouth and squinted into the darkness. "Cool," she said.

"Our own private hotel room," he said. "Just like I said." Luke didn't intend to waste a bunch of time. "Now, Nelly Moses, you come over here." He sat on the edge of the bed and spread his legs.

The obliging Nelly stepped into the vee of his legs and put her hands in his hair, while Luke slid his hands under her tee to lock onto her breasts. Breasts that made a little B&E worth it.

The kiss was damn good, too.

They started to strip, and when his zipper snagged, Nelly giggled again. "You know what you're doing, right?"

"Isn't my first time, if that's what you mean." He was glad it was dark, because his face was hotter than burned rubber. He got the zipper down, and Nelly pulled off that skimpy cotton thing she wore over those hooters of hers.

In seconds he was on top of her and buried deep.

A second after that, a hand grabbed a fistful of his hair and yanked him out—and upright. Nelly covered her breasts and scrambled back against the headboard. A knife tip gouged under his chin and a trickle of sticky warmth ran along his neck. His sixteen-year-old cock withdrew like a threatened turtle.

"Hey—"

"Shut up." The knife moved, made another shallow cut. "You've got thirty seconds to get your bare asses out of here or this"—he jabbed again—"will do serious work."

The man's head jerked in the direction of Nelly. "Much as I hate the thought of you covering up them titties of yours, sweetheart, you go first."

Nelly moved as if someone had slammed a hot brand on her butt; she stuffed her legs into her jeans, and yanked on her tee. The next second she was out the window, then she stopped. "You let him go or I'll scream." She sounded scared, and her voice squeaked like a little girl in a schoolyard.

Luke was impressed, until the knife made a short, shallow slit under his ear, and his own hot blood seeped under the neck of his Tee.

"You scream, sweet thing," the man holding him

said, "and your boyfriend is raw meat. Now get the hell out of here."

Luke heard her clang down the fire escape in quick time. The man shoved him from behind. "Now you, limp dick. Get out of here and don't come back. And keep your mouth shut. You tell anyone about this, and I'll fuckin' find you. You got that?"

"Yeah, I got it." Luke made for the window, caught a glimpse of the guy when he straddled the sill on his way out. Shit! The guy was a freakin' mountain!

As Luke scrambled down the fire escape, he heard the man laugh. "Thanks for the beer, dickless."

When the kids were gone, the man picked up the backpack, tucked the six-pack under his arm, and blew out the candle. When he closed the door of Room 33 behind him, he was grinning. *Man, that piece had a nice set on her.*

Maybe hanging around this dump was gonna have some perks after all.

Chapter Two

Joy sat on the edge of her bed and stretched. She was still stretching when the phone rang. She looked at her bedside clock—not seven yet. Almost ten in New York—had to be Connie about that piece she'd just sent in for *Travel World*. What was it again? The Scottish Moors . . . no, Irish castles, that was the one. She slid into work mode and picked up the phone.

"Joy Cole here." She managed to sound brisk before stifling a yawn. A phone call before coffee—what could be worse? She stood, headed for the kitchen.

"It's me."

"Mother?" Joy stopped in the middle of the room, unable to associate Lana's voice with the early morning hour.

A silky laugh traveled down the line. "I knew my call would surprise you."

"Surprise is for popped balloons and tax refunds—this verges on trauma. You haven't got out of bed before ten since . . . hell, you never got out of bed before ten."

"Maybe I've changed. It has been a while, after all."

Nearly six years, but who was counting? But change? Joy didn't think so. "I'm sorry about Stephen. And I was going to call today. What happened?"

"Heart."

"No warning?"

"For Stephen, yes. According to his lawyer, his doctor told him months ago how serious his condition was. He didn't share that with me." Her statements were matter-of-fact, and her tone conveyed neither resentment nor despair. No change there.

Joy had a surge of pity for Stephen. Sick, dying, he must have known sharing his pain with Lana was out of the question, sensed what Joy knew from experience: Lana didn't *do* death and dying—at least, not someone else's. Certainly not Joy's father's.

She went to the window, peeked out into a blinding morning sun, and rubbed her forehead, not knowing where to go next. "I assume you're okay?"

"I'll miss him, of course."

"Uh-huh." Joy doubted it, but maybe in the end it wasn't Lana's fault. She just didn't have any of those still waters that ran deep. More of a summer creek in a drought.

"I tried to call you several times. About the funeral. But you were away." She paused. "Your office said Paris, I think."

"Just got back."

"Lucky you. I love Paris."

"Everybody does." Joy girded her loins, figuratively speaking. "Is there something I can do for you, Mother?" She held her breath. There was always something you could do for Lana. It was the *how much* you had to worry about.

"You can come to Seattle for a visit. That would be a start."

"Can't. I'm leaving for Australia any day, and I've got

a lot of prep to do." Okay, so she did make it sound more imminent than it was, but as a buffer, it was all she had.

Silence.

"This isn't about me, Joy."

She sounded annoyed, which was odd. Lana seldom got angry. She was often hurt, saddened, prettily confused, painfully thwarted, terribly disappointed, and on occasion elegantly resigned—each emotion carefully choreographed—but never plain old mad. "What is it about?"

"Stephen. He left you a hundred thousand dollars and a hotel. You have to come and take care of things." Her tone was without inflection or emotion.

"He *what?*" Joy's lungs imploded. "Why would he do that?"

"I have no idea. He also left you a letter which I'm to give to you. Maybe it will explain things."

Joy unthinkingly tugged on the blind pull, freeing it to flap and crash its way to a tight roll at the top of the window. The sun exploded into the room to fry what was left of her brain cells.

"The hotel—it has to be the Philip."

"Yes. Ghastly place. It should have been taken down years ago."

Joy remembered it. She'd been there once when she was twelve or so. Old, run-down, dirty, and smelly, as if everyone in the place survived on boiled cabbage.

"Are you still there?" Her mother's voice jolted her out of the foggy memory.

"I'm here," she said and rubbed the lines, bow-tight now, between her eyes.

"Good. I checked, and there's a ferry leaving Victoria for Seattle in a couple of hours. Can you be on it?"

She exhaled, felt a part of her hard-won life slip out on the breath. "No."

The word shocked them both into a brief silence.

Lana's tone was measured when she responded. "I'm afraid you have to come, Joy. Stephen, for some inexplicable reason, tied our fortunes together. The will really can't be settled without you."

Joy's stomach headed south. She cursed inwardly, not liking the word "tie" the least bit. "Then it will be next week. It's the best I can do." She wanted her life for a while longer yet.

Lana let more silence filter along the line. "Fine. I'll see you then."

Click.

Joy stared at the phone in her hand, listened to the dead connection for a second or two, then signed off.

A hundred thousand dollars and a hotel.

She made for the kitchen; even an inheritance didn't stem her need for her morning coffee. She fiddled with the thick pad of coffee filters, her fingers unable to do what they'd done for years—pull one from the pack.

She rested a thigh against the red-tiled kitchen counter, set the filters back on it, and tried to level off her emotions.

It would *not* process. Stephen Emerson had been her stepfather for five years, most of which she'd spent alone in that ridiculous big house arguing with the staff and growing her horns of independence by smoking cigarettes, failing exams, and, for a time, running with a damn dubious crowd. Of course, no one noticed.

And now this insane inheritance—after one drink in a hotel bar. It made no sense. The man must have had more money than he knew what to do with or there were major strings.

Joy hated strings.

And that old, beat-up hotel. What in heaven's name would she do with the thing? She'd been in enough hotels to last her a lifetime—she certainly didn't need one of her own.

* * *

Wade stood outside Room 33, Lars and Rebecca beside him.

"We're not kidding, Wade, something went on in there last night. Maybe two o'clock or so." Lars spoke urgently. "You should take a look at least."

Wade wondered how the hell he'd let himself be elected caretaker, when he hadn't even run for the damn job. He'd started cleaning the place for something to do, and the next day, somebody in the hotel—he suspected it was Sinnie—dropped a set of keys off at his door and anointed him king. His dumb luck, the management company supposedly responsible for the place hadn't bothered to replace the former caretaker who bolted months ago. So here he was, standing at Room 33's door with a ragtag contingent of tenants breathing down his back.

Maybe Room 33 was one of the things that had drawn him back to the Phil, but he never planned on visiting it with an entourage.

"I didn't hear anything," he said. "And I'm only two doors down. And"—he tried the door—"the room is still locked. Maybe you heard me sleepwalking."

"You sleepwalk?" Rebecca said. "Cool."

"Rebecca, he's kidding," Lars said. Rebecca rolled her eyes. "And as for the lock," he gestured toward the bulb-shaped keyhole, "this one's original—you could open it with a paper clip."

"Tell me again what you heard," Wade said.

"A couple of thuds, as if something dropped, then someone rattling down the fire escape—in a big hurry. They made a hell of noise."

"That outside fire escape hasn't been used for years. Not since they put fire stairs inside in the sixties."

"Someone used it last night, Wade. I can't believe you didn't hear it," Lars insisted.

Wade hadn't heard it, because he hadn't been here at two o'clock, but he wasn't about to tell Lars and Rebecca that. When he couldn't sleep, which was damn near every night, he walked, sometimes ran, until he was exhausted. Better that than counting stains on the ceiling. Counting his sins.

Lars and the very pregnant Rebecca lived in Number 26, along with two cats, a snake-mean parrot, and ten tons of art supplies. They'd been living in the Philip for a couple of years. They were maybe twenty or so, generally broke, crazy about each other, and cause-happy. The first week Wade was here, Rebecca had proudly showed him a newspaper photo of Lars chained to a towering cedar in Oregon, where they'd spent time saving trees.

"You think there's anything to that 'room of doom' stuff?" Lars asked.

Wade's head snapped up. "Where did you hear about that?" He hadn't heard that stupid phrase in years.

"Found an old clipping behind the front desk."

"Yeah, well, don't believe everything you read."

"I don't, but I thought maybe you did. You still haven't opened the door," Lars prodded.

Wade's gut contracted, and something with a thousand legs crawled along his spine. But it wasn't an urban legend inspired by an old newspaper piece that was holding him back. What did was his business.

Mike came up behind them. "What's goin' on?"

Wade turned, looked up. Ex-wrestler, ex-con, Mike was a huge man. Mostly gone to fat, but Wade, judging from how easily the man moved, knew there was lots of muscle under the blubber. "The artists here say they heard something in here last night."

"Yeah—me, too. Let's take a look."

Wade decided to get it over with and turned the key in the lock, but it was Mike who pushed the door open, and it protested every inch.

"See?" Rebecca said to Lars. "I told you I heard creaking."

Mike gave the door one final shove to open it fully, and everybody peered in. Nobody walked in.

Morning sun filtered through the dirt on the high, narrow, and undraped windows, and dust motes, set loose by the draft coming in from the hall, shivered and rose to dance dully in the paltry light.

Wade immediately looked toward the bathroom. The door was ajar, open enough for him to see cracked black-and-white floor tiles and the edge of the old, claw-footed tub; its lion paws clenching grimy glass balls. His breath jammed in his throat.

"This place stinks." Lars sniffed the air, rubbed his nose. "When's the last time someone was in here?"

"Last night, according to you." Wade stepped into the room. "Before that? Who knows? Years." Wade hoped the questions would end there.

"How come?" Rebecca asked.

"Superstition. Stupidity." He shrugged.

"The 'room of doom' thing, right?"

"Partly." He'd give her the abridged version. "There were more incidents after that piece came out. All explainable, but the press got on it and wouldn't let it go. Pretty soon nobody wanted to rent it, so they locked it up. In the sixties, I think."

"The 'they' being your grandfather, right?" Rebecca said.

"Yes." No one in the Philip would even know of his relationship to the hotel if it weren't for Sinnie's loose lips. The woman knew more about the Emersons than she had a right to. Probably a hell of a lot more than he did.

Wade walked to the window. "Broken lock," he said, changing the subject. He nodded toward the mussed bed. "Looks as if somebody came in and bedded down for a few hours." He spotted a beer can on the floor near the window and bent to pick it up. Some of its brew spilled on the threadbare carpet.

"Could have been a homeless," Mike added.

"Maybe." Wade took a screwdriver from his tool belt, reset the screws, and secured the window. He wanted out of here, the sooner the better. Then he spotted a few mottled stains on the windowsill. Blood. Had to be. And not that old. He ran a hand along the sill. No dust. Just more dried blood. He wouldn't have said anything, but he caught Lars watching him. "Whoever was in here must have scratched himself, been bleeding when he climbed out the window."

"Heard somebody in the hall maybe, got scared and ran off," Mike contributed.

"Whoever it was, they're gone now. With no real damage done." Not that he gave a damn.

"Your grandpa sure had taste, Wade," Rebecca said, turning her head this way and that, taking in every corner of the room. "This place is something. Look at that chest of drawers, Lars. It's awesome. And the four-poster bed! I can't believe this stuff is still here. All the other rooms in the place are decorated in flea market rejects. This is really classy." She ran a finger along the marble-topped bedside table, looked at it, and grimaced. "Classy . . . but dirty."

For the first time since he'd stepped into it, Wade studied the room: the faded green-and-white striped silk wallpaper, oak wainscoting, the three framed pictures of dead game hung on the wall by fine chains, the fan-shaped wall sconces. All of it wrapped in a gauze of dust and cobwebs. Sealed off in the sixties and having escaped redecorating and upgrades, it was a thirties time capsule—and, beneath the grime and neglect, in near-perfect condition. Except for the smell, a soup of odor that hadn't had a stir of fresh air in so long, it had damn near calcified.

It was the same the last time he'd been in here—eighteen years ago—but then the blood was fresh and there had been a lot more of it.

So much blood.

Wade evened out his breathing, fought the gloom descending over him like a closing curtain.

"Look," he said, "this little tenant meeting is fun, but I've got work to do." He gestured toward the door with his head. "Let's go."

Mike ambled out first, followed by Lars and Rebecca. When they were all in the hall, Wade locked the door. He figured no one heard the rocky intake of fresh oxygen he took to clear his head. Too bad all the oxygen in the world wouldn't make him forget how much he hated this fucking room.

Lana looked across the outdoor table at David Grange.

The night was warm, the barest of breezes drifting in from Lake Washington, and the restaurant was comfortably casual. She was glad to be away from the house, pleased David had insisted on taking her to dinner this evening. But she wished he'd stop talking about the will and that awful hotel. There was nothing to be done until Joy arrived, and Lana had other, potentially more satisfying, things on her mind.

"I still can't understand Stephen's rationale," David went on, shifting back in his chair. His brow furrowed as he sipped his "very fine" merlot, a wine selection he'd discussed *ad nauseam* with the wine steward. There'd been a time Lana would have been impressed with a man who spent so much time on a wine list; now it bored her. But David Grange, despite his occasional lapse into pretension, didn't bore her at all. He was handsome, amusing, clever, ten years younger than she, and necessary.

"Perhaps the letter will explain it. Joy will be here

next week. We'll know then." She twirled her wine, watched the rich fluid make ruby waves against the sides of the long-stemmed glass. "For now there's nothing to be done."

He studied her curiously. "You're so calm about all of this. Aren't you angry?"

Her shrug was slight and elegant and made her scoop-necked silk sweater slip over her shoulder. David's eyes slipped down with it. Lana was pleased. "What good will anger do? It won't change Stephen's will."

"But you need money to live on." He stopped. "The house is yours, isn't it? He did do that much." His questioning gaze returned to her face.

"Yes."

"Thank God for that." He went on, "But cash flow? In that respect you could be in serious trouble. You do understand that, don't you?" He stared at her as if she were an exotic plant, not a woman with a brain. Joy had often looked at her the same way but with more disapproval. And Lana may have a cash flow problem, but she also had a solution—sitting across the table from her.

She reached over and stroked his hand. "You worry too much, and I appreciate that, but I'll be fine. As you said, I have the house. If I have to, I'll sell it." The words were calculated, brave with just a hint of pain on their edges. But the truth was, Lana's stomach quavered at the thought. She'd spent months with the builder and decorator, going over every detail of its construction and design until it was perfect. Exactly how she wanted it. Nothing would make her leave it. Nothing. Holding David's hands tightly in her own, she lifted her eyes to meet his. "But honestly, darling, I don't want to think about such . . . unpleasant things right now."

David's expression darkened, and he leaned forward. A swag of his heavy blond hair shifted over his forehead. He played his index finger on her palm. "No matter what happens, what that damned letter says, I'll take care of you. I want you to know that."

"I *so* needed to hear that." She touched his cheek. "And there are so many ways of being cared for, aren't there?" She loved him when he was like this, so intense, so committed to her. Men. She adored them. They were so . . . handy. And David touched her in a way no other had. At times her feelings for him made her faintly anxious.

"Are you wearing sandals?" she asked, lowering her voice to a near whisper.

He looked confused. "Yes, why?"

"Because I'm not wearing underwear." She moved her hips forward on the chair. "And I'm spreading my legs . . . just so, under the table. You can't see—but you can feel." She narrowed her eyes, blew him a kiss. She was already warm and dewy.

David glanced around the restaurant. When he brought his eyes back to meet hers, they were hot and hooded. "You're crazy," he said in a low, ragged tone.

"Just the tiniest bit. Do you mind?"

"Not at all." He slid his bare foot between her thighs. She picked up her wineglass; he picked up his. And while Lana concentrated on keeping her eyes open, David concentrated on making her happy.

Things were, as always, exactly the way Lana wanted them to be. The way she intended them to stay.

Joy paid the cabbie, and when he drove off, she turned slowly to survey her mother's recently completed palace: the serpentine driveway, wide ocean view, a brick façade with walls of artfully draped glass, and a cathedral-style entrance with oak doors and hammered black iron hinges that would have been at home in a medieval castle. All of it set in an immaculate garden in full glorious bloom. Down the path, a gardener weeded a brilliant show of geraniums.

Feeling as though some of that hammered iron had made its way to her stomach, she stood at the front doors. Before she had a chance to knock, Lana opened the door.

"Joy, I'm so glad you've come." The requisite hug was executed, and the two women separated as if they'd been caught performing a lewd act in public.

"Mother," Joy said, knowing she should add something, and opted for the expected, and the truth. "You look wonderful."

She touched her face. "The odd wrinkle creeps in no matter how good the fight. But come in," Lana said, glancing downward. "No bag?"

Here we go, Joy thought. "I checked into the Marriott. Left it there."

"I see."

"It's my business, Mother. It's comped. I have a zillion hotels I can stay at for free. I figured I'd stay out of your hair by taking advantage of it for once." *And keep some distance between us.*

For a moment Lana looked confused. "Your business?"

"I'm a travel writer, remember?" Joy felt better already, reminded of just how little anything she did ever mattered to Lana. Hold that thought, she told herself.

"Of course, I'd forgotten." She stepped aside. "But come in. No need for us to stand on the doorstep."

The foyer was, as Joy would expect, suitably grand. "Nice house. You must be happy here."

"Yes, Stephen and I built it about five years ago. I told you that, didn't I?"

Joy nodded, dimly remembering one of those post office change of address cards being forwarded from her old address.

"Come into the sitting room," Lana said. "There's someone I want you to meet."

The sitting room would seat twenty, but it held one man. He rose when the two of them stepped into the room and smiled to display perfect white teeth. Joy looked him over—tall, fair-haired, and sexy. Not bad at all. Mom was doing okay.

He put out his hand. "A pleasure to meet you, Joy. I'm David Grange." His gaze swept her, and his eyes widened in surprise, then narrowed. "You're as beautiful as your mother. You could be—"

"Twins, I know. Thanks."

"You've been told that before?"

"On occasion." About a million of them, and she still hated it. She'd even dyed her hair brown for a while, but the root thing, along with her travel schedule, proved to be more of a hassle than she needed, so she'd let her natural blond come back.

"David is my very dearest friend," Lana cut in, going to his side and locking her arm in his, the gesture overtly possessive. "I couldn't have done without him since your father died."

"Stephen Emerson was *not* my father." The familiar knot of anger tangled in Joy's chest.

"Stepfather, then," Lana corrected smoothly before walking to the bar. "Can I make you a drink?"

"No, thanks. But I'd appreciate your telling me why I'm here."

"You may not need a drink, but I do." Lana looked at David Grange. "Could you do the explaining? You'll make it clearer than I can—and at least there's a chance Joy will actually listen."

David gestured toward the mile-long sofa opposite the fireplace. "You might as well take a seat, Joy. This will take a minute or two."

Joy sat, relieved it was he who'd do the explaining, saving on the emotional brakes she always had to engage during any interface with her mother. David took a place at the other end of the sofa.

Two wide cushions between them, he began, "Your mother has already told you Stephen left you money and a hotel property. What she didn't tell you is he left her absolutely nothing."

Joy knew her shock slackened her jaw. "Nothing?"

"The house, of course, but other than that—no. Nothing at all."

"I don't get it."

"That's just it. Neither do we." He pulled out an envelope from his inside suit pocket. "We're hoping this will explain it."

She took the letter, noted the string of attorneys' names, and turned it over. Lana handed her a letter opener.

Joy started to read, and with every carefully typed line her heart beat faster. Anger, dread, and outright panic made her hands shake. "This makes no sense." She looked at the two people who were watching her as if she held the key to paradise. "He wants me to look after Mother. He says"—she scanned to the second page—"'while you, Joy, have a practical nature, Lana is too utterly feminine and soft-hearted to care for herself financially.' He says if he puts the money directly into her hands, it won't last long enough for her to be 'ensured of the future she deserves.' He says I'm to do whatever I want with the inheritance as long as I take 'appropriate financial care' of my mother." Joy looked up, stunned. "He wants me to be your financial babysitter."

"Did he say anything about how much he loved me?" Lana asked.

Joy blinked, confused by the jump from money to heart. She glanced down at the letter. "Yes. And I quote, 'insanely.' "

Lana looked blandly pleased.

"It seems his *love*," she accented the word and started to read again, "is the reason he dragged me back into the picture. He wants us to 'be friends at the very least' and to 'heal our fractured relationship' before it's too late." Late for what, Joy didn't know, and she didn't bother reading aloud the part that said her mother needed her. It was ludicrous.

"Was there anything else?" David asked, his gaze on the letter.

"Oh, yes." And she didn't need to read it to remember his words. "He says he hopes, by involving me in my mother's future, Lana need never be alone, as he was." Joy shook her head. Stephen must have been on a diet of magic mushrooms, because the odds of Lana staying alone for a second longer than she had to would be measured in zeroes. "He says he's sorry he doesn't have more to leave us, but he's certain I can 'build on' what's left."

"May I see that?" David asked.

Joy handed him the letter, slumped back in the sofa. *Look after her mother.* She was forty-eight years old, and Stephen portrayed her as a dotty centenarian—or an irresponsible, profligate spender. The latter, more likely. Obviously even the frivolous, besotted Stephen had managed a peek or two through the lust.

She heard David curse under his breath. "What?" she said, straightening.

"Stephen took out a mortgage on the house two years ago. A big one." He looked at Lana. "I'm sorry, my love, but unless you come up with major cash flow—and fast—you could lose this place."

Joy had nothing to say to this, but she didn't miss the

"my love" in David's expression of regret. She wondered if there were odds of *less* than zero.

The mortgage news dazed even the endlessly self-possessed Lana. "I don't understand it. Where did all the money go?"

Joy kept her voice calm, had no idea what her eyes said. "My guess? You spent it." She stood, walked to the bar, and poured herself a glass of mineral water. "Let's face it, Mother, you and Stephen made spending an art form. You should have expected this."

"Well, I didn't. I thought there was lots of money. Stephen never said otherwise." She looked abused and uncomfortable—both beautifully done.

David went over, perched on the arm of her chair, and touched her hair. "It's all right. Everything will be all right." When she grasped his hand, he kissed it, before he switched his attention to Joy. "Can we be honest here?"

"No, let's all play let's pretend. That would make me ecstatic about assuming financial responsibility for my mother while she's barely past child-bearing age—and her delighted by the prospect." Okay, it was bitchy and sarcastic, but it was all she could come up with. Hard to think when your head was in a vise.

David Grange said nothing for a moment, then, "Okay, I get the picture. You and your mother don't want to be in each other's faces. Fair enough." He waved the letter. "Fortunately there's an easy way out, and we can all benefit from it."

Joy stopped pacing, instantly curious. Lana gave him an adoring look. Adoring looks were a specialty of hers.

He went on. "Joy, you've inherited a hundred thousand dollars and the Hotel Philip, right?"

"So it seems."

"Now, a hundred thousand dollars isn't much."

Joy looked at him as if he were nuts. She could live

on that kind of money for years—not a lot of years, but years.

"But there is value in the hotel. Before this"—he waved the letter again—"I was prepared to buy the Hotel Philip from your mother, assuming it would be her who'd inherit. Given that's not the case, here's what I propose. You keep the hundred grand. I buy the hotel from you, for cash. You give it to your mother and go about your life. I think that scenario not only satisfies the intent of Stephen's final request, but offers the best solution for everyone, don't you?" He again sat on the arm of Lana's chair as if the whole matter were a *fait accompli*.

Joy rubbed her brow. This arrangement would solve all their problems—he was right about that. But Stephen was barely cold in his grave and the sale of the hotel was already set up? "Exactly how long have you two been seeing each other?"

Obviously it was a question neither of them expected, and one neither was prepared to answer. Finally, Lana took a stab at it. "David has been a friend of Stephen's and mine for some time. It's only natural that since he died, we've become closer."

"Natural for you."

Lana ignored her barb. "David has my best interests at heart." She smiled up at him, dropped the smile when she turned back to face Joy. "I'd prefer you not read any more into it than that."

Joy shook her head in wonderment. She was a force of nature, her mother; her instincts for survival—and continuing prosperity—honed to perfection. Stephen may not have told Lana directly about his failing health, but Joy suspected her mother sensed it, flagged it as a danger to her financial well-being. Enter David Grange, no doubt willing—and, more important, *able*—to ease Lana's way. Like a replacement part for a failing organ.

"I'm not reading anything into it," she said, careful to keep her voice flat. "Simply curious."

Lana tilted her head and a mass of thick gold hair, the same color as her own, tumbled over her shoulder. Her striking azure blue eyes settled on Joy. "Such a waste of time, curiosity."

"When it comes to you, Mother, it's difficult not to be curious—even morbidly so—considering your love life moves at the speed of light." Joy wanted to bite her lip. Fifteen minutes in her mother's company and she was a smart-mouthed sixteen-year-old again. *Civil, she had to stay civil. Figure a way out of this thing.*

"You're being sarcastic. It isn't attractive."

Before Joy could answer, David interjected, "Look, why don't we give Joy time to adapt to her new situation, think on things. And when she's done that, we'll talk again."

Bless you, David, Joy thought, turning away from her mother's now-empty stare. "Good idea." She picked up her bag, which she'd dropped on the coffee table. "I'll meet you both at the hotel tomorrow morning. Say, ten. You can show me around. We'll talk after that."

"You want to see the Philip?" David looked surprised. "What for?"

"I inherited it. Makes sense for me to take a look at it. Who knows, maybe I can refurbish the place, turn it into a going concern. Give Mother a job." She said this to nettle her phlegmatic mother but received only a raised eyebrow in response.

David laughed. "A going concern? Maybe. If your aim in life is to be a slum landlord."

"That bad?"

"Worse."

"Still, I'd like to have a look at it. Is there a problem with that?" she asked, irritated that the man thought her stupid enough to sell him something she hadn't set eyes on since she was a kid. Not likely.

"No problem at all." David lifted one well-tailored shoulder. "It's just there's not much to see. The value's in the land, not the hotel. I'm afraid the old Phil is long past its nineteen-thirties prime. The place hasn't functioned as a hotel for years. Now there's maybe twenty or so full-time tenants occupying the place. Misfits and criminals, mostly."

"Sounds lovely. But I still want to see it." Joy wasn't surprised by David's description. It backed up her own memory of the Hotel Philip rising from the single time she'd been there, with Stephen and his son, Wade. It was only a month or so after Stephen married Lana. An annoyed Stephen had been called to the hotel because of vandalism in one of the rooms—some kind of insurance claim. It was obvious he hated the place. The hotel was a mess then. No doubt it was worse now.

Her memories were spotty, those of a preoccupied young girl who hadn't wanted to be there in the first place. Impressions: cool marble in the foyer floor, small lion heads carved into the trim on the front desk, a towering lobby ceiling . . .

While Stephen bustled about with the insurance agent, Joy was handed over to his son, whom she'd only seen a couple of times before. He was impatient, and rather than stand around and wait in the dismal lobby, he'd taken her up in the clanking, jerky old elevator and shown her around.

He'd told her his grandfather had built the hotel during America's Great Depression, how he'd almost lost it years later. He'd sounded proud, respectful. Wade was maybe seventeen or eighteen then, and, from her almost-thirteen-year-old perspective, major cute. She'd listened to him as if every word from his lips was honey on a stick.

That same night he had a blowout with Stephen, left, and never came back. Joy never saw him again. Nor, she guessed, did Stephen or she wouldn't be standing here today. She wondered briefly what Wade would think of his father's bizarre will.

She pulled herself into the present. "How about we meet at the hotel at ten? If that's too early, we can make it later."

"Ten's fine." David pulled out a shiny blue PDA from his inside suit pocket and entered the appointment.

Lana rose. "Count me out." She pretended to shudder. "I was there once, a few years ago. It was cold and creepy then, probably worse now. I have no burning urge to go back." She met Joy's eyes. "Look around all you want, Joy, but remember, you have a responsibility to me, and I expect you to live up to it. David's suggestion is the obvious solution. It allows you to live your life and me to live mine—exactly the way I wish." Lana gave her a pointed stare.

On a perpetual spend-a-thon . . . "I'll take a look at the hotel, decide what to do then." She told herself she was being practical, businesslike in taking the necessary steps to assess the hotel's worth, but underneath she knew it had something to do with having the upper hand with Lana for the first time in her life and wanting to hold onto it as long as possible. Childish? Absolutely. Because in the end, she'd do what had to be done to satisfy her mother, and she'd do it as quickly as possible.

Then she'd hop the next plane to . . . wherever.

What did she care if her mother was broke again in a couple of years? She would not let that, or a moldy, tacky old hotel, take over her life.

She absolutely would not.

Chapter Three

Wade grimaced while Sinnie perforated his thumb with a needle the size and sharpness of a hypodermic. What the hell ever happened to the concept of using tweezers to pull out a sliver? And judging from her determined expression as she dug into his flesh, Sinnie had a sadistic streak a mile wide.

"Ouch!" He pulled his thumb back, put it in his mouth, and tasted the salt of his own blood.

"Baby," Sinnie charged and stuffed her weapon back in its red tomato pin cushion. "Good thing you tough guys don't have to carry the kids into this world. We'd be a declining species, for sure."

He took his thumb out of his mouth. "We do our part."

"The fun part." She put her battered sewing basket on the shelf under her TV. The woman looked as if she'd had a side order of tacks with her breakfast. She stood and jabbed a finger in his chest. "You should buy the Phil. It's the right thing to do."

Wade gaped at her. "Where the hell did *that* come from?" Buy it? Hell. He couldn't wait to be free of the place. Another few days and he'd have things figured out, some kind of plan in the works. And saddling himself to the Phil wouldn't be part of it.

"You should go to that Lana woman and get your hotel back. Your grandpa would want you to have it. That poor man will be trembling in the dirt, thinking about his hotel in the hands of that greedy piece of baggage your daddy married." Her stare was python-mean.

Wade froze. Even Sinnie hadn't ventured into this territory before. He picked up his tool belt, wondered again what had possessed him to buy the thing. "I'm going up to four—Henry's doorknob has gone missing. I said I'd replace it for him. After that I'm going on mop duty."

"Henry's doorknob can wait and so can your darn mop." She clutched his arm. "What can't wait is this hotel. If you don't do something, we're all going to get our walking papers. The lot of us. Besides that, this place is rightfully yours. If you'd have made up with your daddy, maybe—"

He pried her fingers from his forearm. "Leave it alone, Sinnie. You know, and I know, there's no going back. My father's dead and this hotel was part of his estate. It belongs to Lana Cole now. What she does with it—and when she does it—is her business. My guess is she'll sell the place with the speed of light."

"And won't that be grand!" She glared at him. "We all sit here waiting for our eviction notices, while a shifty-eyed developer makes plans to tear the Phil down and build God knows what."

"You don't know that." Wade figured Sinnie was right, but even so, he didn't intend to set eyes on Lana Cole again. For any reason. Ever. The woman was every man's wet dream, gift wrapped—with the killer force of a radiation leak. Lana Cole had come into his father's life, absorbed him, and destroyed his family with one feline swoop of her eyelashes. Even in the years since, telling himself over and over again how it took two to break up a marriage—that his father was as much at fault as Lana—he still harbored a near-pathological hatred for the woman.

He loosened the buckle on his carpenter belt a notch. "I'm going." He strode to the door.

Sinnie called after him, her voice less strident now. "What's happening here, Wade Emerson—it isn't right. This place should be yours. Your grandpa would've wanted it that way."

Wade's hand was on the doorknob and he kept his face to the door when he said, "Forget my grandfather. Forget about this place being mine. And especially forget about me having anything to do with Lana. And giving her a pile of money for my own family's hotel—assuming I had it to give. It isn't going to happen. You, me, and all the rest of the hotel's exalted clientele will be living in Dumpsters before I go within a thousand miles of that woman."

Sinnie wasn't deterred. "But what if someone else does, Wade? What if someone gets to her before you and grabs the Phil out from under your slow-moving behind?"

"Then good luck to them. If they have to be in the same room as that woman to get it, I'll feel damn sorry for them." He walked out.

"Mr. Rupert, are you there? I've brought Melly back."

"Mind, boy. I'm coming." Christian Rupert touched a button on the side of his recliner, and the chair seat lifted enough for him to reach his cane and pull himself to a standing position. At eighty-nine, his head worked fine, but the body under it was a crumbling mass of brittle bones and spent muscles, the lot of it weighing barely a hundred pounds. Some days he thought maybe he wouldn't bother dying, just hang around long enough to disappear.

"Mr. Rupert," the boy called again. He heard Melly whine, let out a couple of short barks.

"Almost there," he said, and picked up his struggling pace. At the door he stopped and flipped up the cover of his peephole. "Anyone with you, boy?"

"No, sir."

He asked the same question every time. The boy knew he had to come alone, but considering he wasn't right in the head, Christian had to be careful. "All right, then." He turned the bolt and opened the door a crack. The instant he did, cold tines of fear stabbed at his shrunken lungs. When he opened the door wider, the panic grew. It always did. "Quickly, quickly, boy. Get in!"

Melly skittered in, and Gordy turned his big body sideways to force himself through the narrow passage created by the partly open door. Christian closed it behind them, relaxed somewhat to hear the bolt hit home, its solid click like a distant rifle shot in the large room. He breathed as deeply as he could to calm himself.

"You okay?" The boy looked at him curiously, his tone anxious.

Without being aware of it, Christian had closed his eyes while he took his air. Ancient and shriveled as he was, he probably looked like a cadaver—frightened the boy. "I'm fine, Gordy. Will you help me back to my chair?"

"Sure."

Gordy took his broomstick of an arm and walked him to his recliner. He leaned back into it and pushed the button. Down he went. "Melly, my girl, did you have a good walk?" Melly answered with a swirling tail, jumped onto the footstool sitting beside Christian's chair, and put her paws on his armrest. Christian couldn't take the weight of her on his lap, so the footstool, a hand's length away, had to do. He stroked the dog's soft head and crooned, "My pretty girl, pretty, pretty girl."

"Can I have my money, please? My mom wants me at home."

"Did you take the girl for a good, long walk?"

"I did. She likes the park." Gordy smiled at the dog. "She chased a squirrel today. Treed it, too."

Christian stroked the dog's head again. "A real adventure, eh, Melly?" He lifted his head and jerked it toward the table under the window. "My purse is there. Take three dollars out of it and bring the rest to me."

He watched the boy go to the table, click open the small leather change purse, and take out exactly three dollars. He showed the money in his hand to Christian. "This right?"

"Exactly. You're a good boy, Gordy."

Gordy grinned and handed him the purse, then watched while Christian counted what was left in a ritual they shared every afternoon.

A man had to be sure. There was always the chance the man-child pocketed extra when Christian wasn't watching. It was all there as it always was. He tightened the grip on the money in his hand, relishing the feel of it, the power of it, the preciseness of the count.

Christian set the purse aside. "Anything new going on in the hotel?" Another ritual. Daily question period.

"Nope. Same as always." He brightened. " 'Cept somebody tried to sneak in one night. Left a beer can and broke a window."

"Where was that?"

"Room 33, I think."

"Really." He snickered. *Good old Room 33.* He went on, "I heard a hammer earlier. Is something broken, Gordy?"

"Henry's door. He lost his doorknob, but he needed a hinge, too, so Wade was doing it for him."

Christian's head came up. "That would be Mr. Emerson. Am I correct?"

"Uh-huh. He fixes things good around here."

"So I've been told." What he hadn't been told was that the man was still in the hotel. How odd.

"He could fix your stuck window. I could ask him. If you want me to."

"No, that won't be necessary." Christian smiled at him. He was a nice boy, really. Rather pretty. If he were twenty, thirty years younger, he would . . . "What does he look like, this Wade fellow?"

Gordy frowned. "I don't know."

"Does he look like that?" Christian nodded to a sepia-toned photograph in a gleaming silver frame. It sat on a table near the French doors leading to the penthouse rooftop patio. Gordy went to the table and picked it up. Seeing it in his hands made Christian's nerves jump. He wanted to shout, put it down, put it down! But he wanted the lad to look at it even more. He'd tried to stifle it, but the longer Wade Emerson stayed in the hotel, the more his curiosity grew.

"He does. Kind of. Except not so weird." He returned the photograph to the table.

"Farther back." Christian said. "Put it nearer the window. Right where it was."

Gordy did as he was told and came back to stand in front of Christian. He didn't ask who the man in the photo was, but Christian told him anyway. "That's a very old picture. It's Wade's grandfather, Joseph Emerson. We used to be business partners. But that was a long time ago."

Gordy looked around the room, rubbed behind his ear. "Can I go now, Mr. Rupert? My Mom's waitin'."

"If there's nothing else you can think to tell me, you can go. But come back this afternoon at five. All right?"

"Yes, sir." The boy didn't waste time, headed straight for the door.

"No earlier. No later," Christian reminded him, as he always did.

"Yes, sir," he said again and slammed the door behind him.

Christian was disappointed. With Stephen Emerson dead, changes were coming to the Philip. The quake and quiver of them rose from below, inevitable and threatening. His source said not to worry, but worry was what he did best. Worry and plan. He hadn't expected much from the man-child, of course. But he'd hoped to draw him out, tap into any information he might have overheard. Information that might prove useful as the days progressed.

Somewhat agitated, he glanced out the window and settled his gaze on the large, tree-filled planters on his rooftop terrace. They needed cutting back, watering. It was time to call Mike in for some work. Mike would talk, answer his questions—not like Sinnie, who came and went from his home like a ghost.

Yes. Mike would know what was going on. And if he didn't, he'd find out. Christian would see to that.

Silly old fool, he said to himself, settling deeper into his chair, trying to learn something from Gordy, a man whose brain was still in short britches. What would he know about the Hotel Philip . . . or Christian's abiding feelings for Joseph Emerson? And why would the boy in him care? He let his head rest against his chair back and closed his deep-set eyes.

So long ago. Why would anyone care?

Except him. Christian cared. And Christian remembered.

All of it . . . the stir of desire, the fire of ambition, the searing heat of passion—and the trust invested so deeply, so naively, in youthful dreams.

All of it . . . destroyed, ground under the heel of a heartless, uncaring man.

Hatred, like love, had a long shelf life.

And hatred was his friend. It kept Christian alive. It kept him sane—or his version of it.

And it kept him amused.

Joy stood outside the Hotel Philip and looked up. The morning was gray, the hotel grayer. Not the color, that was buff brick, soiled, tired, and showing every decade of its neglect. No, the grayness was in the Phil's attitude, that of a distinguished old gentleman, once proud and natty, now self-conscious in torn pants and scuffed shoes.

The city's pigeons had accented the Phil's decline with their personal brand of scorn, leaving guano to lie like dirty snow over the arched windows on either side of the broad, once-grand entrance. One of the windows was half boarded up and a graffiti artist had been hard at work on the free wooden canvas, drawing ZOOM ZOOM ZOOM and trailing it with wild, wavelike curls in greens and reds. A neon sign was fitted, like a misplaced suture, into the alcove above the door. Buzzing and blinking in a phosphorous blue, it proclaimed Hotel Ph—ip to anyone interested in an introduction. Joy guessed not many were.

Nothing about the Hotel Philip ZOOMed.

It was much—much!—worse than she remembered.

And it was all hers, a woman who owned only what she could carry and rented the rest and who hadn't spent more than six months in any one place in too many years to count. She shook her head. Stephen Emerson had one wicked sense of humor.

She scanned the hotel front again and swallowed. What a waste. Neglect, a thousand sins of omission, and this was the forlorn result. No doubt the Hotel Philip might have been a charmer in its day, but its day was past.

She glanced up and down the littered street, a mélange of pawn shops, Eastern-style eateries, vacant stores, and, strangely, a bright new coffee shop. It looked like a freshly capped tooth in a mouthful of cavities. She knew from her cab ride here that better times were encroaching on this forsaken street. A block away a major revitalization plan was in the works, and a new hotel was rumored to be on the boards two blocks to the east with shops to follow. But, except for the coffee shop, nothing like that was in evidence here.

The cabbie called it the street Seattle forgot. She tended to agree.

A light rain started to fall, so she climbed the three steps to the entrance, sought what shelter she could under the buzzing blue sign to wait for David Grange. Joy didn't trust him, not that it mattered, because she didn't intend the "taking care of Lana" scenario to include a useless vetting of her current lover.

But for her mother's sake—and her own—she hoped David Grange was a prince among men. It would make her own getaway easier. On that thought, a yellow cab pulled up to the curb and disgorged said lover onto the sidewalk. He smiled up at her.

He was definitely pretty, she decided, watching him take the stairs to join her, his wide, white smile locked in place with a politician's ease. He had a dimple and probably, under his conservative blue business suit, a rather worthwhile, gym-hardened body. Not unappealing.

"Sorry I'm late. A meeting ran too long." He opened the hotel door. "Shall we?" He followed her in.

"Cavernous" was her first thought. Ammonia was her

first scent. The place smelled like a hospital on a serious bacteria hunt. Not the stew of odors she remembered or expected.

"This is new." David looked around, eyebrows raised.

"What?"

He waved a hand. "The place is clean. The last time I was here, maybe a month ago, the lobby still had dirt from the sixties." He walked to the front desk, ran a hand along it, then lifted it. "Somebody's been busy. Maybe they finally replaced the caretaker."

Joy barely heard him. She spun slowly, raptly, in place. Time and its ravages hadn't been kind to the stately lobby, but even in its beaten, battered state it retained an old-world elegance. She didn't remember that. Today she soaked it in, marveled at it: the front desk's thick, carved walnut top—now time-blackened—sitting atop a façade of pink marble; the floors, stained and pockmarked by the passing years, showing proud traces of their once-pearly-white marble surface; the ceilings, bruised to yellow by a million cigarettes, soaring high and arched, looking down in dismay.

When she was here last, she was twelve, had felt nothing but idle curiosity; today she felt sadness.

It may be clean. It may smell good. But it was still a mess. So depressing to see how a building once grand and handsome could fall so low.

David pointed to an elevator at the far end of the lobby. "We might as well start at the top and work our way down." He tilted his head. "Unless, of course, you've seen enough already."

"No. I'd like to see it all." Threat of a wrecking crew arriving imminently couldn't drag her out of here. "Every floor."

"This way, then."

In the elevator, David pushed the large black button

that said 6, the last in the series. As the elevator cage clattered and jerked its way to the sixth floor, Joy said, "I thought there were seven floors."

"There are. But the seventh is the penthouse. You have to get off at six and walk up. It's not legally a part of the hotel. Held in perpetuity by a man named Christian Rupert. He'll be there until they take him out in a pine box—"

"You're a lawyer."

"Gave myself away, did I?"

" 'Perpetuity' will do it every time."

He laughed.

"What will happen to him if I agree to sell you the hotel?"

"*If?*" he repeated. "That slum-landlord thing starting to appeal to you?" He smiled down at her. One of those megawatt smiles artfully executed to melt female hearts at one hundred paces.

"Not likely." She gave the barest shrug. "Just curious."

"Rupert will have to go." His expression darkened.

"Can you do that? What about the 'perpetuity' thing?"

"Look." He faced her, his expression sober. "We should get things straight. There's two ways this hotel can go. Spend a few million to renovate and bring it up to code which *might* provide a minimal return at best—or sell and bring in the wrecking ball. The clock is ticking either way. Stephen received a court order over two years ago to make basic safety improvements, mainly electrical and structural. He ignored it. Didn't want to be bothered, I guess. That order will shift to the new owner. You. If you don't comply, the city will step in and *comply* for you—which will cost a fortune.

"Believe me, Joy, the smart thing to do is take my offer and get out now—before the city gets even more cranky." He stopped and his mouth firmed. "As for the old man upstairs, he should have been in a home years ago. Now, he'll be forced to it. Unfortunate, but that's the way it is."

Joy loathed the idea of shoving a helpless senior into a home he didn't want, but the idea didn't seem to bother David. "How does he feel about that?"

"No idea. I've never met the man. I'll deal with him when I have to."

Joy didn't comment, but neither did she miss his presumption. In his mind the Hotel Philip was already his.

He went on. "The thing you need to understand is that unless you have a few million stashed away you're willing to risk on engineers, architects, and a building crew, the only way you can give your mother the cash she needs is to sell to me. It keeps coming back to economic realities—the real value in the Philip is in the land."

"So you keep telling me, but I do have the hundred thousand."

"When it comes to the Hotel Philip? A drop in a *very* empty bucket."

"I see," she said, not sure she saw anything other than a man determined to get his hands on her—and her mother's—property. And while it bothered her, after what she'd seen so far, he might be right. The place was a wreck. Selling was the smart way out. All she had to do was get someone to confirm that Grange's offer was fair, take it—and walk away.

"I hope you're not too disappointed, that you weren't hoping for more," he said.

She didn't have time to answer because just then the elevator jerked to a clanging halt—at the third floor. David pushed button 6 again, and again, to no avail. It didn't work, nor did any of the other numbers. The elevator refused to move, and the grated accordion door, easily seen through, was not so easily opened. After sev-

eral more futile tries, David yelled into the empty hall.
"Anyone there?"

Nothing but a faint, bouncing echo.

David rattled the cage bars, swore under his breath.

Joy studied the brass roof of the ancient elevator, en-
visioned frayed hoist cables anchored by rusty bolts.
Her stomach kicked. They were only three floors up,
but the ceilings were very high. It was a long way down.

David rattled harder. Called out again.

With an abruptness that shocked them both, a man
carrying a bucket and a mop stepped in front of them.
He must have come from the stairs beside the elevator.

"Thank God," David said and loosened his grip on
the cage struts. "Get us out of here, would you?"

Joy, from where she stood behind David, saw the man
reach into the cage and lift a narrow bar, then pull the
accordion-style door open. The elevator hadn't aligned
with the floor properly, so David chose common sense
over courtesy and stepped out of the elevator before
her, then offered his hand to help her with the step up.

He glared at the man with the mop. "If you're responsible for maintenance around here, you should have that
thing"—he gestured back at the elevator—"seen to immediately."

The man, looking amused, slid his gaze from David
to Joy. When it settled on her, the amusement vanished
and every line in his face drew to hostile.

Joy stared at him, couldn't believe her eyes. "Wade.
Wade Emerson?"

He said nothing, and if possible, his gaze grew even
colder; he visibly straightened.

When he turned as if to walk away, she touched his
arm. "It's Joy Cole. Do you remember me?"

He cocked his head, and a look of confusion dis-
placed the hostility. "Little Joy?"

"Not so little anymore." She looked at him, his damp-kneed denims, ratty, sleeveless shirt—the dark green eyes, studying her as thoroughly as hers studied him. Past him, down the empty hall, she noticed the still-wet floor. None of it made sense. "You work here?" she finally mumbled, unaccountably reddening.

"Live here, for now at least."

Wade Emerson living in this rundown heap? Baffled, she had no idea where to take the conversation from here. "Oh, I see."

He gave her a half smile, without a trace of embarrassment. "I doubt it."

Then, thank God, David piped up. "You're Stephen's son?"

Wade's attention, until now fixed on Joy, shifted to David. She knew he'd taken in the salon haircut, expensive suit, high-gloss wingtips, and made some uniquely man-on-man judgment, although he gave no hint of it. "The one and only," he said, his tone even. "And you?"

David thrust out his hand. "David Grange. Friend of the family." He looked at Joy as if for confirmation.

Joy didn't see it that way but let it go. The two men shook hands.

"Been here long, Emerson?" David asked.

"The name's Wade. And I've been here a time."

The two men locked gazes, and while Wade's eyes were unreadable, David's were openly speculative. "Sorry about your father," he said. "Good man. Unfortunate you couldn't make the funeral."

"Yeah." Wade picked up his mop and pail, his gaze again settling on Joy. He didn't seem to like what he saw. "I'll be on my way. Watch the floors, they're slippery in spots."

Joy, still so stunned to find him here—like he was—watched him go without a word. He opened a door a few feet down the hall and walked in, leaving the hall empty, except for patches of dampness on the floor and the faint scent of pine.

"The higher they fly . . ." David shook his head, his expression openly amazed.

"I don't understand."

"I just mean that Wade was up there, *way* up there. A financial genius, Stephen called him. Apparently he made a serious name for himself in the mergers and acquisitions field."

"They kept in touch, then? Stephen and Wade?" This surprised Joy, who'd thought the rift between them complete and permanent.

"No. Stephen tracked him when he could, through the financial pages, old friends, that sort of thing. But he made no effort to reconcile, nor did Wade. Not sure what happened between them, but it was obviously damn bad." David frowned, a flash of concern in his eyes. Then irritation. "I had no idea he was here."

"Did you know him . . . from before?"

"No." He stared down the hall, his expression reflective. "Strange," he said. "And sad, of course."

"Sad?" Joy echoed, intrigued. "Why sad?"

"Stephen's heart started to fail the day they sent Wade Emerson to prison."

Chapter Four

Wade walked to his window, opened it, and did deep breathing.

Life really had a way of broadsiding a guy. For a minute there, he'd have sworn the woman was Lana Cole. Talk about like mother, like daughter. He'd never seen such a resemblance.

He took another full breath and went to pour himself half a cup of leftover coffee. He took a drink and immediately threw the rest of it in the sink. Tasted like liquid soot. He rubbed his temples, eased himself into a chair stationed by his Formica-topped table.

Joy Cole. He'd met her a couple of times before his final blowout with Stephen and her mother. The last time was right here, in the Hotel Philip. She was twelve or so then, which would make her around thirty now—and a real stunner. Just like her mother.

If she was lucky, the resemblance stopped at the physical.

But what the hell was she doing here? Checking out Mommy's inheritance to see what kind of good fortune had befallen the Cole women? If so, she must be one disappointed lady. He smiled grimly. The guy with her had the cut of a lawyer—shiny shoes, firm handshake, calculator eyes. The executor, maybe, showing her around. Maybe Mommy wanted her opinion on what to do with the hotel.

Tear it down, most likely.

He ignored the pain in his gut and looked at the ceiling. "Well, Joe, it looks like the day of the dame. Not too sure how you'd feel about that." He took his tool belt off, emptied the bucket of water into his sink. Nothing to do now but lay low. Let the lawyer show the lady around— and stay as far away from her as possible.

A half-hour later, he heard Sinnie hissing against his door. "Wade? You in there?"

He didn't feel like Sinnie right now, but he knew there'd be no avoiding her. "I'm here."

She marched in, not bothering to close the door.

"Ever see the like?" she asked without preamble, looking wasp-mean. "More damn crust than a bread roll."

"You've met our guests," he said. "I just poured myself an orange juice. Want some?" He took a deep drink, felt the cold orange rip down his arid throat.

"I don't want any juice. I want you to do something." Her voice rose.

"And that would be?"

"Get that woman out of here. Get them all out of here. This place is yours by right, Wade Emerson. It was in your grandpa's blood, and it's in yours."

Wade held his words in for a second. "Sinnie, I'll say it again, one more time and slowly. This place does not belong to me. I have no claim on it. Whether you like it or not, the Phil belongs to Lana Cole."

"Actually, it doesn't. It belongs to me." The voice was low, the words bell clear.

Joy Cole leaned against his open door, her head tilted to one side, her gaze arcing between him and Sinnie.

"Say that again," he instructed, certain he hadn't heard right.

"I said the hotel doesn't belong to my mother, it belongs to me." She didn't move, and her gaze fixed to his, leaving Sinnie gape-mouthed at his side.

Wade put his unfinished orange juice on the scarred counter and scratched his forehead with his index finger. "You're telling me Stephen Emerson left this hotel to you?"

"To put it briefly, yup."

"You're the daughter!" Sinnie popped to life.

"Yup again. Joy Cole, daughter of Lana." She looked at Wade. "What do you think it means, you and I opting for Stephen and Lana instead of good old Mom and Dad?"

Wade had no answer to that or anything else at the moment. He struggled to get a grip on the situation, an angle on the woman lounging confidently against his door. Whatever shock she'd registered at seeing him in the hall a half-hour ago was gone; in its place was total composure. God, the woman looked like her mother, except for the eyes. Lana's were still, kind of a dreamy Caribbean blue; her daughter's were blue steel.

"Well?" She hadn't moved an inch.

"Well, what?"

"If you don't want to talk, how about showing me around?"

He leaned back against the counter. "Can't see why I should, considering you've just had the two-dollar tour, courtesy of the legal beagle."

She shifted away from the door and straightened her bag strap on her shoulder. "I asked him to go. I thought you'd do a better job."

"Absolutely right," Sinnie piped in. "Wade knows everything there is to know about the Philip."

Wade glanced at Sinnie, who for some goddamn reason looked clam happy.

Joy smiled at her. "I know." She looked at Wade again and while the smile drifted from her mouth, it lingered in her eyes when she said, "I remember."

Abruptly caught up in his own memory, Wade stared at her, tried to see the young girl he'd met years before. Instead he saw her mother, leaning over him . . . wrapping her cool, expert fingers around his cock.

He looked away, back again, not sure what she'd see in his eyes. "I'll show you around," he said. "But not today. Today, I'm busy. Come back tomorrow around noon." He sounded like a moron, but all he wanted right now was for her to leave. And if she were anything like her mother, she wouldn't take a step until she had what she wanted.

Joy looked around the small, seedy, very *unbusy* room, then back at him, her expression wry. "Okay. I'll come back tomorrow. Noon. See you then." Without another word, she turned and left.

"Now isn't that something?" Sinnie let out a breath that could be heard clear to the lobby and stared at the open door. "Can you believe it?"

Wade picked up his juice, downed it. "No." He walked to his door, didn't bother to close it, and looked meaningfully at Sinnie. "Haven't you got a rummy game to play . . . somewhere?"

"Okay, I'll go. We'll talk later. Figure things out."

Wade was losing it and losing it fast. He frowned. "Jesus, Sinnie, figure what out?"

She wrinkled her already wrinkled forehead and lifted her thin eyebrows. "Men!" she said in utter disgust. "Dumb as bricks, the lot of you." She glared at him. "We've got a chance, don't you see? If that Lana creature had inherited, we'd be out on our ears in no time. But she didn't, her daughter did. So maybe, if we put our heads together, we can come up with a plan. You can talk to her, maybe get this place back. Romance her, then—"

"—Romance her?" Wade couldn't believe his ears.

Sinnie clutched his arm. "If you had the hotel, every-thing would be all right again." Her voice rose on the last words and her eyes brightened with moisture.

For the first time, Wade saw the fear behind the fire.

Sinnie had arrived at the Phil broke, widowed, and without family sometime in the seventies, and immediately started working for Christian Rupert. She'd been a friend of Wade's grandfather and his mother. As a boy she'd won him over with bags of peanuts, jaw breakers, and more hugs than he'd been comfortable with.

He should have sensed her panic, expected it. She must be terrified by the thought of being tossed out of her home and losing her extra income in one clean sweep of a new broom.

Hell! He put his arm around her shoulders, walked her toward the door. "Okay, Sin, we'll talk later. Okay?" He tried to soothe her and avoid making any promises, because he had none to make.

She left, tears at the corner of her eyes, too proud to brush them away. "Just you don't make that later *too late.* Some people got all the time in the world. I'm not one of them. You hear me?"

"I hear you."

He closed the door behind her and cursed himself into the next century. How the hell had he got himself trapped in this zoo? First a bucket of water and a mop, now an old woman's tears and a load of fresh-laid guilt.

He waited until he was sure Sinnie had cleared the hall before he headed out. He needed to get out of here, take a walk. By the time he was at the front door of the Philip, he'd resigned himself to talking to Joy Cole, finding out what her plans were. He owed Sinnie and the rest of the tenants that at least.

Then he was history. He'd find a new place to nurture his demons and let the hotel and everyone in it go to hell.

* * *

It was close to eleven P.M., and Christian, as was his custom, sat sipping a fine brandy. The night was mild, so he'd left the terrace doors ajar to catch the cool, dark breezes coming from the west. He remembered a time when he would have opened them wide, stood to breathe in the scents from his beloved rooftop garden; there had been roses, verbena, even a potted lilac bush. Its lush blossoms had filled his home with spring.

Back then the open terrace doors caused him no distress at all. He understood no one would come to him through those doors unless they could fly or were ghosts— he grinned flatly—which fortunately he didn't believe in.

Regrettably the panic that lived in the whirls and eddies of his aging mind continued to tighten its grip, miniaturize his world. In due course, his terrace became as much a place of dread as the six floors underneath him. His shudder was involuntary, maddening. From below stairs anything—anybody—was possible. Christian knew he was malfunctioning, that his fears were illogical and chaotic, but the knowledge didn't change anything. He accepted what he'd become years ago. He was old and rich enough for ten lifetimes, so if he chose to coddle his devils, coddle them he would. Then he'd take them to his grave.

The stereo played Bach's *Brandenburg Concerto No. 6*, the strains of the violins in perfect harmony with the soft night winds.

Christian closed his eyes, waltzed his head in time with the soft, vibrant flow of music.

A rap on the door jarred him to a stop. Such intrusions weren't uncommon at this time of night, but they were always planned and expected. This one was not.

And given that Gordy wasn't due back with Melly for another half-hour, it paid to be careful.

Christian slipped his hand down the side of his chair and pulled out the small revolver. His hand was shaky; his spirit was not. He calmed himself, told himself it was probably one of the hotel guests—he always referred to them as guests—coming early to check on him. He paid them well for this service, and organized it on a random basis. These visits formed the basis for his security. He was not without enemies.

He took his time getting to the door, revolver in hand. He didn't look out the peephole; instead, he whispered against the door. "Who is it?"

"David."

Christian was annoyed. David shouldn't be here. He hadn't asked him to come, and it was dangerous, given their plans. Were they seen together, it could ruin everything. "I didn't ask you here." He heard what he thought was a curse from the other side of the door. *Impudent puppy.*

"Christian, it's important. Open the fucking door."

"David, you know I don't like that kind of language." Christian put his hand on the bolt, didn't slide it.

For a second there was no sound, then, "Sorry, I forgot."

Christian stifled his anxiety, slid back the bolt, and opened the door enough for David to enter. David took over from there and slid the bolt shut. Christian tottered back to his chair and his brandy. He put the revolver back in its place between the cushion and armrest of his leather chair. When he was settled, he said, "What are you doing here? You know you're not to arrive unbidden."

"Did you know Wade Emerson's living in the Phil?"

"Of course."

"You're not concerned?"

Christian allowed himself a giggle. "Concerned? No. Amused? Definitely." He aligned the lapels on his velvet jacket, smoothed them down. "And at my age, I take amusement where I can get it. Besides, Sinnie tells me he'll be leaving any day."

"It's dangerous."

"I don't believe so. He has no claim on the Phil."

"He could make one."

"Unlikely in the extreme. Add to that his lack of resources. The man lost everything. But in the improbable event he attempts anything, you can be sure I'll be the first to know." Christian lifted a hand, waved it arrogantly. "Within days, thanks to your preparations and my foresightedness, David, this hotel will be mine. At that time, I'll be delighted to show the last Emerson to the nearest exit."

"I don't like it. He could fuck things up."

Christian winced. What was it about that dreadful word that made its use so ubiquitous? "He's insolvent. A ruined man with nowhere to go but down. He's of no consequence, no consequence at all." Christian often mused on what Joseph's reaction would be to the wreckage of his precious family. "Forget Wade Emerson."

"I don't expect I have a choice. I seldom do."

"Smart of you to remember that."

David paced, looked distracted. "Is Mike working out all right?"

"He'll do. Not the gardener you were, of course. But I had more energy then for the necessary training." He eyed David with interest. "Although I doubt you came here to ask about my latest hireling."

David helped himself to a brandy, and Christian shot him a disapproving look. "I don't believe I offered you that. Please wipe the bottle with the cloth when you're done and set your glass on the tray."

David's expression soured. "I know the drill."

"So, again, why are you here? Surely you can't be that concerned about young Emerson. I assure you, I'm not."

David quaffed the brandy, appeared to suck the fire from his throat to his head. He shook it clear. "Lana Emerson has the will."

"I know that." Christian enjoyed the look of surprise on David's face. It pleasured him to think he still had the upper hand with his protégé. "You are not my only source for information. The question is, why did it take you so long to come and tell me such critical information?"

"I've been trying to come up with a solution before bringing you the problem. Isn't that what you taught me?"

Christian ignored the curled lip, the sniping tone. "Judging by your use of the word 'trying,' you haven't succeeded. So, tell me, what is the problem? No, let me guess—the Emerson woman wants more money." Christian was prepared to increase his offer, had been all along, even while David continued to assure him the woman was prepared to practically give him the hotel.

"Lana didn't inherit. Stephen left the hotel to Joy Cole, her daughter."

Christian's grip tightened on his glass, and he didn't immediately speak. This did indeed add an unexpected variable to their plan. "There's no mistake?"

"No."

"She was here. Today. Gordy told me he'd met a 'pretty woman' in the hall."

"Yes. She asked me to show her around. Then she said I should go, that she wanted to wander around the hotel by herself."

"And you let her?" Christian took note of his quickened heartbeat. He didn't like new people in the hotel. People he couldn't control. Emerson wasn't a problem in that respect, but this young woman . . .

"Short of dragging her out the front door by her hair—which I suspect might have brought a crowd—I had no choice. She's a stubborn bitch."

"David!"

"God, Christian, give me a break about the language, will you? Maybe take one small step into the twenty-first century?"

Christian ignored him. "This girl—"

"Hardly a girl. She's thirty, or close to it."

"But she'll go along with her mother's wishes, will she not? And sell you—us—the hotel?"

"I've convinced her there's no value in the building— which in fact there isn't, Christian, to anyone other than you," he said, his tone disparaging. "She's also got a serious case of wanderlust—and a job that feeds off it, so, yes, I think she'll sell."

"You 'think' so," Christian echoed, his words laced with disapproval. "My dear David, you'd best soon come to *know so* for both our sakes. I've waited half a century for the chance to own my home." His pulse pounded against the thin skin of his throat; he put his fingers against it, applied pressure. "If it weren't for me, there wouldn't be a Hotel Philip; it's mine by right. And I will not have what may be my last opportunity lost because of a stupid young woman and the even stupider Emerson who willed it to her. This is my home, and I do not intend to *ever* be removed from it." He shifted his gaze to the terrace where the wind rustled the leaves of the trees in the large planters. A handful of leaves skipped and danced over the patio stones. "Such a bore, moving. So many things to dispose of."

In the still, strained atmosphere of the penthouse, the pump of David's lungs could be heard over the soft notes of Bach—over the clink of David's glass when he poured himself more of Christian's fine brandy. "The day I met you was the day I was cursed." David's look was venomous.

"We curse ourselves, David, didn't you know that?" Christian showed his teeth in a full yellow smile, then went back to the business at hand. "This Joy Cole, is she married? Does she have children?"

"No." David tossed back another shot of brandy.

"Other siblings or blood family members?"

"Not that I'm aware of."

"Then make yourself aware, and in the event she's foolish enough to reject your offer, we shall have a plan B. While this may be a small snag, it is not a catastrophe. Simple, really." Christian stroked one bony finger with another, considered his position, and formulated his instructions. "If the daughter chooses not to sell to us, you dispose of her. Her nearest relative, her mother—who I presume you're still sleeping with—inherits and all will be as it should."

David stared at him as if he didn't understand—or wouldn't. He exhaled sharply.

Christian watched him. He enjoyed those moments when a man's self-interest collided with his conscience. Such fun.

David stood in the center of the large room, empty brandy glass in hand, his face a map of distaste and loathing. "Did I hear you right? Did you just tell me to *kill* Joy Cole."

"I simply gave you a plan B. I'm certain a man with your looks and charm can convince a 'pretty girl'—if that halfwit man-child's description is to be believed—into doing things your way. You've done so well with the mother."

"A mother who'd kill me if she caught me sniffing around her daughter."

"Afraid of a woman." Christian's thin lips twisted up. "How droll." He took the smile off his face. "But hear this, and hear it well. You'll do what has to be done to get me this hotel. The time is now. This place would have been mine years ago if not for that worthless Stephen's promise to his thieving father to keep the Philip in the family at all costs." *And never sell it to me.* Christian's voice rose and his stomach tensed as it always did when he thought of the injustice done him. "I didn't encourage you to become part of Stephen's—and his harlot wife's—life for your sexual pleasure—"

" 'Encourage?' " David echoed with a snort. "That's a good one."

Christian ignored him, went on, "You were there to provide me with information and results. So hear me well—I won't have the Hotel Philip slip through my hands. You will do whatever it takes—copulation or mayhem—to secure it for me. Do you understand?"

David glanced away briefly. "I'll need time."

"Look at me, you fool! Do I look as if I have time?" Christian dug his fingers into the chair arms, stemmed his unhealthy agitation, and lowered his voice. He was displeased with David's reluctance. Very displeased. "Just do your job. Get that girl's signature on the sale agreement."

"Or?"

"Kill her." Impatient with his evasions, his refusal to obey, Christian shifted his gaze to the terrace. "Do we understand one another?"

David crashed his glass down on the top of the liquor cabinet and headed for the door.

Christian saw his chest heave with the effort not to throttle him. Of course, he wouldn't. Christian's mouth contorted to a sneer. Men. So predictable—if you handled them deftly. As he always had.

At the door, David stopped. "You're a viper, Christian. The most cold-blooded son of a bitch I've ever met. It must have been a slow day in Hades when they welded you together, because they did a first-rate job. From hell's point of view, you're fucking perfect." He opened the door wide, held it a moment, and stepped out.

Christian's ancient heart found its rhythm a few minutes after the door closed. David was becoming tiresome, not as malleable as he once was. The thought didn't please him. He hoped David wasn't developing a conscience at this stage in the game. Not that it mattered. The Cole girl must be dealt with quickly.

The heat of Lana's embarrassment crawled up her neck, flamed in her cheeks. "You're sure?" she asked the sales clerk.

"I'm sorry, Mrs. Emerson, but I've tried it three times." The woman's face had to be a mirror image of her own, a pale shade of fuchsia. "I can try again . . . or you could call. I'm certain there's a mistake."

"Yes, but no matter. I have other cards. I just don't have any with me. Please hold the clothes." She took her hand from the large plastic bag on the counter of the exclusive shop. "I'll come back for them tomorrow."

The woman put the bag behind the counter, smiled. "Happy to. As I said, it's probably a computer mixup. These things happen all the time."

Not to me. "I'm sure that's it." Lana took the useless credit card the woman handed her and put it in her bag. "Tomorrow, then." She walked out of the store, careful to walk slowly and keep her head high. A few minutes later, she went into one of the zillion coffee shops that decorated every corner of Seattle. She bought herself bottled water and took a seat.

She was broke. And she was dependent on her daughter to change that. The bill for those summer tees was less than five hundred dollars—*a measly five hundred dollars!*—and she couldn't afford them. There was David, of course. She could go to him, ask for money; he *had* said he'd take care of her.

She thought about this, but decided it would be a bad move. It was too soon after Stephen's death to appear desperate, and if she handled her money problem badly it could ruin things. She'd appear weak, needy, perhaps even grasping—traits that frightened men off faster than bad sex. No, she had to wait for him to offer the money, *insist* she take it.

Last night, when he'd called, he'd been edgy—angry again—because Joy hadn't committed to selling the Philip. Adding her money problems into the mix would increase his stress level, perhaps turn his anger toward her. The smart thing to do was to be supportive, get in his corner—and start handling her damn daughter.

She glanced out the window, saw the top of the Marriott. The hotel wasn't more than a couple of blocks away. Lana stared at it a long time, slowly sipped her water, and tapped her polished nails on the table. Finally, she rose and picked up her bag.

Stephen had asked Joy to take care of her, and, having considered her other options, Lana had no choice. She would ask Joy for money.

As she walked up the street toward the hotel, Lana's dearest wish was that Stephen were still alive—so she could kill him herself.

Chapter Five

Joy opened her door and stood back, amazed. "Lana . . . I mean, Mother! What are you doing here?"

"Visiting. May I come in?"

Joy stepped aside, and as usual when she was in the same room with her mother, her stomach muscles tensed. "I just got back from meeting Stephen's lawyer. It seems even wills need to have paperwork and X's in all the right spots."

"It's done, then?"

Joy nodded. "I was just having coffee. Would you like some?"

"No, thanks." Lana walked into the luxurious hotel suite and looked around. "Nice. There must be more money in travel writing than I thought—either that or you're already into that hundred grand."

Joy looked away, clamped down on her temper. "Like I said, it's comped. Sometimes I get lucky."

"Obviously." Lana strolled over to the window, looked out and down onto the busy street below. It was close to noon, and the lunch crowds were already rushing the crosswalks. She turned back to Joy. "I need some money."

Her wide-set eyes rested on Joy like drugged butterflies, bright, pretty, expressionless.

The taut muscles in Joy's stomach eased off. She'd expected this, just not so soon. "How much?"

"You could give me the hundred thousand."

"I could, but I won't."

"It's mine. Stephen meant for you to give it to me."

"He meant for me to *take care* of you—financially. And he left it up to me to decide how best to do it. That's going to take a few days. In the meantime, how much money do you need to get through the next month?"

"Forty thousand."

Joy's breath caught and then she laughed. It was the only logical response. "I said a *month*." She shook her head. Some things—like her mother's spending habits—never changed. "I'll make your mortgage payment and give you ten. That should put a few cans of soup in the cupboard." Joy got her checkbook from her briefcase, wrote out the check, and handed it to Lana.

Lana took it, barely glancing at the numbers on it. "This isn't going to work, you know. Me coming to you for handouts."

"It's going to have to. For now, at least. Trust me, I don't like it any more than you do."

Lana slipped the check into her bag. "You toured the Philip yesterday. What did you think?"

"I think it might have . . . potential." Joy hadn't meant to say it aloud, particularly to her mother. She wasn't even sure it was the truth. But after touring the hotel yesterday and listening to David's pitch, she'd decided to keep her options open. Temporarily, at least.

"You're not thinking of keeping it! You can't be." Shock tightened Lana's mouth.

"Relax, will you? I said I was 'thinking.' The place is a dump, you know that, but I'd be stupid not to look at all possibilities."

"I'm stunned. Out of my shoes stunned. You'd consider turning down David's generous offer, so you can run a seedy old hotel in one of the worst parts of Seattle. That's the stupidest thing I ever heard."

Joy's patience thinned dangerously. "And what makes you so sure Grange's offer is all that generous?"

Lana's eyes narrowed. "This isn't entirely about money, is it? What you really want to do is get back at me for your father—" She stopped abruptly.

"The smart thing," Joy said, her words as icy and tight as the coil curving around her heart, "is for us not to go there. The smart thing is for us to get on with our lives—which means me figuring out your financial mess as intelligently as I can, so you and I can call it quits on this pretense of a relationship once and for all."

"You're an unforgiving little bitch, Joy. Did you know that?"

Joy concentrated on breathing, didn't respond.

Lana's gaze rested on her, as still as snow on a mountaintop. "And if ending our 'relationship' is what you truly want, the quickest way to accomplish it is to sell that stupid hotel and give me the money."

"No doubt you're right, but for now, I've decided to be the 'practical person' Stephen expected me to be and take time to think things through." She nodded at the check in Lana's hand. "What you've got there"—Joy nodded toward Lana's bag—"is it for now, so I'd suggest you make it last."

Lana, after giving her a frigid glare, walked toward the door. Once there, she swung back. "I'll have to talk to David, tell him you're taking some time."

"He knows. He called this morning. I told him the same thing I told you—that I'm thinking things through. He wasn't thrilled at the news."

"That property is important to David. He has time constraints, and his partners are getting anxious. He has reason to be disappointed." She raised a brow, the gesture only mildly impatient. "How long will this 'thinking' of yours take?"

"A month?"

"Then you'll come to dinner four weeks from today. I'm asking you not to make a final decision—*or any commitments whatsoever*—until David and I have a chance to present our case. Do we understand one another?"

Trapped, Joy nodded again. "Fair enough."

When the door closed behind Lana, Joy walked to the bedroom, stripped off her clothes, and stepped into the shower. She put having dinner with her mother and David in the same category as a full body peel followed by a salt rubdown.

She lifted her face to the cascade of water coming from the showerhead and wondered, not for the first time, what the hell she was doing.

She had less than an hour before she met Wade at the hotel. Maybe it was just a whim, and maybe she'd learn nothing to help with her decision-making, but a half-hour or so without David's ambition and her mother's greed and impatience would be a blessed relief.

No doubt selling the hotel to Grange provided her the quickest exit—if she could trust him and his offer. But she didn't. She needed an outside opinion and an independent evaluation. And she intended to get them.

One thing was sadly obvious: the buffer—a solid framework of time and miles—she'd built between her and her mother had crumbled within seconds of their being in the same room.

She stepped out of the shower and toweled off.

But this wasn't *all* about Lana and their miserable relationship. There was something else.

Yesterday in the Philip, when her initial shock at the

condition of the hotel had worn off, and after she'd gotten rid of David, she'd spent more time in the lobby.

The images remained.

Scarred oak floors, cracked and broken windows, stained marble too many years from its Italian quarry, decorative plaster moldings, once set so meticulously in the joint between floor and wall, now shrunken and split.

A faded, dusty ruin basking in the scent of clean, fresh pine.

On the fourth floor, she'd stopped at a door with a shiny new brass doorknob; it radiated like a small sun in the dark, depressing hall. When she'd run a finger over it, she'd gotten a lump in her throat as big as a lemon.

Why a brass doorknob made her think about her father, she couldn't imagine. But it had. Painfully so. And she'd remembered those times he'd let her come into his garage workshop, helped her build magical, foolish kid things. How they'd laugh together . . .

Alone in the halls, her heart—territory she'd barricaded off and guarded fiercely for years—had raced, whirred in her chest as if it were one of those windup toys a parent gives a two-year-old for Christmas.

Then there'd been the snippet of overheard conversation, the woman saying, "yours by right, Wade Emerson, your legacy . . . in your blood."

The words stuck in her mind, sharp pins tipped in regret. Joy Cole, so cool, so quick-lipped and reluctant to connect, and always on the move, had lived thirty years and could honestly say nothing was "in her blood" except the required red and white cells.

By right, the Phil should have gone to Wade, and it angered her that Stephen's insane request had embroiled her as much in his life as it had in Lana's. It made her feel guilty.

She took a few breaths and told herself there was nothing she could do about that. What was . . . *was*. Her odd reaction to the hotel, to seeing Wade again, her surging memories of her father, her nomadic, chilly life—none of it mattered.

All that mattered was the care and feeding of Lana Emerson—and doing the right thing.

Today she'd inspect every last inch of the decrepit hotel. It was time she and *Phil* really got to know each other, and she couldn't have a better person than Wade to introduce them.

She went to the closet. She'd already laid out a pair of khaki slacks and a silk shirt, but was suddenly indecisive. Maybe jeans and a tee would be more appropriate.

What the hell did a woman wear to tour a dilapidated building with a financial genius? And ex-convict.

Christian told Mike to sit down. The big man obeyed, folding his hands together between his knees. He looked nervous. Christian liked that.

"Well, Michael, have you thought about my offer?"

Mike nodded.

"You understand what I want."

"Yeah, you want me to do the gardening, like I have been doing, and keep an eye on things, let you know what's goin' on in the Phil." Big Mike nodded his head. "I can do that."

"And keep quiet about it? That's critical."

"Sure, no one here worth talkin' to anyway."

Christian picked up the remote control from his side table, turned down the volume on the sound system. He needed to be heard—and, more important—understood. "You'll have to quit your other job immediately. I need you here, eyes and ears open all the time. You understand that?"

"No problem."

Christian stared at his newest recruit, watched him carefully. He hadn't planned to promote him so early, but his choices were limited. "I'm told there was trouble in Room 33 the other night. Did you have anything to do with that?"

"A couple of kids got in, using the outside fire escape. I rousted 'em."

"Ah." He could see by Mike's proud expression how much he'd enjoyed the incident. A good sign. "You didn't hurt them, did you?"

Mike dropped his eyes as if he weren't sure what Christian wanted to hear. "Not too much," he mumbled.

"Just as well, all things considered." While he would have enjoyed seeing 33 come to life—or death—again, things were unsettled. Police nosing around would be inconvenient.

"Huh?" Mike said, obviously confused by his response.

Christian ignored him. He was big and stupid, which disappointed him. But he was still useful. He went on, "Gordy tells me there was company in the hotel yesterday. A man and a girl. A pretty girl, he said."

"He got that right."

"He said the girl stayed after the man left. Is that so?"

"Yeah, she walked around by herself for a time, then went to Wade's room."

Christian's heart jumped, and he took a second of silence to calm himself. "And what went on there?"

"Not much."

Christian raised a brow. " 'Not much' isn't the type of answer I'm paying for."

Mike frowned, appeared to think a moment. "Wade didn't seem happy about her showing up. That's for sure. Sinnie was, though."

"Sinnie was there?" Unpleasant news.

"She was raggin' on Wade about his grandpa and all.

About how he should own the Phil. How he should get off his butt and do something about it. He pretty much ignored her. Like everybody." He shrugged. "Sinnie's always goin' on about somethin'."

"Is she?" To calm himself, Christian turned up the volume for a moment, enjoyed a particularly fine movement in Bach's Concerto in C Minor. *Dear, dear, Sinnie. Will you never learn to do as you're told and mind your own business?*

"And the girl?" he asked finally. "What did she want from Mr. Emerson?"

"Wanted him to show her around. Lucky bastard. Said she'd come back tomorrow." He hesitated. "That'd be today, around noon."

"This girl, Michael. Just how pretty is she?"

He rubbed his crotch, grinned broadly. "Prime booty, Mr. Rupert. A man could sink his dick in that and just fuckin' leave it there."

Christian's stomach heaved, but he kept his voice modulated. "There's no need to be tasteless. And you should know I abhor foul language."

The smile dropped off Mike's face.

"Now, if you'll be good enough to sweep off my terrace and water my trees, I'll have an envelope ready for you when you're done."

Mike stood, gaped down at him, but didn't move.

Christian waved a hand, the gesture short and impatient. "The terrace, man. Do my terrace. And be sure and close the door behind you." Christian couldn't wait to get rid of him. Money bought all kinds of things, all kinds of people. The trouble was, they were all of the most repellent ilk.

He watched Mike through the window as he swept, watered, and hand-weeded his planters.

Christian's mind went back to the "prime booty" the man had so grossly described. Women, as a sex, had never held his interest, but Christian understood the dangerous thrust and pull of sexual attraction. Respected its power.

And more than anything, he feared it.

The risk of such an attraction between Wade Emerson and Joy Cole, the current owner of the Hotel Philip—his hotel—was not one he would tolerate.

Wade stood in the Philip's lobby and glanced at his watch. She was five minutes late; he'd give her ten.

When his watch told him fifteen, he moved to go, but stopped when the hotel's one good door thrust open. The other was nailed shut in the interests of safety. Joy Cole breezed in, wearing jeans and a navy blue tee. She looked hot and hassled as she stepped briskly to him.

"A lot of foot traffic in this town. I misjudged the walking time." Her smile was brief, unapologetic, and she offered him her hand. "Thanks for waiting."

He took the outstretched hand. Small bones. Soft skin. Firm grip. He gave it back and looked down into her keen, bright eyes. Hard to believe the sour-faced twelve-year old had turned out this good. "You look thirsty. It's hot out there. Let's go." He took her arm and walked her back toward the door.

When he pushed the door open, she protested. "I thought we were doing a tour of the hotel, not the neighborhood."

"Good idea to have a look at both."

"I guess." She stepped out in front of him.

Wade closed the door behind them, and he couldn't not pick up the pop can and fast food wrappers someone had stashed in the entranceway. He dropped them in the trash can a few feet from the door.

He knew she watched him, but she didn't say a word.

"Where are we going?"

"There's a coffee shop up the street. I could use one." He looked at her. "And you could use . . . what? A Perrier. Evian?"

She smiled slightly, pushed a long strand of hair behind her ear. "Something like that."

When they were settled, him with his dark roasted coffee, her with her bottled water, he said, "So, little Joy inherited the Philip." He drank some coffee, studied her.

She didn't flinch. "That's what the will says."

"You happy about that?"

"A Marriott or Ritz would've been better."

He laughed. She didn't.

Her gaze turned curious. "Aren't you angry?"

"About what?"

"About how things worked out. Your dad, my mother. Now this hotel thing." She turned her bottle so the label faced her, then away again, not taking her eyes from his. "You must be bitter."

"Now there's a word." He appeared to consider it. "But no, not bitter."

"What, then?"

"Surprised my father didn't leave it to Lana." Hell, he'd given her everything else she wanted and disposed of what she didn't. Like his mother.

"Not as surprised as I was." She hesitated, looked uneasy. "You didn't go to Stephen's funeral."

"No."

"Why not?"

"Ever try beating around the bush?" It surprised him how comfortable he was with her, which was damn stupid, considering her genes.

Her lips quirked up. "Not my style."

She added nothing, waited for his answer with the patience of a heron dining at the seashore. He took a breath. "I figured your mother would be there." He drew his lips to a tight seal. Enough said. Too much said. Nobody needed to know it, but he had visited his father's grave that day—after everyone had gone. He'd touched the fresh earth, said what passed for a prayer . . . something about how he wished things hadn't turned out as they did, how he hoped things were okay on the other side. It was the best he could do. He wasn't much good in the forgive and forget department.

"You don't like my mother." Joy's tone was even, the words calmly said.

"As an understatement, that'll work." He drained his coffee. In Wade's opinion, Lana Cole was an A-list predator and the most narcissistic, opportunistic woman he'd ever met. She cared about two things, sex and money. And she'd do anything to get all she could of both. He didn't see the need to share his opinion with her only daughter.

"I guess you've heard about how it takes two to break up a marriage," she said.

"Yeah, I picked up on that."

"But you don't believe it?"

"I believe there are people who know how to capitalize on the weaknesses of others and don't hesitate to do it to get what they want."

"And you think my mother is one of them."

He said nothing, had already said far more than he intended.

For a moment it looked as if she were going to launch a defense, then she said, "Your opinion. Everyone's entitled to one."

He shoved his empty coffee mug away from him. "So how about that tour you were so hot on?" He eyed the full bottle of water in front of her. "You can take that with you." When he started to get up, she put a hand on his arm. The warmth of it stilled him.

"Do I take that as a change of subject?"

"I'm not much for history."

"Fair enough, but there's something you should know before you show me the Philip."

"Go on."

"I've had an offer on it. That man I was with yesterday? He wants to buy it."

"And?"

"Then he wants to bring in a wrecking ball. Take it down. The money's in the land, he says."

It was the inevitable end for the Philip; Wade knew that. What pissed him off was her words slammed into his stomach as if they were the damned wrecking ball she alluded to and left a queer throbbing in its wake. "Probably the smart thing to do," he said, his voice as flat as his gut reaction allowed. "Good bucks for you, I'd figure."

She frowned at him, her expression puzzled. "That's it? That's all you feel?"

"There's not much point in my feeling anything."

She studied him as if he were a science project and she an A+ student. "I don't think I believe you."

He recognized that unwavering gaze. Although deeper and more intense, it was exactly like her mother's, and it irritated the hell out of him. "Look, the jaunt back to yesteryear was fun, but I've got work to do. So, how about we head back to the Phil, I give you your tour, my two bits' worth of opinion, and we part company."

He might as well have not spoken; she didn't move. "Do you remember the last time we saw each other? I was twelve, you were maybe eighteen? Your grandfather had died the year before—I remember you telling me that. I remember how sad it made you look, and how the sadness lifted when you talked about the hotel, how your granddad had built it, how it almost ruined him, but he'd succeeded despite the biggest depression the country had ever seen. You were so proud . . ." Her voice trailed off. "Anyone could see how much he meant to you, how you felt about his work."

Wade labored to breathe. How the hell had the little squirt registered all that? She was just a kid, with the biggest, moodiest eyes he'd ever seen. The last memory came with a jolt and brought more. He'd talked his ass off that day and those moody eyes had stayed with him for every word. They were with him now, urging more words from him, words he couldn't hold back if he tried.

"I loved him," he said. "I'd never deny that. He was more a father to me than my own. He was a hardworking, never-say-die kind of man who kept his word and met his commitments." He paused, wanting her to be absolutely sure of his meaning, when he said, "But the Phil was his life, not mine." There might have been a time he'd thought otherwise, but Stephen put an end to that.

In the space between them lay the buzz of the coffee shop, the hiss of the milk steamer, cups hitting saucers, the chatter of the servers, and the scrape of plates shoved across the counter to waiting customers. It might as well have been the silence of the catacombs.

Joy chose to break it, her tone cool and glass level. "That's too bad, because I'd like to consider all the options on this property. One of them being—if it's financially viable, of course—to renovate, bring it to compliance with city standards, and reopen." She'd thought about it all night, but saying it aloud brought a rush of enthusiasm she wasn't prepared for.

Wade stared at her for a long time. She saw the emotion in his eyes, surprise replaced by suspicion, suspicion replaced with intense speculation. "And why would you want to do that?"

"I don't know yet whether I do, but if I feel it's a good business move . . ." Uncertain where to go from there, or whether to mention her childlike emotional response to the Phil, she stopped.

"You know how many people go broke using 'feelings' to make financial decisions."

"Yes, I do, which is why I'm talking to you. I don't plan on doing anything stupid. If it turns out the smart thing is to sell, that's what I'll do. Right now, I need input, a professional's analysis, to see which idea is most viable—hold and renovate, or sell. According to David, you're a 'financial genius.' Exactly what I need."

"Tell me why I should give a damn about what you 'need?' " His face darkened. "I'm not my father. The care and feeding of a Cole woman isn't high on my priority list."

The air in Joy's lungs shifted. He'd used the exact words she'd used when she'd been thinking about her mother earlier. It was suddenly disturbingly clear how much Wade disliked Lana. He'd hate the idea of the proceeds from the Philip being used to ensure her financial future. But with barely a month to make a decision, she needed his expertise and knowledge of the hotel. She decided not to tell him. "That wasn't fair," she said. "I'm not my mother either."

"You're right. Sorry." He didn't look sorry, he looked irritated.

She left his apology to float alone for a second. "Is there a chance we could talk about this—without the ghosts of Christmases past getting in our way?"

He locked his gaze on her. "Did David also tell you I recently spent time behind a wire fence?" Those mixed emotions again, shooting through his eyes, shame replaced by pride. Defiance.

"He told me." She took a drink of water. "He didn't tell me why." She was curious, knew it showed.

"You're better-looking than my first cell mate, but you sure sound like him. 'What ya in for?' " he mimicked, then laughed, sharply with an edge of sneer.

"You're not going to tell me, are you?"

"No."

"I can find out on my own."

"I'm surprised you haven't already. A smart girl like you should have figured out the risks of asking an ex-con for advice. For all you know, I'm an axe murderer."

"Doubt it. I read the papers. Hasn't been an axe murder in years."

His lips ticked up as if at a private joke. "Maybe not, but the thought did cross my mind once or twice."

"So you don't want to talk about it?" She wondered if he meant that smile to be so seductive.

"You could get me drunk, take me to bed. That might loosen me up. After sex, I'm a sucker for pillow talk."

His playful innuendo crossed the table between them like a gust of hot wind. Joy's mouth went dry. "I don't use sex as a bribe." She'd intended her comeback to be light, breezy. Instead, a preacher on the witness stand couldn't have sounded more righteous.

"What do you use it for?" There was humor in his eyes, along with undisguised male interest.

Her stomach fluttered. A change of subject was in order. "How did we get from my interest in renovating the Hotel Philip to sex?"

He cocked a brow. "It's a guy thing."

She couldn't help laughing. "Yeah." And when this guy talked sex, this girl wanted to listen. Bad idea. Very bad idea. She wanted to drop her gaze, but couldn't.

He watched her for a moment; then, with an abruptness that caught her off guard, he stood. "Let's get back to the hotel. We'll talk there."

"You'll think about my idea then? At least consider bringing the Phil back to life? If the economics work, of course?"

"There's more than economics involved."

"Like what?" She stood, scanned his face. The man's mood changed with the speed of light, or the turn of a phrase.

"People. Years back, the Philip stopped being a hotel, stopped being about nightly room rates and profit and loss. It became home to people who don't have a lot of choices. You don't just toss people into the street for the sake of a few bucks." He started for the door. "Let's go back to the Phil. I'll give you your tour. We'll talk after that. And talk is all I can promise."

Chapter Six

"You look troubled, David." Lana touched his bare shoulder, ran her hand down to squeeze his hand, shift it to a more interesting place on her naked body—a body still torrid from lovemaking. He obliged her by deftly drawing his finger through and over her sex-moistened pubic curls. She arched into his hand. "But not too troubled . . ."

"You're the most beautiful woman I've ever known, Lana, and you feel like silk." He dipped his fingers into her, and she drew in a near painful breath. "How can I be troubled with you stretched out in front of me like a feast. A very mouthwatering feast." He moved his hand from her pubis to her breast, tugged on a nipple and bent to kiss its tip. He let out a breath then and propped himself on his elbow to look down at her, his face drawn, his eyes dark.

Lana couldn't get enough of David Grange. She took his head between her hands, drank in his deep but worried gaze. "You say such perfect things," she whispered against his mouth, before kissing him until she weakened.

"Maybe making love with my ideal woman brings out the poet in me." His breath hot against her cheek, he pulled back from the kiss.

She couldn't stop looking at him—his finely chiseled face, midnight blue eyes, the sensuous mouth designed to give her so much pleasure. In so many ways.

Fear rooted in the lower region of her stomach.

She called him her blond beauty, knowing it both irritated and pleased him. But he was beautiful and he was *hers*. She stroked his thick, golden hair, tried to suppress the fear unfolding in her depth. She was dangerously close to being unable to live without this man— perhaps even in love with him, an emotion she'd spent a lifetime avoiding. So much better being the one loved than the lover.

Abruptly, David swung his legs over the side of the bed. He looked worried again. She wished she hadn't told him about her and Joy's conversation at the Marriott. He'd been troubled since the words were out of her mouth. He massaged his eyebrow, as he always did when he was preoccupied.

"She's actually thinking of renovating that old place. I can't believe it."

"Thinking is not doing, darling. Forget it. Joy's always had a tendency to overanalyze things. It's her nature. It doesn't mean a thing, just makes her feel smarter than she really is. She's being her usual mulish, inconsiderate self, that's all."

"She's got to sell me that hotel," he said. "She damn well has to."

Lana sat up, rested her head on the headboard of her king-sized bed. She was tired of talking about the Philip, and about her stubborn daughter. If Stephen had done the right thing, none of this would have happened. "That stupid, stupid will."

"It's not your fault." David finger-combed his thick blond hair, and stood beside the bed to look down at her. Naked—and marvelous—he began to pace. She watched him, enjoyed the sway of his large penis—another of his many attributes. He filled her in a way no other man had.

"I should have paid more attention," she said, adopting a rueful expression. "But Stephen and I had drifted apart in the last year or so and—"

David sat on the bed and stroked her cheek with the back of his hand. "You can't blame yourself for that," he said. "I had something to do with the 'drifting apart,' as I remember."

She smiled. "Yes, you did."

"Do you think he knew about us? Had suspicions?"

"No. Absolutely not." She refused the idea. She was much too clever for Stephen, always had been. No. It was more likely he saw himself as truly doing Lana a favor by forcing a reunion with Joy. The man was such a dreamer! And God knew—as Lana did—people staring death in the teeth became strange as their time drew near. Often ridiculously nostalgic.

David kissed her and she drifted away again, to that place he took her so effortlessly. A place with no money problems, no disturbing old hotels, and the only *joy* was her body releasing, releasing . . .

When David stretched out beside her and put his arm behind his head, Lana draped herself across his chest. "I did do one smart thing," she said and nibbled on his perfectly served nipple. She heard his breath stall.

"What's that?"

"I insisted she give me a time frame. A month. Not a day more. And"—she licked him before lifting her face to meet his eyes—"I made her promise to let us know before she made any commitments whatever. That will give us time to maneuver if she decides to do something foolish—which I really don't think she will."

"That's great." He rolled up and over her and his eyes were brighter, his worried frown eased. "It will buy me time with my investor, for now at least."

Lana didn't answer, tamped a surge of impatience. All these plans of David's were so mysterious. He'd mentioned partners, but never by name. Pools of capital, but not from where. Boring, every bit of it. She never encouraged him by asking questions, because to Lana only one thing mattered: how much money would eventually end up in her bank account when the Phil was sold.

"Can I ask you something?" David propped himself up again.

She lifted a brow.

"How do you really feel about Joy?"

"Feel?" Trick question, Lana decided. David knew there wasn't a traditional mother-daughter relationship, but that wasn't the same as appearing as an uncaring mother. "We have our differences, you know that. But she's my daughter. I love her, of course." Truth was, she didn't like to think about her feelings for Joy—or anyone else. It was easier to think about herself.

He studied her. "That's what I figured." He closed his eyes a moment, then he opened them. "Then what I'm going to ask of you won't be too hard."

She scraped his chin softly with a long, red fingernail. "And that would be?"

"Keep in touch with Joy. Get closer."

When Lana raised a questioning brow, David smoothed it straight. "I'm not asking you to knit afghans with her, sweetheart. Just to stay abreast of her thinking. I wouldn't want anything to happen to her—"

"Now there's a bit of melodrama. What on earth

could happen to her?" She ran a palm over his chest, downward, determined to change the subject. Close to Joy? He might as well have asked her to bed down with a crocodile.

"I meant to say I wouldn't want anyone to get to her, encourage her in this stupid renovation idea she's come up with. It's important or I wouldn't ask. Will you do it?"

"If that's what you want," she said. But then she'd say anything to end this conversation, get on with more meaningful pursuits.

He kissed her lightly. "I owe you one."

"Yes, you do." She ran her hand down between their heated bodies, wrapped it firmly around the length of him, squeezed until his hot flesh quivered and jumped under her hand. "And you'll be happy to know you can take it out in trade."

He buried his face in the hollow at her throat, and she could hear his efforts to control his breathing. Her heart wanted to leap from her chest when he kissed under her ear and said. "Christ, Lana, I don't think I could live without you"—he thrust into her, closed his eyes—"without this."

He moved inside her and so did her fear. If this was love, Lana preferred lust. Lana Cole Emerson didn't know what to do with love.

Wade stood in front of the last door of the day. They'd been in the hotel for over three hours.

After a tour of all the unoccupied rooms—which was most of them—Wade had taken Joy into the weirdest and mustiest basement in Seattle. He rapped on, and talked about, the Phil's bewildering maze of pipes, vents, and electrical wiring until Joy's brain was thick with information. None of which she'd yet put in order. A hotel, she'd learned, was much more than a haven for the weary traveler, it was a marvel of engineering and planning.

By the time Wade opened the double doors on the grand ballroom, Joy was dusty, dirty, and eager to see more. He stepped back to let her go in first.

"Wow." She walked in and did a slow spin. "I don't remember this from when I was here."

Wade closed the doors behind them, looked at the ceiling some thirty feet above them. "I don't think we came in here. Look." He pointed upward and her eyes followed to see a painted ceiling that would rival the finest of those she'd seen in the galleries of Italy. But instead of cherubs and angels, it was the towering trees, rich waters, and jagged coastline that cradled the home of Seattle in the mid-nineteenth century. It was brilliant.

"Wow," she said again and heard him chuckle.

When she turned to look at him, the steadiness of his gaze made her briefly self-conscious. "What?" she asked, stepping away from him.

"You like that word," he said. "And I like the way your lips move when you say it." He kept his interest full on her. Now she felt edgy.

She walked to the center of the cavernous room and away from his scrutiny. "So this is the grand ballroom?" she said and did another turn.

He smiled before going along with the change in subject. "Yes. This is the nearest to original of any public part of the Phil. Like any business, through the years changes were made. Some good. Some bad. The worst during the late sixties. That's when the shift started toward permanent residency. Once that happened, this room was closed off. My grandfather said even if the rest of the place went to hell, he wanted this room to stay as it was."

"That would be Joe Emerson, right?"

Wade nodded.

"Then your father must have felt the same way. He didn't change it, either."

He shrugged. "He pretty much ignored it, like he did everything else to do with the Phil. He inherited more interesting things to play with." Wade took another long look around. "As for grandfather, I think it had something to do with my grandmother loving the room so much. I said as much once."

"And he replied?"

A smile, part amusement, part nostalgia, curved his mouth. "He said 'Fiddlesticks.' Old Joe wasn't your sentimental type—on the surface, at least."

"How long were your grandparents married?"

"Over fifty years."

Joy started to say *Wow* again but thought better of it. "That's amazing." She walked to one of the windows. She could hear the traffic on the other side, but the heavy velvet drapes caked in dust muffled it. She shoved one of them aside to reveal windows that appeared to be covered on the outside.

"These windows look interesting, but why are they boarded up?"

"The hotel was resurfaced along the outside of this room somewhere along the line, and the windows were covered over. I don't know why." He came to stand beside her.

"Can you pull the drapes farther apart? I'd like a closer look."

The drapery track was a good twenty feet over their heads. Wade reached as high as his six-foot-plus frame allowed, grasped a fistful of fabric, and gave a strong tug. It didn't move, so he tried again.

This time draperies, track, and sixty years of powdery grime came down with a swoosh to completely envelop them. When they'd fought their way free of the heavy, dust-laden velvet, they looked like a pair of chimney sweeps. Joy's eyes were running like taps and she couldn't stop coughing.

"Are you all right?" Wade pushed the last of the drapery off her shoulders.

"I've got something in my eye," she said. "It feels like a clod of clay."

"Come on. Sinnie'll have something to help. She's the ship's doc."

Joy kept a hand over her dust-stuffed eye and followed him out of the room. "Was that Sinnie I met yesterday?"

"Uh-huh." He took her in tow.

"She's a doctor?"

"Actually, she's more of an Igor, but we like to indulge her."

"How reassuring."

"She's on five. Let's go."

Sinnie opened her door on the first knock. Even with only one good eye, Joy saw her shock. "What in heaven happened to you two? Fall down a coal shaft?"

"Joy's got something in her eye. I thought you could help." Wade said.

"Come in. Come in," Sinnie took Joy's hand, pulled her forward. "Come to the bathroom, girl, I've got eyewash in there."

As they disappeared into Sinnie's tiny bathroom, Joy heard Wade say, "Hi, Mike. I didn't see you sitting there. Not working today?"

"Got laid off."

If Wade answered, Joy didn't hear. She was sitting on the toilet, and Sinnie was flushing her eye out with enough liquid to raise the level of the Pacific. When she had Joy completely blind, she closed the door.

"Glad you're here, Miss Joy Cole, because I've got a few things to say." She handed her a towel.

Joy blotted her face, glanced in the mirror over Sinnie's sink to see hair layered in dust and dirty gray streaks running from her eyes to her chin. "Talk away. But do you mind if I try to get rid of this grime?"

"Here." The woman handed her a soap pump.

Antibacterial. Strong enough to strip paint. "Thank you." Joy didn't relish the idea of washing her face with it, but it would have to do. She turned back to the sink. "What's on your mind?"

"That man out there."

"Wade?"

"This place should be his, not yours."

Joy put as small an amount of soap as she could on a clean facecloth. Or what was a facecloth ten years ago. It was thin as gauze. "I agree with you, Sinnie. But it isn't."

"Would have been if he'd made up with that useless father of his. Hadn't gone to jail, which makes him pretty stupid, too."

Joy rinsed her face, her interest piqued. "Why did he go to jail?"

"Told you. He was stupid."

"How stupid?"

"Eighteen months' worth. And all because of a woman."

"He hurt a woman?" Joy couldn't believe that. She'd spent the afternoon with the man, and other than a killer wit, she didn't detect violence.

"No! Wade wouldn't ever hurt a woman! And it was her should've gone to jail." She gave Joy a hard-eyed look. "He just picked the wrong female, like his daddy before him. But Wade's paid his dues. And he doesn't need another Miss Fancy Pants to come along and take what's his, mess him up again."

Joy folded the facecloth, set it on the sink, and faced her. "That 'fancy pants' being me?" She came very near to smiling but managed a straight face.

Sinnie's expression shifted and she cocked her head. "You're a cool one, aren't you?" She looked as if she approved.

"I didn't come here to 'mess up' Wade's life, Sinnie. I'm here because his father left this place to me. Right now, I'm trying to figure out the smartest way to deal with it, and I've asked Wade to help. That's it."

"You want my opinion?" Her gaze was steely.

"Can it be avoided?" This time she did smile. She liked this woman.

"Give the Phil to Wade, and don't waste any time doing it. It's the right thing to do."

Joy studied her for a minute, saw the love there. Envied it. She thought of Lana, her endless needs, and her own responsibility, courtesy of Stephen, to meet them. "It's not that simple, Sinnie." And neither could she ignore her own growing feelings for the Phil. Amidst all the neglect and decay, there was a handsomeness to the place, a wry charm. And no matter how many broken windows she counted, how many ruined halls she walked, that charm captivated her.

There was a knock on the door. "You all right in there?" Wade called.

"Coming," Sinnie said, then whispered for Joy's ears only, "I like you, young woman, I truly do. But the 'smartest' thing for you to do is leave this place to its intended. And I'll say this, too—you hurt that boy out there"—she jerked her gray-topped head—"and you'll have me to answer to."

Wade banged on the door again and Joy opened it, glad for the diversion; it hid her grin. Joy hadn't answered to anyone since she was eight years old, yet the idea of being accountable to this fierce old woman held a peculiar appeal.

When the door opened fully, she looked up at the six feet of "boy" Sinnie was so protective of, then into his green eyes. Until now his eyes had been watchful, quiet. And while they'd teased and humored her throughout the tour of the Phil, they had given away nothing about the man behind them. But in this moment they held concern—for her.

She was no more used to being concerned about than she was to being accountable.

"Need anything?" Wade caught her chin with his knuckles and raised her face to his, turned it to and fro, scanned it thoroughly, worriedly. "There's a drugstore up the street."

"No, I'm fine." Unless you factored in a strange weakness in the limbs or a pair of eyes suddenly incapable of leaving his.

"Good." His voice lowered, and he lifted his hand to push her hair back from her temple; the gentle connection held until he'd run his fingers through the length of her hair and brought a handful of it to rest below her shoulder.

For a frozen moment, they stared at each other and neither spoke. Still loosely holding her hair, Wade rested the back of his hand just above her breast. A heavy, warm stone radiating heat. Joy, gazing up at him, was dimly aware of her own shallow breathing, her narrowing focus. Wade drew in a heavy breath, his gaze dropping to her mouth.

Sinnie coughed—loudly—and spoke sternly. "She had a bit of dust in her eye, Wade, she wasn't flattened by a falling piano. And you aren't looking so good yourself, in case you haven't noticed."

Joy felt her color rise up, far enough to meet the befuddlement between her ears. She still couldn't get her breath.

Somebody laughed.

Joy turned from Wade, who hadn't stopped looking at her and didn't look the least flustered, to the other man in the room. She'd completely forgotten he was there.

"This is Big Mike," Sinnie said without preamble. "He lives on four."

"Mike. Nice to meet you." Joy hated the look he gave her—one of those centipede-under-the-collar kind of looks.

The burly man nodded, held onto his smarmy smile.

Joy turned to Wade. "I think I've seen enough for today, but I was thinking . . ." She hesitated. This idea of hers had seemed like a good one—before the time warp she'd entered with Wade a couple of minutes ago. Now she wasn't so sure.

Wade waited for her to finish. She glanced around to see both Sinnie and Mike equally as interested. *Oh, hell, in for a penny . . .* "I was thinking it might be a good idea for me to stay here—while I figure things out."

Wade's eyebrows shot up as if they'd been pulled by wires. "You want to stay here?"

"Makes sense to me. I can take my time looking around, really get to understand the place."

"I don't think so."

"Why?" She didn't bother to tell him it was her hotel and she really didn't need his or anyone else's approval.

"There's not a decent room in the place. You've seen that today." He shook his head. "You're better off at the Marriott."

"Room 33's in good shape," Mike said. "Rebecca sure liked it."

"No." Wade said.

"No." Sinnie said, their voices a beat apart.

Joy looked at them both, intrigued by their vehemence. Then she remembered. "You didn't show me that room today. Said you didn't have a key."

"I didn't have it on me. Not that it matters—the room's a mess. It's a bad idea." Wade's jaw was set to rock-hard.

"Wade's right," Sinnie piped in. "You've got a good, safe room where you are. This is no place for a woman alone."

"You're alone, Sinnie," she said, a comment that brought a scowl dark as a rain cloud. "And believe me I've stayed in worse places than the Phil through the years."

"There's a room on four, right next to mine," Mike said. "It ain't too bad. I'll look after her."

Wade glared at him. "Joy's fine where she is. At the Marriott." He stated the last as if his words were etched in stone.

Joy eyed them all. Three more people trying to tell her what to do in her own hotel. "Let's take a look at four. And while we're there," she said, turning to Wade and smiling, "you can get the key to Room 33."

Chapter Seven

Wade walked Joy to the front entrance of the Phil. He was stewing. The idea of Joy staying in Room 33 rested in his gut like a leaky tanker in a sea of oil. But nothing either he or Sinnie said had budged her resolve. As he was discovering, Joy Cole was not easily swayed.

Joy stopped abruptly at the door. "You haven't said a thing since this—" She dangled her new room key in front of his face. "What's the problem?"

He took the key from her hand. "*This* is the problem." He copied her, lifted and dangled the key.

She grabbed it back, tossed it in her tote.

"What the hell was wrong with the room beside Mike's on four?" he asked.

She sighed one of those long-suffering, impatient sighs women were so good at. "Let's just say it's a girl thing, Wade," she said and feigned a mild shudder. "I'd rather take a cot in the basement."

"I can arrange that." His tone was caustic.

She laughed, then studied his face. "You can't possibly be afraid of that 'room of doom' thing, can you?"

"Where'd you hear about that?" The Phil might have been built to last forever, but its walls sure had ears.

"A guy named Lars told me. When I was trying the doors yesterday, I met him outside 33." They'd arrived at the front doors. "Quite a story," she added. "On a par with being swallowed whole by a boa in South Africa or eaten by dingoes in the Australian outback. You don't buy into that kind of stuff, do you?"

Wade didn't bother to answer her. Room 33 and his opinion of it wasn't her business. He was overreacting, and why the hell should he care where the woman slept?

When he opened the door, sun speared through to temporarily blind them both—and stop the questions. Joy dug for sunglasses, put them on, and stepped outside. Wade followed. She took the first step down and turned to face him, her perfect skin sheet-pale in the brilliant sunlight. "Have we stopped talking?"

"One of us has."

She allowed a time lapse, then said, "What about the Phil? The renovations I'm thinking about? Are you going to help me run a few numbers or not?" Her eyes questioned, her chin was high, and her stance was still as stone.

Wade wanted to say no, but today's tour of old halls, shuddering pipes, and cracked plaster walls—and all the obvious potential attached to them—stopped the word behind his clenched teeth. Not that he intended to be involved.

When he didn't answer, she went on, "Then I'll find someone else. They won't have the firsthand knowledge that you have, of course. But I'll manage."

Wade didn't want her to find someone else, and the certainty of his opinion rocked him. "We'll talk tomorrow." He grimaced. "When you move in."

"I won't be moving in until next week sometime. I've

got to go back to Victoria, talk to my boss, and make arrangements for some time off."

"Just as well." Wade was relieved. "It'll give me time to think things through."

"Good." She started down the street.

"And, Cole"—she looked back at him—"I hope you've got deep pockets. Any kind of workable plan for the Phil won't be cheap."

She waved, appeared totally unconcerned, and turned the corner.

Wade went back into the Phil's lobby. He was thoroughly pissed with himself. He hoped to hell he wasn't thinking with his dick again. God knows, Joy Cole had made that long unused part of him stand up and take notice.

But that aside—and aside was where he intended it to stay, he didn't feel good about this idea of hers, didn't feel good about it at all. The woman had no idea what she was in for.

She was dreaming—and more fool him—he was going along for the ride.

Joy walked the few blocks back to her hotel, enlivened. After studying every nook and cranny of the Philip, after being dumped on by a dust cloud, and after a day with Wade Emerson, she'd fallen in love . . . oh, not with Wade—despite her attraction to him, she wasn't that much of a fool—but with the Hotel Philip.

After the first hour, she no longer saw the scars and warts, she saw bright new carpets, fresh paint, polished oak, and a front desk with customers lined up to check in. It was an exciting vision and she saw herself—

She cut that line of thinking. This wasn't about her, and growing attached to the Phil or any of its tenants would only make complications. The plan was to get the hotel to generate revenue, then turn it over to a hotel management company so it would provide Lana with a respectable income, although probably not even close to the one required to support her current lifestyle. Lana might not like it, but it was a practical solution. The trouble was, Joy wasn't feeling practical, she was feeling ambitious, turned on, and excited.

She picked up her pace and within minutes she was in the Marriott's smartly appointed lobby.

"Joy, I was hoping to catch you." It was David Grange. His grin was wide and friendly, but his gaze widened when he took in her dusty, disheveled condition.

"David," she said. "What brings you here?"

"I'm meeting your mother a couple of blocks away, so I thought I'd come by. Buy you a drink?"

"As you can see, I'm not in top condition." But David was, thanks to Boss and Armani. She eyed him. "Are you ever casual?"

"In the right circumstances." He reached over and flicked some dust off her shoulder. "Why don't you go up and change. I'll wait."

"Are you going to pitch me on selling you the Philip?"

He laughed. "Do you want me to?"

"No."

"Go freshen up. I'll meet you in the bar."

Joy watched him walk across the lobby. So did a few other women. That would please Lana, Joy thought, stepping into the elevator. She liked trophy males.

She showered, changed into blue slacks and a white silk blouse, knotted her hair at her nape and was downstairs in twenty minutes tops. Her one nod at vanity a brush of lipstick and a pair of gold hoops.

David rose from his seat upon sighting her. When she reached the table he pulled out her chair. "You really are very beautiful," he said from behind her. "I'd love to have met your grandmother."

"She was short, dark, her name was Francetti, and she never shaved her legs."

"You're kidding."

She gave him one of her mother's looks, slow and empty.

He grinned. "Got me."

The waiter appeared, and David raised his brows in Joy's direction. "Scotch, please. Neat," she said.

"Double that," he said.

When he turned his attention back to her, she asked, "Why are you here, David? What is it you want?"

"To get to know you better?" He sat back in his chair, casual and at ease.

"I doubt that. I think you'd like it if I caught the next bus to nowhere."

"I'm sorry if I gave you that impression."

She shrugged, noticed he didn't exactly deny it. The waiter brought their drinks. She sipped. Waited.

He sat forward in his chair, cradled his drink. "There are things you don't know about the Hotel Philip, Joy. Things you'll never know."

His expression was intense and Joy assumed he was about to launch into a list of the Phil's structural sins and shortcomings to dampen her interest in upgrading. She had the urge to quaff her Scotch and head for the exit, but if she did that, she'd fall on her face. She'd tough it out and be courteous . . . if her patience held. "I don't know about a lot of things, but I'm pretty good at filling in the blanks as I go along."

"Sometimes blanks are best left empty."

Joy's senses sharpened, and the bar, busy with the after-work cocktail crowd, seemed to quiet. She matched his soft tone. "I don't agree with you. Speaking for myself, I've never met an empty space I've liked."

"Your mother told me you were stubborn."

"I prefer 'tenacious' and 'determined.' Traits my mother and I share, by the way." She sipped her Scotch. "Now, what is it I should know about the Phil—in twenty words or less, please. I've had a long day." So much for courtesy.

"That you're going to sell it to me now, or you'll sell it to me later. And now would be the smart time, the safe time. Better for all concerned." He leaned back in his chair, took a drink.

The bluntness of his statement, the implied threat, made Joy pause. His words were clear enough, yet he looked oddly nervous, distinctly uncomfortable. She'd thought him a pretty boy, smooth, a bit too clever, but it seemed he was more than that. "Interesting choice of the word 'safe.' Maybe you'd like to explain it?"

He looked away for a moment as if to gather his thoughts. "Your mother is on the financial ropes," he said. "Add to that, she's very tense about your involvement in her life. I'm worried about her. Afraid she might do something drastic. If we can finalize things, it will ease her mind and be better for everyone."

Joy burned down the Scotch in one gulp—to avoid spewing it across the table. " 'Drastic?' You're not serious! You actually believe my mother would—" She couldn't finish. The idea was too insane to say aloud.

"You've been away a long time. You don't know her the way I do."

"I know her well enough to know if they gave out survivor ribbons, my mother's would be blue." She set her glass on the table and stood, angry now. "And as an effort to coerce me into selling you the Philip, David, the quiet little drink together idea was a misfire. I've told my mother, and I'll tell you—I'll do what I think best to look after her interests." She put both hands on the back of her now vacant seat and stared him down. "If that means selling the property, I'll do that, but *not* until I've explored all possibilities and done due diligence."

His face was tight. "Are you negotiating with me on price, or are you really thinking of reopening the hotel?"

"Both." She lifted her hands from the chair. "I've got a month to make my decision, and I intend to use every minute of it." She turned to go, then turned back. "Oh, and you should know I'm checking out of here in the morning. I'm going to Victoria for a few days and when I come back I'll be staying at the Philip."

Genuine alarm tightened his handsome features. "That's a bad idea. You have no idea *how* bad."

That made the third person today telling her she shouldn't stay at her hotel. She lifted her chin. "We'll talk in a month." She walked out.

A few days later, Christian put on a pair of white gloves and tottered across the room to his desk, where he opened the second drawer and pulled out an envelope. He went from there to stand before a large oil painting of an isolated and windswept beach. He moved it aside and opened his safe. He took out one of the stacks of bills and carefully removed twenty small bills. He put three of them in the envelope.

He heard the familiar rap on his door. The boy was punctual, he'd say that for him.

Christian let Gordy in through the door he half-opened for the purpose, calmed himself, and bent to pet Melly. "Good girl. Daddy's good girl." He looked at the man-child who was smiling at Melly. "Where did you take her today, Gordy?"

"We went with Sinnie to that clinic place. It was a long way." Gordy's eyes widened with his smile. "Melly was real good." He patted the dog's soft head.

Christian went back to his chair. He was so stiff. He told himself he needed to walk more, but he never did. Even his beloved terrace had become too intimidating. Who knew what the winds would deposit there? "Is Sinnie sick, Gordy? Is that why you went to the clinic?" Christian liked to keep tabs on Sinnie. She'd cleaned his home for years, but she seldom spoke to him. Not that he was bothered by that. He enjoyed her silence, considered it a benefit of her distaste of him.

"No. Not sick. She said she needed a paper to get more medicine for her cranky old joints." He chewed on his upper lip. "A prescr . . ." He trailed off.

Christian smiled. Gordy was so amusing. "A prescription. She needed a prescription."

"Yeah, that's it."

Christian rested his head back, suddenly tired and bored with Sinnie's cranky joints. "Get your money, boy. It's where it always is."

"Thanks."

Christian heard him rustle around, watched from under hooded eyes until satisfied with the count. "Come back this afternoon at two." He let his eyelids again drift to a close.

"Can't, Mr. Rupert. I'm working for Wade today."

"Doing what?" He hoped this wasn't the boy's day for idle chatter.

"He's cleaning up for the new tenant. I'm helping," he added proudly.

"New tenant?" Christian's head came up. He'd heard nothing about a new tenant.

"Yeah, the pretty lady who was here last week? She's moving in."

Christian stared at Gordy, at first unable to identify the emotion roiling through his body. Surprise? Indeed. Anger that he hadn't been informed? Certainly that! But his next feeling was glee. The stupid girl was playing into his hands. Here, he could watch her, be more in control. And it made it so much easier to prepare the stage for David to do what in the end Christian knew must be done. There must be no mistakes, no back-tracking—and no witnesses.

"What room is the pretty lady taking, Gordy?"

"Thirty-three."

Christian's laugh quickly became a series of shallow wheezes. The boy looked alarmed, until Christian pressed a lace handkerchief to his mouth. His bent, spidery fingers held it there until he'd regained his composure enough to say, "Get along with you, boy, and tell Mike to come up. I need him . . . to water the terrace planters."

Wade didn't hesitate outside the door to 33, just jammed in the key, turned it, and strode to the room's center. Gordy followed him in, bucket and sponge in hand.

"Start with the bathroom, Gordy, and do a good job. Women tend to be fastidious about bathrooms."

"What's that 'fast' word mean?"

"Super clean. Real fussy."

"Like my mom."

"Probably," Wade answered absently, and walked to the window to look at the latch he'd fixed last time he was here. Like he figured. Not good enough. He'd have to reset the screws.

"Wade."

"Uh-huh."

"Could you come here? There's something in the tub."

"What?" Wade swallowed, kept at the latch, sank the new screws deep.

"I dunno. It's sort of red. Come look."

Wade took a breath and walked toward the bathroom.

He stopped in the doorway to see Gordy puzzling over the bathtub. "Yeah?"

Gordy pointed. "What do I do about that stuff?"

Wade ignored the white storm gathering behind his eyes, the hair standing upright on his forearms, and peered into the tub.

"It's rust." He relaxed, told himself he was ten times a fool. "Shake some of that white powder on it. Let it sit a bit, then scrub it. It'll come away." Maybe. If it doesn't, the woman's going to have an orange ass. Serve her right. She had to pick this room. Well, good for her. He'd do what he had to do and get the hell out of here.

Wade went back to the window, tied his mind up with insetting screws, and didn't hear Mike step in through the open door. "She comin' in today?" he said.

Wade tossed him a look, kept working. "So the lady says."

Mike went to stand over Wade, managed to block the light from the window. "Handy for you." He gestured at the room's open door, gave Wade an obnoxious grin. "Being across the hall and all."

"You mean something by that?" Wade gave the screw a final turn, didn't bother to look up until it was set deep.

"I mean she's one damn fine bitch. I was hoping she'd take the room on four." The man looked as if he were salivating. "But I guess one floor don't make much difference when a man's dick is thick."

It's a girl thing, Wade. Joy's words echoed. "Well, she didn't go on four, Mike. She's on three. My floor." Wade straightened, but even at six-foot-one, his gaze didn't level with the big man who had it over him by at least three inches and forty pounds. "And if you want to keep that square head of yours on your shoulders, you'd be smart to leave her the hell alone."

Mike didn't move a muscle, just grinned as if all that

muscle and fat he was encased in would stop a bull at a full run and he damn well knew it. "Sure, Wade. Anything you say, Wade." He looked at the newly installed window lock. "Good job. That'll keep the bogeyman out." He grinned again and rolled himself out of the room.

Wade watched him go, restrained aggression a tight twist in his stomach. *Son of a bitch!* It looked as if Joy Cole was a much better judge of character than he was. He'd been around Mike for weeks, but they'd never exchanged more than hallway salutes. Wade thought of him as big, harmless, and none too bright. Time to rethink the harmless bit. If he hadn't been wallowing in his own damned misery, he'd have picked up on the brute, the slime of him, those dull photocopier eyes of his—as if he were imprinting events on his brain for review later when he had time to figure them out. Well, he'd picked up on him now, and he was suddenly damn glad Joy—if the obstinate woman had to be in the Phil—was directly across the hall.

Gordy came out of the bathroom. "All done. What's next?" He looked at the door. "That Mike?"

Wade nodded.

Gordy dropped his bucket, ran to the door, and yelled, "Mike!"

Wade heard a "Yeah" from down the hall.

"Mr. Rupert wants you to go up and see him."

Another "Yeah" and the sound of a door banging.

Wade looked at Gordy. "Why does Mr. Rupert want to see Mike, Gordy? Did he say?"

Gordy came back in the room, picked up the abandoned bucket. "Wants his trees watered or some sweeping done." He shrugged. "Something. I don't know."

"Hmm." Wade tried to picture Mike with a broom or a hose. Had real trouble. "You see Mr. Rupert a lot, don't you?" He eyed Gordy. "Walk his dog, stuff like that."

He nodded.

"Is he nice to you? A good guy?"

His face brightened. "Oh, yeah, he gives me money . . . shows me stuff."

"What kind of stuff?"

"He showed me a picture of your grandpa once. It was kind of brown, though."

"He's got a picture of my grandfather? You sure?"

"Uh-huh. It's on his piano."

Wade found that strange. Through the years Rupert's name would come up in the Emerson family—when there'd been a family—as the weird eccentric who owned the hotel penthouse. The man who, as far as anyone knew, had stopped going out sometime back in the seventies. But every time his name came up, his grandfather would growl something about him being a mean old bastard and kill the subject. He'd never indicated there was any kind of shared history between the two of them other than a legal document giving the "mean old bastard" title to the penthouse. Wade knew Joseph Emerson saw hard times in his early years, particularly while he was building the Phil, so he assumed the title to the penthouse was a financial arrangement, one Joe had come to regret later on. Pure speculation, of course, because when it came to Christian Rupert, his grandfather had absolutely nothing to say.

"What ya want me to do now, Wade?" Gordy asked.

"Nothing. Finish what you're doing in the bathroom and head home. Your mom told me you've got a dentist appointment."

Gordy made a face. "Okay." When Wade headed for the door, he asked, "Where're you going?"

"Be right back," he said, stepping into the hall. "I'm going to get the vacuum cleaner."

"Real men don't vacuum," Joy said when they collided outside the door. "Didn't you know that?" She had a suitcase in one hand, a computer case strap over her shoulder, and was towing another bag behind her. She wasn't laughing, but she was smiling, and Wade had the sense her smiles were rare.

He held her by the shoulders, felt his big hands warm and fold over straight bones and trim muscle. He didn't want to let go. "I said I was getting it, didn't say I was doing it," he said. "I figured I'd leave that to you." She'd steadied under his hands, so he reluctantly dropped them to his sides. He was adolescently glad to see her. "Although I could be bribed . . ."

"I think I've heard that one before."

"Just wanted to be sure the message got through." He should have stopped himself, but he didn't. He ran his knuckles along her jaw and wondered if the rest of her was this intriguing mixture of soft and firm.

"You're anything but subtle, Wade."

"And here I thought I was being Mr. Smooth."

She tilted her head, gave him a speculative look. "You're smooth enough, all right. Maybe too smooth."

He let that go, and took her bags from her hand. "The place is as ready as it's going to get. You won't change your mind, take another room?"

"Nope."

He shook his head, stepped aside to let her pass, and followed her into the room. He set her bags down near the bed. "Okay. Real men know when they're beat." *But you can bet I'll be keeping an eye on you.* He took her hand, led her back to the open door. "That's my room across the hall. Anything, anyone, bothers you, shout."

She stood beside him and peeked out. "I will."

"And did you know my door is never locked?"

"I do now," she said in a tone husky enough to rattle his male cage and lay down hope as hot as melting gold.

They looked at each other. Wade heard Gordy banging around in the room behind them, but like that day when Joy came out of Sinnie's bathroom, streaked and grimy, he couldn't take his eyes off her. And everything male in him told him she had the same problem.

He knew his voice was dark when he said, "Something's going on here. Between us. Are you getting it?"

The slightest hesitation. "Yes, I'm getting it"—she shook her head, and her smooth forehead creased into a frown—"but I'm not sure it's smart to do anything about it."

The elevator door clanged shut down the hall; metal slammed against metal. Like a cell door closing, like a hundred cell doors he'd heard every night for eighteen months. And it reminded him of what he was. What he'd done. He pulled his gaze from hers.

What the hell was he thinking, playing with this woman? He turned away. "You're right. It's not smart," he said and headed down the hall. "I'll get you that vacuum. If you need anything, ask Gordy—he's the guy cleaning your bathroom. He'll be happy to help."

He knew she didn't move, knew she watched him go with a big question mark in her eyes, but he didn't look back.

He'd been out of jail for less than three months. His life was a fucking mess. He might need sex, but this sure as hell wasn't the time to start messing with a woman like Joy Cole—a keeper if he ever saw one. He wasn't in the market for one of those.

Maybe she did look like a gift from the gods, and maybe she was. If so, the gods' timing was brutal.

She was a complication he didn't need—and she came with a mother who made his damn stomach turn.

Christian was frustrated that his illness forced him to rely on fools and cretins. He settled his ancient eyes on his latest recruit. "Michael, you've let me down. You didn't tell me the woman was moving in. I had to hear it from Gordy. Pure chance. I don't like chance. Do you understand me?"

Mike shrugged, a flash of brutish anger heating his dull gaze.

Christian prodded him. "Say, yes, Mr. Rupert. Anything you say, Mr. Rupert."

The big man looked as if he'd explode and Christian restrained a snicker. So much aggression, quite enticing in a sick kind of way.

When he didn't comply with his suggestion, Christian went on, his voice flat and hard. "I'm your lifeline, Michael. If you forget that for a second, I'll not hesitate to toss you to those nasty creditors of yours—or make a short phone call to the proper authorities. I don't think you'd care for either option, would you?"

"No." The word shot out like a dry, acrid nut.

"I take that to mean you'd like another chance?"

Mike glared but nodded.

"Very well, then." When he'd told David he needed added security, he'd found the perfect candidate, a man who had three choices: go back to prison for parole violation, get a knife in his back from a local drug ring he'd been stupid enough to steal from, or do whatever Christian Rupert told him to do in order to stay alive on this side of prison bars. He detested Michael, of course, but right now, he needed him. There were preparations to make.

"I want you to do something for me." Christian slapped the envelope against his thigh. "And to show there's no hard feelings, there's something extra in it—if you do it well."

Mike said nothing, but Christian knew he had his attention. He went on, "How many guests are in the hotel? Right now. This moment."

Mike looked at the ceiling, started to count on his fingers. "Old Henry, them Millars down the hall from me, Sinnie, Lars, and Rebecca . . . Cherry and Gordy, Wade, me . . . the owner-broad. Then there's four or five on six, a couple on five and on two, I think." He stopped, looked confused. "I don't know, maybe twenty, twenty-five in maybe twelve or thirteen rooms."

"That's all? Christian hadn't realized his below stairs flock was so depleted. He grew momentarily uneasy, not sure how he'd cope if all the space below him were empty. When the hotel was finally under his control, he'd have to think on this. David would help. But right now he had instructions to give.

He handed Mike a set of master keys for the hotel. Mike tossed them in his hand. "Don't need these, ya know. I can get in anywhere."

"Yes, but I'd rather you do it quietly. Now, listen carefully. I have tasks for you to perform. For now at least, you are not to trouble the 'owner-broad.' What I want you to do is this—in precisely the following order. First, you . . ."

Lana took a sip of her cool Chardonnay. "You're not kidding. She did that? Moved out of the Marriott and into Hotel Horrible, one star and falling?" She gave her bikini top a tug to settle it in place—and get David's flagging attention. The man was obsessed with the do-ings of her daughter. Such a bore.

David's eyes dutifully followed her languid reorgani-zation of her breasts within the strip of silver ribbon that formed her bikini bra. "She moved in today. Two suitcases. Wade helped her."

Lana frowned. "Wade?" She lifted her head, then her sunglasses to better see David's face. "You can't mean Wade Emerson."

"He moved in two, three weeks ago."

"You didn't tell me."

"Should I have?"

Lana merely raised a brow to look mildly chastising. She wasn't happy, but she didn't let it show. Joy's independent thinking neither surprised nor frightened her. In fact, she'd expected it. But the last person she'd expected to show up was Stephen's son. This created a completely new scenario.

When she didn't answer, David rested his head back on the navy linen-covered double lounge chair they shared. Lana knew he was trying to look relaxed, but he wasn't doing a good job of it. This morning, for the first time, his lovemaking had lacked his usual attention to detail. And there was no better place than bed to observe a man distracted.

She sat up on her side of the lounge, spread her legs, and assumed a lotus position she knew would get his attention. She rested her hands on her knees. "How does Wade look? He was quite young when he left, but I remember him as quite . . . delicious."

"I tell you there's an Emerson loose in the Hotel Philip and you use the word 'delicious?'" A twist of a smile turned up his lips. "Then you'll be happy to know he looks just like his father. Taller, maybe. Maybe more—"

"More what?" she prodded, but it was as if he'd seen something in her face that made him stop.

He pulled her hair loose from the artful topknot she'd created after their swim. "More 'delicious' than you remember. All filled out. Probably has a cock a mile long." He looked at her crotch, the wisp of strap barely covering her sex. "Not that you're going to have a taste anytime soon." He shoved the strap aside and penetrated her with a playful finger. "You're mine. Don't forget that."

Lana, accustomed to men being possessive, let him play for a time, then moved his finger aside and got up. "I'm not in the mood," she lied.

David gave her a disbelieving look, a slow smile. "You're always in the mood, baby. Come here."

She ignored him. Fear had taken hold, troubled her. Stephen's son had been *delicious*.

Lana knew that from Wade's last visit to Stephen, not long after their marriage and the night of the final father and son blowout. At eighteen, Wade was strikingly handsome, intrinsically sexual, and completely unaware of his appeal. So tempting. Too tempting.

She supposed it had been a mistake—her wee hours trip to his bed. Although it certainly worked out well enough.

Wade Emerson . . .

Tall, lean, with thick, coffee-colored hair. Smoky jade eyes and the walk of a restless panther. Long legs wrapped in denim . . . and between his legs a fullness the denim showed to advantage. A fullness she'd ached to discover.

At seventeen he'd been intriguing; she could imagine him as a mature male, experienced, his potential realized, his sexual prowess at its peak.

She turned back to David.

"I think you should have told me he was back."

David put an arm under his head, looked up at her. "Forget about Emerson. Stephen sure as hell did. Not only is the man fresh out of prison, he's broke. I don't think he has a dime to his name. He's not a player."

"Perhaps. But he could become one very quickly, my darling—if he starts fucking my daughter."

Chapter Eight

Joy crossed the hall and put her ear to the door of Room 36, Wade's door. Since she'd moved in three days ago, she hadn't heard a sound from this damn room. And he sure as heck didn't respond to her whacking on his door.

But he was in there now; that muffled curse she'd just heard proved it. She had him treed.

He'd been avoiding her and she was fed up with it.

Come to think of it, the whole hotel population was avoiding her. Why should he be any different? Other than an ugly leer from Mike as she sidestepped him in the hall, the only one who'd spoken to Joy since her arrival was Sinnie. She'd come around the first day and offered to clean her room. Figuring the elderly woman wanted the money, she said yes, and Sinnie had shown up every day at ten o'clock since.

But it wasn't Sinnie on her mind now, it was Wade Emerson. She was going to roust him if she had to stand here all night.

When he didn't answer her polite knock, she gave the door a good bang and yelled, "I know you're there,

Wade. That four-letter word was a dead giveaway." They'd agreed to work together, and she had a limited amount of time. He knew that. Maybe she should have gone elsewhere for her advice. Maybe she still should. But if nothing else, she'd find out what was going on. She banged the door again.

Finally, a mumble. "It's open."

She opened the door and stood in the doorway. He waved her in, but didn't look up from the papers strewn over his pockmarked red Formica table.

He'd pulled a lamp close to its edge, and the cord, six inches above the floor, formed a trap line between him and the kitchen. He was keying intently into a new laptop—the open box was at his feet. The computer's bright screen contrasted sharply with the paltry light seeping onto the table from under a fringed lampshade. Abruptly, he pushed it back, finger-combed his hair. He studied the screen silently until it morphed into an aquarium with brilliantly colored fish swimming in a too-blue ocean,

He stood then, but neither looked at her nor smiled. "Your timing's perfect. Do you want coffee, or are you one of those no-caffeine-at-night types?" He headed for the kitchen area, remembered the lamp cord just in time, and stepped over it. He looked as if he were shaking loose from a fog.

"I'll take the coffee," she said. "But what makes now so perfect? It's after midnight. Most sane people are in bed."

He glanced at the clock over the sink, frowned, shoved his hair back again. Obviously, when Wade concentrated, his hair took a serious thrashing.

"You've been avoiding me," Joy said. "Why?"

"Take a look." He nodded toward the laptop.

She strolled over to the computer, hit a key to bring the working screen back. When she saw what he'd been working on, the columns of numbers, intricate calculations, her heart added extra beats.

"That," he gestured at the computer again, "took time. I didn't want to be interrupted." He poured coffee into two mismatched mugs and gave her the one proclaiming the wonders of Eddie's Plumbing. She sipped; the coffee was hot and strong. Just like the man who handed it to her. She swallowed the errant thought along with a deep draft of caffeine.

"I thought we were going to work on the hotel figures together. I do know how to add and subtract, you know. Very good at it, as a matter of fact."

"No doubt. But I'm better." He was leaning against the kitchen counter, but he shoved himself away from it and went back to the table. "What I've done here is a couple of worst case scenarios. If you're as good at dealing with city hall and the trades—and the moneymen— as you claim to be with numbers, you should be able to come in under budget." He picked up a computer disk. "The Hotel Philip can be a viable operation—and a profitable one—but it will take work and smarts—and investment." He shoved the silver disk into the laptop and started messing with keys.

He was quick and able with the system, and in seconds Joy saw the copying graph stream across the screen. "I've given you two scenarios," he said. "The first is the cost to restore the Philip, bring it back, give it the full thirties treatment. The second outlines a different approach, a renovation for the purpose of producing a workable economy hotel. Less risky, obviously."

He popped the disk out of the side of the machine. "There are two big problem areas. One is the state of the roof—you'll need a professional to price that out— and the air conditioning, also on the roof. My grandfather installed it in the late seventies. I've assumed—to be conservative—it needs replacing. But again, you'll need a professional opinion."

"Any recommendations?" she asked. She'd never

heard him string this many words together at one time. It was as if he were impatient to get it over with, get her out of his room.

"There's a couple of names in the notes section. I know you brought a computer with you," he went on, his voice businesslike but without inflection. He handed her the disk. "This is a copy of everything I've done. Take it back to your room, give the numbers a going-over. If you've got questions, suggestions, whatever, I'll be around tomorrow. Keep in mind most of it is educated guesswork. You'll want a second opinion."

When she took the disk from his hand, he stepped back to lean against the counter. He stood there, still and silent, as if he couldn't wait for her to leave. Joy put the disk on the table, followed it with her coffee mug. "What's going on here?" she asked, genuinely curious.

He picked up his abandoned coffee, drank, and over its rim settled his gaze on her, his eyes dark, guarded. "Budgets, cash projections, rough construction estimates. What else is there?" He tossed the dregs of his coffee into the sink.

"You're playing dumb, Wade. And not well."

"Actually, you're wrong. I'm not playing dumb. I am dumb—about as dumb as a guy can get." He gave her a look so scorching, her knees weakened.

"Care to explain?"

She saw his jaw shift and tighten, and his eyes glittered, then dimmed to a sensual glow. "I want you, sweetheart. And there's nothing smart about a man letting his goddamn cock do his thinking, especially when it hasn't thought of anything else since you hauled your sweet ass into the Phil."

He made no move toward her. Joy sensed his words were intended to repel her; instead they attracted, tugged slender, sensitive strings anchored deep in her body. She could barely draw in air. "I figured that might be it," she said, and knew she sounded stupid and vain. And she wondered about her choice of words. If she were honest she'd replace the word "figured" with . . . "hoped."

He looked disgusted. "That obvious, huh? Just another guy, in a stream of guys, lusting after a Cole woman."

"No! That's not it. And I resent that 'Cole woman' remark." This was not the time she needed to be reminded about his hostility toward her mother.

"Resent whatever the hell you like, but the best thing right now is for you to go back to your room and leave me to mine." He gestured to the disk. "Take it and go."

She picked it up, took the few steps to the doorway, and opened the door a couple of inches.

Wade glared at her from across the room, his face tight and drawn, the barest of tics enlivening his jaw.

"What if I don't want to go?" she said and raised her head to meet his stark gaze directly. She was testing, she knew that, and it was foolish. Dangerous, perhaps.

Music from somewhere along the Phil's darkened hallways filtered into the room. A guitar, Joy registered, being played badly. She closed the door, kept her hand on the knob, and waited for him to answer.

"You want to go, all right, you just don't know it." His words were low and clipped.

She considered his words, the chill in his eyes. "The jail thing, right?"

He averted his eyes briefly, brought them back to her, colder than before. Pride and anger each seeking a place in them. "According to records in the great state of New York, I've defrauded a bank and obstructed justice."

"Did you?"

His laugh was harsher than his expression. "Everybody who goes to jail is innocent, don't you know that?"

She ignored his non-answer. "Sinnie said there was a woman—"

"The day that woman's mouth closes someone ought to raise a flag."

"Was there? A woman?"

"A man says he wants to have sex with you and you want his life story. This a new approach?"

"Maybe the woman is interested and wants to know what she's getting into."

His face unreadable, he studied her for a long time. "What she'd be getting into would be a bed, sweetheart, where she'd have sex—as good as it gets, more sex— then a long good-bye kiss. You want that?"

"The word I used was 'interested,' Wade, not yes with a capital Y and an exclamation point." She took a giant mental step back, sorry she'd opened her mouth. There was something in the way he kept looking at her that told her to be cautious—with an exclamation point.

Silence, long crazy beats of silence.

His eyes hotly speculative, Wade raised an eyebrow. Trapped in his smooth, knowing gaze, Joy busied herself by flipping the disk pancake-style between her hands, trying to think. Finally, she blew out a breath, and irritated, raised her eyes to meet his directly. She was no ingénue—why act like one? "Okay, I admit it. I've been thinking about it ever since I saw your sweet ass that first day in the Phil."

"The 'it' being sex? With me?"

She rolled her eyes.

He smiled as though he couldn't help himself, but it dropped off his face as fast as it appeared. "There's always a woman."

"And?"

"And she's my business, not yours."

Joy thought about her own past, her own painful mistakes—the responsibility she had for her mother, how much Wade would hate the idea of his efforts being to Lana's advantage. How much she needed his help. She stood. "You're right about that." She retraced her steps to the door. "And you're right about something else. You and I diving under the sheets would be a bad idea." She tossed a smile at him from over her shoulder, determined to lighten—and inject common sense into—what had to be a working relationship. "No matter how interested we are in each other's 'sweet asses' . . . Good night, Wade."

Wade's night was anything but good. His bed was a rack, pulling the lower half of his body into a sexual hell and the top half into ambition central. Neither arousal made him happy. His mind went from Joy to the Philip and the neat row of numbers he'd created to prove the viability of Joy's plan. He hadn't been smart; he should have walked away from this place the day the will was read. Who the hell was he kidding? Thinking he could stand by like a damn eunuch and watch the Phil be brought back—and him have no part in it.

For weeks he'd ignored Sinnie's harping, filled his days with mops and buckets, convinced himself he didn't give a damn. Enter Joy Cole with her crazy "possibilities." From there all it had taken was a computer spreadsheet, a bunch of "what if's," and a gust of fresh hope.

He swung his legs bedside, stuffed them into running shorts, and pulled a sleeveless tee over his head. Time to run a thousand miles, clear his head, and do some serious planning. He did his best thinking working up a sweat.

He went to the fridge and drank orange juice from the carton. About to put it back, he heard a thump on his door.

"Wade, you in there?" It was Sinnie.

She poked her head in.

Feeling grim, he forced a smile. "Hey, Sin. You're up early."

She eyed him. "And you look as if you've been run over by a truck. One of those big ones."

He stowed the orange juice. "Didn't sleep."

"Why not?"

"Too much noise in the alley. Must have been a dozen cats out there."

Sinnie made a clicking noise with her teeth. "You should marry the girl, you know. That way, you'd get your hotel back. And everything would be . . . over."

He blinked. "Jesus, Sinnie!"

"Don't curse! And you'll be pleased to know I'm not here about your love life—or lack of it," she went on. "Old Henry's gone and a couple of people from six. The lot of them cleared out without so much as a by-your-leave." She plopped herself down at his table.

"And, you're telling me this because . . ." Wade ambled over to his coffee pot. Might as well make himself one, because it looked as if Sinnie was going to be here a while.

"Something's fishy. Henry wasn't feeling good, and he had a doctor's appointment tomorrow. I was taking him. He wouldn't have just left."

"I hate to break it to you, Sinnie, but there are a few people in this world who don't clear their decisions through you. Henry's probably gone out for a wa—"

"And I'm telling you, Mr. Wade Emerson, the man is gone." She pulled her chin back, and gave him her teacher look. "And the people from six? Same thing. Poof!"

"Poof?" Wade shook his head. He wanted to laugh—instead he smiled.

Sinnie shook a bony finger at him. "Don't you snicker

at me." Her voice lowered and her expression tightened to a worried mask of well-used wrinkles when she added, "Something strange is going on here. Something *very* strange."

Wade stopped his coffee-making. Hell, why not humor her? He could use the distraction. "Okay, Sin, let's go take a look." Secretly he figured Henry had just got tired of Sinnie being on his back and gone on a bender. The couple on six? Probably skipping on the rent.

He and Sinnie stepped into the hall at the exact moment Joy opened her door. Wade sucked up his irritation, sent one of those male, *What the hell did I ever do to you, Lord?* prayers heavenward.

The woman looked like gold-plated sin.

She smiled at Sinnie, then said, "Wade, I was just coming to see you." She lifted the papers in her hand. "I have some questions."

"Is that them?" He gestured at the papers.

"Yes, I printed them out."

"Shove it under my door. I'll look at them when I come back."

Her eyes went all fiery. "Back from where?"

Sinnie piped up. "Something funny's going on 'round here. We've got ourselves some missing tenants. We're going to check. You can come along if you want."

"Missing tenants?" She looked alarmed. "What happened?"

"Most likely nothing, but Sinnie here"—Wade attempted to kill her with a look—"has concocted a conspiracy. Aliens, I think."

Sinnie glared. "You'll see."

"I think I will come along," Joy said, and gave him an I-dare-you-to-stop-me kind of look.

It was his turn to glare. "Fine. Let's go."

They went to Henry's room first. The door was unlocked—not unusual for Henry—so they walked in.

"See?" Sinnie said, but her tone was more worried than triumphant. "I told you it was strange."

Wade didn't answer, but he did take a good look around and Sinnie was dead right—it was strange. He bent to pick up a broken lamp and return the table it had sat on to an upright position. He went to the kitchen counter, much like his own. Someone had eaten a sandwich and left all the fixings out. Old Henry was a drunk, and he didn't have much, but what he had was always neat and clean. He kept his room trim. Navy training, he'd told Wade proudly. Wade checked the closet and bureau. Empty.

"What's goin' on?" Big Mike walked in.

Wade glared at him, but kept his curse in lockup. Did this asshole have a goddamn tracking system up his butt, or just a severe case of bad-penny syndrome?

Mike moved close to where Joy stood by the lamp table Wade had just righted and smiled down at her, a big, toothy smile that made Wade want to belt him. Joy quickly moved to the other side of the room.

"Something funny's up, that's what. Old Henry's gone," Sinnie said, her tone apprehensive.

"Yeah, I know. He left last night."

Wade swung around. "You talked to him?"

"Passed him in the hall. He said somethin' about goin' to his sister's place in Portland."

Wade turned to Sinnie. "Does he have a sister in Portland?"

"Yes. Doris." She looked confused. "Don't know her last name. Not sure Henry did. The man couldn't stand the woman. He'd never go there."

"All I know is what he said."

"What time was that?" Wade asked.

Mike appeared to think. "Ten o'clock. Maybe later. Not sure, exactly."

Wade looked at Sinnie. "Makes sense."

She stared at Mike as if he'd grown two heads, then turned the same look on Wade. "Makes no sense at all! I'm telling you, he wouldn't go there. And he sure wouldn't head for Portland in the middle of the night."

"Ten o'clock isn't the middle of the night," Wade reminded her.

"It is when you're seventy years old," she announced.

He couldn't argue with that. "Let's check out six." He moved toward the door, and Sinnie and Mike fell in behind him.

"He left his suitcase," Joy said.

Wade shifted his gaze back to her. "What?"

She pointed at the shelf on the top closet. "Looks like a suitcase to me."

"Maybe he didn't need it," Mike said. "Man didn't have much of anything."

"He must have used something for his clothes. His bureau's empty." Sinnie looked at Mike as if his brain was leaking.

She was right, which didn't make Wade feel any better. "Let's check out six."

At the door, Wade eyed Mike. "You must have something better to do than follow us around."

"Can't think of nothin'."

Through gritted teeth, Wade reminded himself it was a free country.

Room 68 was in worse shape than Henry's place. Someone had trashed it. But no mystery here, just traces of white powder, burnt spoons, and hypodermics.

"Junkies," Mike announced the obvious. "Probably went out for more drugs and just didn't come back. Might yet." He picked up a spoon, sniffed. "Bad stuff. Real bad stuff."

Wade ignored him, looked around. Must have been one hell of a party, because there was enough drug paraphernalia for ten users.

"Tragic," Joy said, more to herself than anyone else in the room. "Just damn tragic that people continue to kill themselves this way."

"Did you know them?" Wade asked Sinnie.

"Sort of." She looked uncomfortable.

He waited.

"Her name was Marianne and the fellow's name was Bruce. Cherry was working with them, trying to get them into one of those addiction programs."

"Maybe that's why they bolted."

"Maybe," Sinnie conceded. "But Cherry's going to feel really bad about this."

Wade looked around the dirty, chaotic room in disgust, caught the trace of a smirk on Mike's face. "Now that we're satisfied"—he looked at Sinnie and quoted—"there's nothing 'funny' going on other than everyday life at the celebrated Hotel Philip, let's get out of here." Mad as hell, he strode toward the door. He hated this aspect of the Phil, the decay and relentless deterioration that made it a home of last resort for people whose next stop was the street. They deserved better and so did the Phil. He shut down his thoughts. Not his hotel, he reminded himself. Not his problem. But after last night, he found shutting down harder to pull off. "I'll come back later and clean the place up," he said, his voice brusque.

"Why bother?" Joy said and followed him into the hall along with Mike and Sin. She lifted the sheaf of papers in her hand. "If this works out, we'll have a clean-up crew in here next month. Leave it for them."

All eyes turned to Joy. Sinnie's set on her fast and hard. But before Wade could stop her, Joy went on. "In six to eight months, the Hotel Philip could be completely renovated with people lined up at the registration desk, and—"

"*Joy.*" Wade snapped out the word. This wasn't the

way to let people know their homes were about to be decorated and rented out from under them.

Joy's gaze shot to Sinnie's face, then to Mike's. "Oh, God, I'm so sorry."

Sinnie looked as if she'd been punched; it was the first time Wade had seen her at a loss for words. Mike looked thoughtful, which made him look as if he were lifting boulders in a rock quarry. Wade didn't give a damn about Mike, but he did about Sinnie. And he didn't like to see her with that panicky look on her face.

"I'm *so* sorry, Sinnie," Joy said again. "I didn't mean to blurt things out like that. Nothing's for sure yet. But it's only fair you know I'm thinking about reopening the Phil. As a hotel. But if it happens," she said, touching Sinnie's arm, "you'll be welcome to stay on, if that's what you want. If you don't, I'll help you find a place you like and pay the rent for a year."

"What about everyone else?"

"I'll offer the same arrangement to anyone who's made their home at the Phil for over five years."

Sinnie said nothing, still dumbstruck.

"It will work, Sin," Wade said, relieved Joy had opted for his recommendations on the tenants.

"This your idea, Wade?"

Joy answered, "Yes, it was Wade's idea—and a good one."

Sinnie shot a nervous glance in Joy's direction. "So you're really thinking of operating this old place as a hotel again?"

"Yes."

"Where you going to get the money?" Trust Sinnie to be direct.

Joy glanced at Wade—he could have sworn she looked guilty—then said, "I've got the money, or at least most of it."

This was news to him. "You did read those numbers, didn't you?" The estimates he'd worked on—which excluded final figures on the air conditioning and electrical—said close to a couple of million was needed to get the ball rolling.

"I know the numbers"—she glanced at Sinnie and Mike—"but I'd rather not discuss them standing in the hall."

"Your place or mine," he said.

"Mine." She looked uncomfortable and quickly added, "But tomorrow. I'll be more, uh, certain about things then."

"You got it." Wade knew there were as many questions in his eyes as there were secrets in hers. He hadn't imagined that shot of guilt.

"Well, kids, helluva tour, but I'm outta here," Mike said. Two seconds later he trudged down the hall and disappeared into the fire escape stairwell. Sinnie watched him go, her expression troubled.

Joy went one way down the hall and Wade went the other, a thoughtful unusually quiet, Sinnie at his side.

Outside her door, without warning, she grabbed his forearm and dug in her nails. "Don't let her do it. You do it. This is your hotel. Not hers. She's just a girl." Her voice was low, earnest.

Figuring he was in for another of her lectures about his "legacy," he loosened her grip, touched her anxious face. "It's all right, love. Everything's going to be okay. You and I both know the Phil can't survive as it is. Change is inevitable. And better Joy Cole than a wrecking ball." He kissed her cheek. "If she can make it work, you and all the rest of the tenants will be treated fairly. That's all you can ask." He opened her door, gently shoved her inside. "Just think about it before you set that hard old head of yours against it, okay?"

"Oh, I'll think on it, all right. Won't be thinking about much else from here on in." She closed her door in his face.

Wade headed for the Phil's front door, questions drumming in his head. He'd figured when Joy had time to digest the financial demands for renovating the Phil, she'd bolt or at least contact Grange and start the selling process. She hadn't.

The woman was full of surprises.

Outside, the morning was bathed in sunlight, and with Old Sol levering his way still higher in the east, it promised to be a sweltering day.

Wade stretched, eased his tense muscles into more fluid movement, then started to run. He pushed Joy Cole and her scheme for the Phil to a back corner of his mind. And when he'd freed up his more rational thinking, the first person who came to mind was Henry.

Wade might tease Sinnie, and the woman might drive him crazy, but she had the instincts of a CIA agent. If she thought something was wrong, it probably was. When he finished his run, he'd check Henry's room again, this time without an entourage.

He jogged easily to the corner, crossed the street, and ran into Blackberry Park. He picked up his pace—didn't spot the cab following him, nor was he aware of the azure blue eyes tracing his every movement.

Chapter Nine

Lana watched Wade's strong legs and powerful stride take him to a tacky little park not far from the hotel; then she leaned back into her seat.

He was better than she remembered. Any woman in her right mind would want him all over her. Want all of him. She doubted her so-smart, so-cool daughter would be any different. When a man who looked that good wanted you, you wanted back. Of course, he'd want Joy, if for no other reason than she looked so much like Lana. She smoothed her hair and refreshed her makeup.

The situation was troublesome.

When Lana glanced out the cab window at the Hotel Philip, she didn't see a stolid, lusterless hotel with broken windows and a dirty brick façade; she saw a very large check made out to her.

If Wade seduced Joy, if they slept together—and if he was as physically commanding as she remembered—that check, along with a lifestyle she was determined to maintain, was at risk. Lana wasn't fond of risk.

"That horrible, hideous hotel," she said, unaware she'd spoken aloud.

"Where to, ma'am?" the cab driver asked, looking at her through the rearview mirror.

She gave him her address, and he pulled away from the curb. Lana gazed blindly out the window, tried to think what to do next. One thing was imperative. She had to keep her eye on things; she couldn't sit by and wait on pins and needles for Joy's decision. If she and Wade were fucking each other's brains out, she needed to know.

Which meant getting closer to her daughter.

She put a hand on her stomach, applied pressure to settle it. *Close* wasn't something she did well.

But it would make David happy. He'd wanted her to "keep abreast of things," but she'd put it off, not relishing the task of spying on her daughter, and not thinking it necessary.

That was before she knew Wade was in the picture.

Lana hadn't seriously believed Joy would take on the hotel, had convinced herself she was being her usual difficult self, solely to irritate Lana. After all, she had no money, no business experience, and chronic wanderlust. She'd thought her contrary, maddening, and inconvenient, but never the threat David thought her to be.

Wade being on the scene changed that.

He regarded the Philip as his by right, had been fixated on it since he was boy. When Stephen disowned him and threw him out of the house that night, he hadn't cared about anything except the Philip. "Keep all the other crap," he'd said, referring to what at the time was a substantial fortune. He'd been so calm, so determined. "But the Philip is mine. It's what Grandfather wanted. It's what I want—for me and Mom. That's all. You and your whore of a wife are welcome to the rest." The boy was fiercely protective of that cow of a mother of his, she remembered.

Stephen, enraged by Wade calling her a whore, said hell would freeze over before Wade saw a penny of Emerson money or the deed to the Phillip. He'd told him to get out, said he never wanted to see him again. He never did.

Lana put her head back against the headrest.

Now he was back, and he'd been handed the perfect opportunity to get *his* hotel and get laid at the same time. What man would resist that? None that Lana knew of.

The cab driver pulled up outside her house. She paid him and walked the short distance to her front door.

Inside she went into the living room and sat heavily in a chair. Dear God, this whole business was tiresome. She was exhausted by it.

But exhausted or not, Lana wouldn't allow Wade to seduce his way to her money. She'd stop him, by any means available. And, of course, with a man the means was *always* available, conveniently located behind a zipper. She smiled, knew the chance of her righteous daughter taking her mother's leavings to her own bed were less than zero.

But before that, she'd do the mother thing, find out what was going on in her daughter's perverse, high-minded brain.

First thing Monday morning, Joy took a seat across from Jarvis Deane, her banker. His desk, glass-topped, was surgical clean—not a paper on it except a file with her name on its tab.

Her married name. Joy Marie Sheldon.

"Mrs. Sheldon," he said, his tone breezily formal. "It's nice to see you again."

"Call me Joy, please—and it's Cole, Mr. Deane, not Sheldon. Hasn't been since . . . the marriage ended." Joy ignored the stones in her stomach.

"Yes, of course. It's been a while, hasn't it?"

"Eight years."

"Really? Time flies and all that." He pulled the file toward him and opened it. "Let me see what we've got here." He opened the folder, swiveled the computer on his desk to face him, and keyed in the number from the file folder. His eyebrows lifted. "Very nice."

She wanted to run but instead asked, "How much?"

He put a finger on the screen. "One million, nine hundred and forty-two thousand dollars and . . . twenty-six cents." He closed the file in front of him and smiled at her, as if he'd just delivered her a healthy set of twins.

Joy emptied her lungs in one loud swoosh and crumpled back in her chair. "That much? Really?"

"Really. Behold the miracle of compound interest and a conservative investment strategy. Combined, they've come close to doubling your money in eight years." He swung the computer aside, fisted his hands, and plunked them on her closed file. "So you're here, Mrs. Shel— Joy. Which means you have plans for your money. How can First Bank help?"

Joy left the bank a half-hour later, her emotions tangled—satisfaction in the knowledge she had the money to begin work on the Philip in the same stew as an overwhelming regret she was about to use money she'd tried to forget she had for nearly a decade.

She looked up at a sky slowly shifting from summer blue to gray. *You said I'd be glad I had it one day, Matt. You were right. Thank you.*

And there was her mother . . .

When Lana discovered the source of Joy's wealth, she'd revel in how her "high-minded prig of a daughter"—a description she'd used more than once—had taken a man for a pot-load of money.

It didn't matter.

What mattered, suddenly more than anything, was the Philip, the work and challenge of bringing it back, making the old new again. What had started as a slow-building dream during her tours of the Phil had come alive in Wade's carefully thought out numbers. The Philip could come back. And Joy could make it happen. How ironic. All the years of traveling on trains, boats, and planes—and the endless stream of nondescript hotels—yet it was a hotel, a decaying ruin of a hotel, that now felt like home.

She wouldn't let her mother, or the origin of her money, ruin that.

While she walked, the sun flitted in and out from behind gray clouds. It was sultry hot. But it wasn't the heat that made her mind stop on one thing that, strangely, bothered her more than any other. If she wanted his help—and she did . . .

She'd have to tell Wade.

Wade had spent the weekend thinking and Monday morning running. By the time he got back to the Phil, it was after ten and Sinnie and Gordy, Gordy's mom, Cherry, and Lars and Rebecca were camped in his room. No Mike, thank God.

Sinnie had made them all coffee and doled out his cookies, and except for Gordy, who was watching television, they sat around his kitchen table eating as if it were their last supper or a funeral watch. He didn't need this. He had serious thinking to do. He'd been running for hours, and his head was clearer than it had been in years.

He had the rudiments of a plan rooting in his brain, and he wanted time to forge it into something more solid than wishful thinking. He did not want a roomful of people.

"What's this about?" He stood in a runner's sweat in the middle of the room and called on his limited patience. He raised a hand. "If it's about plumbing, I don't want to know. I don't do plumbing."

Lars laughed. Sinnie gave him her fish-eye. "Five's empty. Everybody's gone."

Wade stopped on his way to the bathroom, where he was bent on taking a shower. "What do you mean, gone? And who's everybody?"

"Everybody but me, that's who," Sinnie said. "I'm the only one left on five. Phyllis and Jack from 53 are gone and that nice Doddie woman from 51. Pretty, with the red hair?"

Wade didn't know, but he came around quickly to Sinnie's "something strange" theory. These defections made it six people leaving within a couple of days. Unlikely statistics. Wade looked at the people sitting around his table. "Anybody here know anything about this?"

As one, they shook their heads. Then Rebecca spoke. "I think Nick and Natalie are going, too. I saw her bringing in boxes from the market down the street."

"Did you talk to her?"

"She said she was cleaning up, getting rid of stuff." Rebecca's voice was soft when she said, "I didn't believe her. She looked—she looked scared, is how she looked."

"Rebecca," Lars interjected. "Don't start imagining things."

"I'm not—" She rubbed a hand nervously over her rounded belly.

Wade held up a hand. "The one thing we don't need is a domestic dispute." He looked at Sinnie. "Any chance you've let it loose in the hotel about Joy's plans?"

She opened her mouth as if to deny, then muttered, "I might have mentioned it."

"Sin!"

"You think that's the problem? What about Henry? He didn't know anything about that."

"Maybe Henry's case is different, but there's the strong possibility that more than one tenant will skip rather than hang around and wait for an eviction notice."

"That's possible," Lars said. "I know since Sinnie told us, we've had our eye out for another place."

"That's hogwash and you know it, Wade Emerson," Sinnie added.

Gordy piped up. "What time is it?"

Cherry, who was about to join in the dispute, turned to her son instead. "Almost ten-thirty, Gordy. You better go."

Gordy got up from where he'd been sitting on the floor in front of the TV. "Yeah, Mr. Rupert doesn't like anybody late." He stretched, a tall man stretch, and looked at Wade. "I got a new job. Mr. Rupert wants me to do the ten o'clock check and the three. And next week maybe the five o'clock, right before his dinner." He smiled at Wade as he walked out the door. "Standard rate, too."

Wade looked at Cherry. "What's he talking about?"

"Everybody here does checks on old Rupert. Door knocks, we call them. He sets them up, changes them all the time." She took a bite of her sandwich. "We knock, he answers, we go away. When Sinnie goes to clean his place, he gives her an envelope for everyone who's done knock duty. That's what we call it." She stopped. "I guess he's afraid of getting sick or something. Kind of sad, really, poor old guy."

Sinnie gave a disparaging snort. "There's nothing poor about Christian Rupert. That old man's got enough money for a hundred lifetimes."

Wade studied her. "How do you know that?"

Sinnie looked down, as if she'd said too much, and Cherry laughed. "Sinnie knows everything."

Wade bought that but decided he'd leave his Rupert questions for later. "So, how long has this door-knocking routine been going on?" he asked.

"Since the old goat quit going out. Years ago, now." Sinnie poured herself a mug of tea. "He gives me a list from time to time, names of the people he wants to knock, times, that kind of stuff. He calls it 'the schedule.' Sometimes there's odd jobs. Window cleaning, the odd repair of something or other. Stuff like that. Most everybody's okay with doing it. Money's good."

"So he picks the people?"

"Uh-huh." Sinnie looked away. "He's particular about that."

Lars interrupted. "Old Rupert isn't going to be happy about all these people going off. Especially if Natalie and Nick leave. Nick's been cooking for him—all that special stuff he likes so much."

Wade leaned against the bathroom door he hadn't managed to escape through. But suddenly, he wasn't in any hurry. He was curious. "It seems the old man keeps people pretty busy around here. Door knocks, dog-walking, cooking, cleaning—"

"—gardening," Cherry added. "Mike takes care of that."

"Right, Gordy told me that." Wade scratched his chin idly. "I should be insulted. He's never offered me a job."

Sinnie piped up, "Who cares about old Rupert and his jobs, anyway? The big thing is why's everybody leaving the Phil? What's happening around here?"

Sinnie was right. Rupert wasn't the issue, but he'd definitely caught Wade's attention. He pushed away from the door and stared at the assembly in his kitchen. "If you guys will vacate my place, I'll have a shower. Then I'll do some checking and see what I can find out. My guess? The people on five got nervous about what they heard"—he arched a pointed look at Sinnie—"and moved on." He wasn't sure he believed it himself, but he couldn't see the point in everyone being upset without knowing the facts.

They all filed out, but as usual, Sinnie had the last word. "Where's the Cole girl?"

"How the hell should I know?"

"You should be nice to her. Maybe keep her close—and an eye on her."

"Go, Sinnie, just go." Slowly, he closed the door on Sinnie's ham-handed attempts at matchmaking. He and Joy had made their decision. Hands off. He intended to abide by it. Besides, he was about to become a busy man.

He was going to buy the hotel.

It wasn't going to be easy, but he knew if he took his head out of his armpit long enough to think it through, he could do it.

Hurdles? Sure. One of them money. Zero collateral and a shiny new prison record wouldn't help, either. But Sinnie was right. The Hotel Philip was in his blood as it had been in his grandfather's before him.

If buying it meant lining Lana's pockets, he couldn't have done it. But Joy? Not a problem. Hell, he'd be doing her a favor. Once he convinced her of how much work was involved, the time it would take, the extent of the risk, she'd be glad to take the money and run. Especially if he made her an offer too good to refuse.

And maybe, when he was on his feet and the hotel was operational, they could—

He cut the thought. First things first. And the first thing was money. Money to buy the hotel, and money to refurbish. Wade had some but not enough.

But Sinnie had given him an idea. And it hadn't been about the missing tenants. He'd keep his promise to check up on them, but right now he had other things on his mind.

If Christian Rupert had the money Sinnie said he

had, he was a logical choice as an investor. Wade would put in what remained of his cash, then offer Rupert a straightforward business deal for a loan with a fixed repayment schedule with interest higher than the going rate.

Those terms, and the assurance the old man would never see a wrecking ball raze his home of over half a century, made a solid offer. Wade saw no reason he wouldn't take it.

Joy got back to the Phil shortly after noon. It had started to rain through the sun, cloudbursts that created steaming sidewalks and damp summer clothes. To the east the sky was dark, bundled clouds rolling across the sky like a herd of black bulls.

Anxious to get back to the hotel—her hotel, Joy didn't stop for lunch. Her mind buzzed with plans, and questions—how to tell Wade about the money, how to tell Lana she was going on an allowance while Joy built up the hotel.

She skipped the elevator and took the stairs, noticed a few light bulbs were out. She'd see to that herself, not bother Wade with it. When she pushed open the fire door leading to the third floor, it was even darker. Lights out here, too. Odd. She was sure there hadn't been so many burnt-out lights when she'd left this morning. Her mind shifted from plans to place—then puzzlement. Maybe most of the bulbs had been replaced at the same time, she thought, or maybe she needed to use a higher quality bulb.

The heat and rain had made the windowless hall muggy and uncomfortable. Joy quickly walked the few steps to her room, anxious to open a window.

She reached for her doorknob—yanked her hand back as if she'd touched a flame. Her door was ajar. Her stomach tightened, and she took a step back, looked up and down the dark, very empty corridor. Unlike the other tenants at the Phil, Joy always locked her door. Some habits weren't worth breaking.

Light from her room seeped through the partially open door to draw a thin blond line on the hall floor.

Every light in the room had been off when she left this morning, she was sure of it. Her heart pounded in her ears, and she looked across the hall to Wade's room, considered knocking on his door, but decided against it. She'd faced worse situations than this in some of the seediest hotels in the world. She'd handle this one. But it was nice to know if she screamed loud enough, he'd be there.

She moved back toward her door, listened intently for several minutes. Heard nothing. Then, preparing herself for a run down the hall—and that scream, if necessary—she gently pushed Room 33's door open wide enough for her to see most of the room. The hinges gave a dull scrape of complaint, and she paused again. Still no sound. Her chest stopped heaving.

"Anyone in there?" she said, both deepening and raising her voice.

Nothing but silence.

Joy pushed the door open, suddenly and so forcefully it slammed the wall with a loud crack. She flipped on the overhead light.

The room was empty.

Except for the stark, blood-red words scrawled on the wall above her bed.

"GET OUT AND STAY OUT!!!"

Joy dropped her bag on the table and sat heavily in one of the chairs, her heart resuming its loud thump within her chest. Who would write such a thing? Who would want her out of the Phil? And why?

She swallowed her unease, told herself to think things through.

She'd locked her door and the lock was intact, which meant whoever did this had a key. Other than Sinnie, the only other person she knew for sure had keys was Wade. He had keys to all the rooms—she'd seen him use them. But even though he'd made it plain he didn't want her here, particularly in this room, she couldn't make herself believe he had anything to do with this.

A clap of thunder brought her to her feet, every nerve jangling.

"What the hell!" Wade stepped into her room through the still-open door.

Joy's hand flew to her hammering heart. "God, you scared me."

He scowled at the harsh red scrawl over her bed, his expression ominous. "And that didn't?" He gestured rigidly at the writing.

"I was just trying to figure it out."

"What's to figure? Pack your bags. Go back to the Marriott."

"That"—she pointed to the words on the wall—"is unfriendly, Wade, not threatening." She gave him a direct look. "Although listening to all that bristling authority you just dished out, I might think it came from you." But somehow his exercise in control had calmed her.

"I'm more of a modern guy. I'd e-mail." Then he scowled at her. "I'm assuming that question was a joke?"

"The best I could come up with."

"Bad joke. One that follows your bad move in actually moving in here. I should never have let you take this room in the first place. Big mistake."

"I hate to remind you of this, but I own this hotel and I chose to stay here. You had—and have—nothing to say about it." She matched his glare with one of her own.

He blew out a breath, looked mad as hell. "Yeah, you

made the choice, but it was a lousy one." Then he added, more softly, "I don't want you in here. This damn room is jinxed."

Her mouth dropped open. "You can't be serious."

He looked grim but said nothing.

"You *do* believe it. All that 'room of doom' stuff." She couldn't hide her amazement. Mister calm, cool, and controlled, believing in ghost stories.

"I didn't say that."

"But you're not denying it," she said.

He twisted his lips, absolutely glowered at her.

"Look, the Phil isn't in the best of neighborhoods—anybody could have picked the lock and played a prank. That"—she gestured with her chin at the defaced wall—"doesn't mean the room is infested with evil spirits. You don't honestly believe someone is going to come in here and do me in, do you?" She would have laughed if his expression weren't so stoic. "Rooms aren't jinxed, Wade. You're overreacting to somebody's idea of a bad joke."

He looked at her a long time, as if considering a set of options. When he finally spoke, his voice was strained, his expression dark.

"My mother committed suicide in this room"—he waved a hand toward the bathroom—"in there, a year after my father married your mother."

Chapter Ten

Joy's body weakened as if drained, reeled as if punched. She'd heard Stephen's wife had died not long after she and Lana moved into Stephen's home; she hadn't known her death was by her own hand. No one had told her that. Wade's face was hard, tight.

"I'm so sorry," she said. "I didn't know."

"Sit." He pointed to the loveseat against the wall. "We might as well get this over with."

She didn't know what he was talking about, but she did as he said and sat down. He took time to think before he started talking.

"When you first asked me about the 'room of doom' thing, I ignored you, because it's a question I've never been able to answer. But after my mother," his gaze slid toward the bathroom door, then abruptly back to her, "I researched the place. There were the incidents written up in that old clipping, sure. But there were more through the years. Mostly during the late fifties and sixties. This little piece of real estate"—he waved a hand around the room—"has hosted fires, vandalism, robberies, drug overdoses, suicides—my mother's wasn't the only one—and three violent deaths. Add to that list two other murders in which the bodies were found elsewhere, but the victims were last seen in this room. The press never let it go and eventually the Phil's business started to dry up. My grandfather, who'd always resisted closing the damn room—pure stubbornness, I'd guess— finally did. But it was too little, too late."

"But your Mom died in—"

"In '86." He nodded, walked to the window. His back to her, he said, "She was always fascinated with Room 33, talked about writing a book on it. No one in the family was surprised she chose it." He looked back at her. "She had a sense of humor, my mother, about everything except Lana Cole taking her husband. That, she couldn't handle."

"With all the other . . . ugly things that happened here, was there ever any doubt it was—" She stopped, somehow unable to say the word.

"It was suicide, all right. Her note made that clear. She said she didn't want to wake up anymore, didn't want to go on pretending she was stronger than she was."

"So she came here and—"

"Ran a tub of warm water, stepped in, and cut her wrists open." His eyes were stark. "She was missing for two days before we found her."

Joy got up from the old sofa and crossed the room to stand in front of him. She held herself very still. "And she blamed my mother?"

The pain in Wade's eyes morphed to anger. "I don't know who she blamed. There was nothing in the note, no one named specifically, just what she saw as her own failure to make my father happy. But I know that if human hearts actually do break, hers did. And she chose this room, and Stephen and Lana's first anniversary, to kill herself." Wade narrowed his gaze on her. "How I see it? When my father's weakness—coupled with his then-substantial fortune—collided with your mother's greed and selfishness, my mother didn't stand a chance. Lana played Dad with the touch of a master. If I could even once believe she gave a damn about him, maybe . . ." He shrugged.

"But he let it happen. He must have wanted it, too." It was a small defense, but all she had.

Wade jerked his head in reluctant agreement. "My mother spoke to yours once, did you know that?"

Joy's stomach lurched. "No."

"She asked Lana to leave her husband alone. Your mother laughed, said she 'never left a man alone if she could help it.' She suggested my mother get rid of the 'pig fat' she had around her middle, learn to give a decent blow job, and find herself another man."

Joy went to stand at the foot of the bed, clutched one of its tall foot posts, and held on. She didn't want to think about her mother's acid tongue and cold heart, afraid she'd retch. The bold letters spit at her. GET OUT AND STAY OUT!!! She had the fleeting notion that Wade's mother had scrawled the words from the other side.

He came up behind her, put his hands on her shoulders. "I don't usually talk about any of this. Too damn hard, I guess." He nodded to the words on the wall and his voice firmed. "If you insist on staying here, will you at least look around the hotel, take another room?"

"I could, but I don't think it would make any difference. Every one of them has walls to write on. And at least here I'm just across the hall from you. I don't feel I should cut and run. If I do that, Room 33—"

"Room 33, what?"

"Wins. Room 33 and all its rumors and old secrets wins." She took a breath. "Everything you've talked about? It's in the past. I think it should stay there."

"I can't change your mind?"

The word "yes" trembled on her lips, but she shook her

head to indicate a negative, too aware of the weight and heat of his big hands sliding to the base of her neck, resting there, before massaging her nape with his thumbs.

"Then you can bet I'll keep my eye on you, Joy Cole. That okay with you?"

"Okay." She smiled, turned to look at him.

"Good." He paused. "And for what it's worth, I don't confuse you with your mother. Not anymore." He squeezed her shoulders and streams of warmth traveled down her arms, to pool in her chest. "You're much more beautiful."

She gave him as direct a look as possible, given his nearness and the disparity in their heights. "You and this room aren't the only ones with secrets, Wade. There are things you don't know about me, and like it or not, I *am* my mother's daughter. Nothing will change that." Through the gathering sensual mist in her brain, she saw that dark light—the money. He'd know then how much like her mother she was. She should tell him but . . . later.

She'd tell him later.

He stroked her lower lip with his thumb, studied her mouth. "Nothing will change this, either." His head came down and his lips, firm and slightly open, moved over hers. "You believe in fate, Cole?"

She couldn't breathe, let alone talk. She was suspended, waiting for his mouth to center, find hers, claim it. "Fate . . ." She let the word out on a slow exhale. "Never thought much about it." She shifted closer, until her breasts pressed into his chest. He was hard, taut muscle, above and below. He parted his legs to hold ground, receive her flush against him. Enfold her.

The heat—

Too sudden, and with it the reflex to hesitate, pull back, the sense she was going into perilous territory. But to say no against Wade's mouth was impossible.

She wanted him, every female sinew and nerve in her body shouted it at her with sure sexual conviction. She found her voice again. "What about you? Do you believe in fate?"

Wade caressed her skin, brushed kisses along her cheek, her jaw, her parted lips. "I do now. There's something about us together. Something inevitable." He lifted his head and his dark eyes poured heat into hers. "I like the taste of you, Miss Cole, the feel of you in my arms. And I've been wanting more of both since you"—he smiled—"hauled that sweet ass of yours into the Phil."

He took her mouth in a kiss so scorching it seared her mind, her heart—the soles of her feet.

Joy forked her fingers through his heavy hair, her heart stammering, her mouth taken—conquered—by its first contact with his tasting, probing tongue.

"Jesus . . ." he muttered and released his hold to look down at her. "You're like a mainline aphrodisiac." For a moment there was something close to fear in his eyes, then his gaze, heavy with desire, dropped to her lips. He shook his head, half in resignation, half in wonderment. "I think I'm fucked." A slow smile turned his lips. "In the best possible way, of course."

Lana met his eyes, tried to smile back through the sexual mist adrift in her mind. "Not yet, you're not. But hold that thought." She pulled his mouth back to where it belonged. When they parted, breathless, she said, "This—us thing—it has to happen. I want it to happen, but no promises, no illusions. Okay?"

"Sweetheart, I gave up on promises and illusions the day I went to prison." He kissed her again, a kiss of heady sensual potential. Then he lifted his head and leaned his forehead against hers. "But there's no chance I'll make love to you in this room." He stepped back. "And, much as I want it to be, it isn't going to be now."

"Places to go and people to meet?"

"Something like that."

She traced his ear with her finger. "If this is your idea of foreplay, I'm not impressed." She stood on tiptoe to kiss his ear, nibble his lobe.

"Hmm . . . if you want to settle for a quickie and a pat on the rump as I hustle you out of my room, it can be arranged."

She cocked her head and stepped back. "Enticing as that sounds, I'd prefer something more substantial. And I—" She hesitated, defensive but compelled to be honest with him, even though her name in this room seemed sacrilegious. "My mother called. She wants to see me. I'd only come back to make myself a quick lunch and . . . pick up some papers. I'm due at her house in an hour."

His eyes stilled, then he nodded. "Later, then?"

"Later." She frowned when a thought came.

"What?" He traced a line on her forehead, smoothed it with his thumb.

"I was just thinking. I've never made a date for sex before. Coffee. Lunch. Dinner and a movie. But never specifically for sex. I'm not sure how I feel about it."

"I'll buy a bottle of cheap hooch and roll out the cheese and crackers—will that help?" He tilted his head.

"More intriguing foreplay. I've found myself a master."

"Nope." He brushed a soft kiss across her lips, grinned. "More of an accomplished amateur who takes his sport very seriously."

"Ah, and modest, too. I can't wait."

They were still smiling at each other when her door, which had been ajar since Wade came in, was opened wide.

"You in there, Wade—? "Mike leered at them. Keeping one hand on the doorknob, his gaze jumped from her to Wade. He looked pleased. Joy had the feeling he'd been standing outside that door longer than he'd admit.

Joy stepped back, trapped in a kid feeling of being caught playing with something she shouldn't be. Wade didn't move at all, briefly tightened his grip on her shoulders and released her. "You know those things at the end of your arms, Mike? They're called hands. Most people use them for knocking."

When Mike continued to stare, Wade added, "What the hell do you want?"

"Sinnie sent me. She wants you to take a look at Gordy, maybe take him and Cherry to the ER. Somebody cut him in the park."

Three hours later, Wade brought Cherry and Gordy back to their room, and helped settle the wounded boy on the couch. At the hospital they'd filled out a report and talked to the police. Wade hadn't gotten the impression they planned to do much about it. The fact Gordy was cut protecting Rupert's dog from a fried-eyed crazy who wanted to use him as a football, because the dog barked at him, didn't rank high on their priority list.

"You okay, partner?" Wade asked, helping the big guy get settled on the ratty sofa in their room. The wound was a deep slash across his upper thigh, and judging from Gordy's crabby expression, the stitches hurt like hell. "Can I get you something? A soda, maybe?"

"No sugary pop," Cherry said. "I'll make him soup."

Wade figured hot soup in this weather was overkill, but he left that decision to Cherry, who bustled to the counter and started banging around with pots. "I've got to go, Gordy. You take care, okay?"

"Okay." He moved his leg, the bandages bulging under his shorts. "Melly's okay, huh? Really?"

He'd asked this same question a dozen times since

the incident in the park, and every time his brow
scrunched with concern. "Melly's fine. You looked after
her real good. Mike took her back to Mr. Rupert."

"Melly doesn't like Mike. Who's going to walk him
tonight?"

"Mike, maybe?"

Gordy's scowl deepened. "Melly doesn't like Mike,"
he repeated, then looked up. "You do it, Wade. You walk
Melly. She likes you. Please . . . please."

"Okay, Gordy. I'll take care of Melly." Fate at work
again. This was his chance to meet Rupert—he'd be a
fool not to take it.

"You gotta be there at eight. Mr. Rupert doesn't like
late people."

"Eight it is. Now rest that leg," Wade said. "You're
going to have one hell of scar to show off."

Gordy smiled at that, then turned his attention to his
ever-on television screen.

Wade strolled to where Cherry was stirring soup into
a pan. He kissed her on the cheek, spoke quietly. "Keep
your door locked tonight, sweetheart. Will you do that?"

She stopped stirring, nodded. "Yes, I will." She glanced
at her son, lowered her voice. "What do you think is
going on around here, Wade? Why do you think everyone is leaving?"

"I'm not sure yet. Probably just a pile of coincidences,
people skipping rather than giving notice, but in the
meantime, better safe than—"

"—sorry." She nodded. "I agree totally. Will you tell
the others? Or do you want me to?"

"I'll make the rounds. You stay with Gordy."

"I will, thanks."

Wade walked the shadowy fifth floor hall after checking on Sinnie. He'd filled her in on Gordy's condition

and gave her the same advice he'd given Cherry. For once she'd given him no argument.

In the stairwell heading to the third floor, he was obliquely aware of a lot of lights burnt out. Something else to check into.

But the thought didn't stick. The idea of fate did, and it was coming at him hard and fast. A dog, a boy, and his birthright had converged. Tonight he'd meet Christian Rupert. He had other options for raising the money, but it was possible that Rupert—if he was interested—would be the best—and quickest. It was worth a shot.

As was Joy Cole.

The thought of her wouldn't leave him alone. When he'd gone to her room earlier to tell her more tenants were gone and seen that ugly scrawl above her bed, he'd damn near lost his breakfast. Fear had clawed his guts ever since. And he was damn glad she'd left the hotel when he did—even if it was to visit her mother.

He opened the fire door to the third floor. A single light burned at the far end of the hall. The rest were black.

Lights out. Henry gone. Other rooms vacated without notice. He hated to admit it, but Sinnie was right. Something was going on around here. Someone wanted everyone out of the Phil. And those ugly words smeared across Joy's wall said she might be next on the list.

Tonight—if Wade had his way—she definitely wouldn't be sleeping in Room 33. If common sense wouldn't work, maybe sex would. And if that failed, he'd damn well chain her to his bed until he figured out what the hell was going on around here.

Christian slipped on a pair of clean white gloves, picked up the phone, and dialed. "Mr. David Grange, please."

He was fortunate enough to be put through immediately.

"What do you want, Christian?"

David's abrupt question rankled but didn't deter Christian from his goal. "I'd like a status report on the progress of my property acquisition." Christian chose to be circumspect on the telephone. One never knew who might be overhearing at the other end.

"I'll get back to you on that, of course, but I will tell you the party in question will be coming to dinner with Lana and me at the end of the month. We'll know for certain then, but I'm confident things are going well."

It pleased him that David was also being prudent in the choice of his words. Although he did hear that irritating note of impatience in his tone. "Really? Perhaps you'd be good enough to share the reason for that confidence with me."

"For God's sake, I said I'd get back to you." His voice started to rise; he lowered it to continue. "And I will. Get off my back."

Christian ignored his impertinence. "Another question. Equally important, I believe. Did you discover any next of kin for that young woman we discussed?" Christian had to wait for his answer, another impertinence.

"Only her mother."

"Good, then rather than you and I argue as to whether or not the party will sell, I suggest we meet to consider a move on to Plan B."

Christian heard a sharp intake of breath. "Why?"

"I've heard rumors of planned renovations and a blossoming relationship. Activities and a relationship that would not be to our mutual benefit. I've decided it's best we take care of it sooner rather than later." Christian could use Mike for the job, of course, but he had other uses for him before he was disposed of. And David had grown arrogant of late, wasn't as malleable as he should be. He hadn't been the same since he'd entangled himself with that Emerson woman. It was time for a lesson in humility. David would balk, but David would perform. He was Christian's man, and he must not be allowed to forget it. Killing his lover's daughter would be the perfect reminder.

Another breath, long and deep this time.

"David, are you there?"

"I'm here."

"Come by tomorrow night. Midnight. We'll discuss the details then."

Christian hung up before David had a chance to argue and turned to Mike, who sat placidly picking at his thumbnail. "You've done well. Carry on with the, uh, evictions. I want the hotel empty by this coming weekend. That gives you four days. Leave the boy and his mother until the last. Melly needs her walks. And you are to leave Miss Cole and Mr. Emerson alone—completely alone. Have I made myself clear on that?"

"Uh-huh."

Christian pulled off the white gloves, dropped them on the table beside his chair. "As for tonight, don't do anything other than watch. If—and when—the girl does go to his room, I want to know about it."

Mike smirked. "Watch, huh? I can do that."

Odious creature! Another minute, he'd be drooling all over his Persian carpet. "I don't expect they'll invite you into the room, Michael."

"I got my ways."

Christian lifted his gaze to the heaven he'd forsaken as a youth, and tried to stem his repulsion. He'd come to a new low in his life, having to deal with the likes of this disgusting specimen. When it was over, when the hotel was his, he'd make certain the guests were of a much higher caliber.

He wanted this stupid beast out of his sight as quickly

as possible, but he had one more item of business—a question to ask. Were he a younger man, he might not ask it, perhaps even fear the answer, what it might require of him. But he wasn't young, he was very old, and he would not, could not, abide divided loyalties. "About Sinnie, Michael. Is she playing a part in this relationship between the Cole girl and Mr. Emerson?"

"Sinnie? Yeah," Mike said, and laughed. "I heard her tell Wade he should marry the bitch so he could get his hotel back. His legacy, she calls it."

What warmth remaining in Christian's blood turned to sleet.

Sinnie had given Wade Emerson good advice. If he heeded it, there would be trouble—and heeding it would not be difficult. Not only were the Emerson men attractive, they were notoriously weak when it came to women. Joe had been positively idiotic over that sow of a wife of his, and she for him. Loathing, thick and bilious, simmered low in his stomach at the thought of her. As for the tall, handsome Stephen, that wastrel had been picked off by the worst harlot in a bad lot. He suspected the young Emerson would also be sexually appealing. And if the woman's legs were shapely enough and open at the appropriate angle—and she had his grandfather's hotel in her portfolio—what would stop him from fornicating his way to ownership?

Bile rose to Christian's mouth, acrid and bitter, and his heart stumbled behind his dry ribs.

Women. They were always in his way.

The young Cole woman had inherited his hotel, had plans to renovate, fill it with people—too many for him to organize, keep track of. He shivered, fear slithered snakelike around his bones. And tonight, if Michael were correct—she was going to have sex with Joe's grandson—right under his feet.

And now Sinnie. His Sinnie, despite his unending kindness to her, had deceived him, told him Wade Emerson was moving on. All the while encouraging the pup to woo and marry the little Cole slut to get his hotel back.

His hotel. The words tore along his mind on metal skids, sparking and burning a path to the root of his avarice, the core of his hate.

Stupid, stupid woman. She'd poked her nose in where it didn't belong for the last time. He calmed his turbulent emotions. Sinnie had said too much, been disloyal.

She was dead to him.

He looked at the hulk of a man sitting across from him, his ham hands hanging between the open wedge created by his thick thighs as he awaited Christian's bidding.

And very soon she'd be dead to everyone else.

Lana tied the terry robe around her slim body, and answered the door. Already annoyed. "I expected you earlier, Joy."

"I got tied up. Sorry." She didn't look sorry.

Even in coming to see her, the girl was inconvenient. Lana was expecting David in less than an hour. She stepped back from the door to let her in. "If I'd known you were going to be late, I'd have put this off until tomorrow." She disliked feeling pressured, but it was past time for the mother/daughter bonding routine to start, and she'd pull it off if it killed her. Wade Emerson was not going to get her hotel. She calmed herself, readied herself for the hour ahead. "I wish you'd called."

Joy stepped into the high-ceilinged foyer. "Actually, the last time I called you was on your forty-fifth—or was it sixth—birthday, and you told me you didn't appreciate the reminder."

Lana laughed, surprised she actually enjoyed her

daughter's acerbic humor. "You're right. Let's go out to the patio. A drink?"

"Iced tea, if you have it."

"The ready-made kind."

"Perfect."

Joy followed Lana to the kitchen. Done in a combination of white, maple wood, and with stainless steel appliances, it looked as if it were completed yesterday. "It's in there, I think." Lana waved in the general direction of a cupboard and took one of the high seats around the center island. She watched her daughter move with skill around a room she rarely frequented. "Do you cook?" she asked, suddenly curious.

"Yes."

"What? What kind of things do you cook?"

"This and that." Joy went to the fridge to get ice cubes. "When I'm ambitious I tackle French, maybe Thai."

"I'm impressed. Although I do boil a mean egg."

Joy gave her a sideways look. "I don't remember that."

"I've only done three. I suspect you were away." Lana was pleased to see a smile, however brief, turn up Joy's lips. Lana wasn't much as a mother, as the boiled egg story testified. And Joy was difficult, but, looking at her now, seeing how beautiful, how like herself she was, a sliver of regret made her think some kind of friendship would have been nice through the years. Lunch. Shopping, maybe. But Lana was a realist. Her daughter didn't like her, perhaps even hated her—all because of her father. In Joy's eyes, Lana might just as well have killed the man with her own hands. "Let's go outside," she said, using the spoken word to negate the useless thoughts in her mind. "We'll sit beside the pool. It's stuffy in here after that rain. Thank God, the sun has come out."

"Sure, lead the way."

When they were settled, Lana in a lounge chair, Joy in an upright one by the patio table, Lana said, "You should get out of the sun." And to her surprise, Joy nodded and pulled her chair to shelter under the table's umbrella. To even more surprise, her daughter's easy compliance caused a small lump in her throat. She set her gin and tonic on the table beside the chair. Two sentimental bouts were enough for one day. Any more would be maudlin. "So tell me, have you decided to sell the hotel to David? Let me take the money and run?"

"We agreed on a month. It's been barely two weeks."

"Just curious." She watched Joy purse her lips, a habit of hers when she was thinking. She'd done it as a child and was doing it now.

"Did you know that Stephen and I had a drink together a few months ago?" Joy asked.

The abrupt change of subject caught Lana off guard. "No," she said. "He didn't mention it."

"We met by chance in San Francisco a few months back. We talked for an hour or so."

"It must have been a hell of a conversation, considering it was enough to have him change his will." Her tone was sharper than she intended. And though she wanted to know what went on between the two of them, she wouldn't ask. No point. Ancient history. She settled herself casually, more comfortably, on the double lounge.

The look Joy leveled on her was faintly impatient, and she paused before adding, "We talked for a long time. He must have been ill then, although he didn't mention it."

"Hmm." Lana didn't want to talk about Stephen. He was dead, gone—of no value to her now. If she were to live as she always had, resolutely in the present, resolutely for herself, she didn't have time to reminisce about Stephen.

Joy sipped her iced tea but kept her gaze on her mother. "You really don't care, do you? Eighteen years of living with him, and you don't give a damn."

"Stephen's gone. Dead. I don't see the point in talking about him now or rehashing whatever we had together."

Joy's look was more startled than disapproving, although Lana knew the disapproval was there, a twisted root curled around her daughter's soul. A soul very much like her own, strong and cautious—and self-protective. Perhaps it was a family trait. "I thought you loved him," Joy said.

"I did, in my way. But the truth is, people come and people go from your life. Attaching too much of yourself to anyone is a waste of emotional energy."

Her daughter fixed that unnerving stare of hers on her, kept it there. "You're afraid of people leaving, aren't you?" She spoke softly, seeming awed, as if she'd just discovered the Holy Grail. "God, I should have seen it before. It's textbook psychology. You're afraid of being hurt—so you walk away first. Hurt first."

"Don't be ridiculous. And Stephen died, in case you've forgotten. He left me—the hard way. It sure as hell wasn't the other way around." If this was mother and daughter bonding, it was a pain in the ass. She wasn't about to let Joy beat her into a corner, judge her.

"But you were already having an affair with Grange, marking your exit," Joy went on.

Lana briefly considered lying but decided it was pointless. It wouldn't make Joy's opinion of her any worse—or better—than it was. Besides, she'd learned long ago, silence was much more effective than lies. She shrugged, hoping her nonchalance would deter her bulldog of a daughter.

"Do you love him, Mother? Like you loved Dad, the

men after him, Stephen?" Her tone was rife with sarcasm, disbelief.

Lana got up from the lounge. "Why all the questions?
What do you want from me?" This getting together idea
looked like a major mistake. She should have known
Joy would try to control things, make them go her way.

"Me? Nothing. I haven't wanted anything from you
since the day you took me away from my father. But you
invited me here. We've never really talked before"—she
sighed—"so I thought I'd make the most of it."

"And here I thought you were just being your usual
pain in the ass."

Joy met Lana's gaze, her eyes no longer so coolly determined. Now there was something else. Confusion?
Lana couldn't be sure. She hadn't spent much time learn-
ing to read people. Never saw the point—and it took
her attention off what mattered. Herself. A fact she
never apologized for.

"You fascinate me," Joy said, suddenly quieter, less accusatory. "Did you know that? I've never met anyone
who comes close to your degree of selfishness. But even
knowing that, I look for more from you. But you always
disappoint. When you left Dad—"

Lana held up a hand. "Oh, please, let's not go back
to the Bronze Age in your pubescent search for truth."
She dropped the hand, angry that her stomach muscles
flexed and contracted with no command from her. "I
am what I am. I look out for myself, because I'm the
only one capable of doing it."

"The miracle is that these men don't see that. They
all love you. Stephen did. Dad did, and God knows how
many others there have been. And now, of course, David
Grange."

David. Did David love her? She squashed her moment of doubt. Of hope. Refused it. "What can I say,

I'm a goddess." She opted for sarcasm, intended it to sideline the direction of this conversation.

"Yes. A goddess." Joy's smile was wry. "That's what Dad always called you."

"You remember that?"

"I remember everything." She wrapped her arms around herself. "I just don't understand." She leveled an empty gaze on Lana. "Like why you walked out on Dad when he was dying. Why you never told me he was sick. Never let me see him again."

"I thought it was best." Lana turned away from her daughter's fervid scrutiny, went back to relax on her lounge chair.

"Best," she echoed. "Best for you. And that's what counts. That's what always counts. I would have stayed with Dad. I wanted to, but you lied to me, took me away."

"You were a kid. You needed to be with your mother." Lana couldn't believe that pap had come from her own mouth.

Joy's eyes widened, and for a moment it looked as though she might laugh. "You're serious. That's how you saw it? You and I needing each other? I don't think so, Mother. I needed my dad. I needed to be there for him." Joy's expression was one of bottomless regret, sickening distaste. "Hell, you didn't even take me back for his funeral."

Lana tried another shrug, pulled herself into the now. "You don't know . . ." she said, still trying to hold back, go to that silent place deep inside her where anything not good for Lana was shuttered out.

But like thick, black tar under intense pressure, those years of hell bubbled up, worked to force out words Lana never wanted to say.

Chapter Eleven

Joy watched her mother in amazement, the rapid play of emotions on her normally sanguine features. She looked angry, frustrated, pained, and terrified. All of it at odds with her languid posture on the chaise lounge.

"Then tell me, Mother, tell me what I don't know," she pleaded softly.

Lana's glance shifted sideways. "You're not going to let it go, are you?"

"No."

A long silence fell between them.

"I watched my mother die," Lana said, and Joy could see her muscles tense, the lines in her face straighten. It was as if she were staring barefaced into a winter wind. "It took her three years." Her gaze was opaque, her tone board flat. "Do you know how many bedpans that is? How much vomit and bile? How many changes of sheets? Bed sores?" She closed her eyes. "How many screams of pain."

Joy's eyes widened. "You never told me."

"My father didn't believe in doctors and my mother only believed in my father—the original iron hand.

Minus the velvet glove, of course. I'm like him in more ways than I care to admit. As are you, I think. When Mother got sick, he told her to go to bed. When she got sicker, he told her to stay there. I was told to 'see to her.' " Lana breathed slowly, as if to regain her equilibrium. "There was no one else, so I did." She stopped and her gaze turned cool and distant. "I quit school to watch my mother die, daughter dear. And it's a graduation I wouldn't recommend."

"How old were you? When you quit school?"

"Thirteen. I was sixteen when she died. My father said it was too late for school, so he got me a job cleaning house for a woman—a woman who became his new wife within a month of my mother's death. When they married, I walked to the nearest highway, I-5, I think, and put out my thumb." She looked at Joy, her expression defiant. "Your father picked me up. I guess you didn't know that, either. He was decent enough, so I stayed. From then on, I never looked back."

Lana glanced around, and her eyes, more expressive than Joy had ever seen them, lingered on the stately home, the swimming pool, the blur of brilliant red geraniums bordering her fence. "And I'm not going to ever again." She lay back in her luxurious lounge, settled in as comfortably as a freshly fed cat, as if she hadn't spoken of such terrible things. Closing her eyes, she looked calm, comfortable in her silky, pampered skin, the daring bikini most twenty-year-olds would shy away from.

"Did you love her? Your mother?" Joy had to ask, drawn to peer deeper into the fissure Lana had opened.

Silence.

After a deep breath, Lana opened her beautiful eyes. Her voice was distant, achingly soft, when she said, "I adored her. She was long-suffering, patient, giving, uncomplaining, and utterly unselfish. She accepted her death, her long, painful good-bye to this life—under my father's orders—totally alone and with the dewy-eyed innocence of a saint. She was a fool, ten times over, and I loved her with all my childish heart."

She seemed to consciously still her mind, and her gaze steeled when it met Joy's. "She was the *last* person I loved. The last person I will ever love. Do you understand that?"

The mother now stretched out before her was the one Joy had always known, focused inward, untouchable, and eerily serene. "Including me."

Lana didn't lift her head. "You were a mistake. I never intended to have a child. But your father was determined, so I went along with it. I was barely eighteen. I figured it was as good a way as any of hanging on to a man." She curled her lips. "I've since learned a much more effective method. I had two abortions before I finally and permanently ended my childbearing days. Thank God for the miracle of the knife."

"So when Dad got sick, you left—"

"Got it in one. I'd already had enough bedpans to last me the rest of my life. I wasn't looking for more."

"But I begged to stay with him, and you took me with you anyway. Why?"

"A good question. And the only one I've never been able to answer. You were a burden then, and you still are." Lana closed her eyes again, but Joy saw the tension, the deliberate flexing of her hands, as if they'd tightened uncomfortably. "Now that we've had this marvelous sharing experience, can we get down to business? Talk about the hotel."

"I'd still like to know—"

Lana glared at her. "For God's sake, drop it, Joy. The psychotherapy session is over. Let it go."

Joy, her senses numbed by the first real conversation she'd ever had with her mother, knew when she was

beaten. Lana wouldn't say any more. Her head thick
with confusion and revelations, she could only mumble,
"I brought a file but I left it in the kitchen. I'll be right
back." She stood on weakened legs and made her way
off the patio.

In the monstrously unappealing kitchen, she located
her file, but suddenly rubbery in the legs, sat down
when she realized she'd lost something else—her old
perception of her mother.

Lana was self-absorbed, manipulative, and cold—every
one of those things in spades, but she *had not* singled
Joy out for rejection. She'd rejected loving—anything
or anyone—long ago. In a twisted way, knowing this
lightened her mood, hinted at possibilities.

Or maybe she was picking at emotional crumbs.

Nothing had changed, yet everything had changed.

There was even the chance, if Joy could make her
plans and dreams for the Phil understood, perhaps be
more conciliatory and less combative, that her mother
would go along with them—that something remotely
close to a mother-daughter relationship could come out
of this mess. She smiled. Exactly what Stephen had intended by his bizarre will.

With the barest flicker of fresh hope, she picked up
the file and headed back to the pool area.

David had arrived, having let himself in by the side
gate, and the kiss he and her mother were sharing definitely wasn't meant for an audience. Joy stepped back
out of sight until it was over. Which was pointless, because she suspected neither of them knew what embarrassment was.

When David saw her, he got up from where he'd been
sitting on the side of Lana's lounge chair. "Joy. Your
mother told me you were here. Nice to see you again."
Dressed casually in tailored shorts and a labeled golf
shirt, he was photo-shoot ready. Again she wondered

exactly who David Grange was out for, himself or her mother, or both.

"David." She acknowledged him with a brief nod. "I'm glad you're here," she lied. She actually wished he were a thousand miles away so she could talk to her mother alone. But the way Lana gripped his hand told her there was no chance of that. "I have an idea for the Philip," she went on. "I was going to go over the numbers on it with Mother, but she'll want your opinion anyway, so your being here will save us all time." She handed her mother a recap of Wade's projections and budgets.

"Numbers." Lana barely glanced at them before handing them to David. "Your strength, darling, not mine." She got up from the lounge. "Drinks?"

David was already scanning the papers, didn't raise his head when he said, "A gin and tonic, if you have it. Thanks."

"Done. I'll throw some clothes on and be right back."

When she was gone, David lifted weary eyes to meet Joy's. "You have no idea what you're doing, do you?" He rubbed the center of his forehead as if he didn't expect an answer. "You had help with these. This isn't something you could have worked up yourself so quickly."

"Wade Emerson helped."

"Shit!"

"I don't think so." She took her seat at the table she'd been at earlier, sipped her now-tepid tea. "I think he knows what he's talking about, and he knows the history of that property better than anyone."

"He's an ex-convict, for God's sake. Fraud, obstruction of justice. What the hell are you thinking, Joy?"

She ignored his outburst, didn't bother to tell him she'd done her own checking on Wade's criminal record. "I'm thinking of making the Hotel Philip a viable operation so I can provide my mother with the income she needs to live. Makes sense to me." She didn't mention her feelings about the Phil, her strange and growing sense of belonging—the pride of ownership that grew day upon day. She doubted David would understand, or care, when his own vision was of an implosion and a blur of roaring bulldozers.

"It makes no goddamn sense at all. With this"—he gave a wild wave of the file—"you're more likely to put her in the poorhouse. It's insane."

It was Joy's turn to get mad. "Insane or not, I can do whatever I damn well please with the Philip, David, and you have no say in it."

David took a moment, apparently to calm himself. "Okay . . . let's assume for a moment these numbers make sense—which I don't believe they do—we're talking a few million here. Where do you plan to get the money?"

Lana came back wearing cotton slacks, a silk tank top, and carrying David's gin and tonic.

"Did you hear this?" David asked, waving the file, again.

Lana handed him the drink. "I heard enough." Lana stared at Joy, her gaze as flat as the water in her pool. "And David asked a very good question, Joy. Where will you get the money? From sleeping with Wade Emerson?"

Joy felt her jaw drop, and when she scanned from her mother's face to David's, she saw his had done the same.

He spoke first. "Lana, what are you saying?"

"Nothing." She took a chair at the umbrella-shaded table and crossed her long legs. "I'm not saying anything. I'm *suggesting* that Wade Emerson is behind this plan of Joy's, that he's not above seduction to get control of what he sees as his birthright. So . . . I'm asking." She turned goading, speculative eyes to Joy.

Joy hadn't found her tongue, was afraid she'd swallowed the damn thing. The leap from Lana's earlier revelations, to David's brash interference, to her sex life was like trying to digest a tough cut of beef dipped in chocolate. She grabbed the file from David's hand, her own hand shaking. "My mother has sex on the brain, David, having discovered long ago that the way to man's heart—and wallet—is through his erect penis." So much for being less combative, more conciliatory.

Lana laughed.

David swore.

Joy grabbed her tote bag, stuffed the file in it.

"Don't do this." David said. "It's a mistake. And if you're counting on Emerson for the money, forget it. He doesn't have any. I've checked."

Joy spun, zeroed in on the two of them. "I am not sleeping with Wade Emerson to get his money—" She stopped.

Her mother, knowing her words came out wrong, laughed again, before settling her flawless face to a smug smile. "I watched him run the other day, you know. Very nice. You have good taste." She sent one of her smoky gazes toward David, took his hand. "Like mother, like daughter. And with a man who looks like Wade, has a body like Wade, I'm sure there is at least *one* other long, hard reason to go to his bed."

Joy didn't have an ounce of violence in her, but if she had, she'd have slapped the smile from Lana's face. Instead she raised her eyebrows and matched her mother's bemused expression with a carefully composed dead-straight one of her own. Control was a game anyone could play. "Who I sleep with and for what reason is my business. But just to set your minds at ease," she said, her tone biting, "you'll be pleased to know I have money— two million dollars, to be exact."

Joy savored David's shocked—frightened?—eyes, scanned the mask that was her mother's face. "You know,

I came here today to talk things over, get your input on the idea of renovating instead of selling, which is the way I'm leaning right now. But just to keep you in suspense—and to keep my promise—I'll save my final decision and any more attempts at communication until the end of the month as we agreed."

She gave her mother a withering smile. "It's been fun. A very educational afternoon. I hope you and David enjoy the rest of it."

"See you in a couple of weeks, darling daughter. Don't do anything with Wade that I wouldn't do."

Joy's anger turned to disgust, and because she couldn't find a printable response to her mother's implication, she took a step away.

David reached for her arm, gripped it tightly. "And for God's sake, don't even think of keeping that hotel. It would be the biggest mistake of your life."

"I'll do whatever I decide to do." She yanked her arm free of his grasp and swept out, her whole body rigid with tension and forced bravado.

When the massive front door closed behind her, she leaned on it briefly before bolting for her rental car.

She steadied her hands on the wheel, drove two blocks, pulled over, and cried for twenty minutes.

When did a grown woman stop wanting her mother? And why the hell, when she found her—or at least a small piece of her—did it hurt so much to lose her again?

Suddenly chilled, Joy put the car in gear and drove and drove and drove. . . .

When she finally turned the car back to Seattle's city center, the sun had slipped below the horizon, and she'd shoved Lana and the increasingly inscrutable David Grange to the back of her mind. She'd have to think everything through, make some decisions, she knew that. But not now.

Now she was going home. To the Phil. And tonight she would sleep with Wade Emerson, for reasons that had nothing to do with money and everything to do with strong arms, deep kisses, and a soul she sensed was in lonely concert with her own.

Or would be until he learned how she'd come to be in possession of almost two million dollars.

Like mother, like daughter.

Wade took the elevator to six, got off, and jogged the steps up to the seventh floor. He looked at his watch as he walked the few feet to Christian Rupert's door. Five minutes to eight. He knew Rupert didn't like late, but nobody had said anything about early. Standing in the dim light over the penthouse door, Wade rapped three times. If he did get invited in, it would be the first time he'd set foot in this part of the hotel. Christian Rupert's inner sanctum. Hell, his grandfather, if he weren't already in his grave going on twenty years, would have apoplexy.

"You're early, boy. Come back in five minutes."

The voice sounded muffled as if it came from a fair distance away. "It's not Gordy, Mr. Rupert. It's Wade Emerson. Gordy's leg is pretty bad. He asked me to walk Melly."

Silence greeted this announcement, so Wade waited a second before adding. "I'm happy to do it, if Melly's up for it. And I'd like to talk to you, if you have time."

More silence, then, "Just a minute."

It was exactly eight o'clock when the door slid open about four inches and a gnome of a man, almost half Wade's height, looked up at him from behind the heavy chain securing the door. His ancient eyes, pale gray, were deeply set in a wizened face that looked older than a face was ever meant to be, but there was nothing ancient in his sharp gaze; it was icily intelligent. "Emerson, you say?" he asked, his eyes watery but unblinking.

"Yes. Wade Emerson."

"We haven't met," Rupert said, as if it were an accusation of sorts, and he made no move to unchain the door.

"No. Maybe I should have come up, introduced myself." And maybe he should have, he thought, but he'd fallen easily into the Emerson pattern of pretending Christian Rupert didn't exist.

"Yes. That would have been right."

Duly chastised, or as chastised as an over six-foot-tall man could be by someone three times his age and half his height, Wade nodded amiably. "About Melly. Would you like me to walk her?" The dog was snuffling at the lower part of the door, whining and pawing.

"Are you alone, Mr. Emerson?"

"Yes, and the name's Wade."

"Wade Philip Emerson. I know. You were named after this hotel. I knew your grandfather. I'm sure he mentioned me."

The last was said with force and maybe a touch of wistfulness. "Yes, sir, he did." He didn't bother to mention in what way he'd been mentioned. And as to the "mean old bastard" label, Wade would form his own opinion.

Rupert stared at him as if the fate of the free world depended on his decision to open the door or close it in his face. Wade had the sensation of being x-rayed without a radiation guard. A full minute passed before the man closed the door, slipped the chain, and opened it again. Not much wider than the first time.

"Use as little of the opening as you can to come through, please. I don't want the hall breeze in here. All the dust. Germs, etcetera."

"Sure," Wade turned sideways, inched his way into

the room while the old man pressed the door against his chest. Wade heard the shallow, erratic rasp in his lungs as he slid past him and stepped into the room. The poor guy was terrified.

In a second, Melly was all over him, and Wade's attention was diverted to the excited dog.

When Melly settled down, Wade offered Rupert his hand. He stared at it in apparent confusion.

"Oh, yes, the handshake custom. You'll have to excuse me, I don't do that." Rupert tottered back to an automated recliner chair that sat nearly dead center of the large room. When he sat in it, it dwarfed him.

Wade idly rubbed his rejected hand on the side of his jeans and looked around, intensely curious. As far as he knew he was the first Emerson ever to be in here. When he'd been a kid, his grandfather had ordered him to stay as far away from the penthouse as possible. But even now, he was stunned by the size of it. It had to be five thousand square feet. And it was so damned . . . thirties. Except for the recliner Rupert sat in, the place was like a museum.

"This is quite the place," Wade said.

"Yes, I like it. Look around, if you like."

Wade did, couldn't have resisted if he wanted to. The ceilings, as in the rest of the Phil, were very high, but here the walls held a series of soaring, arched windows with stained glass inserts at their tops. Tonight, despite the show the sun made, sinking slowly into the west, only one window—matching the others but serving as double doors leading to the terrace—had its draperies partially pulled back. He moved to the window, curious to look outside.

The terrace was spacious, encompassing most of the hotel roof. A brick wall on one side hid the air conditioning unit and a roof access door, installed in the seventies sometime, and sealed a few years later. To Wade's knowledge, that door hadn't been opened since. Two deep rectangular containers, lushly planted, formed the other two sides.

Unlike the rest of the decaying hotel, everything was in top condition. He was impressed. "You've lived here a long time."

"Most of my life. It suits my needs."

Wade nodded, abruptly aware of something else going on in the room, something other than a look-around and words of superficial hospitality. The room was warm, charged. Strangely uncomfortable.

Except for the pool of light cast by the lamp burning beside Rupert's chair and the finger of sunset that made it through the half-opened drapes, the cavernous room was deep in shadow. Christian Rupert sat ramrod stiff in his over-large recliner, his intense study of Wade overt and unblinking.

"Step into the light where I can see you," he instructed.

Wade decided to humor him, walked to the window and stood in the light from the lowering sun.

"Oh, yes . . ." Rupert took a deep, noisy breath and closed his eyes; he seemed transported. When he opened them, he said in a hushed voice, "You are very much like him. Very, very beautiful."

Wade frowned. This was a first, a man calling him beautiful. He put it down to the man's age. "I assume you mean my grandfather. Gordy told me you had a picture of him."

"There." He pointed to a grand piano, draped with a fringed green cover, beside the terrace doors.

Wade saw it immediately, picked it up, and carried it toward the light. "This is him, all right. Although I've never seen this exact picture before." He studied it a moment longer and set it back on the piano.

"No, you wouldn't have." He gestured at the picture.

"A little farther back, please. Where it was before you picked it up."

Wade did the best he could with the picture. "Exactly how long have you lived here?"

"I stopped counting the years sometime back—made the passing of them easier to bear." The barest smile crossed his face. "But I moved in not long after the hotel was built."

"That's over sixty years."

"I expect it is, Mr. Emerson."

"Wade, please."

"Of course, things are so much more informal now. And you may call me Christian." He gestured to a liquor cabinet. A glass tray and a decanter sat on its top. "I have brandy, very good brandy. May I offer you one and prevail upon you to serve one to an old man who now hoards his strength with a miser's concern?"

"Happy to." Wade poured the brandy. Christian was right. It was very good, two-hundred-dollars-a-bottle good. He handed him the glass, noticed that while he'd been getting the drinks, Christian had donned a pair of white gloves. Weird old duck, definitely obsessive/compulsive, but so far not the "mean old bastard" his grandfather described.

"Thank you," he said, taking the brandy from Wade. "Now, sit down, Wade Philip Emerson—in the light where I can look at you . . . such memories you bring back." He stopped. "Then tell me, what brings you to the Philip? And more to the point, what brings you to me? You wanted to talk, you said."

Christian was sharp. Wade admired that, and he admired people who got to the point and skipped the subtlety. He sipped the brandy but ignored the chair Christian gestured to. "What brought me to the Philip originally was curiosity. I wanted to see how the old fellow had stood up through the years." More of a truth than he'd admitted when he arrived at the Phil's front door. "What brings me to see you is a business proposition."

"A need for money, you mean."

Wade smiled at the man's directness. "My need for money, your need to retain your home as the sanctuary it's always been for you. As I said, a business proposition. One that will benefit both of us."

Christian sat back in his chair and started to laugh. The laugh became a cough, then a series of harsh, painful-looking wheezes. Rupert clutched his chest, seemed to fight for his breath, tears streaming over the thin skin of his cheeks.

Christ, he was turning blue. Wade moved toward him, no idea in hell what to do, but Christian raised a hand, rasped out, "Don't! Don't touch me. I'm fine."

Relieved, Wade saw color return to his face and heard his breathing steady. "Are you sure?" Wade eyed him, still uncertain whether or not to call 911.

"Yes. Perfectly fine." Christian sipped his brandy, used a tissue from the table beside his chair to wipe moisture from his runny eyes. "I thank you for that. It's been a long time since I was so highly amused."

"What was so funny?"

Christian set his pale eyes on him, repeated, " 'A business proposition. One that will benefit both of us.' Your grandfather said those same words to me over sixty years ago." His mouth quivered before forming a nasty twist of a smile. "And young, arrogant fool that I was, I went along with it." He wagged his head, raised cold, rheumy eyes to Wade's. "And I've cursed him and his grasping, selfish spawn every day of my life since. And you are that spawn."

Silence, thick and dark, filled the room.

When the shock of his words wore off, Wade put down his brandy glass. This was what he sensed earlier.

Hatred. Frigid and unadulterated. Wade had firsthand experience with hatred, but usually going out, not coming back at him. "Obviously there's a story behind that. One I don't know. I'd like to hear it."

"I don't think so. But I'll tell you this. I saved this hotel for your grandfather. If it weren't for me, he'd have lost it right after that grand opening of his." He looked around with the distaste you'd show an unclean sty. "I financed him, got him and this hotel out of debt, and all I received for my efforts was this prison."

"He didn't pay you back?" Wade didn't buy it. His grandfather was a scrupulously ethical businessman— with an intense distaste for debt. This crap from Rupert didn't wash.

Christian shot him a look of pure loathing. "Get out and don't come back here, Wade Emerson. I let you in to satisfy my curiosity. I've done that. Now get off my property. Better yet, leave this hotel. You have no rights here. No rights at all!" His breathing flattened to the point of disappearing. Still his ancient eyes were fixed on him, dark with a hatred nurtured for more than half a century.

Wade, the hotshot in a thousand go-for-the-jugular business meetings, recent graduate of Prison U, and a world-class hater himself when it came to the blue-eyed blonde who'd torn his family apart, did not know what to say to this sick old man. Rupert was so small and frail, he'd have a heart attack if he poked him with his finger. "I take it you don't want me to walk your dog."

Christian's head came up at that. "You're a cool one, aren't you? Just like Joseph."

"Better like him than you, Rupert." Wade had had enough. "But you'll be disappointed to know I won't be leaving the Phil anytime soon. I intend to buy it."

Rupert looked unfazed, amused. "That takes money, boy. Something you don't have and won't get." He paused. "Most people don't like doing business with jailbirds."

Wade studied him with new respect. "You really keep up on things from this aerie of yours, don't you?"

"I keep advised of what affects my interests, yes."

Did he mean Joy? Wade's mind started to race, a slab of dread laying in across his lungs. "Mind telling me what exactly those 'interests' are?"

"The one most critical to me is that an Emerson never again owns the Hotel Philip." Rupert's face flattened to the dull matte of a cracked plaster mask. "As to the rest, they are no business of yours. Now, I'd appreciate your leaving my home and never coming back. You're the last Emerson I ever want to see."

Wade looked down on him, shook his head. Obviously there was no shelf date on hatred. "Grandfather was right."

"Really—about what?"

"You *are* a mean old bastard."

Rupert laughed harshly. "It came to that, did it? That's what he thought of me." He said the last to himself, before nodding toward the door with a tired lift of his head. "Good-bye, Mr. Emerson."

Wade took the fire stairs down, but it wasn't until the third floor that it occurred to him—his plan for buying the Philip had been knocked sideways. Whatever happened between Joe and Rupert had obviously been damn bad, fueling hatred powerful enough to last over half a century.

He thought of his own feelings about his father—Lana—grew uncomfortable when he realized how long he'd been carrying his own load of disapproval and loathing.

He tried to force his mind back to his goal, ownership of the Hotel Philip—and money. But his thoughts refused to think of anything or anyone except Joy.

He'd bet she was one of those "interests" Rupert kept his beady eye on. And he'd also bet Christian Rupert was a dangerous man.

No way did he keep that level of malice contained in his penthouse. This was a man who would act on his instincts—or get someone to do it for him.

Wade opened the fire door to the third floor.

But it was unlikely Rupert was behind the threat on Joy's wall. Hell, he had to be elated that someone other than an Emerson owned the hotel.

No, Joy was no threat to Rupert or his "home." The only thing he needed to worry about was a wrecking crew with a load of dynamite, not a woman who wanted to renovate and run the hotel—which meant honoring his right to the penthouse.

Which took him back to the question. Who the hell had written on Joy's wall?

Joy stripped to her panties and bra and headed for her bathroom. She turned on the water to run a bath and unclipped the clasp of her bra. She wanted a bath badly, desperate to wash away the confusion and pain of the afternoon with her mother.

She stared at the tub, chilled suddenly when another mother came to mind.

Wade's mother had chosen to die in this bathtub. Joy watched the water rise, the steam paint itself on the mirror over the old pedestal sink, felt the humidity thicken in the confined space, and tried to rein in her too-vivid imagination and unsettled emotions.

She reminded herself the suicide was almost twenty years ago, that she'd been using the tub for days already; but all her logical thoughts didn't work. Today, knowing what she knew, the idea of taking a bath in it seemed disrespectful, faintly ominous.

She sat on the edge of the tub, bra dangling from her hand, and turned the water off.

She heard a knock on her door, and glad for the interruption, donned her cotton robe and went to answer it.

It was Wade, carrying a box of crackers, cheese, and a bottle of red wine.

He cocked his head. "You want to spoil all my fun?"

"Huh?"

He smiled, reached out, and touched the lacy bra dangling in her hand. "Don't you know how much a man likes taking these things off?"

She was suddenly very glad he was here. And when he leaned down to brush a soft, too-brief kiss across her mouth, she smiled back. "I was going to take a bath, but—" she stopped, not knowing how to finish.

He glanced behind her, and his expression darkened briefly before he smiled again. "Come over to my place. You can use my bathroom"—he lifted the wine and cheese he held in his hands—"while I cook."

"If opening a box of crackers is your idea of cooking, we could be in trouble."

"We can go out for dinner first, if that's what you want. Or we can subsist on wine, cheese, and sex for a couple of hours and then eat. Your choice." A half-smile.

"Let me see . . . sex first—or romance. Tough call." She joked, while her stomach tightened and her legs quivered. Between those legs, a small pulse throbbed and constricted.

"Not for me, Cole. I've been feeling romantic for days now. I figured you already picked up on that." He kissed her again. With his hands full, it was lips only, mouth to mouth, breath to breath. It was tenuous, so fleeting it made her ache for more. Wade put his mouth to her ear, whispered, "But when a woman dangles a frothy bit of bra in front of a man, he tends to fast-forward things." He walked across the hall, looked back when he got to his door. "When you've decided the order of things, just knock."

Before he disappeared, she called out, "Wade."

He turned.

"Run a bath for me, will you?"

He tilted his head, grinned. "You're my kind of woman, Joy Cole," he said, then disappeared behind his door.

They had a date, to make love, with no preliminaries, no requirements—unless you counted cheese and crackers—and she was happier than she'd been in weeks.

The thought occurred to her that having Wade Emerson to look forward to at the end of a bad day would be like waking up to a Christmas tree every morning.

Joy went back to her own bathroom and drained the tub.

Two minutes later she opened Wade's door.

Chapter Twelve

When Joy walked in, Wade was leaning against the counter, arms crossed. His gaze slid over her, from naked toes, belted midsection, to uncombed hair. His smile was gorgeous, seductive—and oddly terrifying in the effect it had on her already unsteady nerves.

He made no move toward her.

Anticipation was the only sound in the room.

She closed the door, pressed her back against it, and kept both hands behind her.

Years of being on her own, the constant travel to exotic and not-so-exotic places, and more than the average number of lovers taken for expediency and sexual gratification, had made her self-sufficient, sure of herself, and too damned *liberated* for her own good. Independence was good. So was confidence—but the sexual test runs? She could neither name nor count her gains from them. Unless cynicism and a growing loneliness were defined as bonuses.

She was no timid virgin and had long ago given up the games surrounding sex, concluded its sole value was physical release. You didn't need hearts and flowers to get there. On a cold, forsaken night in Moscow, you didn't even need a man.

But here, now, under Wade's level, burning gaze, she wilted as if untried, sexually naive, as if what was about to happen between them was of . . . consequence, vital in a way nothing had been before.

As if Wade were her first man—or her last.

He crossed the room and pulled her hand from behind her. What he did next surprised her and set wings aflutter low in her belly. He raised her hand to his mouth and kissed her palm. "I'm glad you're here," he said.

"Me, too," she muttered and meant it with all her befuddled heart, now wild and crazy in her chest.

"This way." He tugged her toward his bathroom. Once there, he let go of her hand, knelt on one knee, and turned on the old chrome taps. To test the water temperature, he let the water pool and flow over his open palm. "Do you like it hot or tepid?" he asked, running his other hand from the back of her knee to her ankle.

"Hot," she said, and knew neither of them was talking about water temperatures. Her concentration focused on Wade's caressing hand, the strings it pulled as if by magic in the nether recesses of her body.

He stood. "Me, too. The hotter the better." He gave her a potent sideways glance. "I'll leave this for you to finish. Towels are there." He nodded to a shelf over the tub. "Red or white?"

She looked at him, her mind a blank.

"Wine. Merlot or chardonnay?"

"The chardonnay, thanks."

"You got it." He strode to the door, glanced back at her. "And you've got your privacy. Yell if you need anything." Hand on doorknob, he grinned. "You should know I majored in back scrubs." He closed the door behind him.

Joy dropped her robe and stepped into the tub. When it was full enough, she turned off the noisy, complaining taps and sank under the water to drench her hair. Her own temperature was so high, the hot water felt as cool as a morning lagoon. She stayed underwater until she needed air and popped up.

And when she popped up, so did the thought of the two million dollars she had in her First Bank account.

Wade wasn't going to understand. She didn't understand it herself. Why had she taken it? Anger, rebelliousness . . . greed? Or because her own genes swam in the same pool as her mother's. She went under again, as if the guilt could be washed away by hot water and a promised glass of cool white wine. She'd have to tell Wade, and in an odd way even wanted to, but not tonight. Unpleasant truths were best served whole, in the morning sunlight, when there were no shadows to hide in.

Tonight there was only Wade.

She lathered her body, gave her thoughts to the present; the clean forest scent permeating Wade's bathroom, the liquid seduction of the deep, old tub, and the glide of the soap bar, slick and foamy, over her sensitized skin. Quivery and agitated, she closed her eyes, listened to the soft piano jazz now coming from the next room, tried to relax. But with her eyes closed, her imagination, all heat and flashing images, heightened every sense until she trembled.

When she ran the soap over the curls of her pubis and along her cleft, the sexual jolt shocked her eyes open. She looked down at her hard-jutting nipples, felt the heavy throb between her thighs—the deep fever of wanting.

And there was no need to wait.

No need to hesitate.

She rested her hands on the sides of the tub, inhaled to calm herself, and looked at the closed bathroom door. She took another breath. "Wade. Are you there?"

A couple of seconds passed. "You need something?"

She knew from his voice he was outside the door.

"I've been thinking about that back scrub," she lied, knowing her real thoughts were X-rated and, for now at least, best kept to herself.

The door opened and Wade stood in the doorway. He wore jeans, a denim shirt with half the buttons undone, and he was carrying a bottle of white wine and two glasses. "Back scrub, huh? Can I take that as code for the beginning of phase one?"

She pulled the facecloth she had covering her breasts under the water. "You can."

His gaze slid to her water-slicked breasts and his eyes went dark. She saw his chest heave. Wine bottle now dangling from his hand, he looked at her as if he never wanted to stop. "I sure as hell hope you're not expecting too much in the way of foreplay." He smiled but something more serious was going on in his eyes.

The light in the bathroom was white and harsh and the water without benefit of bubbles; Joy leaned back to let him see all of her. Her nipples were at the waterline, shifting above or below the water on each breath. "I'm expecting to have a good time," she said, denying to him and herself any possible need for more. She pushed her wet hair back, lifted it from her nape, and leaned forward in the tub. "And as I recall, you're the one who mentioned back scrubs. Now you're reneging?" Joy's throat was tight with half-truths and the effort to act as if none of this mattered. Because it did matter, so much more than she wanted to admit.

Wade didn't move. "Just thinking."

She lifted her eyebrows. "Can you add something to that? I'm not getting it."

He set the wine and glasses on the floor near the door, and stood over her, his expression strained. "I haven't had sex in almost two years, Cole. I thought I could handle it"—he scanned her naked body through the clear water, his gaze uncertain—"now I'm not so sure.

That good time you want? It's not going to be the first run out of the gate. You ready for that?"

"A man who apologizes in advance for bad sex. That's a first." She managed a smile, ran a hand along his thigh, felt it tense, saw the damp stains her wet hand left behind.

He smiled back and rested his hand over hers. "Bad for you, sweetheart. Heaven for me. That body of yours is an oasis after a very long time in the desert." He popped the studs on his denim shirt. He had it off in a nanosecond. His jeans and briefs were next. He was beautiful, his body long and lean with muscles to match.

And his erection was astonishing.

He glanced down at her. "I can guarantee I'm healthy, but if you're worried"—he held up a condom—"or need protection?"

She shook her head. "Pill."

He tossed the condom, looked at the high bathroom ceiling, and let out a long breath. "I must be living right. Slide down," he instructed. She did and he took a position behind her, spread his legs as wide as the old tub allowed and pulled her against him, pressing his hard length against her buttocks and back.

"Jesus, you feel good." He kissed her back, fitted her nipples between his fingers and squeezed them gently, until her lungs emptied of air and her eyes closed. He plucked her stiffened tips before running his hand down between her legs to cup her. "So good . . ."

Her head fell back against his shoulder, the muscles no longer able to hold it upright. She moaned and arched into his hand.

He let her go, gripped the sides of the tub. She thought of a white-knuckle flier bringing a 747 in for a landing.

He swore, and the breath he let out across her shoulder was as ragged as if it had been wrung from him by thumbscrews. "This is going to be worse than I thought."

He rested his head back against the tub. "Give me a minute."

The tub was wide enough for Joy to shift around and make a turn. When she faced him, she reached under the water and ran her index finger the length of his erection, then leaned close to whisper against his mouth. "How about the first time is for you, and the second time for me?" She lifted herself, drew his need to hers, and centered herself over him. He grabbed her by the waist, held her above him and stared into her eyes, his own half wild. "You sure about this?"

She heard the rasp of his breathing, felt the heat of his grip to the marrow of her melting bones. "Just fuck me, Wade." She closed his eyes with kisses, and trailed a finger along his cheek to touch his lips. "After that . . . we'll make love."

He arched up, and at the same time pulled her down hard, filled her completely.

Water sloshed over the edge of the tub. He thrust up, tested her limits, and Joy gasped, her inner walls stretching to take his penis, deep. Deeper. Inside he touched all of her, his hot, internal strokes rubbing, pulling . . .

Her body closed tight around him, claimed him, and throbbed mercilessly in its need for more. She clasped his shoulders and hung on—gave herself in a way she'd never given to a man. The ride was fierce and wild. She was for him. All for him.

Her nails curled into his straining muscles.

He groaned, thrust upward again, his penetration straight, deep, and powerful—his ejaculation explosive. Water from the tub erupted, showered the walls, cascaded to soak the bathroom floor.

Wanting more, she crumpled against him, panted to cool her denied release.

Holding her close, Wade rested his forehead against hers, and for a few minutes all he did was breathe. "I don't know whether to cheer or apologize." He shifted back, touched her face, his gaze dark and soft. "Will a very sincere thank-you do?"

"For now," she murmured. Her words sounded alien, forced out while she still tried to cool down, soothe the throbbing ache between her legs.

"I owe you, Mizz Cole."

"You do." She shoved his dark hair back from his forehead. "And very shortly"—she pressed herself into the cradle of his thighs, made a circular motion—"I plan to collect."

"And I'm looking forward to servicing my debt. But not here." He pulled her face to his and kissed her. When she wrapped her arms around him to deepen it, his chest expanded and contracted in a series of uneven breaths. "Somewhere I can do you justice." He ran his hands over her water-slicked buttocks, squeezed. "Although if we stay hip-locked much longer that might not be an option."

Reluctantly, she let him go and stepped out of the tub. The mirror over the bathroom sink held traces of steam, as did she, and it wasn't the draft coming from the open bathroom door making her shiver. It was the emptiness between her legs.

Wade followed her out of the bath and immediately wrapped her in a towel. Ignoring his own nakedness, he grasped the edges of the towel, pulled her close, and held her to him. Joy tried to control the tremors, the shifting, clamoring need for him coursing like a mad thing through her blood and sinew. She pulled in a deep grounding breath, released it, and reminded herself she was a patient woman. Trouble was, right now she didn't feel like one.

Wade took a step back from her, tilted his dark head to look into her eyes. "You're in trouble, aren't you?"

"Good trouble. And nothing that can't wait." *About* sixty seconds.

He pulled the towel away from her, dropped it on the floor. "Turn around." He gripped her by the shoulders, guiding her until her back was to him. "Lean back on me." He moved the sodden hair from her nape and kissed her, and she felt him harden against her. His voice was rough when he whispered in her ear. "Open for me." He ran his hands down and across her stomach to cup her, exerting pressure with the heel of his hand.

Joy let her head fall back against his shoulder. The coolness brought by the draft against her skin burned off by the furnace stoked by Wade's deft hand.

Her skin feverish, she rolled her hips forward, put her hands behind her to grip his muscled buttocks and spread her legs.

"That's good," he murmured into her neck.

"This is a bit"—she gasped when he slid his finger through her damp curls, ran it through her cleft—"more"—he tugged her engorged nub, and she bucked into his hand. The part of her brain controlling speech was set to *off*. She moaned, her body's focus on the sexual strings Wade played within her, the expert fingers separating her folds, forcing her clitoris into small, needful circles.

Taut and out of her mind, she panted, strained wildly toward a crescendo, the dark magic of release.

Her lungs filled, then emptied. "Oh, God, Wade . . ."

Moisture came with a heated rush, and when his long, expert fingers entered her to probe and stroke, Joy climaxed in a blur of gasping, grasping lungs and fevered exultation. When her knees started to buckle, Wade held her tight, one big hand enfolding her pubis, the other splayed across her belly. His growing erection pressed against her backside, he turned her to face him. His smile was slight and lopsided, his own breath patchy when he asked, "You were saying?"

She took a breath or two, and when she could speak

with something close to a normal tone, she wrapped her arms around his narrow waist, and met his eyes. "I can't remember exactly. But I think it was something about the . . . sex between us, being more, uh, bold than I expected, for a first time. I'm not usually—" She stopped, wondered how far to go. "So . . ."

"Hot?" He caressed her face.

She nodded, stunned by a blush snaking its way up her neck. She *never* blushed. And after what she and Wade had done, pink was a monumentally stupid choice of color.

"We wanted each other." He took her face in his hands and his eyes rested on her, at first quiet and warm, then with a growing intensity. "And as for the hot part, you sure as hell weren't alone."

"I noticed." She smiled at him.

He looked vaguely embarrassed before grinning and reaching down to pick up the wine and glasses. "At least these escaped the tsunami."

She followed his gaze, saw his jeans and shirt and her robe were soaked from the tub water. He put a fresh towel around her.

"Come on. I'll get us dry clothes." He took her hand and led her out of the bathroom.

Joy followed him to the main room. All the Phil's rooms were originally suites, with a sitting area, a bedroom, and private bath. All had been luxurious in their day, and all—except for hers, Room 33—had been bastardized into live-in apartments with cheap kitchens added to the sitting area as time and the tides of fortune beat the Phil into economic submission.

Wade went to his closet, pulled out a cotton robe, and tossed it at her, while he stepped into another pair of jeans. Not bothering with briefs, she noticed, and, semi-aroused, very careful of the zipper.

She wrapped herself in the robe and settled on his

sagging sofa while he poured them both a glass of wine. He joined her, rested a plate of cheese between them on the sofa.

"To bold sex." He lifted his glass, grinned. "And plenty of it."

Joy laughed and the sound of their glasses clinking filled the quiet room. The sex had been bold, without promises, and unlikely to lead to anything but more of the same. Exactly what they'd planned, what she'd wanted. She should be satisfied, not confused. What had happened between her and Wade was supposed to be just sex, heavy on the *just.* No life stories exchanged, no connections made—other than physical—and no ambitions for anything more.

Joy's hand trembled when she raised her wineglass to take another drink. Maybe she was more like her mother than she realized. She might not use men by diving into their wallets, but she'd used her share as conveniences for sex, occasionally for company—without ever truly knowing them or caring to. Until now. Now she wanted to know everything about the man in front of her. She didn't know what this unusual and intense curiosity meant, but she knew she had to satisfy it. And there was a better-than-even chance Wade wouldn't appreciate her inquisitiveness.

Her chest tense, simmering in fear, she sipped her wine and considered how to take the next step.

Wade's head was a sandstorm. For a man who prided himself on his cool, he felt like an adolescent who'd graduated from looking at breasts in *Playboy* to copping his first glorious feel. Joy Cole was TNT, and she'd landed on his doorstep unlabeled. He didn't want her to leave anytime soon. But someone sure as hell did. Joy was in danger in the Phil, and he'd better put his acne-faced feelings on hold until things were sorted out.

He looked at her, pensive as hell across from him on the sofa—within arm's reach. And reach for her was what he wanted to do, but he also wanted to give her a rest.

He'd been rough in the tub. Hell, he was getting hard again thinking about it. He wasn't a small man, and she'd taken all of him, fast and deep, given him exactly what he needed the way he needed it. Not many women would do that.

He loaded a cracker with creamy brie and handed it to her. "Why so serious?"

"I'm fighting an uncontrollable urge to ask you questions." She munched on the cracker. "I don't usually do that."

"Eat crackers? Or ask questions?"

"You're sidestepping."

"Some." Wade knew what was coming, and figured now was as good a time as any to face it. For one thing, if he was going to buy the hotel from her, she deserved to know his past.

He fixed himself a piece of cheese, moved the plate to the low table holding a lamp beside the sofa. "You want to ask about my jail time. Right?"

"Yes."

"And if I don't want to talk about it?"

"I'll understand." She tilted her head. "Although you did say you were a pushover after sex."

He smiled. "I did, didn't I?"

She nodded.

He got up, gripped his glass by the rim, and walked to the table. He set the glass down, and took a chair to face her. "You know the charges?"

She waited, her big blues fixed on him, holding him like one of those sci-fi tractor beams.

"From merchant banking, I set out on my own. Started a company to specialize in financial consulting and mergers and acquisitions. Emerson Inc. No points for a cute name. The economy was hot. The markets were hot. The company was on fire, and I was trying to do everything myself. I was living on a plane and working hundred-hour weeks. I knew I couldn't keep up the pace, so I hired a Chief Financial Officer—"

"Enter the woman?"

"Deanna Nash." He met Joy's intense gaze. "She came with degrees and experience to burn. I gave her the financial end, while I looked after the growing list of clients." He poured himself another glass of wine. "I was still living on planes, but I figured I had the home base covered.

"Deanna was so damned efficient it was scary. The more work I gave her, the more she asked for. We were a good team." He stopped, remembered those heady days. Hot sex, piles of money, and a seriously bloated ego. What an ass he'd been.

"You slept with her."

"I thought I wanted to marry her." He watched Joy's gaze slide away, then back again.

"And?"

"The short version? She took me. Big time. And I was stupid enough to let her. I found out later she'd come to Emerson's owing some not-so-nice people a lot of money. To pay them she siphoned off clients' funds. After she'd paid them off, she started to pay herself."

"How did you find out?"

"I didn't. The IRS did. Then the banks."

Joy shifted on the sofa, and the robe fell away to show one clean, shiny knee. "And then?"

"At first I didn't believe it. I stood by her—which ended up helping the D.A.'s obstruction charge big time. Deanna swore she never made a move without consulting me—that my signature was on every transaction." He pulled an earlobe, hard; he hated revisiting his own idiocy.

"And had you signed everything?"

"Yeah. I trusted her. And I'd stopped reading the fine print." Just about the time they started sleeping together. He stopped, not sure where to go from here. Even he couldn't admit aloud how he'd let his cock negate his common sense. "Reading the fine print was my job. It was right I take the fall."

"What happened next?"

"I paid back all the money, and what might have been an eight-to-ten year sentence translated into under two and a hefty fine."

"And Deanna?"

"She got a slap on the wrist for not standing up to the big, bad boss, and walked into the sunset with a much heftier Swiss bank account than she had before she joined me." He laughed, although even to him it sounded hollow. "She married my defense attorney."

"Good." Joy's eyes hadn't left his face—now they did. She set her wineglass on the table and stood. She walked over to where he sat and, standing over him, ran her fingers through his damp hair. "Sounds to me as if you got off easy. You should count your blessings."

"I do." He grasped her hands, kissed her knuckles, and pulled her onto his lap. "Especially the blessings you gave me in the tub." He parted the flimsy cotton robe, exposed her breasts, and took one in his hand. Smooth, firm, and high, it begged to be kissed. He turned her to straddle him, lifted her until her nipples were mouth level, and licked the one most convenient before sucking it in, hard and deep. Her stomach contracted and she tightened her fists in his hair.

"Enough about me." He looked up at her, smiled. "Let's talk about you. Tell me in detail everything that's gone on in your life since you were twelve and I was eighteen." He went back to work, took her nipple into his mouth, suckled, drew on it until she gasped. He ran his hand between her legs, then a finger between the satin folds shielding her clitoris. She was wet. Heaven in his palm. He took his mouth and tongue from one breast and transferred them to the other. "You're not talking," he murmured against a slick, pebbled nipple, bit her softly.

"And I might not . . . ever again." She kissed his head, then sat back to look at him. "You're good at this, Emerson. A girl could get used to this kind of treatment."

"I sure as hell hope so, because I don't plan on stopping anytime soon." He blew softly on her moist nipple, licked it. "We have a long night ahead of us." And considering he was hard as an oak slab, he was definitely going to be up for it.

She let out a half breath, pulled it back in with a sharp gasp. "How about"—she put her mouth to his ear—"more bold sex, life story to follow." She paused. "In the A.M."

He took her face in his hands and looked into her eyes, eyes languid with passion and a touch of humor. Wade's heart bounded, tried to claw its way out of his chest. He kissed her, tasted her, first softly, then with the urgency his body forced on him. Their tongues met, mated, and drew apart. "You're not the only one who could get used to this." He wasn't smiling, wasn't teasing, and his own words scared the crap out of him. He didn't want to want this woman—this hungrily. And he hadn't the damndest idea how to stop the craving. "I want you again. I want to be inside you. Deep, deep, inside you."

Their gazes met, locked.

Joy reached over, stroked his jaw. "Bed, Wade. Take me to bed." She fisted her hands in his hair, pulled it. "Now."

Wade glanced at the red digits on the clock radio beside his bed. Three-forty A.M. He should be sleeping the sleep of the dead or damned, because his body was, for the moment, sexually sated. Actually, "numb" would be a better word.

Yet he still couldn't keep his eyes closed.

Joy didn't have the same problem. They'd made love twice more, and she'd conked out on him seconds ago. Now, cradled in his arms, she slept as if in a coma, her breathing unlabored and deep, her expression as soft and innocent as a child's. He touched her face and pushed a few long strands of hair to a place behind her ear. He couldn't stop looking at her. And he couldn't stop thinking he was going down fast. He cursed softly, lifted an arm to prop his head, and transferred his gaze from the sleeping beauty in his arms to the ceiling.

That was when he heard it.

He lifted his head a fraction, heard it again. A scratching sound from the wall behind his bed, then a shuffling. He shouldn't be hearing anything from the adjoining room; it was empty. Had been for years.

"You hear that?" Joy asked, her voice thick with sleep.

"Yes." He pulled his arm from under her and got to his feet. "I'm going to check it out."

By the time he shucked into his jeans, she was wrapped in his robe and standing beside him. "What are you doing?" he asked. "Go back to bed. No need for both of use to miss shut-eye."

She shook her head. "I'll come with you."

"Why?"

"It's my hotel. Why wouldn't I?"

He had no answer to that. "Then stay behind me." Wade knew the hotel got its share of street people wandering the halls, looking for a warm place to hang out. Most of them were harmless, but he wasn't taking any chances.

Joy rolled her eyes. "You, Tarzan, me Jane?"

"For the next few minutes. Yes."

The hall was empty. Wade put his ear to the door the

sounds had come from and listened. "Nothing. Probably a mouse on a midnight hunt."

She didn't look convinced. "Maybe. But have you got your keys—which, by the way, I'd like a copy of when you get around to it." She rattled the door handle. "I'd like to take a look."

"Why?"

"It's my—"

"—hotel." He finished the overused phrase for her.

She smiled slightly, but her expression stayed one of puzzlement and curiosity when she looked at the door to the suspicious room.

"I'll get the keys."

When they walked into the room a few minutes later, he knew his own expression carried the same puzzlement. The uncovered window allowed enough street light into the room for them to see a can of beer and a bag of potato chips, both of them on the floor next to a chair, about a foot from, and facing, the wall separating the room from Wade's.

"What the hell?" Wade flicked the light switch but nothing happened. Probably no one had been in here to change a light bulb in years. He picked up the beer can, empty. The potato chip bag was two-thirds gone, but the contents were fresh.

Someone had been in this room, and judging from the positioning of the chair, they were getting their rocks off tuning in to the events taking place in Wade's bed. He needed a closer look, but he didn't need Joy looking over his shoulder. "Check the window, would you?"

Joy crossed the room and left Wade to himself. He quickly ran a hand along the cracked plaster in the wall eye-height from the chair.

A goddamned peephole!

Judging from the angle, whoever was in here didn't see everything, but they'd damn well seen enough.

Chapter Thirteen

A nerve jumped and ticked in Wade's jaw; rage coursed along his tightened stomach muscles.

"Find anything?" Joy came back to stand with him.

"Nothing." He lied, not about to tell her they'd been on something close to *Candid Camera* for the past few hours. "You?"

"The window is secure from the inside. Painted shut, by the look of it. Whoever it was didn't come in that way, which means they had a key." She pursed her lips, paused, then said, "But I think I know who was in here."

"I'm listening."

"Big Mike." She put a hand to her stomach, rubbed as if to calm it.

Wade's stomach got even tighter. "What makes you say that?" He waved a hand around. "Hell, it could have been anyone." And he hoped it was, because there was something seriously ugly about knowing the person who'd ogled them through a peephole.

"It smells like Mike."

He stared at her. "Smells like?"

"He has a kind of rancid odor, then he piles on a

cheap scent. Aftershave, maybe. It makes him smell like stale cigar smoke and lemon. He's always drenched in it." She shuddered. "In lieu of a shower, I think."

Either Wade's nose was out of kilter or he'd never been close enough to the man to get a good whiff of him, but he was impressed. "I'll talk to him. See what I can find out. But for now, let's get out of here." He decided he'd break the man's nose before he tossed him out the damn door. Sick, perverted bastard!

Before Wade could get Joy out of the room, her gaze hit on the chair near the wall. When she spotted the gap made by the cracked plaster, her eyes went wide. "God, he was watching us, wasn't he?" Again she pressed her hand against her stomach, briefly closed her eyes. "I think I'm going to be sick."

In the dim light, Wade couldn't make out her skin tone, but judging from her voice he put it at green for nausea. He took her hand, pulled her to him, and kissed her forehead. He held her for a long moment, then walked her out and into the dark hall. "Don't think about it." He shut the door and locked it. As soon as he got Joy settled, he intended to go to Mike's room, but what he planned for the asshole wasn't something he wanted Joy to see.

They went back to his room and Joy went immediately to the bathroom. Wade checked his wall. When he found the peephole—hard to see among the busy vines in the scratched and torn wallpaper—he blocked it with his bureau.

When Joy came back in the room, he was already in bed. Waiting. "Are you okay?" he asked.

She stood beside the bed. "As okay as I can be after starring in my first live porn act." She rubbed her freshly washed face with both hands, then set her mouth in a stubborn line. "Tomorrow that pervert is out of here."

" 'Tomorrow' being the operative word. Okay?" But

it would be a lot sooner if Wade had his way. He reached out a hand for her, and she took it, her own cold and tense. "Right now you need sleep." And the sooner she was asleep, the sooner he could bust Mike's face in.

Joy looked down at him, her face grim. "Wade, I don't want you to get all macho about this. The Hotel Philip is my responsibility and it was my"—she looked aside briefly—"bare behind on display. I'll handle it my way. If you have any other ideas or plan on a little dragon-slaying on my behalf, I'm asking you to forget it. I'm used to handling things on my own."

Wade considered her request, mulled over the idea of lying, checked his adrenaline gauge—high—then made the mistake of looking into her eyes. Proud eyes. Fierce, independent eyes. "How about we handle it together, Cole. Yours wasn't the only butt on display, you know." And no way was he letting her face down that behemoth on her own.

"Fair enough." She crawled in beside him and snuggled under his arm. "And I agree tomorrow is soon enough. We're both too tired for dragon-slaying, anyway."

Wade pulled her close, kissed her hair. He'd go along with her on this, but as far as he was concerned, there was far too much interest in Joy Cole—and none of it was healthy. Once they'd dealt with Big Mike, he had to get her out of the Phil.

Just after nine A.M., someone attempted to break down Wade's door. At the first loud thump, Joy came away with a start, disoriented, her heart racing in her chest. Wade, his dark head coming up with a jerk, was right behind her.

"What the hell . . ." He jumped out of bed, dragged his jeans on, and was at the shuddering, thudding door in five strides.

"Come quick, Wade. It's Sinnie. She's hurt. Hurt bad."
Gordy grabbed Wade's hand at the same moment Joy
got to his side.

"Where, Gordy? Where's Sinnie?" Wade let the boy
pull him—to Room 33, Joy's room. The door was half
off its hinges, wide open.

"There." Gordy pointed to the bed. He was crying.
"You've got to get her, Wade. Get her. Please."

"Dear God!" Joy spotted Sinnie first. The old woman
lay crumpled beside Joy's bed, unmoving, blood seeping out from under her head and shoulder. Joy put her
face close to hers. "She's breathing, but barely."

"Get your mother, Gordy." When the boy didn't move,
he yelled. "Now!" Gordy bolted down the hall. Joy knew
he'd told the boy to get his mother to stem his panic,
give him something to do.

"She looks bad," she said. "It looks like her head and
upper shoulder are cut." She ran to the bathroom to get
towels, rushed back and pressed one against the visible
shoulder wound. She was afraid to move her head, scared
she'd do more damage than what had already been done.

Wade hooked his fingers around Sinnie's frail wrist.
"She's got a pulse—weak, but a pulse. But she's ice cold.
Shock, I think." Wade got up, pulled the blankets from
Joy's bed, and covered her. "Call 911, will you?" He put
his hand over Joy's, freed her from holding the towel, a
towel turning blood-red as the wound oozed.

"I'm on it." Joy retrieved her cell phone from beside
the bed. When she'd completed the call, she knelt beside Wade. His face was pale and grim.

He stroked Sinnie's hair, leaned in close, and said,
"Hang on, Sinnie. Help is on the way. Hang on, love."

For the first time, Joy looked around the room.
Obviously Sinnie had come to do her cleaning as she'd
been doing for the past couple of weeks, and someone
had surprised her. The wicker basket she always carried

was tipped over, the brushes and other cleaning supplies splaying out from it across the room's threadbare carpet.

"We need another towel," Wade said, not looking up.

"Done." This time, when she rushed back from the bathroom, she glanced up. Another message was added to the one she'd discovered yesterday and hadn't had time to remove. This one was in the same hand, in the same red felt pen.

YOU HEARD ME. GET OUT. GET OUT NOW!!

The last exclamation point snaked to the floor, close to where Sinnie now lay, breathing shallowly and clinging to what was left of her life. She must have interrupted the person who was doing it, and knowing Sinnie, she wouldn't have retreated. She'd have barreled in and . . .

Joy didn't want to think about what happened next. But it was her fault. Maybe Wade was right, maybe she should leave the hotel. It seemed as if nothing had gone right since she'd come here. Sinnie might die because Joy had stubbornly insisted on staying in Room 33.

When Joy passed Wade the towels, she noticed Sinnie's hand and bent down to look more closely. Her fingers were curled tight around a pen.

A red felt pen.

She glanced at Wade, who was concentrating on switching the towels, and gently opened Sinnie's hand and took out the pen. She was still in confusion about what it could mean when the paramedics strode into the room—all business and efficiency. A second later, Cherry and Gordy arrived, to stand quietly by the door while the paramedics did their work.

In no time they had Sinnie on a stretcher and were giving her oxygen. Joy stuffed the pen in her pocket. And watched Wade, his face sober, talk to one of the men. She'd sensed a bond between Sinnie and Wade, but until now hadn't known how deep it ran.

When the paramedic nodded, Wade turned to Joy.

"I'm going to follow the ambulance to the ER. I'll fill out a police report there. I don't know how long I'll be." He strode toward her, kissed her quickly, and squeezed her upper arms. The look he gave her was intense and serious. "Go with Cherry. I'll call you as soon as I know something. I'll call you at her place. Stay out of this room, Joy." He shot a glance at the defaced wall, his expression hard. "Promise me that."

Arguing in times of crisis was foolish, so she nodded.

"And promise me you'll leave the Mike thing until I get back. You'll stay away from him."

Joy hesitated, but nodded again. Considering what had happened to Sinnie, she needed to think, and the idea of confronting that huge, miserable excuse for a human being without Wade at her side didn't sound smart.

"Good." He looked relieved, glanced at Cherry. "Keep an eye on her, would you?"

"Don't worry. You take care of Sin." Cherry, looking as if she were going to cry, stepped aside to let the paramedics wheel the unconscious Sinnie out of the room.

"I will, too, Wade," Gordy said, sounding determined and more mature than his innocent mind said he was.

"I'll call," Wade said again and followed the medics and stretcher down the hall.

Joy frowned and looked at Cherry and Gordy. She didn't react well to orders. "I can look after myself, you know."

Cherry didn't flinch. "Of course you can—you're a smart woman. But add that"—she gestured at the threat on the wall—"to all the other weird stuff going on around here, being smart translates into staying clear of this room for a while." She took Gordy's hand, the gesture as natural as if he were four feet tall instead of six, and stepped out the door. In the hall, she looked back and added, "And I'll even throw in breakfast. Bacon, eggs, the works."

"And a big pot of coffee?"

"Done."

"You're a smooth one, Cherry Ripley." Joy worried the pen in her pocket but couldn't stop a smile. The pen and what it meant would have to wait.

"Yes, I am. And judging from the fact that you're wearing Wade's robe, so is he."

Joy looked down at herself. She'd forgotten. "Give me ten minutes."

"I'll go put on the coffee." She looked up at Gordy. "Will you wait in the hall for Joy, sweetie? By then it will be time for you to go and walk Melly."

"If she's not dead, where is she, Michael?" Christian's blood ran cold, thick, and slow. Things were not going as planned.

Mike's eyes darted around the penthouse like a pair of birds looking for the cage door. "I dunno. Some hospital. It was that stupid kid, or whatever the hell he is." He held a wad of tissue to the cut and bruise on his forehead where Sinnie had slashed him with her broom handle. "Shoulda done him, too," he groused.

"You're referring to Gordy?"

The man grunted a yes, looked venomous.

"Did he see you?"

"Nah. All of a sudden he was hollerin' at the door. Maybe he heard something, I dunno. Anyways, I got myself into the bathroom. Then the old bat—couldn't believe it with the blood and all—shouted the kid's name. Then the dumbo broke the door and barreled in, right away started shouting for Wade. When he crossed the hall to get him, I got my butt out of there fast."

"And then?"

"I ducked into a room down the hall. Hung tough. Until they came and took Sinnie away."

"Alive. You're sure?"

"Not for long. At least that's what I heard one of the medics say. One of them said, 'Too old to take that kind of hit.' Or something like it."

"And you. Of course, she saw you."

"She ain't going to make it, Mr. Rupert. No way. And if you want, I can go to the hospital. Finish the job."

"For now, all I want you to do, Michael, is keep your dimwitted suggestions to yourself, and leave me to think things through." The idea of this burly, hideous man shambling through hospital corridors was a thought not to be borne. No doubt he would make a mistake and drag half of Seattle's police force into Christian's home. Police at his door—unstoppable—entitled to entry. Out of his control. Christian's heart spiked and plunged at the image.

Although it was not in his nature to pace, rage and uncertainty forced him to movement, and he pushed himself out of his chair. With help from his cane, he shuffled toward the windows overlooking his beloved terrace, worked to settle his mind.

The afternoon sun burnished the electric blue glaze on the planters, flickered among the new leaves on the trees. The morning rain had marked the patio stones with damp shadows, making them frames for unknown silhouettes. So inviting, so . . . terrifying. He used to go out there, feel the fresh air on his face, touch the crisp, new foliage; now he could not. His mind wouldn't allow it. And now his world was cut by half.

The overlarge, coffin-shaped planters, so lushly treed, were his pride. He'd designed and commissioned them himself. On the day they'd arrived from Italy those many years ago, they'd caused quite a stir in the Philip. No one had ever seen anything like them—their immense size, the cobalt brilliance of their glaze.

Over the years, he'd watched the plantings in them grow from saplings to trees over six and twelve feet high. Of course, during the incident a few years ago, a couple of the trees were replaced, but they were foliage-rich now. The varying shades of green shooting out from the bright blue of the planters to rustle in the rooftop breeze always delighted him. Although under Michael's clumsy paws the trees were not clipped and pruned as neatly as Christian would have liked.

There was a time when David tended them. He'd come to Christian as a young boy, not more than twelve. So pretty. And as eager and smart a boy as was ever born. His mother sent him up a day or two after they'd moved in to ask for some paying chores. Christian set him to caring for his terrace and his beloved trees. He'd had a knack for it, he remembered, and under his hand, the trees and plants flourished.

David had a knack for many things.

Christian sighed, regretful—angry—at the change in their relationship. He'd cared for the boy as if he were his own son, put him through law school, and his reward was neglect and ingratitude. David needed to be chastised, brought to heel, because all his plans hinged on David.

Christian's legs were weakening—and his mind was wandering—so he walked back to his chair and settled himself.

He knew what he had to do. But first he had to get rid of the useless creature in front of him. David had made a mistake in choosing him, a decision that had put Christian and his home at risk. It was up to David to rectify the situation, and Christian intended he would do so. But he did have a question and one more use for the repellent beast.

"Last night. Emerson and the Cole girl, did you watch them? Did they fornicate?"

It must have been the only nine-lett ord the brute knew, because for the first time this ses n, he relaxed, comfortable in the lascivious territory he so obviously preferred. "Oh, yeah. Went at it like a pair of horny, oversexed—"

"Enough." Christian raised a hand. He wasn't interested in the details or any more conversation with this man than was necessary. "How long were they together?"

"All night. She was with him when he found Sin. Came out of his room."

Christian felt his face flatten, his mouth tighten. He'd been afraid of this. Oh, he knew their having sex might mean nothing. After all, everybody partook of carnal pleasure at their whim in these modern times. But this particular carnal union was between Joe's grandson and the woman who held the title to his hotel.

The risk was immense. Unbearable.

"How far along are the evictions, Michael?" he asked.

"Just a couple left."

Christian would have preferred a more precise answer, but there was little point in asking, and watching the imbecile count on his fingers was more than he could bear. "I want you to accelerate the process. I want this hotel empty. Everyone except the boy and his mother, Emerson and the girl. And I *do not* want you seen. Do you understand?" He needed the boy for Melly—for now.

"Got it." His head bobbed like an apple in a barrel.

"When you leave me now, leave this property. Use the back way. Don't go back to your room. You have two nights to complete the eviction process—but you must *not* be seen in this hotel again. Do you understand that?"

Another bob of the head.

"Assuming you are successful, come here Thursday, *promptly* at eleven P.M., and I'll have a bonus ready for you. One generous enough to allow you to move on. I suggest you then take yourself as far from this hotel as possible, as I will no longer require your services."

Mike grinned and got to his feet. "You're a good guy, Mr. Rupert."

Christian didn't have to force his ironic smile. He was many things, but a "good guy" wasn't one of them.

At the door, Mike stopped. "What about Sinnie?" he asked. "You want me to go to the hospital? Finish her off?"

Christian made note of the contraction in his chest, the ice coating his lungs, but it was advisable that he consider the brute's question. Sinnie was against him, and that was insupportable—as was her life.

But for now she was out of the picture, and that would have to do. If and when she did come to, she'd name her assailant as "Big Mike from four." Of course, there was a chance she would associate them, but by then Michael would be . . . unavailable, and it would be impossible for her to implicate him. "No," he finally answered. "Leave these premises as quickly as possible. I'll take care of Sinnie."

And he would—at his convenience.

It was early afternoon before Wade made it back to the Philip. He parked his Explorer in the parking lot behind the hotel. When he turned the motor off, he put his head back, took a minute to enjoy the silence. The ER at Harborview Med had been a zoo.

Amidst the madness, he'd waited until they'd moved Sinnie, still unconscious, to the private room he'd gotten for her, arranged for the bill to be sent to him, and filled out a police report. Wade figured it was as likely to find its way into the lower bowel of a computer data bank as it was onto a cop's hot sheet.

There was a rap on his car window. It was Joy, with a worried look in her eyes. He opened the door, got out.

"How's Sinnie?" she asked, scanning his face.

"Hanging on." He paused to loosen the tightness in his chest. "Barely."

She wrapped her arms around him, held him close.

He cradled her head against his shoulder. She felt so damn good, it scared him. Joy Cole, in his bed, in his arms, was more than he'd bargained for.

"She's almost eighty years old. Who would have done such a terrible thing?" She moved back to look at him, but kept her arms around his waist.

"Good question. But like everything else going on at the Phil, there's no damned answer."

"I can't help thinking it has something to do with me. Me inheriting the hotel. Me moving into Room 33. Everything was fine before I came along."

If she'd wanted a denial, he couldn't give it. She was right and it made his gut ache. What was going on at the Phil was one tightly tied knot with Joy in the center. "I think you're right. Which is why you should pack up and leave the Phil."

"Don't think I haven't thought about it, but really"— she took her arms from around his waist—"what good would that do? Besides it's—"

"Don't give me the my hotel speech, okay? The fact is, it's not safe here. The smart thing to do is clear out."

"That's not going to happen. You're not the only one who cares about the Philip."

He considered arguing with her, but decided on another tack. "Then you'll stay with me, because I don't want you sleeping alone in that room. And I don't want you wandering around the hotel alone."

"Yes to commandment number one. But I won't be shackled to your bed."

"I hadn't thought of that."

"Don't. I'll stay with you because I want to, and because I have no attachment to that creepy room. But other than that, I do what I want and I go where I want."

We'll see about that. Frustrated, Wade tried another angle. "You saw Sinnie this morning. Whoever's behind this mess isn't afraid to spill blood, Joy. I don't want it to be yours."

"Neither do I." Her look was unflinching. "But I don't intend to be 'run out of Dodge,' either. If I'm the cause of this problem, I want to be in on the solution."

Wade wasn't happy, but he sucked up his loss. "Okay, but I intend to keep you in my sights." And he intended that watch to be 24/7.

She smiled slightly. "I wouldn't have it any other way."

He wanted to shake her, but settled for shaking his head. "And before we start working on that 'solution'— which starts with locating Mike the peephole pervert— I badly need a shower, a shave, and a change of clothes."

"A man with a plan. I like that. But stop at Cherry's first, okay? Lars and Rebecca are there, and they're all anxious to hear about Sinnie." She looped her arm in his and they started down the alley toward the rear-door entrance of the Phil. When he cast a sideways glance at her, he could see she was preoccupied.

He stopped at the door, turned her to face him. "Last night. We haven't talked about it, and I want to say—"

She put a finger on his lips. "Don't. I know."

"Know what?"

"That we shouldn't make it any more than it was."

"What it was, was damned important. At least to me. What about you?"

"Wade . . ." She looked as if she were locked in finger screws.

"Wade *what*?"

Silence.

He lifted her chin to get a look at her eyes. "Now this is interesting. You're all hot to trot to face some maniac who's loose in the Phil, but you can't face what's happening between us. You're damn well terrified."

"Okay, I'll admit it. You're right, I am terrified. A few weeks ago I was heading for the South Pacific, my life, such as it was—on a familiar course. A good contract, a laptop, an airline ticket—"

"—and now?"

"Now, with you, I don't know where I'm heading, but I know there are no maps and no guidebooks."

"I'm falling in love with you, you know." The words tumbled from his mouth without his thinking, but once said, he rested easy with them and had no desire to call them back. The truth was like that, he guessed. "Actually, the fall is pretty much complete."

She looked anxious, like a bird eyeing an open cage door. "It's too soon. You don't know me."

"I know enough—unless you've got a secret prison record." He kissed her lightly, wanted more, but there was no time. "Say it."

"I'm probably going to regret this"—she took a deep breath—"but I think I love you, too."

He could have sworn his smile started at his ankle bones. "That wasn't so bad, was it?"

She shook her head. "Not for me, but for you? I'm not so sure." She looked around the alley; dingy brick walls, boarded-up lower windows, and garbage cans. "And I would have preferred a more romantic setting. Dinner, fine wine, candlelight . . ."

"To hell with the setting." He kissed her long and deep. When he lifted his head, they were both breathless. "After we talk to everybody, and before I take that shower, we'll clear out your room. Bring your stuff over to mine."

"You're determined to protect me from the big, bad wolf, aren't you?" But at least now there was amusement in her eyes.

"Nope. It's about the big, bad wolf having you within arm's reach—so he can ravish you any time he wants." Not anywhere close to a lie, but not exactly the truth, either. He did want to protect her. And he didn't want her out of his sight.

Her lips ticked up. "Okay, but before I do that, I want your promise to keep me clued in on what's going on. Believe it or not, this"—she rapped her head—"works pretty good."

"Deal." Wade opened the door for her, and they stepped into what was once the kitchen of the Phil. It was dim and cluttered with trays, cooking utensils, steel serving carts, and boxes of god-knew-what. He kissed her again, tilted his head, and smiled into her eyes. "I take it you're okay with the 'ravishing' clause."

"Definitely."

Two days later, on an overly warm Thursday evening, Lana sipped a glass of wine and waited in her living room for David. When he finally rang the bell, she glanced at her gold-and-diamond watch. Twenty minutes late. A first.

David had never been late before, and she wasn't sure how she felt about it—or what it meant, other than that she didn't like it.

She opened the door wide and smiled at him. And her heart faltered, lost a beat or two. She wasn't sure how she felt about that, either. Or any of the other bewildering emotions centered on David.

"Hi," he said, leaning down to kiss her softly.

"Hi, back." She wrapped her arms around him, deepened the kiss until his breathing roughened.

He pulled away. "Maybe it would be a good idea if I came in. Either that or we can make out on the doorstep?"

"I wouldn't mind." She stepped aside, and he walked in. He looked breathtaking. Immaculately dressed for their dinner date, he carried flowers. A dozen or more lush white roses.

In the living room, Lana set about pouring him a drink. Giving a brief nod at the flowers he still held in his hand, she asked, "Are those for me, darling? Or a late date?"

A cloud passed over his face. "For you. Although I've no doubt my late date would appreciate them equally as much." His tone was dry.

Lana handed him his red wine—a very fine one she'd sought out and hoped he'd like. "You actually have a late date? Tonight?" She kept the disappointment from her voice, analyzed facts instead. David was late. David was going somewhere after having dinner with her. None of this was good, but she would not let it upset her. No man was worth it. She sipped her wine. Perhaps it was time to move on from this relationship, make new plans. It surprised her to discover she had no enthusiasm for the idea. Her enthusiasm—such as it was—remained settled on David. And, of course, the money to come from the sale of the Philip.

"More of an appointment than a date." He looked at her, his expression tense, angry. "And it's not one I'm looking forward to. It's about the damn Philip. My investors are edgy as hell. This delay of Joy's is becoming a real problem."

"She doesn't trust me"—she ran a finger across his chest—"and she doesn't trust you." Lana always figured the truth, whenever possible, served better than fiction. And she didn't want to talk about Joy. She wanted David's full attention.

"She trusts Emerson well enough, and he's an ex-con, for God's sake."

"Yes, she does. But she won't do anything until she talks to us. We have her promise. That should calm those investors of yours." She sipped her wine, smiled at him over her glass.

He lifted her face to his, held her chin too tight. "Damn the investors anyway. I'd rather come back here after dinner and spend the night making love to you."

"An idea I'd be happy to go along with." She set her wineglass down and wrapped her arms around his waist. "But if you must go, I'll understand." *And I won't claw at you with questions—especially when I might not like the answers about these so-called investors.*

"You're one of a kind, Lana. I wish to hell I'd met you years ago." He kissed her hair. "We could stay here, not bother with dinner."

There was nothing Lana wanted more, but she smiled up at him and said, "And miss dinner at Cristobel's? I don't think so." A small revenge, but a necessary one.

"You turning down sex for food? I don't believe it." But at least he was smiling.

"Maybe it's a whole new me." She fondled him through the rich fabric of his Armani. "And I am very hungry."

He closed his hand over hers. "And you want to make me suffer for that late meeting I have."

She squeezed him and let him go. "That, too, darling. That, too." She picked up her coat. "Shall we go? The reservation is for eight-thirty, and it's at least a half-hour drive."

David laughed. "My meeting's not until midnight, Lana. We can manage a—"

"—quick fuck before you have to run off?" She said it sweetly. "I don't think so. Besides I feel a headache coming on." She caressed his chin and smiled into his eyes.

David laughed, then dragged her—coat, bag, and all—into his arms and crushed her there. "You're wonderful. Have I told you that?"

"Not nearly often enough." She kissed him, happily aware of the hard ridge of him upright behind his zipper. "But if it is quick fucks you want, you'd be wise to make it a practice."

She pulled back and he let her go. Her reward was that she knew he didn't want to. He was a man, after all.

Not exactly complicated machinery.

Chapter Fourteen

"Come in, boy, and be quick about it."

Gordy let Melly go ahead, then wedged his big body through the narrow opening Christian provided.

Christian shut the door, took his calming breaths, and bent stiffly to pet Melly. She enjoyed her walks with Gordy. Quite liked the boy, he was sure. But Gordy, like everyone else in the hotel, had to go. And when he filled it again—with people of his own choosing—he'd make sure one of them was right for Melly.

He walked unsteadily back to his chair. The man-child followed him. "Gordy, my boy," he said, once he was settled in his chair, "would you like to earn a little more money?"

His eyes brightened. "You want extra walking for Melly?"

"That, yes." He shifted in his chair, leaned forward. "But there's something else I'd like you to do, and it might take a bit of muscle." He smiled to engage the boy's attention. "More than I have, in any event."

"I got muscles." Gordy flexed an arm, weight lifter style, and grinned.

"Yes, you have, which is why I'm asking for your help." Christian pointed a bony finger at his terrace where, through a narrow opening between drapes, the sun was beginning its descent. "Out there, behind the planter with the biggest trees, there's a large storage box." He opened the drawer in the lamp table beside his chair and dug out the key. "Take this—you do know how to use a key, don't you?"

Gordy looked insulted. "Yes, sir. You think I'm stupid?"

It was the first time the boy had been anything but agreeable. So droll, his getting angry when his intelligence was threatened, considering he had none. Ah, human nature. "No, no, my boy," he said, softening his tone. "I apologize if it sounded like that. You're bright as a shiny nickel, and Melly and I couldn't do without you." He offered him the key. "Now, please, go out to the storage box, open it, and inside you'll find a large tarpaulin. I'd like you to bring it here."

Gordy took the key, turned it over in his hand, and headed for the terrace.

"Close the door after you, boy! Don't forget."

Gordy came back a minute or two later with a bundle of blue plastic and, thank God, he'd been obedient about closing the doors. How odd that a few days ago, Christian could tolerate the terrace doors being open, and now he feared the very air they unleashed, even though the night was far too warm. He wondered idly if he were sinking further into decline, or simply ridding himself of another threat to his life and health.

"This what you want?" Gordy held the tarpaulin in both hands.

"Yes. Now if you'd be kind enough to open the ties and spread it directly in front of me. So it covers my carpet completely. Nice and flat now," he added, "with the edges straight."

Christian watched the boy work, insisted he get on his knees to smooth the last of the wrinkles from the tarp. "That's fine. A very good job." He surveyed the tarp, perhaps twelve feet by twelve feet. Big enough. He told himself not to be bothered by its uneven, puckered surface. "On the bureau, as usual, there's your pay for walking Melly. And another five whole dollars for the work you just did." Christian smiled at the boy.

"You going to paint something, Mr. Rupert?" he asked, heading for the bureau.

"A little touching up."

And garbage removal, he added to himself.

Joy and Wade were lucky—at least Joy thought so. They'd been given a table in the corner with a window giving them a clear view of the waters of Lake Washington—and hope of catching a spectacular sunset.

Wade didn't seem to notice. They'd dropped in to visit Sinnie in the hospital before dinner, and he'd been as quiet as a tomb since. It had been two days since the attack, and Sinnie was no better. Add to that the fact that neither Wade nor she had made any headway on finding out what was going on at the Phil. They'd covered the hotel from top to bottom. And people were still disappearing, without notice, and leaving no forwarding addresses—including the loathsome Mike. No loss, but Joy would have relished the chance to get rid of him personally. Still, with so many rooms empty, the place was eerie. Wade had insisted they go out tonight—to get away from it.

The only good thing about the Philip in the last two days was sleeping with Wade each night—not sleeping with him was even better, because Wade Emerson was the best lover Joy ever had. There were times when simply looking at him made her mind go blank. It probably wasn't a good thing, long-term, but even if she tried, she couldn't think beyond the now—the strange happenings at the Phil, and Wade's slow, expert hand in bed.

She shifted in her chair, drank some ice water. "Sinnie's going to be okay, Wade. I'm sure of it," she finally said, wanting to break the silence, reassure him. "If she's made it this far, she's bound to improve."

"I hope you're right."

"You've known her for a long time, haven't you?"

"Forever. She was a friend of my grandfather—and my mother. And mine." He smiled slightly. "After my mother died, she took me on as her pet project."

Joy tilted her head, waited.

"She wrote me every week I was in South Woods—that's where I served my time. New Jersey. She never missed. Of course, most of the letters were to give me hell, but . . . every week." He looked out the window to where the sun was lowering in the west. "She's the main reason I ended up at the Phil. I'd been out for a couple of months. And with no place to go and nothing to hold me where I was, one day I got in my car and ended up in Seattle." He looked away again before turning back to face her, his eyes unreadable. "I never intended to stay."

"Why did you?"

"You showed up, for one thing." He reached across the table and took her hand. He smiled fully then, a tease of a smile she knew was intended to change the subject.

"Flattering, Emerson, but you'd been there weeks before I arrived on the scene." She stopped. "It was the hotel, wasn't it? It was the Phil that held you." *Like it held me.* A prickle of unease followed. Sinnie said the Phil was in Wade's blood. His legacy, she insisted on calling it. If that were true, he might not be as amenable to her ownership as he appeared.

"The place needed help. Still does. Hell of an opportunity for occupational therapy."

"Did it work?"

He considered her words a moment. "Yeah, I think it did."

The server came to refill their water glasses.

When he'd gone, Wade said, "I've been doing a lot of thinking about the Phil." He paused, rubbed his chin. "Hell, I guess this is as good a time as any."

"Good time for what?" Again that prickly sensation at her nape.

Only the barest hesitation, then, "I want to buy the Philip from you, Joy. And I want to know if you'll entertain my offer."

Joy's jaw slackened, and she pulled her hand from his. She hadn't known what to expect, but it hadn't been this. "I don't know what to say."

"'Yes' would be good."

"But I thought you were . . ."

"Broke?"

"Yes."

"Not quite. I have enough to give you a substantial deposit, and I can raise the rest." His expression turned cynical. "If there's one thing you learn in my business, it's that there's always money around. It's just a matter of finding it and structuring the right deal with the right people. I'll work it out. I wouldn't expect you to take a cent less than the property is worth."

"But your—" She hesitated, her mind stumbling over what this meant: her own emotional connection to the Phil, the sense of home it gave her, how for the first time, walking those neglected halls and counting broken windows, she'd found a purpose in life. "You have a prison record . . . for fraud. Won't that make things difficult?"

"Difficult, not impossible. No one lost any money dealing with me. I saw to that. Actually, I already approached

Rupert about the deal. Big mistake. Turns out there was bad blood between him and my grandfather, and the last thing he wants is an Emerson owning his 'home,' as he calls it." He reached for her hand. "Or maybe he thinks you make a prettier landlord. In which case, he'd be right." He turned her hand in his and ran a finger slowly across her palm.

She quivered at his touch but said nothing.

"I take it from all your questions you're open to a proposal?" His eyes turned sober, oddly speculative, and they left no doubt he was dead serious.

"I, uh, don't know." She stalled, tried to clear her head. "And I did promise David Grange the chance to outbid any other offers." It would be easy to say no to David, but to Wade? The man who should have inherited the property in the first place. Still she needed time to think, hadn't realized until this moment the strength of her connection to the Philip, how much it figured in her future.

"Fair enough. I'm not looking for special consideration or a special price."

She fidgeted with her napkin. "There are things you don't know about the will." Like how the proceeds, either by sale or operation, were intended to support a stepmother he detested.

"I'm listening," he said.

Joy looked for a way to start, the right words, but before she could find them . . .

"Well, well, look who's here." Lana's voice slid into their conversation like a playful ferret. Joy almost knocked over her glass. Wade's grip on her hand tightened to near-painful before he released it.

When he looked up at Lana, his expression went from light to dark in a blink. He did not stand. Joy knew this wasn't going to be good. "Mother," she said, giving the barest of nods to acknowledge David.

Lana stared openly at Wade. "It's been a long time."

"Not long enough."

"Ah, I see I'm still the mean stepmother."

Wade looked at her in contempt. "I don't know what you are, Lana, but I'm sure 'mean' doesn't cover it."

"Oh, dear," Lana purred. "And I always speak so highly of you." She paused, lowered her lashes. "All of you."

It looked as if Wade exerted all his control to stay in his seat, but he said nothing.

"So what brings you two together, monkey business or business . . . business?" Lana's steady gaze, "calculating possible risk," held Joy's.

"Nothing that concerns you, Mother," Joy lied, and looked at David, whose gaze, like Lana's, hopped between herself and Wade. "David looks hungry. Why don't you go to your table?"

David nodded. "Good idea. Let's go, darling." He tried to take her arm, but she refused to move, her attention fixed now on Wade.

"If you must know," Wade said smoothly, "I'm planning on taking back the Hotel Philip. I just made an offer to buy it from your daughter."

"What the hell is going on here?" David's voice rose.

"I see," Lana said, her response as subtle as David's was blunt.

Joy knew from her mother's terse reply, her shuttered gaze, she was stunned—as was Joy.

Wade had overstepped himself. Joy had agreed to nothing. She looked at him. His face was fixed into stubborn lines, his gaze locked with Lana's. A slow, dangerous simmer churned in her stomach. Before she could speak, David leaned over the table, loomed above her.

"What you're doing. It's stupid," he said. "If Stephen had wanted Wade to have the hotel, he'd have left it to him, not you and Lana."

Wade's eyes shot to David. "What?"

David started to answer him, but Lana interrupted. "I warned you, David." She gave him a sly look. "Although in the end, I suppose Wade's money is as good as yours. No harm in a small bidding war, is there?"

Grange looked shell-shocked, gaped openly at Lana, and didn't say a word.

Lana stared at Joy, her expression blandly malevolent. "For things to have gone this far so fast, all I can say is he must be even better in bed than he used to be."

Joy, who'd been about to state that she wasn't selling anything to anyone, closed her mouth with a snap. She'd heard her mother's words and, snakelike, they coiled in her throat until she couldn't breathe, couldn't make sense of them.

She stood abruptly.

She'd had enough of her mother, David, and Wade—all of their self-serving maneuverings to gain control of the Phil. "Excuse me," she said. She picked up her coat and bag and strode double-time across the crowded restaurant. In seconds, she was outside, hailing a cab.

A second after that, Wade grabbed her arm and swung her around to face him. "What the hell do you think you're doing?"

"Let go of me." She yanked her arm from his grasp, raised it again.

He took her arm down, held it this time. "Where are you going?"

"Home."

"The Philip?" He gave her a dark look.

"Yes, the damn Philip. Although I'm beginning to wish I'd never set eyes on the place." She tugged her arm. "I said, let go of me. Or I'll damn well scream my head off."

He didn't let go; instead he lifted her chin and forced her eyes to meet his. "Scream at me when we get home. And considering I deserve it, I promise to take it like a man."

"Was that the soft echo of an apology I heard?" *Not enough, Wade. Not nearly enough.*

"It was."

She shook her head to release his grip on her chin. "And now I'm supposed to forget you were arrogant and presumptuous in there."

"Do or don't. Your call. I was wrong and I'm sorry."

"The Philip is mine, Wade. Not yours, not David's, not my mother's. Mine. I'll be the one making the decisions, and it would be best if you"—she cocked her head toward the restaurant door—"and everyone else would get that straight."

His look was dark, unreadable, and after a second or two, he gave her a curt nod. "Message received. Now if it's all the same to you, I'd like to stop by the hospital again, then find something to eat." He gestured back to the posh restaurant. "Unless you want to go back in there."

"I'd rather eat curried maggots."

"Agreed." He paused, rubbed the back of his neck. "And from what your mother said in there, I'm guessing you have questions for me."

"Not even one." She looked determinedly unconcerned, which wasn't easy because her body felt turned inside out. Her mother's words—*better in bed than he used to be*—might be a flashing neon sign in her head, but she'd swallow her tongue before asking Wade for the gritty details. Pride? Maybe, but somewhere down deep was a sense of ruin, a feeling she wouldn't admit or dare expose. All she could hope now was that her plan to make the Phil her work, her home, and a source of financial security for her mother wasn't a useless dream, as feathery and unlikely as the dreams she'd begun to spin around Wade.

"Okay, but let me say this. It's not what you think. I *did not* sleep with your mother and would not if she were the last woman on earth."

"I don't need your sexual history. I thought we'd agreed on that."

He cursed. "Fine. We'll drop it—for now. But leaving things unsaid isn't an option."

"I'd say that depends on the 'things.' "

He gave her a sideways look, half curious, half irritated. "Are you generally this damn stubborn?"

"Not generally, always."

"Good to know." He smiled slightly. "We'll do a last check on Sinnie, sort out what the hell is going on at the Phil. And when we've both calmed down, had time to think, we'll talk." He took her elbow and started them both down the street toward his car.

"You generally so damn bossy?" she asked.

"Always."

A half a block away, they reached his Explorer, neither adding anything more to their aborted conversation.

But Joy couldn't get past it.

Better in bed than he used to be.

He'd denied it, but Joy knew her mother. Knew the power she had over men and how she used it.

Wade was right—they did need to talk, and he wasn't the only one with explaining to do.

She looked out the window. There was the matter of the two million dollars she had in the bank. Money given to her by a man—in exchange for three months of her time.

No one knew about that.

It was after ten o'clock when Wade and Joy slid into the booth at a diner a few blocks from the Phil.

Wade felt like crap. Sinnie's condition hadn't improved, and Joy had barely said a word to him since they'd left Cristobel's. A glance in her direction told him that wasn't going to change anytime soon. He didn't push it, because he was a goddamn coward and didn't look forward to telling her about his relationship—or whatever the hell it was—with her mother.

For now, he'd settle for the deafening silence.

They both ordered burgers and two glasses of milk. The burgers arrived at the same time Joy's cell phone rang.

"It's Cherry. For you." She handed the phone to Wade. He had a fleeting thought he should get one of the damn things again. He hadn't bothered since prison.

Wade listened for a time, then cursed. "Stay in your room, Cherry. Lock up tight, and don't answer the door to anyone. Not anyone, you understand?" He listened some more. "We'll be back in half an hour—less. Just do what I said, okay?"

Joy's eyes were big when he handed her the phone. "What is it? What's wrong?"

"The only people left in the hotel are Cherry and Gordy, and us. Everyone else is gone."

"Not Lars and Rebecca! They'd never leave."

"Yesterday I'd have agreed with you. Today they're gone." And if Wade would have bet on anyone to hang in there, it was Lars. Whoever the hell was behind this exodus, and it was damn sure someone was, they knew exactly what strings to pull.

"I don't get it." Joy slumped back in the booth, stared at her untouched burger. "It makes no sense. Any of it."

"There's more."

"More?"

"They found Henry's body down the alley from the Phil. Behind a Dumpster. The police came by about an hour ago, to check out his room. Ask questions. But from what Cherry said, they figured he was another aging wino who'd had one too many, got himself in a brawl, and crawled off to rest. Died instead." Wade's gut denied it. Henry's M.O. was to drink alone and fall asleep. Never hurt a soul—except his own.

Joy went stark white.

He gestured to her burger. "You might want to take a bite or two of that. I think we'd better get back there."

She ignored his instruction, kept her eyes fixed on his. "Mike has to be part of this, Wade. Has to be!"

"If he is, he's smart enough to make himself scarce. Right now he's just another missing Phil tenant." *Which leaves no avenue of proof.* Wade picked up his burger. He didn't have much of an appetite left, but he figured it was now or never.

Joy sat back against the booth, food untouched. "The only sure thing is that all this trouble has to do with Stephen leaving me the hotel." She chewed on her bottom lip. "It can't be Sinnie. It can't."

He put down his burger, gave her his full attention. "Sinnie?"

She dug into the bag sitting beside her. "I didn't want to tell you—you were so worried about her and everything. But this"—she held out a red felt pen—"was in Sinnie's hand the morning we found her in my room. I didn't know what it meant, wanted to think about it. But thinking hasn't helped. I'm more confused than ever. But it was Sinnie who wrote the messages on my wall. I'm sure of it."

Wade rolled the big, red pen between his fingers. *Sinnie? Try to scare Joy away?* "It doesn't wash. For one thing, she was too busy matchmaking. The day she set eyes on you, she wanted me to propose. She wanted me to marry you so I could get the Phil back. That's how Sinnie's mind works. Not to scrawling ugly words on someone's wall."

Joy looked shocked. "She wanted you to marry me?"

"Not the worst idea I've ever heard."

"To get the Phil back?"

"That part is Sinnie's concoction. She thinks the hotel should be in Emerson hands."

"Obviously, so do you, considering your offer to buy it."

"The business part of this relationship is separate from the personal part. About as separate as it gets." Although after tonight, he'd have a hard time convincing her of that.

"Still, that pen"—she gestured with her chin to the pen he rolled between his fingers—"was in her hand for a reason. It's possible she knows something we don't."

Wade didn't believe for a second that Sinnie had anything to do with what was going on at the Phil. But Joy was right on the rest; Sinnie knew more about the old place than anyone else alive.

"I think we should check out her room," Joy said.

He took a last bite of his burger, left the other half on his plate, and slid out of the booth. It didn't look as if Joy was going to eat anyway. "Why not? We've checked everywhere else. Let's go."

The night was warm and humid, but the penthouse was sealed tight against any breeze that might make its way in to cool things down.

Christian turned the kitchen light off, which left only his table lamp to work against the gloom in his large living room, and shuffled along the hall to his chair. He didn't need light; he knew every step and corner of his home as a blind man would. Indeed he'd begun to wonder at its safety; gas gathered into a vacuum certainly didn't sound healthy.

He set a glass of cool water on a coaster beside his chair. He approved the use of bottled water—much more sanitary than the tap—and considered himself clever to have adopted the practice of having one of his hotel guests supply him with a case at regular intervals. The water glass centered accurately, he settled back in his chair.

With Lars gone, he'd have to find someone else to handle water delivery on a steady basis. No doubt he'd have an unpleasant period of adjustment until the new guests arrived to take up the various tasks he required. Until then he'd taken the precaution of having Michael bring a case with him when he came tonight. Good insurance. Another successful Plan B.

He glanced out at the terrace, where Michael was doing his final gardening chore, aerating and loosening the soil in the large planter. He worked under a portable work lamp rigged to the eave of the rooftop stairwell entrance. Christian wondered how David would feel, taking up the gardening tasks again. Not that it mattered. David would do what he was told; kill the silly girl, do Christian's gardening, and . . . take out the garbage.

Mike opened the terrace door—too wide. A gust of fresh air wafted across Christian's face. He had the briefest moment of enjoyment before unseen, dangerous microbes nettled his flesh. "Close the door, Michael. Quickly." He'd wanted to yell but had contained himself. Containment was everything. "Are you all done out there?"

"Yeah."

"Come here, then. We'll say our good-byes, and you can be on your way. I have your money ready." Christian held out the envelope with his left hand.

The hulk of a man took a step closer, until he was directly in front of Rupert's chair. He glanced down at the tarpaulin rustling beneath his feet. "Doin' some painting?" he asked, reaching for his money.

"Yes. A little spatter work." Christian lifted his right hand, the one with the Smith and Wesson, and fired three times. The first two bullets went into Michael's fortu-

E.C. Sheedy

nately very large chest, and he crumpled to his knees, wide-eyed. The third shot was to his forehead—slightly off center, Christian noticed, but close enough to finish the job.

Christian set the gun on the table beside him to cool and took a sip of water. He looked at the clock. Perfect. He tucked his carpet slipper-clad feet under the edge of the tarpaulin to lift it, reverse the blood flow.

He watched the blood ooze away from him and frowned. He hadn't expected so much. It was troubling. No matter.

In minutes David would be here to clean up the mess.

Chapter Fifteen

"You're good at that," Joy said, after Wade had closed Cherry's door behind them and they were walking up the hall. Wade had insisted on checking on Cherry and Gordy before heading to Sinnie's room.

"Good at what?" He gave her a puzzled look.

"Calming people down. Saying the right thing."

"Cherry's made of the right stuff."

"Yes, she is, but I think Lars and Rebecca being gone really spooked her," Joy said.

Looking fiercely preoccupied, Wade didn't answer. He pushed the fire door to the stairwell open. She knew he was thinking about Henry, and after Cherry telling them how badly beaten the police said he was, so was she. Together they climbed the dark stairs to the third floor.

"The lights? Didn't you replace all the bulbs yesterday afternoon?"

"Yes, and they were gone this morning."

"What do you think it means?"

"I think someone likes to do his dirty work in the dark."

"Cheery thought." The idea of someone slinking around the Phil's dingy halls made the hair on Joy's nape rise.

In the third floor hall, Wade said, "I'll get the keys." He disappeared briefly into his room, came out sorting through a handful of keys.

They were in the stairwell heading up to Sinnie's place on five when they heard it. Both stopped abruptly. For a moment they only looked at each other.

"Backfire?" Joy asked, not quite able to believe the old stairwell had just nicely magnified the sound of gunshots.

"Not unless there's a road race on the roof."

"The penthouse? Where that poor old man lives?"

He didn't answer her question; he grabbed her hand. "Let's go." He tugged her up the stairs to the seventh floor.

He stopped outside a door in an entrance hall lit only by what Joy guessed was a forty-watt bulb hanging from a cord a foot above their heads. Whoever had been turning out the lights on the Philip hadn't bothered with this one.

Wade rapped on the door. When there was no response, he knocked again.

"Yes?" Someone said from inside. Quite a few feet from the door, Joy guessed.

"Are you all right in there?" Wade shouted.

"Who's there?"

"Emerson."

There was a moment of silence. "Go away."

"We heard shots fired," Joy said, adding her own shout to Wade's.

"Who's that?" The tone was sharp, the voice closer now, against the door.

"Joy Cole, Mr. Rupert," Joy said, raising her voice.

"I'm the new owner of the Philip. We wanted to be sure you were okay."

The door opened a crack and in the yellow light cast from the single bulb, Joy saw an ancient face—parchment skin, eyes deep-set under hooded lids, and a lipless mouth. White hair grew in sparse patches on his liver-spotted head. Shorter than her five-foot-seven, Rupert stared up at her from behind a thick chain that stopped the door from opening more than six inches. "The new owner, are you?" His lip curled with scorn, and he studied her with unconcealed distaste.

"Yes, I—" She stopped, his animosity hitting her in waves. Either they'd woken him up and he was irritated, or he'd hated her on sight.

Wade spoke from behind her, his voice low. "We heard shots, Rupert. And they came from here."

"They did not. Now please leave this floor. You have no rights here." He stared through Joy. "Neither of you." He started to close the door.

"Are you sure you're okay—" Joy reached out, her knuckles glancing off the hand he had curled around the door edge; he gasped, looked at her hand as if it were a strike-ready cobra. She yanked it back.

"Go away. And don't come back here," he snapped. "This is my home. Stay below stairs, and don't come here again." He closed the door in her face. She heard bolts slam.

Joy looked at Wade, grimaced. "Not exactly the welcome wagon."

"Don't take it personally. He's not crazy about me either."

"Maybe it was the TV." Joy rubbed the hand she'd inadvertently touched him with on her skirt. Somehow the old man had made it feel dirty.

"Did you hear one?"

"No."

"Neither did I." Wade stared at the door as if he'd like to break it down. He raised his hand to knock again. Joy stopped him.

"The old man was more than angry, he was terrified. From what I hear, he's agoraphobic. Given his age— and that kind of fear—it might be dangerous to push ourselves on him." She still held his arm. "Unless we have to. Let's check six," she added. "The shots could have come from there. Or it might have been backfires after all, and the stairwell acted as an echo chamber, magnified them."

He looked doubtful, but nodded. "Okay, we'll check six, then we'll go to Sinnie's." They took the few steps to the stairwell door and opened it . . .

. . . on a stunned David Grange.

"David," Joy said when she gathered up a few working neurons. "What are you doing here?"

"I was looking for you." He smiled, and Joy could see him rally from his shock, pull his slick brand of cool around himself like a magician's satin cape.

"Up here?" Wade eyed him with suspicion. "This is a long way from the third floor."

"I thought if I couldn't find her, you'd be somewhere about, and I could leave a message. I didn't want to leave the evening as it was." He looked at Joy. "Your mother was upset, Joy. I should have stepped in. I'm sorry."

"You came here to apologize for my mother." She didn't bother phrasing it as a question. Something was wrong here. But then, something always felt wrong when she was around David Grange.

"That and—" He glanced at the door behind Wade. "Can we get out of here?"

Wade's gaze followed his to Rupert's door. "Fine by me. We'll go to my room."

When they were settled in Wade's room, Joy sat across from David at the table while Wade lounged against the kitchen counter. "Tell me again why you're here, David—crawling around the Phil's halls at midnight," she asked.

"Okay . . . let's start with this. I'm in love with your mother, Joy—"

"Of course you are." Joy had heard these same words from Stephen and others like him through the years. Her mother's allure was universal. And every man she'd ever caught in her web had been compelled to air his feelings to her daughter. A puzzle Joy never solved, as mystifying as their inability to see in Lana the tiniest of faults. She hated to think of Wade among them.

"And she loves me," he went on. "But when you marched out of the restaurant tonight, your mother was upset, and I realized how big a wedge there is between the two of you. And a big part of it centers around this place." He cast his eyes around, looked disgusted. "This damned decrepit, old hotel."

"That you're so hot to buy from me," she reminded him dryly.

"More so than ever."

"And why's that?"

"It's dangerous here. I tried to warn you days ago, but you wouldn't listen. There are people—" he stopped abruptly.

Joy paused to study him. He sounded serious, and for the first time, actually sincere. And maybe nervous?

"What people?" Wade stepped closer.

David stood and the two men faced each other, eye to eye, evenly matched in weight and height. Neither prepared to back down. "I've said enough. And I can't tell you what I don't know."

"It seems to me you know a hell of a lot more than you should, Grange." Wade's eyes narrowed. "And I think you'll do whatever you think needs doing to get your hands on this place. Including threatening Joy."

"I want this place, sure—and the profits to come with it. Personally, I can't wait to demolish this hellhole." He looked at Joy. "As for harming you to make that happen"—he half-smiled—"that wouldn't make your mother happy, would it? And right now, making her happy is all I care about. I asked her to marry me tonight, Joy, and she said yes. You're looking at a happy man. A very happy man."

And he looked to be exactly what he said he was.

Joy shouldn't have been so surprised. Nothing her mother did shocked her anymore, but accepting another man's marriage proposal when your husband's body was still cooling in the grave reminded Joy—again—of the shallow ground on which her mother built her life. Then she remembered the kiss she'd caught between David and her mother. Even through the jaded eyes she'd come to use when studying her mother, she'd seen the passion between them, the warmth in Lana's eyes. She wondered if it were possible that her mother and this man were truly in love.

"Does my mother know about these 'dangerous people' who don't want me to own the Phil?"

"No. But I know she'd want you safe."

"Let me guess. And for me to be safe, I should sell you the Philip, give her the money she believes is 'rightfully hers,' and leave town."

She cast a glance at Wade. She wanted to know what he was thinking, but his face gave nothing away—except a dark interest in the conversation between her and David

David went on, his voice forceful. "This isn't all about money, it's about your being . . . protected."

"That's it," Wade said. "You've said all you're going to say, Grange, so get the hell out of here. If the lady needs protection, you can bet she'll have it." His face was a tight mask of anger and threat. The air around him hummed with it, but he didn't shift a muscle.

David got up, settled a cold gaze on him. "I'll go, but not before I add this. You don't have pockets deep enough to buy this place, Emerson. No matter what you bid, I can top it."

Wade's gaze was steady. "We'll see about that."

He shook his head. "You're fools. Both of you," he said, and with that was gone.

Joy stared at the door he'd closed behind him. "Do you believe that?" she whispered, more to herself than Wade.

Wade pushed away from the counter. "That guy's got an agenda." He paused. "As, apparently, have you and your mother." His jaw worked and a muscle ticked. "But all that's best left for later. Let's go to Sinnie's room. Our question-and-answer session can wait. People dying can't."

"You're late." Christian's mood was sour. It was after twelve-thirty. He'd spent an hour looking at the obscene sight at his feet. The blood was beginning to agitate him. He slipped the chain on the door, and David pushed his way in, opening the door far too wide for Christian's comfort.

"I met some friends of yours outside your door a few minutes ago. I had to double back."

"Ah, yes, the 'new owner' of the Phil. Christian danced the words out of his mouth in a little-girl voice. "She looked to be no more than twelve years old. The presumption of her!"

"Everybody looks twelve years old when you're as ancient as you are," David said, then squinted. "Damn, it's dark in here, Christian. Why the hell don't you turn on some lights? Or are you terrorized by them, too?"

"Don't be stupid," Christian lied. "I have the lights off for a reason. I do everything for a reason."

"Don't I know it," David said, his voice tired.

"Come with me."

David followed him from the penthouse foyer to the living room. He stopped abruptly, stared stupidly at the hulk of a corpse at the base of Christian's chair, gorily illuminated by the pool of yellow light cast by Christian's lamp. "Jesus . . ." he said, the invocation drifting out on a ragged sigh. "You're crazy, you know that? You're fucking crazy, Rupert. What the hell have you done now?"

"I've disposed of an obscenity." Christian took his chair. "And I'd appreciate your taking it from here."

David's face blazed with anger. "You brought me here to get rid of the body?"

Christian smoothed his velvet lapels. He felt better now that David was here, but he wished he weren't so transfixed by the human waste on the floor. "Among other things, yes. It's not as if you're inexperienced in such matters." He gestured toward the terrace. "There's a large box behind the biggest planter—the one the tarp came out of. Put him in there. I'd have you bury him in the planter itself, but I have no intention of having the dearly departed Michael as a permanent terrace guest. One of those is enough. Tomorrow you can arrange for the proper equipment to remove him from the building. You'll need a dolly, I expect."

David rubbed his forehead. "You expect me to get a body out of this place without being seen?"

"I expect you to get a *box* out of here without being seen." Christian eased the tension from his bony shoulders. David was so recalcitrant. "Your risk of being discovered is minimal, as I had the foresight to have the deceased"—he pointed at the corpse—"clear the hotel in preparation. The only people left are the boy and his

mother on two, Emerson, and, for obvious reasons, the
Cole girl on three. You'll have no difficulties."

"You've gone a bit far, haven't you?" David's chin
lifted as if surprised. "What about your precious security, your endless parade of door knockers?"

"Rest assured, I've taken care of every eventuality."
Christian said, slightly alarmed by the intensity in
David's gaze. "There's a pair of overalls hanging in the
storage box. Put them on to protect your clothes. The
shovel is where it always is."

"And what if I say, fuck you, Rupert, and walk out of
here?"

"I'll ignore your profanity, David—for now—because
I know how grateful you are to me. How much you owe
me." Christian picked up his glass of water, sipped, and
put it down. "Now, please get this"—he pointed at the
Michael thing with his toe, careful not to touch it—"out
of my home immediately. When you've done that, we'll
discuss my plans for the Cole girl. To save you a trip—
you see how considerate I am—you can take care of her
tomorrow night, when you come to remove Michael. I
want to wake up Saturday morning with all this chaos
behind me."

"Forget about the Cole girl. I'll get your goddamned
hotel. There doesn't have to be any more killing."

"I'm afraid I've lost confidence in your approach,
David—and patience. I want you to kill the girl, and I
want it done tomorrow." He paused. "Am I clear?"

David stood in front of him and Christian watched a
war rage across his face, heard the hard tug of his lungs
at the cool night air. The long, hoarse exhalations. The
sound of impotence. It was good to have control.
Christian wondered idly how anyone lived without it.

After more silent seconds passed, David took off his
jacket and started to work on the tarp, his face set to an

expression black as Hades. But even in this emotional milieu, he performed beautifully. In minutes the corpse was swaddled and tied.

"Please ensure the box is securely locked. And double check the binding on the tarpaulin. I don't want leakage."

David shot him a killing glance, dragged the blue-tarped body to the terrace, and, without a word, closed the door behind him.

Christian relaxed back into his chair, knowing David had his work cut out for him, loading and securing that abhorrent bulk for removal. When he was done, they would discuss how Christian wanted him to kill the girl.

Finally, everything was coming together—as it should. Within days, the Philip would be his, as it was meant to be from the very beginning.

"This is harder than I thought," Wade said, standing over Sinnie's three-drawer bureau. "I feel like a sneak thief."

"I'll do that," Joy said, and stepped up beside him. "You check the top shelf of the closet. People always hide stuff there."

"You've seen too many movies," he said, but took her advice and went to the closet.

Joy opened the first drawer and was immediately impressed. Sinnie's drawers would make Martha proud, everything neat as a pin. But not much there. "What are we looking for, anyway?"

"Damned if I know," he said, then, "Bingo."

She turned. "I told you people put things up there. What have you got?"

"A photo album."

He sat on Sinnie's bed and adjusted the bedside lamp. Joy sat beside him. The album was old, and well-organized, every picture tucked into slots provided by gold corner stickers.

On the third page, Wade stopped, pointed. "That's my grandfather. Old Joe himself." His finger trailed off the page.

"Is this your mother?" Joy pointed to a picture of Stephen with his arm around a small, pretty woman.

"Yes. In better times."

"She's lovely."

Wade nodded, touched the picture, and turned the page. "But what have we here?"

"Sinnie. I think." Joy looked closer at the picture. It showed a young girl of maybe fourteen and a boy, older but shorter. Both smiling for the camera. Behind them was a grand house and beyond it what looked like the ocean.

Joy slipped her nail under the photo and carefully lifted it out of its golden corners. She turned it over, read, *My brother Christian and I. Montauk, N.Y. I was fourteen.*

Wade sat back, shook his head. "Whoa! This is news. Sinnie and that nightmare in the penthouse related. And she never said a word."

"Why, do you suppose?"

"I don't know." He looked baffled. "I always had the impression she didn't like him very much."

Still holding the picture, Joy turned to the next page. And the next . . . There was nothing more of interest until the last one. Here, Sinnie had constructed a pocket using heavy paper and clear tape, and judging by the tears and yellowing, she'd done it a very long time ago. Inside the makeshift pocket were newspaper clippings. All of them about Room 33, including the "room of doom" article.

Wade pulled one of the magazine clippings from her hand. It had a picture of his grandfather—much older than the picture in the album. "I remember this," Wade said. "It was a few years before he died. The Philip was a mess and he was pouring money into it to keep it going, hanging on by his bloodied fingernails. This guy—the writer—was doing a piece on ghosts or some damn thing. He'd latched on to the 'room of doom' article and came to interview Joe." He paused as if to remember. "Joe never talked about that stuff, never believed a word of it. To him it was always a run of bad luck. But this time he wanted to explain things. Make a point about how irresponsible reporting had damaged his hotel's reputation."

"And did he? Make his point?"

"No." He stopped. "Truth is, the press *wasn't* the problem. It was that 'run of bad luck' Joe talked about. It destroyed the Philip and when it failed, the neighborhood failed."

"Look at this." She handed him a list in Sinnie's handwriting of all the tragic events that had taken place in Room 33.

Wade studied it. "There's some here even I didn't know about." He pointed to one. "Joe never mentioned this."

"Family of three murdered in the 'room of doom.'" Joy read and shuddered at the image. "I can see why. I wouldn't tell my grandson either." She looked at Wade. "But I don't think all this"—she ran a finger down the list—"had anything to do with bad luck. This smells like a plan." Uneasiness burrowed into her stomach. David's warnings lit up in her mind.

"A plan that goes back a long way. A very long way." Wade rose abruptly.

She started to put the album back together, but when it came time to put the list and the photograph back, Wade said, "Hang on to those."

She knew what was on his mind, "You think we should

ask"—she pointed toward the ceiling—"Rupert—Sinnie's brother, about her list, right?"

Wade's face was closed, angry. "We sure as hell can't ask Sinnie. And that man either knows something, or worse yet, he's had a hand in things around this place for more years than I like to think about."

"He's not going to be thrilled to see us. If he even lets us in." She remembered the size of the chain on his door. It would keep out a SWAT team.

"I know a way." Wade glanced at his watch. "But it won't work tonight. So let's go. We'll get some sleep and think about this in the morning."

The events of the evening, her mother's sexual intimation, rushed back. Her throat tightened. "That's all we're going to do. Sleep. Until things are sorted out. Do we understand each other?"

He nodded, but he didn't smile.

Lana sat in her car, craned her neck to look up at the hotel. There were only three lights on in the whole place that she could see, an outside light on the rooftop, one in the lobby, and another on the third floor. Other than that, the Philip was shrouded in black.

It was one-thirty in the morning, and David still hadn't come out. She could imagine what he was doing in there, but Lana didn't go in for imagination—she preferred facts. Tonight, on the way to dinner, he'd proposed to her and she'd accepted; then, after the scene with Joy and Wade in the restaurant, he'd turned to stone. She'd never seen him so angry. Of course she'd left him to stew—until it came time for his late meeting that *wouldn't* wait.

Curiosity made her follow him; fascination that the meeting was held in the Philip at this time of night held her in place.

Joy was in there.

She thought about her daughter, her strikingly beautiful, very young daughter—as a potential rival. It didn't seem possible. But she needed to know, and sitting here accomplished nothing. She opened her Mercedes door and got out. The street, deserted except for a couple down the block who'd reeled out of a tavern, was dark. A chilly breeze kicked trash along the gutter, and she pulled her silk sweater tight to her shoulders as she walked toward the hotel.

She reached the main door as David came out of it. "Lana, what in hell are you doing here?" He clutched her upper arms, didn't look pleased.

"I could ask you the same thing," she said.

"Business. I told you that." As if pulling down a blind, he covered his initial shock at seeing her there with a frustrated glare.

"Care to tell me what kind of business brings you to this awful place in the middle of the night?"

"No." He took her arm.

"I thought not."

When she pulled away from him, his smile was cool, taunting. "But I can tell you I bumped into Joy. We had a very nice talk. Beautiful girl, your daughter."

Shock was such a rare sensation for Lana, she barely recognized it. Jealousy—rarer still—made her stomach curl. "And what exactly did you two talk about?" Lana knew her voice was level, prided herself on it.

He took her arm, none too gently, and led her away from the hotel doors and across the darkened street. "After your performance in the restaurant, I thought I'd best plead my own case." His eyes were cold. "What the hell did you think I'd do, with you mouthing off that Wade's money was as good as mine."

"It is. But there isn't a chance I'd ever see a dime of it. Which is exactly why I said that."

"What the hell are you talking about?"

"Wade detests me, David. Always has. Blames me for the death of his mother . . . among other things. Now that he knows the Philip money will bleed through to me, he'll withdraw his offer—and probably get out of my daughter's pants—at the speed of light."

David looked suspicious. "You're sure?"

"Trust me on this. I'm absolutely sure. After tonight, Wade is out of the running."

"Why didn't you tell me this earlier?"

She smiled. "Because you were angry, miserable, unreachable, and you annoyed me."

"I had reason to be angry. Still am. And you'd better be right about Emerson, because if there's one thing my investors won't tolerate, it's more delay."

He opened her car door, his expression still sour. "I told Joy about us, by the way."

"Don't you think that was my job?"

He lifted one of his expensively clad shoulders and dropped it. "Maybe, but it's done. Believe it or not, I was actually excited about it." He swung her to face him, gripped her upper arms. "I love you, Lana. I'll do anything for you—anything—but I have to get that hotel. No matter what it takes. Do you get that?"

She'd never seen him so strong, so forceful. "I get it, my darling." She stood on her toes to kiss him, ran her tongue along the tense line of his mouth. "And all I'm trying to do is help. Believe me, after tonight, you have nothing to worry about."

His mouth softened and he took hers in a deep kiss. "You drive me crazy, you know that."

"I certainly hope so."

"Are you going to tell me why you followed me tonight?"

"I doubt it." She lifted her wide blue eyes to his, filled them with sexual promise. "But you're welcome to come home with me and do your best to make me talk."

He smiled, and opened the car door wide. "Get in. I'll follow you home." He leaned in and kissed her again. "And believe it or not, I'm glad you came."

"Me, too," she said. *You lying bastard!*

Joy came out of Wade's bathroom. She wore his robe again and with the light and steam of the bathroom behind her, she looked like an emerging dream.

He stuffed a pillow behind his head and shifted up to lean against the headboard.

She slid into bed beside him, warm and soft from his bathtub—and wearing pajamas. Damn!

They needed to straighten things out—before pajamas became steel armor. And it wasn't going to be pretty. "I think we should get this over with." Lousy introduction, but all he could come up with. She visibly tensed.

"The 'this' you're referring to being Lana's involvement in the Philip?" she said.

"Uh-huh."

"All right. But tit for tat."

"Sure." He knew she was referring to his and Lana's relationship. Big, fucking, deep hole there. He wasn't sure he could climb out of it. He also knew he couldn't avoid it. "But you first."

She seemed to consider this, then pushed herself up to sit beside him. "Why not?" They looked like a pair of seventies sitcom characters. Except he sensed there'd be nothing comedic about their conversation. "You've probably figured it out already. Your father left me the Hotel Philip and a hundred thousand dollars—and lots of strings." She smoothed the blanket over her knees, and started to talk. He left her to it for the next ten minutes.

When Joy finished explaining how Stephen intended Lana to benefit from Joy's ownership of the Philip, Wade's breath had cratered in his lungs. And one searing conclusion occupied his brain. If he bought the hotel from Joy, the last of his cash would flow through to Lana, the woman who destroyed his family and humiliated his mother.

He had trouble getting his words out. "That letter. It's not binding, you know. It's not attached to the probated will."

She didn't look at him. "I know that."

Unable to stay still, he got up, shoved his legs into jeans, and turned to look down at her. "But you don't care."

"It's not about caring. It's about obligation. It's what your father wanted." She moved to sit on the edge of the bed, her back to him.

"That doesn't make it right."

She propped a knee on the bed, looked at him. "Maybe it is right. They were married for eighteen years, Wade."

"Eighteen years and over forty million dollars." His snort was derisive, disgust and anger a hard lump under his ribcage. "Let's see . . . that's a burn rate of two million a year, give or take."

"Forty million." Joy's wide-eyed gaze shot to his. "That much?"

"And every cent of it made by my grandfather."

"I didn't know." She rose, walked to where he stood by the window. They both looked down into the shadowy street. "But it doesn't change anything. I can't ignore your father's request." She ran her hands through her long, blond hair, then leaned against the windowsill. "But I can interpret it in my own way."

"Which means?"

"I don't intend to sell the Phil and hand the money to my mother. I want to reopen it, make it profitable, and pay my mother a monthly dividend from the proceeds."

"What's in it for you?"

"A home. A goal . . . a solid place to live my life. Some kind of foundation. It's difficult to explain."

She didn't have to. Wade understood perfectly. It was the same reason he'd wanted the Phil, but unlike her, he knew what he was in for. "The Phil is a seedy old hotel in a lousy part of town. It might take years to get it back to where it should be. Not to mention a hefty budget. It's a hell of a way to get a life, Joy." He prodded her resolve, didn't know why. None of it mattered now that he knew Lana's stake in it.

"Maybe." She stood, crossed her arms under her breasts. "But it's the life I want. I'll take care of Lana, and I'll take care of myself. And I won't sell to David Grange." She lifted a brow, studied him. "I take it your offer is off the table?"

"Every last nickel of it. Your mother's financial well-being might be your concern. It sure as hell isn't mine. I don't care if she—" He stopped. Enough said.

"I think the normal finish to that sentence is 'rots in hell?' "

He said nothing, and she fixed those wide, truth-seeking eyes on him—and honed in on a dark spot he'd hoped never to visit again.

"Which leads us to your story," she said. "Tell me. What did she mean when she said you must be 'better in bed than you used to be?' "

"Maybe you should ask her." He was stalling and knew it.

"Do you really want me to do that?"

"No." He didn't, but neither could he make his damn mouth work.

Silence filled the room, heavy and bleak—accusatory.

Finally, Joy closed her eyes against it, against him. Her words came out on a chilled whisper. "You did sleep with her, didn't you?" She licked her lips as if they were dry, and her gaze met his—not with the anger he'd have been comfortable with, but a bone-deep, terrible misery.

"I did not sleep with her." That much was true. He couldn't describe what they'd done, but he knew one thing—it had nothing to do with sleeping.

Chapter Sixteen

Joy's blood coursed through her veins, a river of ice.
Wade was lying and she knew it. He looked angry,
guilty, and frustrated. No doubt he was all of them. Just
as she was sickened, disappointed, and strangely pan-
icked. She had the insane—or smart—urge to grab her
clothes and run. But before she could be sure that her
brain still controlled her legs, Wade stepped up to her.

"Sit down," he said. "I might as well get this over with."
His expression was forbidding, his mouth a thin seam.

He exerted light pressure on her shoulders to make
her sit on the edge of the bed. With the anger and pain
in her head blocking a sane decision process, she sat.
He stood over her. They both took some deep breaths.

"I was seventeen when your mother married my dad."
He stopped. "This isn't going to be pretty, and I'm not
going to watch my words. Can you handle that?"

"Oh, I can handle it, all right. The truth is, I'm fascinated. It's not every day a girl sleeps with the same man
who's slept with her mother."

"It wasn't—" He stopped again, looked at the ceiling
as if it would offer him the excuses he needed. "I did

not sleep with your mother. At least, not in the sense you're thinking of it."

"I'm thinking of it in the sense of fucking." She managed to lace her tone in sugar and add a smile. It felt like a tear across her lower face. "How are you thinking of it . . . fondly?"

He glared at her. "If you'll shut up, I'll tell you."

She put a hand behind her ear, ignored the building pressure in her lungs. "Go for it."

"I was seventeen—"

"—you said that." When his glare hardened, she didn't care. Anger, cold and vicious, had staked its claim. She turned away from his eyes, afraid of what truth she'd see there.

"It happened the same day you and I met at the Phil. I'd met Dad there that afternoon to go home with him for his birthday dinner the same night. I hadn't wanted to go, but my mother insisted . . . That woman didn't have a mean bone in her body." He paused as if to gather his thoughts. "Before dinner, I hit Stephen's liquor supply, figured I needed liquid courage. I was okay until Lana came in and sat in my mother's chair. Cool as . . . hell, cool as it's possible to be."

"I get the picture."

"I doubt it. Anyway, that cool—and the Jack Daniel's— made me a little nuts, I guess. I mouthed off, said something rude—and probably crude—to your mother. I can't remember, but whatever it was started a fight with my father." He glanced down at her. "You remember that? You were asked to leave the room and you weren't happy about it."

She gave a slight nod. "You broke a glass against the wall."

"Yeah." He pulled his earlobe. "After that, I got out of there and went to bed." He started to pace, then just as suddenly stopped. "I fell asleep pretty much right away. I guess 'passed out' would be more accurate. It was maybe three o'clock when I woke up." He took a breath. "I thought I was having a wet dream, and maybe I was, at first. But then I felt hands . . . working me. I woke up hard as stone with your mother straddling me, trying to—hell. You can guess."

Silence bloated the room, as if there'd been a sudden, shocking death. Even the air thinned.

Wade looked as if he'd been beaten by ghosts—no visible scars but haggard, weak, and exhausted from the battle.

Joy put her head, suddenly too heavy to hold upright, in her two hands. She did not want to know this. Didn't know what to do with the information.

"There's more," Wade said.

She lifted her face to his, her mind blanked by overload.

"When my brain kicked in, I shoved her off me, cursed her with all the colorful vocabulary at my seventeen-year-old disposal—you got a taste of it earlier that night at dinner—and that brought my father to the scene." His expression altered subtly, at once pained and hard, and he ran a hand through his hair. "And what a view he got. A naked kid with a hard-on, railing at his beautiful wife, who was flat out on the floor." His mouth flattened. "She told him I'd come on to her. That she'd come into my room to check on me, and I'd been all over her."

Nauseous, Joy had to ask, "And Stephen? What did he do?"

"He believed Lana and tossed me out of the house." He dragged a chair to face her and sat, trapping her knees between his. He reached for her hands, and she didn't have the strength to pull them away. "My guess is he went to his grave believing I was some kind of pervert." Pain clouded his gaze. She saw him straighten to refuse it entry, work to contain the bitter memory, shove it into the ugly past where it belonged.

"And you blame my mother." Her words sounded dumb, ill-placed, and stupidly accusatory, but she didn't know what else to say, didn't know how she felt, and couldn't hold onto an emotion long enough to identify it.

"I don't know how else to say this—except to say it. My take on it is that all your mother cared about was money, and she married my father to get it. When I think about it now—which is as little as possible—I see that little show in my bedroom as her way of getting rid of me. I'm not going to lie. I more than blamed her, I hated her—maybe I still do." He lifted her chin, forced her to look at him. "The one thing I did *not* do was sleep with her. You have to believe that, or you and I don't stand a chance."

She pulled her face away, got up, and crossed the room to the closet. She started to dress. If she didn't get out of here, the chaos in her brain would close her lungs completely. She needed fresh air, and more than that—she needed to get away from Wade . . . the image of him and Lana.

"Joy, don't do this." He started across the room.

She held up a hand to stop him. "Don't touch me." She put on her robe, gathered up her bag and the dress she'd worn to dinner. A dinner that now seemed like days ago. "And don't say another word."

She finished gathering up her things. At the door she looked back. "And there's something you should know. I have two million dollars in the bank—the result of a brief but highly profitable marriage. So you could say preying on men and their fortunes is a specialty of the Cole women."

Not waiting for his reaction, she stepped into the dark corridor and ran across it to her own room.

Room 33 enclosed her with the harsh, dark purpose of a prison cell, its only light the gray illumination from streetlamps nearly a half-block away down the alley outside her window.

Her blood pounded and stumbled along her veins, and her heart thumped until she couldn't hear over its thrumming beat. She wanted to run, run and never stop, but even in its overtaxed state, her mind registered that it was the middle of the night and a dangerous neighborhood. And she wasn't wearing any shoes. Her shoes were at Wade's, as were most of her clothes, her computer, and her naïve heart.

"Joy." There was a determined pounding on the door. She ignored it.

"I don't want you in that room," he said.

"I don't care what you want." She looked at the door, Wade had installed new hinges after Sinnie's attack. He could pound all he wanted and he'd stay on the other side unless she wanted it otherwise.

"If you won't stay with me, I'll drive you back to the Marriot. You can't stay here." He thumped the door again.

Joy unlocked it and flung it open. "If anyone's going to leave this hotel, it's going to be you. For the last time, this is my hotel, not yours, not my mother's. Mine. And I'll do what I damn well please." She came perilously close to poking him in the chest, but the thought of it was too ludicrous. "Have I made myself clear?"

"Perfectly."

"Fine," She started to close the door and he put his foot in it.

"We haven't finished."

"We are about as finished as finished gets."

"I wasn't talking about us. I was talking about the Phil, about finding out what's going on around here." He kept his foot wedged in the door opening.

"I can do that on my own."

"You probably can." His look was cold. "But some-body hurt Sinnie, and I don't plan on leaving here until I find out who. We can either work together or alone. Your choice."

"You do whatever you like. Alone works for me." Alone, always alone—she was used to it, yet the word slid across her tongue like the bitterest of medicine.

"I did not have sex with your mother, Joy. If you don't hear anything else I say, hear that." He pulled his foot from the door and crossed the hall. "If you're going to sleep in that room, check all the windows and lock your door. I'll leave mine open. If you need me, call." He disappeared into his room.

When she closed the door behind her, she followed his instructions, took off her robe, and crawled under the covers. The bed was cold and too firm, but her resolve was colder—and harder. She lay awake, stared at the shadowed ceiling, and for the rest of the night fought a winning battle against tears.

Lana, for all her selfish ways and flagrant indiscretions, was her mother. She couldn't change that. Nor could she shape her into the milk-and-cookies mama she'd dreamed about as a child. But, mysteriously, as if she carried a gene imbued with the immutability of it, she couldn't stop loving her—and hating her at the same time. Lana had taken her from a father she loved, never let her say good-bye—and now she'd taken Wade.

Wade . . .

In the small hours the anger ebbed, and a wretched, deeply resented, fear replaced it. Joy didn't know if she could ever look at Wade again without replaying that scene in his bedroom.

And she never wanted to see that scene again.

* * *

Lana slipped out from under the covers, too warm to sleep, too indecisive to make plans. She looked back at the man in the bed. A man who, a few hours before, she'd agreed to marry. David was everything she wanted and didn't want.

They were too much alike, she and David. And he'd lied to her, she was sure of it. His deceit left her uncertain, vaguely uneasy.

Lana knew what she was—selfish, cautious, and controlled. She didn't believe in emotional unraveling—except in bed. She took what good sex had to offer—release in a confined period of time—because risking your body, your physical responses, was such a small thing. Lana adored seeing desire in a man's eyes, the want of her. Only her. She'd seen lust in David's eyes the day they'd met, and she'd responded to it, as she'd done many times before.

She'd considered herself fortunate to find him when Stephen's interest in the bedroom started to wane— most likely when his health problems began. She'd thought she and David would last a month or two and she'd move on.

That was a year ago, perhaps more. And tonight she'd agreed to marry him . . . because she was afraid to lose him. That fear was disconcerting. It should be David who was afraid, not Lana Cole. Never Lana Cole.

"What are you doing out of bed?" David's deep voice came out of the dark.

She walked back to the bed and put one knee on it, looked down at him. "Actually, I was thinking about your marriage proposal."

"Regrets already?" He stroked her bare knee, ran his hand along the back of her thigh.

She saw his smile, heard the teasing tone. "Some," she said, and enjoyed seeing his brow furrow, the grin drop from his seductive mouth. It wasn't good for a man to feel complacent. "And I was thinking about the Philip."

He sighed, long and exaggerated. "I told you what I was doing there. You have nothing to worry about. It was business. I'd suggest you drop it."

Lana leaned over him, close enough to see his eyes in the moonlit room. "I don't care what you were doing there, David. I care about the fact that you haven't bought my hotel. And that I don't have ten million dollars in my bank account." Of course, none of what she said was true; she was unnerved by the time he spent at the Phil, his growing relationship with Joy, but she had no intention of telling him that.

"Well, you can stop thinking about it. It's taken care of." He pulled himself up, leaned on one elbow.

"I'm glad to hear that. So tell me this, now that *I've* taken Wade Emerson out of the picture, when exactly can I expect Joy to write me my check?"

"Shit, I don't know. Soon." He stopped suddenly to study her. "How about I knock her off, you'll inherit, and we'll be back to where we were supposed to be before Stephen wrote his stupid will." He eyed her, a raised eyebrow in contrast to the deliberation in his expression.

Silence.

"Very funny," she said, irritated by his attempt at black humor and the quick jump of her heart.

David threw himself back on the bed, covered his eyes with a forearm. "Then the answer to the question of when you get your money is, *I don't fucking know.*" The tension in his voice carried through the pale yellow light in the room.

It didn't surprise her, because in the weeks since Joy inherited the Philip, David had grown increasingly remote. Something was wrong, but rather than probe—

and perhaps become more deeply involved than she already was—she'd treated it with sex. David forgot his troubles when she opened her legs. So much more effective than opening her heart.

Hearing the tired frustration in his voice, a part of her wanted to pull him into her arms, soothe him. But her heart hadn't ruled her head in years. She wasn't about to let it start now. She headed for the guest room. "Well, darling, when you do 'know,' we'll set a date. Until then, I'll be sleeping alone."

"Don't play games with me, Lana. Not now." He sat up in bed, his jaw tight, his expression deeply serious. "You know how I feel about you. I love you. I've never loved anyone like I love you. You'll get your money. It's all lined up."

"So you say—*ad nauseam*. What I'm saying is, 'show me.'" At the door, she turned back, knew she was lit by moonlight. "If you don't"—she stroked her pubis, ran her hands over her breasts, then cupped them in offering—"I'll find someone else to take care of me."

She heard him swear as she walked out of the room.

Between frequent checks of the third-floor hall and Joy's door, Wade had done the toss-and-turn tango most of the night. He felt like road-kill.

The sun dumped into the room from his open window, an avalanche of light that burned his corneas.

His phone rang.

He sat on the edge of the bed, reached for it.

"Yeah," he said, rubbing closed eyelids.

"Wade? Lars."

Wade's eyes snapped open. "Where the hell are you? Are you and Rebecca okay?"

"We're in Bellingham, and, yes, we're okay."

Relief swept through Wade. "What happened?"

"In a minute. How's Sin?"

"Hanging on. The doctors are neutral about her chances, but every hour she's alive increases them."

"That's good. We were worried."

Wade heard him relay the info to Rebecca. "Now, what's the story, Lars? Why did you cut out?"

"We had a visit from Big Mike. He told us to leave or else."

"And the else was?"

Lars breathed heavily into the phone. "If it was just me, Wade, I wouldn't have gone. But he threatened Rebecca." He paused. "Sick bastard has a sewer drain for a mouth. I couldn't risk anything happening to her or the baby, so we split. I feel like shit about it."

"Don't. You did the right thing. Did he say anything? Give you any reason why he wanted you gone?"

"No. Just said to get out right away, because the place had to be empty. Said not to ask questions or 'my pretty little woman wouldn't be so pretty anymore.' Said he really liked 'working with women.' Sick bastard."

Wade rested his head in his hand. "Amen to that." And if he knew where the 'sick bastard' was, he'd *amen* him, too.

"There's something else."

"I'm listening."

"After Mike did his number on us, I kept an eye on him. He went straight upstairs to the penthouse."

Wade showered, dressed, and headed to his kitchen.

Rupert and Big Mike. Things were beginning to make a bizarre kind of sense. Rupert had to be behind the evictions. The trick was to prove it. Mike, if he could find him, was the key.

And he owed it to Joy to let her know about Lars's call.

He stepped into the hall, holding a steaming mug of coffee, and headed for Room 33. Last night was one hell of a botch. He was in a hole deep enough to stop daylight. He hadn't really expected Joy to understand the *thing* that happened between him and Lana, so all he could do now was keep his mouth shut and wait.

He knocked on her door.

She opened it.

The look she gave him was lethal. He decided the wait was going to be a long one. He shoved the hot coffee toward her. She eyed it, eyed him. "This a peace offering?"

"Nope. Coffee." Anger simmered low in his gut. She didn't believe him, and it was damned unjust.

She took the coffee, drank.

"You're welcome," he said.

"What are you doing here anyway?" she asked.

"I heard from Lars. Thought you should know."

That got her attention. "And Rebecca? Are they okay?"

"They're fine." He turned and headed back to his room.

"Where are you going?"

"Back to my room."

"That's it? That's all you intend to tell me?"

He leaned in his open doorway. "I thought you wanted to work alone."

"You're being smug. It doesn't suit you."

"Drink your coffee. And have a nice day. I'm going to drop into the hospital, and then I'm going to do some checking around."

"What kind of checking?"

"Lars and Rebecca took off because Mike threatened them. I'm going to try and find him." He pushed away from the door and started to turn.

"Not without me, you're not. Give me ten minutes." She slammed the door behind her.

He looked at the closed door, his chest tight, regret a knotted band around his heart. *Baby, what I want to do is give you a lifetime.*

They met the doctor coming out of Sinnie's room.

"How is she?" Wade asked without preamble.

Joy saw the worry lines etched into his high forehead. They appeared every time Sinnie's name came up.

"She's doing better. Amazing, really, for a woman her age to survive that kind of brutal attack." He went on, "She was awake briefly a while ago, but she's sleeping again now."

"You're sure she's going to be okay?" Wade asked.

"I'm never 'sure' of anything. But I'm more positive than I was when they brought her in. Good enough?"

"Good enough." The lines across Wade's forehead eased. "Okay if we look in on her?"

"Sure. But let her sleep, will you? She needs the rest."

Wade nodded and pushed open the door to Sinnie's room.

She was sleeping deeply, and Joy watched Wade carefully take her hand in his, bend to kiss her gently on the forehead. "Back later, Sin," he whispered.

Outside the hospital, Wade said, "I don't know how much luck I'm going to have tracing Mike, but I'm sure as hell going to try. After that, I'm going to see Rupert."

"I'm going with you."

"This from the woman who last night was going it alone." He looked disgusted, started to walk away.

Joy tugged on his arm to make him stop. "You're angry." She was amazed. The way she saw it, she was the one entitled to be angry . . . confused. Not Wade.

"Damn right, I'm angry." He turned on her, his eyes dark and hot. "I said I loved you. You said you loved me. Then you threw it all down the toilet because of that damned mother of yours—and something that happened a thousand years ago. You flew out of my bed like a betrayed wife. Yeah, I'm mad . . . *goddamn mad.*"

Joy didn't move. In the bright sunlight, under a barrage of his male logic, she faltered. "She's not my *damned mother*, she's my mother, and she—"

"—sexually assaulted a seventeen-year-old boy. Unless you missed that part." The words were flat, set like stones in concrete. "Do I think she made a habit of it? No. I think she did it for a reason. To come between me and my father—or, more accurately, me and my father's money. And she was successful. But what she did or didn't do has nothing to do with you and me." He stared at her. "She was not the first or the last woman to wrap a hand around my cock, Joy. She's just one I had to tell you about—before she put her own spin on it." He started walking again.

In the deepest part of her, Joy wanted to believe him. Did believe him. But she wasn't sure she could rewind the movie in her mind, put it away. Her mother and Wade. It hurt dreadfully. "Wade."

He stopped.

"I, uh, don't know how to deal with it."

He didn't say anything for a long time. "Tell me you'll try."

She nodded. "I'll try. But no promises."

"Fair enough," he said. His expression rigidly composed, he stood by the car.

She stepped up to him, edgy and uncertain. "Where are we going first?"

"The county clerk." He opened her door and she got in.

"Why there?" Joy buckled up.

"To check the property's tax record. See if anyone we don't know has an interest in the Phil. Maybe purchased a tax lien."

"A what?"

"If a property goes into default, the county sometimes sells tax lien certificates, generally by auction. That way they get the overdue taxes paid—money in the bank. The investor who purchases the lien bets on a good return on investment—and the possibility of claiming the property if the owner doesn't pay up and redeem the certificate in a certain period of time." Wade turned left out of the parking lot. "If there is a lien on the Phil, and I'm betting there is, my guess is Rupert's name is on it."

"Wouldn't someone have told me? Your father when he wrote me the letter?"

"Should have, but my father wasn't much for details. The information would catch up with you sooner or later—generally in a nice little notice like pay up or lose the property within X number of days. Or maybe the taxes are paid. I don't know. But it's worth a check."

"Let's do it," she said, and turned her head to look out the car window. Both she and Wade held to silence in the forty minutes it took to find the right counter in the county clerk's office. An hour later they walked back into what was now a grayed-down morning.

There was a tax lien against the Philip, and it was held by Christian Rupert. The surprise was the person who had been his proxy in the purchase. David Grange.

"David ever mention to you that he represented Rupert?" Wade asked when they were back in the car.

"No, and the connection is hard to figure. David told me from the beginning his plan was to buy the hotel and tear it down. He insisted the real value was in the property, but—"

"Having the hotel demolished is the last thing Rupert wants."

She nodded. "And that first day? When David was showing me around the hotel? He talked about 'the old man in the penthouse,' about how he'd have to leave when the hotel was sold." She paused to remember. "He said he'd never met him."

"So . . . as my grandfather used to say, 'truth lies a-dying between one liar and the other.' "

Joy frowned. "What exactly does that mean?"

"No idea. Sounds good, though. And it looks as though a serious conversation with Grange is on our agenda." Wade put the key in the ignition. "Now that we've found two liars, let's look for the third, our friend Mike."

Chapter Seventeen

It was early evening when Joy and Wade arrived back at the Phil. They'd tried tracking Mike through the references he'd given when he'd rented his room—all bogus. The courier service he'd worked for—for three whole days—yielded even less. Mike was nowhere to be found. Other than the shady connection between Grange and Rupert, they had zip.

When Wade's Explorer pulled to a stop, Joy got out and headed toward the back entrance of the hotel. When they were in the ghostly kitchen, Wade said, "I don't suppose you're going back to the Marriot?"

"No."

"And you won't stay with me—even if I sleep on the goddamned couch."

"No."

"Room 33," he said wearily.

"Yes, because I can't think of a reason not to." But she could think of lots of reasons she needed time away from Wade Emerson—and the idea of the two of them being in the same room without their being all over each other was, to her, patently ludicrous. Sex was already in the mix. She needed to get it out and start over again.

"Does the name Big Mike mean anything to you?" he asked, his tone laced with sarcasm.

"Mike's gone."

"And you know this . . . how?"

"Cherry and Gordy are still here and the last eviction was days ago. I think after Sinnie, he got scared and ran—a very long way. And I think today proves that. And"—she reached deep into her tote—"if I turn out to be wrong, I have this. Meet Smitty."

Wade stared at the gun in her pale white hand. "You're kidding." He looked as if his lungs had burst.

She stuffed the gun in her bag. She hated the thing, the feel of it in her hand, its dark intent.

"Is that licensed? And do you have any idea how to use it?"

"Yes to both questions." She righted her bag on her shoulder. "I'm a woman—"

"I've noticed."

She ignored him. "I'm a woman and I travel alone. I took self-defense classes years ago, and when the world got uglier, I bought this and learned how to use it." Praying all the while she'd never have to. "And if I have to, I will." She started to walk away. After a few steps she realized he wasn't with her. She looked over her shoulder to see him standing in the same place, his hands on his hips. He looked angry enough to eat the hard metal she'd just put in her bag.

"Are you going to let go of this thing?"

"What 'thing' is that?"

"Your mother. Me. That thing."

She walked back to him. "I've spent the night and all today working on that." She smiled but it turned wobbly. "To say my relationship with my mother is anything but . . . unsettled would be a lie. I know she has her failings"—she lifted her eyes—"God, but don't I know. She's no saint, and to her credit, she's never claimed to be. In some ways, she's the most honest women I know. But I can't get the idea of you two—"

"Jesus! There never was a 'you two.'" He looked ready to explode.

"You tell me that, and I believe you—which, by the way, makes you the first man *ever* to come within pheromone-sniffing distance of Lana Cole and not succumb to whatever her lethal attraction is." That last sounded petty and insecure—she knew that—but when it came to Lana, insecurity was a set piece, like black water in a deep cavern.

"I'm attracted to her daughter. That's lethal enough for me."

She stepped away, emotionally weary, not wanting to go any further along this rocky path. "Can we leave it, Wade? Just . . . leave it. Until this business with the Philip is done."

"Yeah, we can leave it—for now." He paused. "It was an ugly thing to have happened, and even uglier to have to tell you. Hell, it's a relief to know you don't hate me."

She ventured forward, kissed his cheek—a chaste, spinster-aunt kiss that refused to ask for more. "If it makes you feel any better, hate isn't part of the equation. It's more a kind of . . . chaos that I can't sort through without some time by myself." She stopped. "And there's the possibility we moved too fast, Wade. I've got the tee shirt—several—from that mistake. I don't need another one."

"We didn't move too fast," he stated flatly, then looked at her a long time. "I still want you to come and stay with me."

She shook a negative.

After a second or two, he nodded. "Okay, I'll help you get your things. Later we'll go and see the old man."

"What do you think the chances of him letting us in are? That chain must have been an inch thick."

"I've got an idea." He pushed open the door to the second floor. "And now's as good a time as any to set things up."

When he knocked on Cherry and Gordy's door, it was Gordy who answered.

"Gordy, what time are you walking Melly tonight?"

"Last walk?"

"Yeah."

"Get him at nine and gotta have him back at ten o'clock. Mr. Rupert asked me to make this walk real short tonight, because he wants Melly back early." He looked worried. "He says he's not feeling so good today. Got a germ, he says. Mom took him up soup for dinner."

Joy asked, "Your Mom's working for him now?"

He dropped his eyes. "Yes, ma'am. Doing some clean-and-cook stuff. 'Cause of Sinnie being gone and the Phil being so empty."

Wade looked at his watch—almost eight. "Gordy, I've got a proposition for you. How about you pick Melly up, bring her to my place, and I'll walk her and take her back"—he dug into his pocket and handed him some cash—"while you take your mom to that movie you're so hot to see. What was it again?"

"*Space Warrior*?" He looked excited, but when he looked at the money, he frowned. "Mom says I'm not supposed to take money I don't earn. Says it's . . . begging. Not nice."

"You did earn this. Helping me fix Joy's door. Remember?"

Gordy smiled. "Oh, yeah. Standard rate."

"That's right. So? We have a deal? You go to the movie, I walk Melly."

Gordy stuck out his hand. "Done." He sounded thirty years old.

"Good. I'll see you around nine, then. Hope you enjoy the show."

"Thanks a lot, Wade."

"One other thing. Don't tell Mr. Rupert, okay?"

"You want to surprise him, huh?" He stuffed the cash in his jeans.

"Something like that." He looked at Joy.

Gordy appeared to give this thought, but said, "Okay. But be on time, okay?"

"Right. Not a minute late."

Christian pulled the blanket over his shoulders, shivered. He was coming down with something, he knew it.

No matter how he tried, he couldn't keep his air clean enough. Surely everyone who came in carried nasty microbes into his home from the dirty streets below. If he could, he'd do without any of them. He certainly didn't like that Cherry woman cooking for him, but of course he had no choice. He had to eat—and with Sinnie gone . . .

Not that he wanted her back. Most assuredly not. She'd betrayed him. It wasn't to be borne.

But the man-child's mother was brash, not respectful enough, and she looked at him as if he were a sideshow curiosity. He didn't like her. And she was the newest to enter his space. It was probably she who'd brought on his illness.

"Eh, my Melly," he said to the dog at his side. "Never you." He remembered David asking him once, why, if he was so afraid of germs, did he have a dog? Christian had no answer, other than he hadn't been without one since Joe Emerson gave him one over sixty years ago.

They'd been friends then, the tall, handsome Joe Emerson with his endless confidence and seductive smile, and the diminutive, anxious Rupert—with his bottom-less pocketbook.

Every man should have a dog, Christian. At least you can always trust a damn dog! That's what he'd said, laughed, and given him a small brown mutt. The little dog was the only gift Joe ever gave him, and he remembered it as if it were yesterday.

He remembered everything about Joe Emerson.

Christian had kept a dog ever since. Of course now, he made sure they were bathed often and sprayed with antiseptic every day. Gordy saw to that. And as his world grew smaller, a dog friend was the only kind Rupert knew.

He sank deeper into his chair, into the blanket. In a few days he'd have new friends. The Philip would host only the best people. Like it used to. And he'd choose between them for the finest service. Life would be good.

This very night David would kill the girl. After that, and sixty-five years of patient waiting, the Philip would finally belong to Christian Rupert.

He closed his eyes, visualized Joe twisting in his grave, his fleshless jaws open in a soundless scream, and his gray, rotting bones jangling in protest.

He laughed into the emptiness of his room.

The sound was so new, Melly got to her feet and barked, swishing her tail excitedly.

David turned the key in Lana's front door, stepped in, and turned off the security system. Lana followed him in and slipped out of her light coat. It was wet, and David quickly took it from her. The sudden downpour had caught them by surprise.

"What a night," Lana said, somewhat dismayed by the water stains on her silk skirt.

David, who'd been preoccupied all night, didn't answer. He walked ahead of her into the living room. "Drink?" he asked, holding up a decanter of brandy.

Lana sat on the sofa. "Don't you have to go?"

"I've got a few minutes." He poured her a brandy and brought it to her, taking a seat beside her. His eyes were dark, unreadable. "And I'd rather spend it with you than the man I'm going to see."

"Really?" She swirled the amber in her glass. "And here I've had the distinct impression I'm dropping lower on your priority list with each passing day."

"It's not the way it seems."

"Then how is it?" She set her glass on the side table. "Maybe you'd like to enlighten me."

He looked tired, shook his head. "I'll tell you this much. After tonight, it will be over. This meeting is the end of it."

"Or the end of us." Her heart stilled at the thought of him failing her. Never seeing him again. It shouldn't hurt so much. She forced her next words out. "I want my money, David."

He brushed his lips over hers. "I know you do, but I know something else." He kissed her again, another soft kiss at the corner of her lips.

Lana willed the rapid beat of her heart, the dull ache between her legs, to stop. She made the rules and she intended to keep them. No money. No sex. "And that is?" She asked the question quietly, in as sweetly a sarcastic tone as she could muster.

"You want me more." He gripped her shoulders, kissed her again, deep and with a fierce sexual hunger.

Lana's eyelids grew heavy, drifted to a close. Her spirit floated toward abandon. But when David's hands slid to her back, started to work on her zipper, she pulled back, dared him with a gaze. "I believe you have another late meeting." She knew her eyes revealed her rising passions, but it didn't matter. Let him see what he was missing.

She got to her feet, straightened her clothes. "And you'd better go."

Temper surged in his eyes. "You're something, you know that?" He stood to face her.

"Yes, I do know I'm 'something'. Something very special. That's why you want me." She brushed his lapel, got up on tiptoe to kiss him softly on the mouth. "And it's why you'd do anything for me."

He closed his eyes, shook his head. "You have no idea."

She headed to the closet. "If you're finished with that brandy, you'd best leave. The weather's foul, and you don't want to be late." She offered him his coat.

He took it from her hands, seized her arm by the wrist, his grip a vise. "*Do not* follow me. I don't like it. And tonight particularly—it would be dangerous." He looked down at her, his face taut. "I want your promise on that."

She pulled her wrist from his grasp. "Whatever you say, my darling." She rubbed her wrist.

"Promise me," he repeated. "Say it!"

"I promise."

She watched him pull out of her driveway. She didn't have to follow him. She knew exactly where he was going. And she wasn't sure she could bear it.

At quarter to ten, Wade knocked on Joy's door. He was relieved to hear the bolt being slid open. It told him she was still being careful. Joy was probably right in thinking Mike was gone. But . . . this was still Room 33.

"You're early," she said.

"A failing of mine. I hate being late."

"Where's Melly?"

"In my room, chewing the hell out of a bone the size of Nebraska."

Her smile was brief. "Come in for a minute, then."

He shook his head, preferring to remain in the hall.

"Suit yourself. I'll get a shirt. It's a bit cool." She walked across the room to the closet. She was wearing some kind of thing with those skinny straps. Her laptop was open on her table. Other than what dying light could creep in through the cloud-shadowed windows, its light was the only illumination in the room.

"You were working," he said, raising his voice slightly to be heard.

"Finishing a piece that was due before . . . before your father's will disrupted my life." She flicked on a small lamp beside her computer. "I owe my editor a completed article on the English canal system before I'm free to become a fully employed hotel owner." He heard the closet door close. "Plus, it keeps my mind off things." She stepped out of her room, wearing a white cotton shirt that looked to be two sizes too big. "Ready as I'll ever be. Let's go."

At the same time the phone in his room rang. He looked at his watch. "Give me a minute. I'll get that and pick up Melly."

He was back in less, something the size of a medicine ball implanted in his stomach. Joy met him outside her room. "Sinnie's taken a turn for the worse."

"Oh, no."

He touched her arm. "Come with me."

Joy didn't move. "It's you who Sinnie needs right now—not me." She gave him a push. "Call me from the hospital."

"Damn it, I don't like leaving you." He glanced over her shoulder at her door, "Room 33" rutted deep into the oak. She followed his gaze, then rolled her eyes.

"Wade, give me a break, and get out of here."

"I'll get back as fast as I can. Lock up—and keep your friend Smitty handy."

"I will. Now go! It'll take you at least thirty minutes to get there. And that's if traffic's light. Go!"

Wade eyed her, torn.

"I'll be fine."

"Don't even think about visiting Rupert alone. We're in this together, right?"

"I promise. Now quit worrying."

He wouldn't do that, he knew, but he also knew during the time it seemed his own sorry life was at an end, Sinnie was there for him. Now it might be her turn. He had to go. And caveman days being a thing of the past, and determined women being what they were, he had no choice.

He had to trust her—and Smitty.

When Joy went back in her room, she locked up, got out Smitty, and put him within hand's reach under a file on her desk. Safety off.

She thought briefly about keeping the *appointment* with Rupert, but knew it would be a waste of time. Even if she did get in, the chances of his talking to her were less than zero. Then she thought about calling Cherry to tell her about Sinnie, but remembered she and Gordy were at the movies and would be for another hour or so.

It occurred to her that for the first time she was alone in her hotel—she glanced at her ceiling as if to look through the floors between herself and the penthouse— if you didn't count the large black spider in the attic. She shivered at the thought of Christian Rupert, blamed it on the cool night, upped the temperature on her space heater, then went back to the table she'd been sitting at when Wade knocked.

God, she hoped Sinnie was okay. She checked to see if her cell phone was on and put it on the table near her open laptop. With nothing to do but wait, worry a hopeless knot in her chest, she rubbed her hands to warm them and went back to work.

Locked behind the door of Room 33, rapt in her piece on the English countryside, she was soon oblivious to the yawning, creaking silence of the deserted hotel and the soft staccato of the rain against her window.

It took Wade over forty minutes to get to the hospital. He parked illegally and ran through the rain to the hospital's main entrance. Damn near mowed down the nurse coming out of Sinnie's room.

"Sorry," he said, holding her by the upper arms to steady her. "Is she okay? What happened?"

The nurse stepped back, rattled by the near-collision. "It's much too late for visitors."

"Maybe so, but I'm going in."

"Hey—"

He pushed open the door to Sinnie's room.

Sinnie was propped up in her bed. She'd been dozing, but her eyes blinked open when Wade stalked toward her bedside.

She reached out a frail hand. "Wade. I've been waiting for you. I thought you were mad at me."

"Not a chance." Wade sat on the edge of the bed, as if it were the edge of a pin. He took her hand. "What happened? Are you all right?" Even in the dimly lit room, he could see her color was better, even though she still looked as limp as one of her ten-year-old towels. He didn't care. She'd pulled through whatever the crisis was; that was what mattered.

"Aches and pains in new places. I'm used to those." She shifted her head to look at him. "It was Mike, you know. He's the one who beat on me. He caught me writing—" She closed her eyes again. "I'm sorry, Wade, really. It was stupid, but that girl, she's got to leave the Phil. You've got to tell her."

"You actually wrote that stuff on her wall? Joy said it was you, but I didn't believe her."

As if he hadn't spoken, she went on. "I didn't want to scare her but I . . . heard things. He wants the hotel—"

"Whoa. Who's *he*?"

"Christian." Her face crumpled and she looked away, brushed at her eyes. "I should have told you. He hated your granddad, you know. Tried to ruin him. When Joe bested him, he hated him more. All those things happening in Room 33 . . ." She stopped. "So terrible. They don't come any meaner than Christian." She gave him a guilty look. "My brother."

"I know, Sin. Joy and I found the photograph. We were looking—"

"—doesn't matter now." A tear oozed from the corner of her eye. "I couldn't ever prove anything. I just knew. And I was scared, Wade. I shouldn't have been so scared." She grabbed his hand, squeezed. "He set Mike on me. He wants me dead. My own brother."

"Why, Sin? Why would he do that?"

"Because I know what he wants. What he'll do . . ." She tightened her grip on his hand. "You've got to take care of the girl. If she won't sell the hotel, he's going to kill her so that mommy of hers inherits. I heard David yell at Chris—"

"Grange?" Wade's heart dropped stone-cold in his chest.

"Christian's very own boy. Always has been. He practically raised him."

"Jesus!" *He'd been set up!* And Grange was nothing more than a front man for Rupert. All his talk of protecting Joy, her safety. Bullshit!

Wade shot to his feet. "You didn't have a setback tonight, did you, Sin?"

She looked confused. "Been getting better all afternoon."

Two nurses, one seriously male, pushed open the door. "You have to leave, sir. And you have to leave now."

They didn't have to say it twice. He leaned over, planted a quick kiss on Sinnie's papery cheek, pushed past the hospital bouncer crew, and flew out the door. There was a phone down the corridor, he remembered.

He called Joy's cell. No answer, and she hadn't bothered with a land line to the room. No point in calling Cherry's place; Wade had sent them to the movies. Cursing himself nonstop, he took the stairs to the hospital's main entrance two, three at a time.

He was outside in seconds.

The rain was heavy, but traffic was lighter now. With luck—and navigation under the radar of Washington's finest—he'd be at the hotel in twenty minutes.

He prayed luck would be enough.

Chapter Eighteen

A few minutes after Wade left, Joy added a couple of notes to the margin of her article and leaned back in the chair. Her stomach told her she hadn't eaten since late morning, and that a sandwich—at least—was required. She was halfway through slathering on the mayo when she heard a rap on her door.

She walked toward it. "Wade?"

"It's David, Joy. I know it's late, but I need to talk to you about your mother and me."

"Not the hotel?"

Silence.

"Okay—that, too. There is something you need to know. It'll only take a minute, but if you're busy, I can come back."

For a few seconds she listened to the sound of rain being driven against her window by the gusting wind, not sure why she hesitated, but she did. The emptiness of the hotel, most likely—or the usual woman-afraid-of-the-dark syndrome. She considered both. Neither was life-threatening, nor was Grange—unless a woman wanted to be bored to death.

She'd been handed an opportunity to dig into the relationship of the slick Mr. Grange and the sick Christian Rupert—she'd be crazy not to take it. She opened the door.

David stepped in smiling, and she closed the door behind him. He scanned the dimly lit room. "I've heard about 33, but I've never been in it. Quite the reputation."

"So they say." Joy went back to the counter and finished making her sandwich. "Like one?" She held it up.

"No, Lana and I ate late. Thanks."

She munched, watched him. "So what's on your mind, David? Another offer on the Phil?"

"Would you be open to one?" He'd been looking around the room; now his attention shot to her.

She drank some milk, but shook her head. "No."

"I didn't think so." He snorted softly. "That would be a stroke of luck—and I seem to be out of the running for those lately. The thing is"—he centered his gaze on her—"you really did bring this on yourself. It's not really my fault." He put a hand in his pocket.

"What are you talking about?" The change in his eyes made her uneasy, made her stomach muscles tighten.

"I'm talking about pressure, Joy. The things we *have* to do, the choices we *don't* get to make."

"Such as?"

"To live or to die. Completely out of our hands, really." He rubbed his forehead, his expression taut, filled with regret. "And unfortunately, you have to die. Tonight. Because that madman who lives in the penthouse says so. And I'd best get on with it before Emerson gets back to play the white knight."

Joy stared, tried to assimilate his words. Only a three-letter one came through. *Die.*

Her cell phone rang. David, obviously startled by it and now abreast of the table she'd been working on,

immediately picked it up, turned it off. He set it down—
right beside Smitty, which she'd stuffed under some papers beside her laptop. Now he was between her and it.
Damn! "Are you saying what I think you're saying?"
Stupid question, but a stall.

"I have to kill you, Joy," he said, his tone flat. "I don't
want to, but I have to. I like you. I do. You're tough,
smart, and determined. Just like Lana." He grimaced
on the name Lana as if in pain. "She'll be sad to lose
you—and I hate that. Hate the idea of hurting her."

Joy's mind went into overdrive. She listened to him
in a state of shock. She had to think, to stall. She steadied her sandwich plate and glass of milk in her hand. As
weapons they were zip, but they were time-buyers. And
time, the next few minutes, were what it was all about.
Milk. A sandwich. And the knife! She'd dropped it into
the sink before the knock on her door. But first she
needed words. A delay. "I don't understand," she said.
"Why kill me?" The words felt rusty, rose from a throat
coated in emery.

"Rupert thinks I'm doing it for him, but I'm not." He
smiled a tight, malicious smile. "When this is over, the
joke's on him."

"What joke? I want to know." She was desperate, brain-
less, plan-less. *Think!* She sidled toward the sink.

The hand David had in his pocket moved. *A gun?*
Every nerve in her body shot to red alert. She froze.

Not a gun.

He drew out a long, silk scarf, slowly, gracefully. It
poured out, a brilliant stream of reds, blues, and yel-
lows. Joy moved again, closer to the sink, and put a
kitchen chair between them.

She tried to think, but mesmerized, her mind was
trapped by David's slow, deliberate advance. The flutter
of silken color across his jacket front.

He wrapped a length of scarf in each hand, taping his palms like a boxer readying for a bout.

She watched, frozen, fascinated, sandwich in one hand, milk glass in the other. *Say something. Do something. Delay, delay! Stay calm.* "David. Why are you doing this?" She raised her voice, inched along the counter.

Her brain was alive with fear. Thoughts meshed into a stark, indecipherable muddle. She had a gun, she'd taken self-defense, she'd bested routine trouble more times than she could remember. But there was nothing routine about David's expression; it was grim with horrific purpose. Her gaze flicked from his eyes, fierce and sad, to the lethal silk he flexed between his hands.

He advanced as if she'd hadn't spoken.

She forced herself to take a bite of her sandwich, and chewed, slowly, very slowly, uncertain if she could swallow. Another inch or two and she could reach the knife. *Time, she needed time.* "Tell me about Rupert, David. You were his proxy for the tax lien purchase."

His eyebrows raised. "Very good. It looks as if you've inherited your mother's cool. Checked on the back taxes, did you? I knew you—or Emerson—would get around to that." He snapped the silk, stopped moving forward. "But to set things straight, that viper on the roof is not my client. He's my blackmailer." He took another step toward her. "He's owned me since I was seventeen years old. And the day I get my hands on this hotel is the day he starts dying."

Joy looked over his shoulder to the door.

"Don't even think about it."

She took another drink of milk, another bite of her sandwich, dry oats and motor oil. "What I'm thinking about is *why* he owns you. Why you'll turn killer to own a seedy property in a lousy part of town."

"I am a killer. A fact Rupert reminds me of every day of my life."

She set down her sandwich and the milk—left her hand to rest on the edge of the sink. She'd have one chance.

"Me?" he sneered. "I wouldn't kill a sick rat for this pile of junk. But getting control of this place is the only way to get free of that bastard. He thinks I'm doing it for him. That's a laugh." He stepped around the chair. "Here's how it really works. I kill you, your mother inherits, I buy—and presto. Lights out on the Phil. Power off. Phones disconnected. No one here to knock on the asshole's door. He's a dead man. And I'm a free one."

He frowned, lifted the silk, and took a breath. "You know, that maniac up there is easy to hate. But I don't hate you, Joy. I don't. If you'd only have accepted my offer"—he snapped the silk—"this wouldn't be necessary."

He lunged, Joy screamed, swept the sandwich and milk carton and glass toward him. She plunged her hand into the sink and grabbed the blade of the knife. It slipped away.

"Don't fight me. Please."

Only inches away, he lifted his arms, the dazzling sliver of fabric pulled straight between them, a design to loop the silk over her head—around her throat.

Paralyzed, her back pressed against the wall, she stared, her muscle and sinew rigid as cable.

Move. She had to move.

He lunged.

She dropped to her knees. The sudden move confused him, stalled him, and before he could react to her not being in his grasp, she head-butted him in the groin and scrambled along the floor.

"Son of a bitch."

She didn't look back. Couldn't get to Smitty.

The bathroom, the bathroom . . . Close the door. Lock it.

Her mind screamed instructions.

In the tiny room, still on her knees, she rolled to her back and kicked to slam the door closed.

Too late! His foot was lodged in the opening, and he was pushing to open it, cursing like a wild man. Pleading with her to make it easy. She braced herself against the porcelain bowl, prayed it would give her enough leverage to hold the door closed, and planted her sneaker-clad feet hard against it.

Hold the door closed. Think!

Suddenly David let up his pressure on the door, yanked hard to withdraw his foot. The door closed.

He was going to ram it.

He'd break her ankles. She rolled sideways.

Grange hit the door full force and without her holding it back, he came in wild, out of control. He stumbled over the toilet bowl, and his knee hit the tub edge with a crack, before he fell—directly on top of her.

His weight crushing her, holding her in place, he didn't waste time trying to loop the scarf around her neck. Joy rounded her body into a tight ball, put her head down and her hands behind it in aircraft emergency landing position. David looped an elbow instead. She curled tighter, tried to work herself into the cramped space between the toilet and the bathtub.

"Jesus, Joy, cut it out. I have to do this! Don't you understand?" He grabbed her by the hair and yanked her from the tight corner. Her eyes watered and her scalp burned as if someone had poured acetone on it. "Get up." He ordered, his fingers fisted in her hair. "Do it. Now!"

Joy grabbed the hand yanking her hair, and shot her foot out, fast and hard. It connected with his ankle. He cursed, but his grasp on her held.

Using her hair as his grip, he rammed her against

the edge of the bathtub. The first shock was to her wrist. The second was to the back of her head.

The universe, stars and colors, danced in her skull, a mad swirl, glittering from gold and red to black. Blacker. Her muscles slackened and she went under.

Only a second, but enough.

The smooth silk circled her throat, lethal as a wire garrote.

Still on her knees, she clawed at it, desperate to curl her fingers into its deadly fold, pull it free.

He dragged her out of the bathroom, along the floor, and across Room 33's sitting area. If she could get to her feet . . .

As if he knew her thoughts, David planted a knee in her back, shoved her face hard into the old carpet. Blood spurted from her nose.

The silk digging deeper into her neck, her eyes bulged and dried.

Her vision blurred and her lungs emptied.

Air. She needed air. Air that lay thick and nourishing on the wrong side of the tightening silk. Gray shadows centered in her eyes, then shifted and rolled as if driven off by a wind even darker. Thoughts splintering.

Her will steeling.

She blinked hard, and from the corner of her eye saw her computer cord. She crawled her fingers toward it and with the last of her strength wrapped a hand around it and pulled.

The laptop crashed to the floor on the other side of the table along with a flutter of files and paper.

No Smitty. No Luck.

The distraction was less than a second, but it was enough for her to suck in a teaspoon of air before he again tightened the noose.

Out of oxygen and options, she sank into a storm of

light and growing splotches of black. And more black.
Blacker.

Then . . . a voice, metal hard.

"David, for Christ's sake, what are you doing?"

Abruptly the silk loosened, and though still tight to
her throat, more air filtered into her empty lungs. The
rush of it made her light-headed. Confused.

"Lana!" David's voice, sharp. Frightened?

Lana here. *Mommy, Mommy . . .*

"Get away from her, David."

"You don't understand. I have to do this. For us."

*More air coming in. Light into blackness. Blood in her
nose.* She tried to move, to turn. Couldn't.

"I said, get away from her!"

A shrill voice, not Lana's. Lana's voice is cool like
quiet water. The knee, deeper into her back. The scarf,
tighter again. Sounds of choking. Hers.

"Trust me, darling, this is for the best."

"You're insane. Killing my only child is for the best?"

"Jesus, Lana. Think, will you? I do this . . . thing, you
get your ten million, and I get what I want—my goddamned life back!"

The silk constricting. A band of steel. A circle of death.
No! she wanted to live. Lana . . . Too tired. Dying. In a
second she'd be dead. Only a second between life and
death. Can't breathe. So cold.

A sharp sound. A bullet sound? Metal singing into
flesh to make blood splatter and fall. Metal to maim . . .
to kill. Then a jerking, grinding spasm of silk at her
throat, searing skin, embedding cloth and color deep
into her larynx.

A gasp. Hers. And a wild, desperate grasp for air.
Carpet fibers joining the blood in her nose. Short, pant-
ing breaths.

A weight across her shoulders. Moans. Not hers.

Blood, warm and slow, drizzling over her ear.

"Joy! Are you all right?" The weight on her back falling off. Pushed off? Someone rolling her over. "God, Joy, are you okay?" Lana was on her knees beside her, pulling at the silk.

Joy could only breathe, not talk. She took deeper breaths, filled her lungs until they hurt. "I'm okay," she croaked. She blinked a couple of times and looked at her mother as if for the first time. Lana's eyes were alive with a wildness Joy had never seen before. *Fear.* Joy knew fear and reached out to soothe it. "Mom."

Their embrace was fierce, too hard. And long. They held each other, neither letting go until their hearts, beating one against the other, found a shared rhythm.

Lana pulled away first and turned her head abruptly, but not soon enough for Joy to miss the sheen in her eyes. The first time she'd ever seen her mother cry. When she again looked at Joy, the sheen was gone, replaced by an ironic wonder.

She glanced at David, supine on the worn carpet, brilliant silk trailing across his broad chest. Her magnificent eyes wide with shock and grim amusement, she said, "My God. I think I just killed the best lover I've ever had." She blinked, gave Joy a slight, curious smile. "You always *were* trouble."

Joy swallowed, tried to smile back, but could only stare.

Wade burst into the room, scanned it, and came to his knees beside Joy. "Are you all right?" He ran his hands up her arms, cupped her face. "Jesus, I'm sorry—I should have been here." He looked, stricken, at David's still form. "He could have killed you."

Lana leaned over David and lifted his hair from his forehead, the gesture careful and tender.

"He tried hard enough," Joy said. "But thanks to . . . my mother, he didn't finish the job." She raised her hand to her throat, touched it gingerly; it felt like a stab. "Help me up, would you?" For the first time she noticed her hand was bleeding. Not badly, but Wade quickly gave her several sheets of paper towel.

Lana said, "He's alive."

Wade went to Lana's side. Joy didn't want to go anywhere near the man. She saw a pool of blood growing slowly under his right shoulder.

"Grange, can you hear me?" Wade asked.

Grange mumbled, "Lana, I didn't want to . . ."

"He's okay," Wade said, looking at her mother. "It looks as if you hit him on or below the right shoulder." His shirt and jacket were bright with fresh blood.

"Lana," he moaned again.

"I'm here, darling. I'm here." She shot a beseeching glance toward Joy. "Call 911 . . . please."

Joy, still weak and unsteady, located her cell phone on the floor among the fallen papers and put in the call for an ambulance, then the police. She got towels, too, and handed them to Lana.

Wade snarled in David's face. "An ambulance is more than you deserve, you son of a bitch!"

David's eyes focused blearily on Wade. "Had to. The old man . . ." Either he stopped or his voice gave out. Joy couldn't tell.

Lana pressed a towel to his wound. "Shush, now. Help is coming."

Wade took Grange's face in his hands, none too gently. "The old man *what*?"

"Let go of him," Lana said, her tone flat and hard. "Can't you see how weak he is?"

"I see a man who tried to kill your daughter. That's all I see. I repeat, what about the old man?" He released his grip, stood back.

David's gaze drifted to Lana. He lifted a shaking hand, touched her face. "I love you."

"And I love you." She kissed his forehead. Reverently, Joy thought. "But it really was a bad idea to try and kill my daughter."

Wade cursed, looked about to explode. "Forget the hearts and flowers stuff." He shot a furious glance at Lana before looking back at David. "What about Rupert? What's he got to do with all this?"

A long silence filled the room. It looked as if David had said all he would, or could. There was so much blood on the carpet a person could drown in it.

"Mike's up there." He raised a limp wrist, managed to point to the ceiling with his index finger. "In a box— behind a planter. Rupert shot him. And the planter . . . there's another one. From before. Didn't mean to. God, I was a kid. A stupid kid." He shot out a hand, grabbed Wade's jacket. "Get him, Emerson. *Get the bastard.*" He passed out.

In what seemed only a few minutes but was probably closer to a half-hour, the paramedics carried David out on a stretcher. Lana, clasping his hand, insisted she be allowed to ride with him to the hospital; the police insisted she go along with them. The cops won. A couple of them stayed behind to learn what they could from Joy and Wade.

Joy studied her mother, but knew she'd never come close to knowing the woman she was. The hush of acceptance settled in her heart. She might never understand her, but she'd heard once that when a person *shows* you what they are, believe them. Tonight, her mother hadn't hesitated to turn a gun on the man she loved to save her daughter's life.

An act of love.

Joy would never again ask her for more.

She sat heavily on the arm of the sofa, and in the next second, felt the weight of Wade's big hand on her shoulder, a gentle squeeze. "Quite a night."

She put her hand over his, squeezed back. "As understatements go, Wade, that's a doozy."

"Mr. Rupert. Mr. Rupert!"

The voice pulled Rupert's attention from the window, the riotous disorder in the street below. He moved to his door as quickly as his useless legs allowed. He put his mouth against it. "Gordy, is that you?"

"Yes, sir. Mom said I was to check on you. 'Cause of all the commotion." He said the last as if he were repeating by rote.

Rupert opened the door—almost too wide—and let the lad in. "You're a good boy, Gordy. Now tell me what you've seen. Who's in the ambulance?"

"A blond guy. Joy's mom shot him with a gun. A real one." He seemed in awe.

"I see. And was he dead? Can you tell me that?"

Gordy looked puzzled. "I don't think so, because his face wasn't covered. They always cover it on TV."

"And everyone else is fine?"

Gordy nodded. "Wade's girlfriend was kinda hurt. And her nose was bleedin' real bad."

Rupert's stomach clenched painfully, and he came near to falling before reaching out to brace himself with a hand on the wall. He was dizzy from standing so close to the window, and his heart jumped behind his ribs, ready to burst through them at any minute. He teetered back to his chair and settled into it.

David had failed. And, damn him, he'd lived through it. It was the only possible explanation. He rested his head, closed his eyes, considered his options.

They would come for him. Strangers in uniforms with papers giving them the right to his home. They would want him to go with them. Outside.

He could not allow it to happen. He put his hand

down beside the cushion, stroked the smooth metal of his protector. He would not go gently into the night . . . or anywhere else.

The Philip! His home. His property by right and by endless heartache. The Cole girl would keep it and there was nothing he could do. She would keep his hotel and through her it would, inevitably, once again belong to an Emerson. Joe's grandson would see to that. And Joe? He would laugh at Rupert from his grave.

Never! If it was the end for him, it was the end for Wade Emerson.

"Gordy, would you do something for me?"

"Sure, Mr. Rupert."

"Take Melly with you." He stroked the dog's soft head, left his thin hand to rest there. "And take good care of her, won't you? She's a very good dog."

Gordy nodded gravely. "Yes, sir. I'll bring her back right after her morning walk."

Rupert didn't answer. "And would you please tell Mr. Emerson I want to see him as soon as possible."

Rupert watched the boy turn, called him back. "Get your money from my purse, Gordy." He paused. "Take all you want."

Wade sat beside Joy on her bed, held her hand. She looked brutally pale, but otherwise okay. The paramedics had bandaged her hand and given her painkillers.

Hell, but he'd be glad when this night was over.

The police were finally wrapping up. They'd been all over the place, but all the statements jelled, so their job was straightforward. Joy agreed to be at the station tomorrow to go over her statement and answer any other questions. Wade thought of Lana Cole, shook his head. What a piece of work.

In the last couple of hours, he'd swallowed a lot of

his distaste for her. Even had a grudging admiration at the woman's bottomless self-possession. More again when he thought of her saving Joy's life. The cops said it was doubtful, given the circumstances, she'd be charged. David—facing an attempted murder rap—wouldn't be so lucky. Wade's gut churned at the thought of the bastard.

Neither Wade nor Joy mentioned—by tacit agreement—his rant about bodies in the penthouse.

It was well after one before Room 33 was empty.

Except for its quota of blood.

Joy left Wade's side to go and pick up her papers and her laptop.

"You okay?" he asked, and got up to help.

She rubbed her throat where the bruises were beginning to show, raw and in full force. "It hurts to swallow, but I'm okay."

"I'm sorry I wasn't here." He stood, said again what he'd said a dozen times already. "I should have been." The bare truth of it was he'd never forgive himself for being such a dumb ass and falling for that bogus hospital call. He could have lost her, and the thought froze his bones.

"Does this mean you owe me one?" She walked over to him, wrapped her arms around his waist, and leaned her head on his shoulder. Felt right to him. "That if I knit you a hair shirt, you'll wear it?" she asked.

"I like blue," he said, relieved to hear the humor in her voice—the forgiveness. He pulled her close, kissed her hair, and breathed her in, pulling the scent of her to the deepest part of his lungs. He'd almost lost her . . . He hugged her tighter, not wanting to ever let her go.

The knock on the door made them jerk apart. Still way too many nerves jangling in this room.

"Probably the police. Maybe they forgot something," he said.

"Yeah." Joy wrapped her arms around herself and took a couple of steps back while Wade opened it.

"Gordy? What the hell are you doing up at this hour?"

"When we got home from the movie, Mom saw all the police and stuff. She sent me to check on Mr. Rupert."

Wade glanced at Joy; she'd relaxed a little and was looking interested. "And did you," he asked, "check on Mr. Rupert?"

"Yeah, he's okay. He said he wants you to come up as soon as you can."

Wade glanced at Joy. She raised her eyebrows. He'd figured he'd had his share of shocks tonight—and here was another. An invitation to Rupert's lair was the last thing he expected. Not that he planned on looking the old gift horse in his toothless mouth. "Thanks, Gordy. Now go home. Get some sleep."

Wade closed the door, turned to Joy. "I'm going up there."

A brief arc of fear crossed her pale features, but she stepped toward him. "I'm going with you."

"I wouldn't have it any other way." And he sure as hell wasn't leaving her here. He'd had enough of this damn room to last a lifetime. Rupert was the last piece in the Hotel Philip puzzle, and he knew neither of them would rest until it slipped into place. And until all this bloody business was over, Joy wasn't going to be out of his sight.

"Let's go."

Chapter Nineteen

The new bulbs Wade had put in the hall cast a garish white light, but at least it was light.

They walked in silence to the stairwell, then up to seven. Wade knocked, knocked again. "Rupert, it's Wade Emerson, open the door."

His voice came from deep inside the room. "Come in. The door's open."

Wade touched the door with one finger; it opened stiffly. He put the flat of his hand on it and pushed it aside.

The penthouse was black as a cave, and even though the light in the hall was faint, their eyes needed to adjust.

Joy groped for a light switch.

"I've turned off most lights," Rupert called out. "All that gas in the bulb is quite dangerous when it heats up, you know."

Joy's useless clicking of the switch confirmed the lights weren't working.

"Follow my voice. I've lit a candle. It should be enough for our purpose."

Wade whispered to Joy. "I don't like this. Stay here."

"No."

Wade sucked up his temper. "Okay, then take my hand."

Hands clasped, they made their way along the murky hallway. After a turn, they saw the candle, its narrow flame licking uselessly against the black in the cavernous room. It was on the table beside Rupert's chair.

Rupert looked in their direction, but Wade was certain he couldn't see them outside the circle of candlelight. Not clearly, at least. Wade decided, for now, to keep it that way. He stopped abruptly, and Joy bumped into his back.

"Come in, please. Join me in a late night brandy."

Wade held Joy behind him, heard the clink of glass on glass. "I'll pass, thanks."

"I understand he's not dead. My David." The tone was mild, matter-of-fact.

"No."

"Unfortunate, given his failure to perform."

Wade, eyes now more accustomed to the poor light, saw him take a sip of brandy, then sit stone-still.

"I must speak to him about that," he said.

"Won't happen anytime soon, Rupert. 'Your' David will be going from a hospital bed to a prison cot in record time. And he'll be there a long time."

"Where, no doubt in an effort to make life easier for himself, he will—how do they say it—spill the beans?"

"He already has," Joy said.

Wade saw the old man straighten, set his glass on the table beside the lit candle. "You have the girl with you." His sharp intake of breath was audible in the dense quiet of the room.

"I haven't been a 'girl' for a very long time, but thanks for the compliment."

Rupert turned his head toward them. "You're impertinent and you're not welcome here." His voice was shrill, agitated. "Please go. My business is with Emerson."

"And what business is that?" Wade asked.

Rupert put his head back, and Wade could hear his stark breathing; when he spoke, he sounded calmer. "Instruct your whore to leave and I'll tell you."

Joy gasped. "Just a minute—"

Wade tightened his grip on her hand. "Why don't you go, Joy. Let Rupert and me talk man-to-man."

"You're kidding."

He whispered in her ear. "Don't go far."

"Oh," she whispered back. "Got ya." Then, in a louder voice, added, "Fine, I know when I'm not wanted. I'll wait for you downstairs." She took a couple of steps backward. In the dark recess of Rupert's hall, she made a show of closing the door.

"Good," Rupert said, sounding pleased. "A man should always control his lovers."

"How do you know we're lovers?"

"Mike had his uses."

"And that makes you what? A pervert by proxy."

Rupert ignored his comment. "Step into the light where I can see you." He waved a hand. "There's a chair, directly in front of me."

"No, thanks. I like to stand." But Wade did move deeper into the gloomy room, edged his way to the terrace doors. "And speaking of Mike, David tells us he's a resident here, that you've been doing a little burial work out on the terrace."

"David should know." He raised his glass. "He's quite expert in 'burial work.' "

Suddenly impatient, Wade said, "What the hell's going on here? Are you going to tell me, or do I go out there and dig up the answers for myself."

Rupert sniggered. "My, my, and aren't you just like your grandfather, full of piss and vinegar."

"I can't see this has anything to do with my grand-father."

"Oh, but it does. It has everything to do with him. Dear Joe." He let the name out on a wistful note. "Like you, he was always up and ready to get the job done, no matter the cost." He snickered. "I suspect you have no idea how up and ready he could be."

"Cost? What cost is there in exposing you for the avaricious, murderous son of a bitch you are?"

"Ah, now there's the question. There's always a cost, young Emerson. Your granddad taught me that. And if you'll be good enough to take the seat in front of me—where I can see you properly, I'll show you exactly what *you're* going to pay—and throw in a rather risqué story about your much-revered grandfather as a small bonus."

Silence pervaded the cavernous room, and for a few moments, Wade let it lie.

But he was curious.

He ambled over to the brandy bottle sitting on the liquor cabinet a few feet from Rupert and poured himself a drink. "I'm listening," he said.

"Sit, for goodness sake!" Rupert kicked lightly at the footstool in front of him. "It hurts this old neck, craning to look up at you."

Wade decided to humor the bastard and carried his brandy across the room to sit in front of him. And, God knows, he was curious about his relationship with Joe—or his version of it. He raised his glass to his lips, waited.

"Let's start in the middle, shall we? It's the best part, really." In the flickering light, his face cratered by shadows, Rupert's smile was wavy, grotesque. "It's when your grandfather became my lover."

Wade's hand jerked and his throat opened and closed reflexively over an inward rush of burning alcohol. "You're lying." He wiped the back of his hand across his mouth.

"Now, why would I do that?" Rupert's milky gaze settled on him like seepage. He was enjoying himself. He raised a white brow as if waiting for an answer.

Wade didn't have one, so he got to his feet and walked to the terrace. He pulled back a heavy curtain and gray city light slithered into the room. Joe and Rupert, lovers. He repeated it in his mind. Couldn't make it stick.

Wade had long ago given up judging anyone on the basis of their sexuality, and he was okay with the close-the-bedroom-door-and-let-consenting-adults-do-whatever-they-felt-like-doing school of thought. But Joe and a male lover? The mean old bastard Christian Rupert to boot? As revelations go, it was right up there with discovering you'd fathered quintuplets during a one-night stand. It would take time to digest. He thought of his grandmother, the obvious love she and his grandfather displayed for one another until her death five years before his.

Rupert cackled behind him. "You're thinking it's impossible."

"I'm trying not to think at all." He chased his brandy burn with another and set his glass on the piano near the terrace windows. "Why are you telling me this, anyway?"

"Because I'm going to kill myself tonight and I feel the need to purge my soul."

Wade eyed the ancient, withered man. "You're going to kill yourself," he repeated, wanting to be sure he heard right.

"Yes," he said. "I think it's the best course of action. I have no wish to be forcibly removed from my home, mauled by strangers. Perhaps dragged to a flea-infested police station. There is no doubt such a process would kill me, so I've decided to handle my passing in my own way."

Wade went back to the footstool. "And how do you plan to bring about your . . . 'passing.'?"

"With this." Rupert pulled a revolver from his side. One very much like Smitty.

Adrenaline jolted Wade's back straight. "Messy," he said, and gestured toward the gun. "For a man of your fastidious nature, I'd have thought you'd pick something neater. A nice crystal goblet full of arsenic, maybe."

Rupert sighed, bobbed his head. "Yes, all the blood . . . That is a downside, I'm sorry to say. Perhaps Sinnie will be good enough to clean up after me."

"I don't think so, considering you sicced Big Mike on her. Your sister's lucky to be alive, Rupert."

"She told you?" He blinked. Obviously it was his turn to be surprised—and annoyed.

Wade nodded, kept his eye on the gun. "What I don't know is why the big secret, or why you treated her like a damn servant all these years."

"Sinnie's a woman, therefore she's a fool. She didn't listen to my father or me. Ran off with that useless husband of hers. My father disowned her and so did I. Then, when she found herself alone and penniless, of course she came crawling back." He stroked the edge of his robe's lapel. "I gave her a job and put a roof over her head, told her she'd have both as long as she understood I was not her brother and she could make no claim on me."

"She's your sister, for God's sake, and that's all you'd do for her?"

"She disobeyed me, and then—"

"Then what? Overcooked your damn bacon?"

"She befriended your atrocious family. Unforgivable, really. I should have thrown her out then, but I found her useful." He lifted the gun, waved it in a slow, uneven arc.

Wade had almost forgotten it was there. Almost. Now it had his full attention.

"But let's forget about Sinnie," Rupert went on. "There are more interesting things to discuss." He centered the gun, leveled it at Wade's chest. "Before I turn this on myself"—he wobbled the gun—"I really would like to clear up a few things."

"Fine." A faint creak came from the hall. Wade swallowed. Joy! Damn, he'd thought she'd left when the gun appeared. He forced his focus back to Rupert, the death in his bony hand, prayed she'd stay in the shadows.

"Your grandfather and I were lovers," Rupert said.

"So you told me." He strained to hear more sound from the hall. Nothing. Maybe what he'd heard was her leaving.

"But did I tell you how reluctant a lover he was?"

Wade didn't want to hear any more of the man's venom, but the gun pointed at his chest narrowed his options.

"He wanted to build this hotel—so very badly. But money was a problem. And, as I'd just inherited a substantial fortune upon the death of my father, I agreed to finance his dream in exchange for this place until the end of my life." He swept the hand not holding the gun in a wide arc. "I was your grandfather's angel, young Emerson, and he was more than happy to take my money. But I wanted more, and told him so. But when I spoke of my love for him, suggested ways of deepening our partnership, he laughed at me, assumed I was joking. I was not. I did love him"—he closed his eyes as if to right his thoughts—"and I intended to have him. I waited until he'd committed the sum I'd promised to his various creditors. Then, the night before I was to sign the final papers for the loan, I informed him I would withdraw my financing, let the hotel project sink unless he came to me, or to be more specific, to my bed."

"Jesus! You are a sick bastard."

It was as if Rupert hadn't heard him. "It was the Depression years, and I knew he'd exhausted all his financial resources before turning to me in the first place. I made certain I was in a position to get what I wanted—as I always do. And I wanted him. In every way possible. He was so beautiful . . ." He stared at Wade, blinked slowly. "As you are, Wade. Very beautiful."

Wade's chest moved. He took in air, but he couldn't feel it; his lungs were blocks of ice.

"You call me a bastard," he went on, his voice growing stronger. "I see myself as single-minded in getting what I want. Always. I gave Joe an ultimatum. Be in my bed by midnight or the front door of his fancy Hotel Philip would never open—and I'd see him, his wife, and his infant son on the bread lines.

"Oh, but he was so gloriously stubborn." Rupert's voice was distant now, dreamlike. "But, in the end, he came, of course. The night was—"

"You odious little prick. He must have hated you."

"I suspect he did." Rupert rubbed his forehead, and his mouth set into a tight line. "Although not nearly as much as I came to hate him."

"I take it he preferred his wife."

"You take it right. But I didn't care. I was young. My love was blind and my passions unbridled. *I would make him love me.* I signed the papers in the morning, confident he'd never meet the stringent terms of my loan, that there would be many opportunities for future liaisons."

"Sexual extortion, you mean. But knowing Grandfather, there were no other *'opportunities.'*" Wade remembered his granddad's boast about how he'd always paid his bills, his stern lectures to Wade to do the same and never be "beholden to any man." Now he knew why.

"No. Joseph made every payment—via a third party. I lived in the hotel, but he never looked at me or spoke to me again. I resolved to ruin him, of course—force him to come back to me. But he remained unyielding. Even Room 33 wasn't enough." He chuckled then. "Although it did offer me endless amusement."

"Room 33?"

"Brilliant of me, really. The hotel was doing well. Joseph was meeting his payments. It grew increasingly unbearable"—he shuddered—"the rooms full all the time, people coming and going—bringing god-knows-what germs in with them. It was about that time I became concerned about my health. Then that wonderfully ridiculous 'room of doom' article appeared, and when I saw how the hotel's business temporarily dropped off, I had my plan. I simply ensured that similar events were staged on a regular basis. The press is such a wonderful source of ideas."

Wade, still sitting on the hassock, gaped at the evil in front of him. "You had a family of three murdered to get back at my grandfather?" Saying it didn't make it comprehensible. He was cold to the soles of his feet.

"He never knew, of course. About any of it. That would have spoiled the fun." His expression clouded. "I'd thought I could break him, that when the hotel failed he'd crawl up the stairs to the penthouse—late one night—and beg me to save him."

"It never happened."

"Sadly, no. I did, however, achieve at least part of my goal. Hotel bookings declined, and I was gradually able to exercise much more control over the Philip's inhabitants. Unfortunately, the caliber of the guests did deteriorate as the years passed." He frowned slightly. "In the end, I suppose you'd call it a wash. Isn't that when you don't get exactly what you want, but enough to justify your efforts?" He smiled then, drew back into his chair. "I'm glad we had this opportunity to talk before we leave."

"You're the one leaving." Wade started to get up, but the gun in Rupert's hand—pointed at his chest with not a wobble in sight—stopped him cold.

"Remain in your seat," Rupert instructed. "I have more to say."

Wade relaxed back onto the hassock, eyed the gun. "Shoot," he said, his tone deliberately ironic.

"Very amusing. Another time and another place and I think you and I could get along nicely."

"Sure, I always bond well with sickos who stick guns in my face."

"It's your grandfather's fault, really. All of it. I was prepared to ignore your presence here, but one of the terms of my 'ownership' of this penthouse is that when I die it goes back to the hotel proper." The gun held steady. "When I agreed to the term, it meant nothing to me. I was young, death inconceivable. And I was stupidly lovestruck. But now—after all I've been put through— the idea of an Emerson owning my home is completely unacceptable."

"It's not an Emerson who owns the Philip, or have you forgotten that?"

"I've forgotten nothing. And I'm no fool. You and the Cole girl are lovers, and I suspect you, Emerson, have a reason for that coitus other than carnal pleasure. You want this hotel—as your grandfather did before you. And it's been my experience that Emerson men always get what they want—if there is a woman involved." His lip arced to sneer. "Women are ignorant creatures. Put some stars in their eyes, they open their legs. Promise them a trip down the aisle, they open their hearts. Once there, *voila!* You have them." His smile was snide, knowing. "And if they happen to own a hotel, you have that, too."

Wade barely heard him. There was a shadow behind Rupert and it moved. Jesus! His heart hammered. Joy hadn't left! He had to keep Rupert's attention on him. "You're dreaming, Rupert." He raised his voice. "The Philip belongs to Joy Cole, and the way things are shaping up, it'll stay that way."

"Yes, it will because I intend to *ensure* it does, by seeing you dead, before I see you wed." A slight lift of the gun barrel.

Wade hurled himself sideways. Rupert fired.

He rolled into the darkness beyond the sputtering candle; his arm burned as if seared by a branding iron. He held it with his good hand to stanch the bleeding. He'd been lucky. Now all he needed to do was breathe, and get Joy the hell out of here.

In the halo of light provided by the candle, Rupert struggled to rise from his chair, the gun tight in his grasp.

"Emerson," he shouted, almost to his feet.

Ghostly, slender arms emerged from the darkness behind him. Pale and disembodied, a pair of hands gripped his shoulders, yanked him roughly back into the recliner.

A waterfall of blond hair fell forward to flow over the old man's head.

"Sit down, you cruel, miserable old man!" Joy had caught him off guard and took advantage of it. She ripped the gun from his hand, and called into the dark room, her voice high, anxious. "Wade, are you there? Are you okay?"

Wade stepped into candlelight range, holding his bleeding arm; she came right toward him. "That looks bad. I'll call 911."

"No, Miss Joy Cole, you will not."

Wade looked past her to see Rupert, on his feet now, a small, glittering pistol in his hand—pointed at Joy.

"Fuck!" Wade said under his breath. "We've got ourselves a senior Rambo. How many of those have you got in that damn chair?"

"Enough. A man is nothing without his Plan B." He took a step closer. "Now, to business. Which of you would like to go first?"

Wade tried to get Joy behind him, but she stepped to his side. Finally, he gave up and moved forward, which gave him a better chance to shield her if he had to move suddenly.

The old man sneered at Joy's stubborn posture. "I guess you're not as good at keeping your women in line as I thought."

"Women have come a long way since your century, Mr. Rupert," Joy said. "That would be the fifteenth, right?"

He ignored her, spoke to Wade. "I've never killed a woman. That was David's forte. All I did was provide a frightened boy a place to bury her body." He gestured with the gun toward the terrace. "Although my act of kindness did prove convenient for me. Whenever I needed something done, I'd simply call my David, and he'd come running. Just like Melly."

Wade experienced a brief stab of empathy for Grange. Living your life in debt to this creature would be a hell. He'd have been better off paying his dues in the legal system. And as for Wade, he'd had it! He didn't intend to spend another minute listening to Rupert's malevolent bile—or having Joy in the sightline of his pistol.

He dropped and lunged, took another slicing burn damn close to the other one, but he took the old man down. No contest. It was like knocking over a stack of kindling.

He shoved him into his chair—none too gently—and turned to Joy. "Now, call 911."

While she dialed, Wade removed Rupert's robe sash and secured him to his chair. He also searched it. Hell—who knew?—maybe he'd stashed a couple of grenades. Wade wasn't taking any more chances.

He stepped back from his task at the same time Joy hung up the phone. Side by side, they stared down at the sullen ancient in the chair.

Wade couldn't resist asking, "What the hell is with you anyway, Rupert? Your parents force-feed you beets? Lock you in a closet? There has to be a reason a man carries around a load of hate as big as yours for over sixty years."

Rupert, until now resolutely looking away from his captors, turned back at Wade's question. His smile was cryptic and cold. "Had my love for your grandfather not transformed itself to hate, I would not have survived. Hatred sustained me, empowered me. It gave shape to my life, a reason for living, and a necessary focus. One can not live a life without passion. And the most passionate of all emotions is hate." A drizzle of frothy saliva seeped from the corner of his mouth; his eyes, already set deep by the passage of too many years, narrowed to hooded slits.

Rupert gestured with his chin at Joy, sneered. "You enter this whore of a girl and your body ignites, every nerve and fiber inflamed, straining for sexual release. You are at an apex, a point of ardor without boundaries. A place so high a freefall is inevitable. You talk of love—as I once did to Joseph—and you believe you have discovered heaven." He shook his head. "You have not. What you have done is expose yourself, the searing weakness of your own need. You have risked all that you are. And what you have found is the gateway to your own hell."

"Jesus . . ." In Wade's heart, the word came closer to a prayer than it had ever been. The air left his lungs and words left his mind.

Joy stood beside him in utter quiet, her shoulder brushing his. If there was a response to Rupert's hate-laden diatribe, neither of them knew what it was.

When they stared down at him in silence, Rupert sneered at each of them in turn and turned his face from theirs. Fine with Wade. In the distance he heard sirens. Even better. The sooner this piece of dreck was out of his sight, the happier he'd be.

Joy went to the table, picked up the flickering candle, and held it high to enlarge the circle of light. When she spotted a lamp, she walked toward it, put her hand under the shade, and flipped it on. Its light was enough to trap the three of them in a watery glow; they looked like escapees from the local morgue.

Joy glanced toward the terrace. "Should we go out there? Take a look?"

Wade shook his head, feeling weak now, and a little disoriented. He pulled himself together. "Let's leave that for the pros. David said Michael was in a large storage box. He shouldn't be hard to find."

"The planter with the tallest trees. Don't forget that one. And dig deep," Rupert said, keeping his eyes averted. "David's little girlfriend is there. Bones by now, I'd expect. But no doubt her parents will appreciate the remains. Such a shame when a teenage boy, testosterone, and tequila come together. Anything can happen. Not David's fault, really."

There was a loud knock on the door, and Joy, looking startled and unnerved, moved toward it. "They've come for you, Rupert," she said.

Rupert's head came up on the first knock. His skin was chalk white, his lungs pumped visibly against his rib cage, and his breath came in short, sharp gasps. He curled his fingers around the armrests of the chair, embedded his nails deep into the fabric.

"Take it easy, old man," Wade said, too aware suddenly of the blood running down his arm, soaking his shirt. "Just breathe." He grabbed his numbed left arm, held it close to his body, and took his own advice.

For a second it looked as though Rupert would say something; instead he set his lips into a tight line, leaned his head back, and closed his eyes.

He was bathed in terror.

Wade was bathed in blood, and his eyes were glazing over. Damn! He was going to pass out and miss the damned finale.

Joy came back, followed by two police officers and two paramedics just as Wade sank to his knees.

"Wade!" she screamed and ran to his side.

Before he went under, he felt hands pulling at his shirt, another on his pulse. Joy's hand on his forehead? He couldn't be sure.

What he did hear was a voice . . . far away now, say, "Greg, get over here, fast! I think the old guy just checked out."

Checking out . . . The Philip. Christian Rupert is checking out.

Chapter Twenty

Wade woke up briefly in the ambulance. "You're a lucky bastard," the paramedic named Greg told him. "Two bullet wounds, one a pinstripe, the other a bit meaner. Some stitches, and you should be on your way. Lost some blood, though." Wade's eyes closed on that bit of news. When he woke up again, he was in emergency, a doctor basting him together on one side and two cops asking him questions on the other.

When his brain opened for business, he did his best to fill them in, and not notice that a certain blond someone wasn't anywhere in the immediate vicinity.

The bigger cop finally snapped his notebook closed. "One thing's for sure, the old Philip's had a helluva busy night. Bodies in penthouse planters, huh? That's a twist." He cocked his head. "You know, my dad was a cop, and he took the odd call from the Phil. He said something about a 'room of doom' thing. Said some people believed the place was actually haunted." He raised his eyebrows and smiled. "You ever hear about that?"

"Yeah, I heard." He winced as the last stitch went in. "What's your take?"

Wade put his head back on the pillow, smiled. "Fiddle-sticks."

"Huh."

"I'll be happy to tell you all about it . . . but another time. Okay?" He'd tell them Rupert's part in Room 33, just not tonight. He was tired. All he wanted to do now was go home and lick his wounds. And he sure as hell wouldn't admit the wound hurting the most was Joy's absence.

"Yeah, okay." He tapped his notepad on the bed. "You take care. Forensics will be around the hotel for a while. So stay away from the penthouse, okay? We get any more questions, we'll be in touch."

Wade nodded.

When he was patched to the doc's satisfaction, they wheeled him out with bandaged arm, a sling, and a handful of painkillers.

The first person he saw outside the ER was Joy. She looked tired, her pale skin in contrast to the purple-and-blue bruises on her throat. She got to her feet and came toward him. For a second it looked as though she'd hug him—which he was all for—but she stopped when she saw his arm.

"Are you okay? Will your arm be all right?" she gingerly touched the sling.

He got out of the chair and said his thanks to the attendant before saying to Joy, "The arm will be fine. I'll have a couple of matching scars. Nothing serious."

"You were lucky."

He looked at her. "I am now—that you're here."

Silence.

"I'm here," she said, giving him an unreadable look. "The question is, for how long? When you're up to it, we have to talk, Wade. About you. Me. The Phil."

He didn't like that *for how long?* comment of hers, but he nodded, then gestured toward his arm. "Now's as good a time as any. Talk's about all I'm good for right now."

"Can you make it to the car?"

"Yeah, let's get the hell out of here."

Wade downed another painkiller while Joy went to her room to get him an extra pillow to prop up his arm.

When she came back, she started to fuss over him, and he reached out his good arm and pulled her down beside him.

"You said you wanted to talk."

She chewed her lip, appeared to gather her thoughts. Her eyes went all bright and watery. He brushed a tear away with his thumb. "Hey, what's this?"

She forced a smile. "In a lesser woman, it would be a tear. For a Cole woman, it's a full-blown catastrophe."

He waited.

The smile dropped from her mouth. "I love you, Wade. I've fallen so hard and so fast, it's frightening. Tonight, when you passed out . . . I thought—"

"Don't go there. I'm fine. Stick with the 'I love you' thread."

"I do—love you, I mean—but there's something about me you don't know."

He brushed a tendril of hair from her forehead. "Go on." Whatever she told him, he'd handle it—if it meant holding on to her.

"I was married."

"You told me."

"I didn't tell you everything." She got up, stood in front of him. "It was years ago. I was twenty-one. His name was Matt Sheldon. We were married for three months, and when I left him I was a million dollars richer."

Wade didn't like the uncomfortable tightness in his chest. "That's a lot of money."

"Yes, it is." She stopped, massaged her forehead.

"That it?" he prodded.

"No." She shook her head. "From the beginning his parents opposed the marriage—particularly his mother, but she never said why. Matt said not to worry, it would work out when they came to love me like he did. But a couple of months into the marriage, he started acting strange. He didn't seem to have any energy, didn't want to go out. Didn't want to do anything. I tried to get him to the doctor, but he wouldn't listen, insisted it was a virus of some kind, that it would pass. A month after that, I found a note saying he was sorry—'he had to go'—and a bank slip showing a deposit into our joint account for a million dollars."

"Generous." Wade knew the word bit the air.

"Yes. Generous." She looked at him. "You're thinking I should have given it back. That three months of marriage didn't warrant that large a settlement. And you're right."

"Why didn't you? Give it back." The question was pure curiosity.

She laughed. The word "mirthless" came to his mind. "At first I was hurt—totally wrecked, to be honest; then I got mad. A week after he left, I called him at his mother's, told him he could have his damn money. He told me not to be crazy, to 'have fun with it.' He said he wanted me to have it, and that someday I'd know why. He said he loved me and hoped the money would make up for what he'd done. I didn't understand any of it, got angry all over again, but by the time I'd got myself together enough to think about talking to him again . . . he was dead."

"Dead?"

"He was twenty-four, and his heart gave out."

"Whoa . . . tough."

"It turned out Matt had a heart condition when he

married me. Knew he didn't have much time left. I
guess I was . . . some kind of last grasp at life. When he
started to get sick again, he went home to die, because
he didn't want me to see him failing." She pushed her
hair back roughly, her face tight with old pain. "I loved
him, Wade. He was funny, brave, and—with me, at least—
full of life. I tried to give the money back—to his mother.
She wouldn't take it, said she'd promised Matt she
wouldn't, that he wanted me to think of him when I
spent it and to remember how much he loved me. The
next day, I went to the bank and told the banker to do
something with it and tried to forget about it."

"A million dollars is damn hard to forget."

"Easier than forgetting Matt. And the fact that he
didn't believe in me, denied me the chance to be there
for him at the end, when he needed me the most." She
swallowed hard. "I couldn't be there when my dad died,
and I wasn't there for Matt . . . It just wasn't right."

Wade wanted to touch her, but she remained standing over him, her arms clasped, her posture rigid. "His
death, Joy. His choice. Put it away. From what you've
said about him, that's how he'd want it."

She nodded, but without conviction. "I ignored the
money for a long time . . . then, when I saw the Phil,
thought what it could do—" She met his eyes. "I don't
want you to hate me, Wade. I don't want you to think . . ."

"You're your mother?"

"Something like that."

"Come here." He held out a hand, and she took it
before again sitting beside him on the shabby sofa.
"That money is yours, sweetheart. It was a gift. You have
nothing to feel guilty about."

"I was afraid to tell you."

"First mistake among the many to come." He kissed
her because he couldn't stop himself, but he was care-

ful to hold himself back. His body wouldn't do him any favors tonight. "There's one thing we do have to settle."

"The Philip," she said without hesitation.

"Yes. I want us to be partners. Fifty-fifty. I want you to sell me half the hotel."

She hesitated, then said, "And my mother? Her support from the Phil? Nothing's changed there."

"Everything's changed there, Joy. First, she saved your life and she has my eternal gratitude for that"—he smiled thinly—"although I'd prefer you didn't advise her of that fact."

"I agree." She smiled back, hers eyes soft, but accompanied by a raised brow and knowing look. "And the second thing?"

Wade's stomach tightened, then released. "Rupert is the second thing. That man carried a load of hate through life that crippled him, destroyed everyone around him." He took her hand in his, squeezed it. "I saw a lot of myself in him, and it wasn't pretty.

"And there's one other thing." He lifted her hand to his mouth. "No more Room 33. No more room anything unless I'm in it. Do we understand each other?" He kissed her knuckles, watched her face.

"Sounds like an order to me."

"Yes, it is."

She smiled then, the darkness leaving her eyes. "But as orders go? One I can definitely live with."

EPILOGUE

Eight months later

Joy cupped her hands over her ears, sighed out the last of her patience. The racket from the floor below made her head hurt and the floor tremble. "How much longer, Wade?"

"Two weeks max. We'll open on schedule." He kept his attention on the penthouse window he'd struggled to open for the last ten minutes. He cursed. "This thing must have seized up fifty years ago. I need a crowbar—probably break the damn thing."

The saws—or whatever weapons the construction crew was using to assault the Phil—stopped abruptly.

The silence was magnificent. And Joy immediately found a better use for her hands.

She wrapped her arms around Wade's waist, nuzzled the warm spot between his shoulder blades, and tucked her fingertips under the front of his tool belt. "You don't have to do that, you know. You could ask one of the carpenters to come up." She massaged him under the belt, slipped a hand lower.

He caught it and turned to look down at her. "I don't want anyone up here but us." He kissed her palm, pulled her as close as his tool belt allowed. "Then I can have my way with you any time it looks . . . convenient." He brushed his lips across her forehead, her cheek, finally taking her mouth, deeply, sensuously.

When he lifted his head to smile at her, she sighed again. But this sigh had nothing to do with patience and everything to do with either releasing some of the happiness ballooning inside her or bursting from it.

"Can I finish fixing our window now?" His lips quirked.

She laughed. "Go for it, tool man."

She hesitated then, not wanting to change the mood, but knew it was unavoidable. "I saw my mother yesterday to give her the monthly check. She was on her way to see David. She says his trial starts in three weeks."

Wade looked over his shoulder, frowned. "You know, I don't get it. The guy tried to kill you—her only daughter. That, plus the fact he planted a body"—he turned, pointed to the terrace—"out there, means he's going away for a very long time. And she's sticking by him . . ." He shook his head.

"When he's sentenced, she wants to buy a condo near whatever prison they send him to." Lana, obsessed with David's situation, had accepted his story. He'd never intended to kill the girl. It had been a horrible, tragic mistake that he'd paid for every day since. He'd been drunk, she'd led him on; then, when she wanted to stop, he'd gotten mad. Too mad. His memories stopped there, started again with him banging on Rupert's door, then his taking charge, telling David what to do. Everything, Lana rationalized, was Christian Rupert's fault, including David's botched attempt to kill Joy. Her mother was as confounding as ever.

"You're kidding."

"She asked me for the money, Wade." Joy held her

breath. "It's extra, I know, and it might be hard right now with all the renovation expenses."

"We'll do it, if it's what you want." Wade put his arms around her.

She nodded.

"Done." He kissed her, tightened his grip.

She never wanted to leave the circle of his arms, wanted him to hold her forever. "But what I really want is to live happily ever after in this beautiful penthouse with you."

"Happily ever after, huh?"

"Uh-huh."

He thought a second, then smiled. "Done."